*For Justin*
*Cheers & Thanks!*
♡  ◡

# I on the ISLE of SOUND and WONDER

## ALYSON GRAUER

### FOREWORD BY TEE MORRIS

♡ *Alyson R Grauer*

Xchyler Publishing,
an imprint of Hamilton Springs Press, LLC
Penny Freeman, Editor-in-chief
www.xchylerpublishing.com
1st Edition: July 2014

Cover Illustration by Egle Zioma, http://daywish.deviantart.com
Cover and Interior Design by D. Robert Pease, walkingstickbooks.com
Edited by Jessica Shen

Published in the United States of America
Xchyler Publishing

# SUCH STUFF AS DREAMS ARE MADE OF

### A Foreword from
### Tee Morris, author of
### *The Ministry of Peculiar Occurrences*

I first met Alyson Grauer on Twitter in 2011. It was steampunk that brought us together; but the more we got to know one another, the more we shared in common. One of those many things—William Shakespeare. Once upon a time, I was terrified of Shakespeare; but then after being cast as "The King" and "Morgan the Interpreter" in James Madison University's production of *All's Well That Ends Well*, I needed to get over that fear. That was when my roommate sat me down and made me watch *Ian McKellen: Acting Shakespeare*.

Yes, Magneto—getting his iambic pentameter on. Like. A. Boss.

Alyson told me some time ago she had begun work on her first novel, a steampunk telling of William Shakespeare's final play, *The Tempest*. With all the stories that she and I have shared both online and (finally) in 2014 when we met, I can't recall if I ever told Alyson of my emotional attachment to that play. I first read *The Tempest* in 1990 while studying in London. One year later, I went on to direct it. I still look back on my production fondly—an island stuck in the heart of the Bermuda Triangle, its fairies lost in time and space, music spanning decades providing a backdrop for intrigue, romance, and resolution.

I wonder if Alyson knew *The Tempest* is one of my favorites of Shakespeare's?

She does now.

Alyson and I have only been friends for a brief time, but I have never known her to turn her back on a challenge. If she doesn't embrace challenge, she leaps on a challenge's back, wrestles it to the ground, and demands it to call her a pretty, pretty girl. She stepped up to the invitation of writing for *The Ministry of Peculiar Occurrences*, and her short story "A Trick of Strong Imagination" stands as part of the Parsec-winning season of the *Tales from the Archives* podcast. She was then tapped to write for *Mechanized Masterpieces*. Her novella "Lavenza, or The Modern Galatea" leveled up the steampunk already present in Mary Shelley's *Frankenstein* in such a way that, I believe, Mary Shelly would have given her a nod and said, "You go, girl."

She made her professional debut as a writer with *The Ministry of Peculiar Occurrences* and drove the legend of Frankenstein even deeper into steampunk. Now, she was going to steampunk Shakespeare's epic farewell to the stage, the play I hold so close and dear to my heart?

Of course she would.

When I read *On the Isle of Sound and Wonder*, I found myself on stage at JMU once again, undertaking the challenge to bring Prospero's Island to life. Characters so very familiar to me emerge from the wings and take their places. Music becomes a tapestry woven specially for my players. The storm rises. The show goes on.

But these once-intimate friends are new to me, now. This island is not lost in time but lost in technology. Its music is a clockwork staccato against an omnipresent harmony of steam. I know this world so well, and yet I am a stranger here. I am not the sorcerer behind the storm this time. This is Alyson's world, and I am rediscovering *The Tempest* all over again.

If you are a fan of steampunk, you will enjoy this lush tale of science and alchemy. If you are a fan of Shakespeare, you will enjoy this adventure of redemption, betrayal, and romance. If you are a fan of both—as I am—*On the Isle of Sound and Wonder* is truly the best of both worlds. Not only the worlds of steampunk and Shakespeare, but of literature and theatre. While Shakespeare once told us . . .

> "These our actors,
> As I foretold you, were all spirits
> And are melted into air, into thin air:
> And, like the baseless fabric of this vision,
> The cloud-capp'd towers, the gorgeous palaces,
> The solemn temples, the great globe itself,
> Yea, all which it inherit, shall dissolve
> And, like this insubstantial pageant faded,
> Leave not a rack behind. We are such stuff
> As dreams are made on, and our little life
> Is rounded with a sleep."

In the case of Alyson Grauer's debut novel, those cloud-capp'd towers, gorgeous palaces, and great globe are all captured in a book. You can return to that world. Anytime.

Thank you, Aly, for this astounding trick of strong imagination.

# PROLOGUE

## 1854

Water poured over the streets of the city, down every roof and every drainpipe into the cobbled walkways and curving arches of Neapolis, while the people huddled in their homes and pretended to sleep soundly. It seemed that days had passed in the torrential downpour and darkness, though it could have only been a matter of hours.

The rains had come, swallowing up the sun, and everything stopped as the city braced itself for a flood. The waves slapped and stung the shoreline, the winds peeled away at the city and its gardens, and even so, the midwife climbed from her home on the outskirts of town up the hill to the palazzo.

The child was coming, and it was coming much too quickly.

\* \* \*

It had been a warm, careless day in spring when the opportunity came to the midwife's door. She answered, one hand ever-closed around her tall and gnarled staff. A serving woman stood in the street at a safe distance, flanked by two of what must have been guards in semi-civilian dress—simple caps and jackets over plain-colored shirts and trousers. Nothing out of the ordinary, but somewhat too clean to be authentic. A second glance revealed to the midwife that they were mechanized men, which meant they served someone rather important, indeed.

1

"Good day to you, good-mother," called the serving woman, who was not much younger than the midwife herself. Her voice was lush and gentle, her expression serene.

"Good afternoon," replied the midwife, eyeing the mechanized guardsmen. The pale gold sheen of their skin betrayed them as more than human despite their haphazard peasant costumes and too-casual posture.

The serving woman clasped her hands loosely before her, her head lifted a little higher than the midwife would expect for one of her station. "I was told you assist in the birthing of children. Is it so?"

"Yes, of course. Are you expecting?"

The bluntness of the question caught the servant off-guard, and she squeezed her fingers together as though to keep her composure. "No, of course not. It is my lady who is with child."

"Your lady?" The midwife's gaze wandered to the servant's shoes—plain, but very clean. Like new. The midwife took a step closer, leaning on the staff comfortably. "A wealthy woman, I presume?"

"Very wealthy. She will pay you handsomely for your advice, your support, and your wisdom." Her gray eyes were pale against her olive-warm skin, her dark blonde hair neatly plaited over one shoulder in a single braid.

The midwife drew a slow, deliberate breath through her nose, smelling the warm sunlight, the drying mud beneath their feet, and a hint of exotic perfume, probably dabbed behind the servant's ears. *Jasmine,* the midwife thought, *and . . . sandalwood? Expensive. Add on the hardly used shoes and the mechanical guards. . . .*

"I would be happy to discuss the terms of service, my lady," said the midwife, with a proper curtsey. "And please, don't be offended. I know a highborn lady when I see one, though your disguise was likely necessary for passing through the city unmolested."

The woman's cheeks grew rosy, but she stood with her back straight, her chin tucked with humility. "Forgive the deception, good-mother," she answered smoothly. "I hope you do not mind. I wanted to come myself. The selection of a . . . skilled midwife is not something one entrusts to a servant, after all. Not when there are matters of the heart and spirit involved. Do you see it as a spiritual process, midwife?"

"It is a highly personal process, to be certain." The midwife waited, wondering if the woman would elaborate.

"Yes, just so. Especially when there is a midwife available such as yourself, who has a great deal of special knowledge to draw from." The lady gave a shy sort of smile. "I would rather not discuss it in the open."

*Ah, so she wants magic to bring her baby to the world safely. Well, that much I can do; I've never lost a child.* The midwife nodded and gestured toward her home: a hut half-embedded in the hillside where she was close to the earth and protected from the wind and weather. "Of course, my lady. Come inside and have some tea. Shall I call you by your title or by your married name?"

"My name is Sophia," offered the lady. "My husband is the Duke of Neapolis."

"My noble lady!" the midwife said immediately, and curtsied again for good measure. "I am very honored, indeed. My name is Corvina."

"A lovely name!" The duchess smiled agreeably. "I am pleased to meet you."

"The pleasure is mine. I am happy to help you in any way I can. How far along are you?"

"Not very," said the duchess, a hint of worry scampering across her expression. "But I have had such dreams since it began. I would like for you to riddle them for me, and ward me against any problems that might arise."

"Of course, my lady, I am at your service."

\* \* \*

Dreams.

Corvina paused in a shop's alcove to catch her breath, bracing herself against either side of the narrow archway as the water rushed around her ankles. Leaves, debris, and bits of trash floated past her, sliding back down the hill the way she'd come. What a storm! Lightning split the sky open once more, flashing bright and cold, and she looked up toward the palazzo—the king's stately palace—high on the hill.

On any other day, she would have followed the duke and duchess' instructions to the letter: she would have ridden on a cart heading into town then transferred to a trolley winding up through the streets toward the heights. She would have walked to the gates of the palazzo to give her name to the tin birds that acted as security for the entrance. They would have flown to the guards waiting inside the palace and inform them of her name and business purpose. From there, an armed mechanical escort would have brought her to the duchess' chambers for the birth. They had spoken of the process a thousand times; she knew every step, every nod, and every movement by heart.

But no one had thought the duchess would go into labor so soon, so suddenly, or that it would be in the middle of perhaps the worst storm the city had ever seen.

The midwife straightened her back, stretching her neck for a moment before shifting her grasp on the staff and heading out into the downpour once again, staggering up the hill, as bent as any old woman. She thought wistfully of how much easier it would be if she could somehow guide the storm away from Neapolis, or stop it from raging altogether.

Her wisdom did not lie with the weather, however; her understanding of the human body made her a healer, and that's what had led the duchess to her. That's also what had brought her to the attention of the duke.

4

\* \* \*

The midwife had just examined the duchess' increasingly swollen belly when she met the duke for the first time. The duchess had dropped off to sleep in her chambers, and the midwife was in the antechamber, washing up.

"How is she?" asked the man at the door, and the midwife turned, only to fold into a slight bow. For a moment, she wondered if it was the king himself; but without a crown, he must have been none other than the duchess' lord husband, the Duke of Neapolis.

He was a handsome, slightly older man, with eyes as gray as stone against his smooth, light brown skin. The palazzo belonged to the King of Italya, but, beloved by him, the duke and duchess took permanent residence there, as well. The duke was a known confidante and advisor to his liege lord.

"She's doing well, my lord," answered the midwife, her eyes lowered, the damp cloth still in her hands.

"Please," said the duke, gesturing for her to rise. "My wife tells me you are very knowledgeable. She says you have great herbs and many tales to tell of their qualities." The duke walked into the antechamber, his steps slow and deliberate.

"This is so," said the midwife, lightly but with caution. She had been ejected from more than one city in her thirty-some years; she did not want it to happen again—not when the duchess was doing so well.

"Sophia also tells me that your hands are gentle, but your arms are tattooed."

The midwife stared straight ahead as the duke made a wide circle around her.

"May I see them?" His tone was cordial—courteous, even, but the midwife had heard snakes speak like this before. She did not know yet if the duke was a snake, but he certainly was no barn swallow.

She gingerly replaced the damp cloth to the basin and reached for one sleeve, then the other, pulling them back as one might peel a fruit.

The duchess had spoken the truth: the midwife's arms were dark by nature, but she was, indeed, covered in faded ink depicting stars, the sun, the moon, and archaic symbols the likes of which ordinary folk would not see in their lifetimes, let alone an average day.

The duke did not touch her, but she could feel his eyes as though he inspected her with his broad fingertips. The midwife itched for her staff, but the gnarled, knotted stick leaned against the wall just behind her and barely out of reach.

"I see," said the duke kindly. "Thank you for your honesty." He moved a little further away from her, but his eyes never left her face, even as she avoided his gaze for fear of insulting or angering him. At last he exhaled deeply, the relief and satisfaction of the noise causing her to look up with furrowed brow.

"Have you always been an enchantress?" he asked.

"I beg your pardon, my lord," said the midwife, dropping her gaze again. "I am only a healer, a midwife learned in how to bring forth babes to the world and heal minor ailments."

The duke stopped pacing and looked sharply at her. "As you saw through my wife's disguise, so I see through yours," he said, his voice grown serious. "I wish to know the truth."

The midwife dared to look up at him again, torn between the severity of his tone and the urge to survive another day in this town. But his expression was not angry, simply questioning. She swallowed the instincts that strained within her chest, pleading with her to escape. "I was born with my gifts," she said, but it was neither an admission nor a confession, merely a truth.

It satisfied him, and he nodded. "I wish to show you something, and ask of your wisdom some advice, if you will indulge me." He gestured toward the door.

6

She hesitated a moment, then reached for her gnarled stick. It fit against her palm as though it were meant to be there. They walked in silence for some time, turning down hallways and slight staircases. Their path was crossed by no one, though, more than once, the midwife felt the eyes of servants slinking by behind them, or in passages unseen nearby. The palazzo was very grand, and the midwife felt a touch of wonder that they could move about so freely without ever seeing another person.

She found herself not terribly surprised when the duke pushed open a door and led her down a brief passage which opened up into a workshop of sorts. Instruments and contraptions adorned the space, hanging from the ceiling and mounted on walls and shelves. Books lined the walls and piled on tables, and a warm fire blazed in the hearth nearby, illuminating the brass, copper, and steel in the room.

"You are an inventor?" she ventured, her eyes roving the room, noting the high-mounted windows on the eastern wall of the workplace.

"Something like that," he agreed, moving toward his desk.

She lingered close to the exit, grasping the gnarled staff, wondering what the Duke of Neapolis, favorite of the king, could want with her. He picked up a book, paging through the large, worn volume in search of something particular.

"What can you tell me about this?" He showed her the page.

The midwife's eyes widened only a fraction, but her heart leapt and shuddered in her chest as she studied the diagram. "You are an alchemist," she murmured.

He chuckled. "Not yet," he admitted. "But I have done much reading and much studying, and still I seek more. Yours is a world I wish to know. Intimately." His gray eyes fixed on her. "I would like for you to teach me. You will be paid handsomely, and I assure you, I am a quick study."

"I should focus on caring for your wife and your child-to-be,"
she said, taking a step back. "I don't know anything about alchemy,
my lord; I'm sorry."

"Don't sell yourself short," encouraged the duke, still holding
the book open. "I'm sure you have much to teach. I am willing to
learn. It is a blissful union of opportunities."

"I thank you for your interest, but I should go," said the midwife, bobbing a little curtsey and turning for the door.

"Wait, please—"

"Thank you, my lord, but I—"

The midwife heard the shift of the air as something came hur-
tling toward her. Instinctively, she turned back and brought the
staff over her face in an upward slash, as swiftly and effortlessly as
if it were a part of her own body. A crack of energy erupted from
it and deflected the flying object, shattering it into pieces. The
midwife looked down; it had been a teacup. Not a dagger, not an
arrow, but a simple china teacup, now broken on the floor. She
looked at the duke, who was still holding the book, his eyes bright
and fixed rapturously on her staff.

"Just a midwife," he echoed. "Of course."

She narrowed her gaze, willing her thundering heart to slow. "I
am no alchemist," she repeated firmly.

"No," he said, with a smile of something like relief. "But you
are much more than a midwife. Please." He took a step toward her.
"Teach me. I want to learn."

"And if I refuse you?"

His smile did not falter, but his eyes were cold and bright. "I
can be very charming. Persuasive, even."

The midwife did not like those words, but she feared being
driven from the city as she had from other cities in the past. She
was wary of the look in his eye. "What will the duchess say of someone like me, teaching someone like you?" she asked in a low voice.

8

The duke gave a boyish shrug. "She is with child. There is only one thing in her mind now, and that is the birth. When the child is born, we will worry what she thinks. For now, we won't tell her. Do we have a deal?" He extended one hand to her.

"I don't know much," protested the midwife meekly one last time.

"Anything at all would be a great help to me," he assured.

With a slow exhalation, she reluctantly clasped the duke's hand.

"Excellent. Oh, wonderful. What is your name, midwife?" he asked, beaming as they shook hands.

"Corvina, my lord," she answered, knowing the cause was lost.

"Please, when we are at our studies, you must call me Dante," amended the Duke gallantly, letting go of her hand. "So. Corvina, then. I should have guessed. A raven's name, to match your fine, dark skin." The duke closed his book thoughtfully and smiled at her as happily as any schoolboy. "And your clever mind, as well. They pick locks, you know—ravens do. And they can use stones to open nuts. Excellent problem solvers. As I hope you shall be to me, Corvina." He moved around the work table and glanced back at her. "Please, do not look so cornered. I don't intend to tame a wild thing." She stared back at him, but his smile was steady. "I simply wish to learn from you as much as you'll teach me. In friendship and all respect, I assure you."

The midwife lowered her head. "Of course," she replied, though she could not quell the uneasiness in her stomach. "In friendship and all respect."

* * *

The lightning flashed again, striking a tall spire nearby as Corvina crested the tallest hill in the town. She ducked lower as it cracked, fighting to keep moving forward and upward. She could see the gates of the palace; they were not far, now. It had been the longest hour of her life, trapped in the unyielding downpour on merciless hills. No wonder she was the only soul about the streets tonight; the storm bellowed all around her and made her progress seem futile.

But the word had come from the tin birds: the duchess was in labor, and she would have to come. She would have written back demanding an escort, some kind of assistance to reach the palace in this terrible weather, but the bird had collapsed after delivering the duke's orders. So, it was on foot that she climbed and struggled through mud.

She could see the outline of the mechanical birds perched on the wrought iron gate of the palazzo, each bearing the national crest on their breasts, their heads cocked at varying angles to observe the streets and the city below. She was closer now, within reach, and could see the lights burning brightly within the palace windows.

The midwife hit a loose stone in the street and went down hard. Her staff clattered away from her, and any part of her that wasn't already wet immediately soaked through to the skin. She pushed herself upright, ignoring the ringing in her ears and the searing pain in her bones from the fall, and scrambled after the staff before it was swept away by rainwater. She pulled it back to her, coughing and spitting, and looked up toward the birds, wondering if they—and through them, the guards—had seen her. The metal animals were motionless. She lurched to her feet, exhausted, and pressed onward.

When she reached the tall iron gates, she sagged against them, grasping a bar with her free hand, the other still numbly clinging to the twisted staff. She craned her head back to look up at the birds and yanked on the gate weakly.

"Let me in!" she croaked against the storm's howl. "The duchess . . . The baby is coming! I am the midwife!"

The birds did not move.

"Let me in," the midwife begged, shaking the iron bars again. The metallic fowl rattled in place but did not turn to look at her. "Please, I have to help the duchess . . . I cannot fail them . . ."

\* \* \*

The lessons with the duke had taken place in perfect tandem to the midwife's caretaking of the duchess and her unborn child. While her belly grew rounder and fuller, her husband learned how to make fire, summon air, and shape water and earth to his will. Small things at first, like making plants grow and bringing water and fire to his aid in little, useful ways; but much to the midwife's surprise, he was as he promised: an eager, voracious student.

More quickly than his teacher was prepared for, the duke mastered complex spells and incantations, beyond what even she was used to performing on a regular basis. She hadn't lied that her experience was limited, that her own knowledge of her gifts was primitive, but he had done extraordinary research for many years before finally crossing paths with someone who could teach him to synthesize the information he'd gathered. The midwife felt something uneasy growing within her in conjunction with their lessons, not unlike the infant growing in the duchess' womb.

Several weeks prior, she had been leaving the palace to return to her home, and the duke had seen her to the door, where the hired tram would take her to the outer reaches of the city.

"Thank you for your guidance, good-mother," he said with a twinkle in his eye. She glanced at him as the mechanical driver halted the trolley before the steps. "You are such a valuable resource and a great comfort, as ever."

The midwife curtsied. "Try to get some rest, my lord. Your wife will need you in top shape when the time comes. You must be strong, and stay awake, if the birth goes long into the night."

The duke smiled widely. "Oh, yes," he chuckled. "I shall be sure to rest up. And you, good-mother, you must also keep up your strength."

"I'll be fine, thank you," she muttered, turning away.

His hand closed like a vise-grip on her elbow, stopping her sharply. "You will not fail us, will you? We're both depending on you, Corvina. For different reasons, of course. You will be greatly rewarded for our mutual success. But, of course, you know that, don't you?"

"Yes, my lord," she breathed. "I understand."

"And you also understand what is likely to happen if you fail us?"

The midwife was silent. He released her, letting his hand run along the back of her arm as he did. *Snake*, thought the midwife. The duke chuckled and stepped back.

"Of course," he smiled. "You're a very clever raven." He turned to enter the palazzo and the midwife descended the stair, climbed into the trundling motorized trolley, and let the mechanical servant drive her to the edge of town.

* * *

The midwife sank against the gate, her breaths strained and desperate, the exhaustion from the hike almost too much to bear.

"You have to let me in," she cried, banging the staff against the gate. It resonated with an unusually deep clang, deeper than it should have been. She glanced anxiously at the knotted head of the staff. The last time she had allowed the staff to sing with purpose had been the last time she'd been forced into exile. She swallowed the fear and old bruises and drew herself upright again, leaning on the gate for a moment before stepping back to get a good look at it.

"I swore to protect that mother and that child," she muttered, "and you'll have to let me in before I'm too late."

The midwife hauled the staff back and slammed it against the gates. With a monastic gong, the gates exploded inward, the tin birds falling to the ground as easily as apples from a tree. Rejuvenated by the sudden surge of magic, the midwife hurried through the gates up to the palace door and, finding no one outside to admit her, repeated the process.

The gong sounded again, shuddering in her bones as it did in the fancy window panes of the palazzo, and the door flew inward on its shrieking hinges. She burst into the foyer, a wild, half-drowned ghost, terrifying servants both flesh and metallic.

In the duchess' chambers, the lady herself was indeed in the throes of labor. Several chambermaids fretted over her with cool rags. The duke himself paced in the anteroom.

"Where have you been?" he demanded, white-faced. His boyish confidence and sly manner of the past months were gone. "She's in pain!"

The midwife flung a hand at him and twisted her fingers in a strange gesture. His mouth clamped shut and he made a muffled exclamation, unable to part his lips. "Shush," she said, her hair wild and wet, her eyes bright. "I am here. Now, go," she added loftily, twirling her hand at him. The duke did an about-face and left the room. She went to the duchess and slid her cold, damp hand into the moaning woman's hot, fevered one. "Sophia, my lady, I am here."

"Oh," Sophia groaned, grasping her hand in joy and terror. "My baby . . . I have had such dreams, again. I fear these visions!" Her eyes fluttered closed again, her brow furrowing. "My belly was filled with dark clouds, a cold wind, and flashes of lightning . . . I dreamed that my baby will be taken from me."

"Sweet lady, do not speak of it," the midwife soothed. "There is no time; we must work." She glanced back, but the servants did not appear to have heard the duchess' mumblings.

"I have dreamed that there is no baby," whispered the duchess, "and that there is nothing within me but a tempest!"

"Sophia, be calm," ordered the midwife. "I am here, now. You must breathe much, much deeper than that if you want to bring this baby to the light. Now, breathe!"

She made another gesture, soft palm and open fingers spreading even wider, and the duchess sucked in a deep breath, exhaling in a loud intonation of pain.

"Good! Again!" The midwife gestured, the duchess breathed again, and the chambermaids cowered against the walls, praying helplessly under their breaths, unable to tear their eyes from the scene.

"Go see to the duke," ordered the midwife, annoyed by the maids' mumbling. When they hesitated, she slammed the staff against the marble floor and sent cracklings of electricity and cold air throughout the room, snapping at their clothes and hair. They shrieked and scattered like mice, racing out of the chamber, the door slamming behind them.

The duchess breathed and cried out in pain, and the midwife began to speak in soothing, foreign words that overlapped and swirled about the room like the tide coming in to the shore.

\* \* \*

In the antechamber, the duke and the maids stared at the closed door. From time to time, lights of varying colors would flicker out from beneath the doorframe. The duchess would scream in pain, or the midwife would sing strange scraps of melodies in peculiar tones. The duke fidgeted, ill to his stomach to hear his wife in so much torment, but paralyzed, unable to do anything to help.

Hours passed, and the duchess' crying died down into quiet, shuddering moans and mewls of agony. All the while, the midwife sang and chanted and hummed and spoke, though never in a tongue any of them recognized. After a time, the storm passed, and the rain slowed, finally stopping.

The duke had fallen asleep and the maids had disappeared into the palace when the door finally opened. It swung outward, seemingly of its own accord, but the groan of the hinges startled the sleeping duke, who scrambled to his feet and lunged into the room.

The duchess lay on the bed, her eyes wide and staring at the ceiling, her hair fanned out about her on the pillows; there was a look of utter wonder and love on her face. The sweat was still damp on her brow, but she no longer breathed or blinked.

He could not take his eyes off of her, his beautiful Sophia, perfectly suspended in a moment of joy, perfectly still.

There was a peculiar silence in the room as he stared at his dead wife. The midwife crouched in the corner, rocking back and forth, humming tunelessly.

Finally the duke looked to her and saw that she held something in her arms—the baby. Had the baby died, too?

"What . . . happened," he managed to say at last, his voice low and very dry.

"Shhhhh," breathed the midwife, and at first he was not sure she had heard his question. He took a step toward her. "Shhh," said the midwife again, lifting her head, her eyes the same pale, sky-blue they had always been, startling against her dark, shadow-cool skin.

The infant in her arms was as bright as a star, as pale as the moon that haunted the sky somewhere beyond the storm clouds. It was small, premature, but sturdy-looking in spite of that, with a swath of dark hair across its round head.

The duke was numb, his breath shallow as he stared.

"I have never lost a child yet," said the midwife, after a long pause.

"It's alive?" he heard himself say. The little thing was so small, he couldn't see it breathe.

The midwife nodded, slowly rising to her feet, shifting the small, bright child in her arms as she wrapped it in one of the blankets from the bed. It was the first time the duke had ever seen the midwife without her staff. The gnarled stick leaned against the bed post, just barely within arm's reach from where she knelt.

"This is your daughter," she murmured, looking at the duke with a strangely distant, peaceful expression.

His heart pounded. "My daughter. But Sophia—"

The dark woman shook her head. "Your daughter was too strong for her. It happens sometimes. Your wife's spirit is in her now," she added.

The duke said nothing. He moved to the door and pulled the bell rope to call the maids again. One of them arrived, gasping when she saw the corpse.

"Please take my daughter to the wet nurse," he said quietly. The midwife shifted the baby gently into the maid's arms even as the poor girl began to weep. She scurried out, sniffling over the little girl in the blanket. The duke moved toward the bed, gazing at the cold, still body of his wife.

The midwife leaned against the window, the rain-hammered glass cool and soothing against her skin. She was exhausted; she felt her eyes flutter shut.

"You did everything you could?" asked the duke quietly from across the room.

"Of course I did," said the midwife tiredly. "Your daughter lives, my lord. Be thankful, at least, for that much."

"Yes, of course. But you did at least try to save my wife, didn't you, Corvina?"

She looked at him sharply, but he still stared sadly at his wife. "Of course I did," repeated the midwife firmly. "I am sorry, my lord."

"Yes," he murmured dazedly. "Yes, I'm sure you are."

There was a pause, and the midwife's palm itched for the staff. She made as though to retrieve it, but quicker than she could blink, it was gone, and she turned in time to see it snap comfortably to the duke's palm. He closed his long fingers around it slowly.

"My lord," said the midwife, startled. "May . . . I have my staff, please?"

"I did try to tell you, didn't I?" muttered the duke, still looking at his dead wife. "I did. I asked you for very simple things, Corvina, and yet, you gave me nothing . . ."

"Nothing?" echoed the midwife, staring at him. "Nothing? I taught you everything you wanted to know."

"You gave me nothing," he repeated, slowly turning to look at her. "Nothing but psychorrax. Heartbreak. You have broken my heart, midwife. And I warned you. Now, I will break yours."

*Psychorrax.* They had screamed that at her in Greccia, when the power of her staff had caused the string of events that led to her exile. She had done nothing but defend herself, but the staff's magic was unpredictable, and many men had died in the events that followed. The women had thrown stones at her and screamed heartbreak. *Psychorrax!*

"No, please, please, my lord, this is not my doing. This is not my work!" The duke advanced on her. "My lord, mercy!"

"My wife is dead," he replied, oddly cool, his hand squeezing the gnarled wood over and over. "I have no mercy left to give."

The staff came down hard, and Corvina fell into darkness.

# CHAPTER ONE

## 1873

A bell rang loudly somewhere above decks as Ferran exhaled the breath he'd been holding and smoothed his palms down his shirtfront.

*Okay, you've got this,* he told himself. *You can do this. You've practiced and you're ready.*

He shut the door of the wardrobe, and the lamplight of the small but luxurious cabin caught the mirrored glass on the outside of the wood paneling as he turned to face his reflection.

*Nothing to be nervous about.*

At eighteen, dressing for dinner was an automated process for him, and it had been years since he required a team of trained valets to wrestle him into various fabrics and fits of proper clothes. He tugged his shirt collar upright to loop the dark green silk around the back of his neck and down the front again.

*The knot is just the icing on the cake. If I look just right, Father will believe that I can take care of myself, and he might let me go.*

The elaborate knot he was about to attempt had been tried multiple times over the last few weeks, and had given him a great deal more trouble than he'd initially anticipated. He'd just barely gotten it right on the day of the wedding, only to have it unravel an hour before the ceremony. His uncle, Bastiano, had to come to his sartorial rescue. Bastiano's nimble, long fingers had tied that tie as easily as some men might saddle a horse or build a boat—with careful, deft movements that came from much practice. It was intimidating, and Ferran wanted all the more to get it right now.

There was a knock at the cabin door as he began to loop the silk around itself. A moment later, the rumpled head of Truffo Arlecin, reluctant fool and sometimes servant, appeared around the doorframe, sleepy-faced and uninterested.

"Highness," mumbled Truffo, "they've gone up to dinner."

"I'm almost done," answered Ferran, glancing at him in the mirror. "I just have to tie this."

Truffo lounged against the wall, yawning, and crossed his arms. "Same knot?"

"Yes." Ferran's brow wrinkled as he carefully began the process of tying the folded knot.

"Why not just a regular one? S'only dinner. No heads of state to impress. Excepting your father, of course," Truffo added.

Ferran did not answer, his brow still furrowed in concentration. Truffo sauntered a little further into the room, his arms folded, eyes idly casting about the chamber. Ferran hesitated as he tried to remember which way the silk folded next. Truffo was staring at him again, dark eyes unimpressed and laconic. Ferran pulled a face and exhaled slowly through his nose. The silk slid from his fingers, dissolving into a loose loop about his neck, and he rubbed the bridge of his nose to hide his embarrassment.

"Staring at me like that really isn't helpful, Truffo," muttered Ferran.

Truffo's eyebrows wandered upward toward his smooth dark hair, which was kept short in the current sleek fashion. He was a few years older than Ferran's eighteen, but his face appeared childishly woeful much of the time. Truffo's hair was black, where Ferran's was an unruly brown, and the clown was an inch or so taller—a point of envy for Ferran. Over the years, the dullness of Truffo's dark brow and slight pout had become a familiar moue which irked Ferran, but for some reason was endearing to Stephen, the valet, and Ferran's father, the king.

"Sorry, Highness," drawled the fool, lowering his gaze demurely.

Ferran turned in exasperation. "Can you do a regular knot?"

Truffo pursed his lips thoughtfully. "Is that the one where the big bit goes over and around and then back into the small bit?"

Ferran blinked. "Yes . . ."

"Nope, can't do that one," said Truffo, and shuffled out of the chamber. "Dinner's served, and all that." The door swung shut behind him, and Ferran sighed.

He wrestled the green silk necktie into a standard sort of knot—although a bit lumpy—and ran his hands through his hair to flatten it down a bit more like Truffo's. The fool might be a bore while abroad, but he was a good-looking fellow, if the opinions of the courtiers were anything to abide by, and Ferran was of an age that found him reluctantly staring at his own wardrobe and throwing furtive glances at himself in mirrored surfaces.

*Someday I'll be king,* he thought grimly. He thought about it often these days. *I don't look like a king. I don't even look like a prince most of the time. Just . . . nobody.*

Ferran made his way out of his cabin and down the long, rosy-lit corridor toward the stairs leading up to the recreational deck, and ultimately the dining hall. This corridor in particular had a nice solid feel to it, despite its narrow length. It was almost enough to make Ferran forget how high up in the air they were. He was not prone to airsickness or seasickness, but thinking in too much detail about the altitude of the *Brilliant Albatross* above the waves made him want to skip dinner altogether.

The *Brilliant Albatross* was comfortable, though, and so far their trip had been smooth, even enjoyable. They had sailed away from Neapolis several weeks ago, then taken to the air once the wind had settled, and ultimately landed in Tunitz for his sister's wedding. Now that Coralina had wedded the prince of Tunitz, most of the wedding party was flying home: Ferran, his father, his uncle, and an assortment of servants, including Truffo, the valet, Stephen Montanto, and of course, Gonzo, his father's advisor.

Everyone was already seated in the dining room while servants poured the wine—everyone but Gonzo, who never really came to dinner, anyway. As Ferran passed over the threshold, his father's keen, hawk-like gaze flicked up and followed him about the room while he took his seat. Ferran did not meet his father's stare, but kept his shoulders down and his chin level as he'd been taught.

King Alanno Civitelli was well into his fifties—a slender, aging man whose body had been well-preserved by exercise and discipline in his younger years. At his left sat his younger brother, Ferran's uncle, Bastiano, a handsome, smiling man in his thirties—the fashionable bachelor of the court. To the king's right sat Duke Torsione Fiorente, a dark, shrewd diplomat whose reputation for success was untainted both at the conference table and in the bedroom.

Torsione and Bastiano were friends of old, well-known for their good humor and loyal camaraderie, although Torsione spent much of his time abroad visiting other lands in the name of the king, while Bastiano stayed in Neapolis as something of a cultural figurehead for court.

The valet, Stephen Montanto, paused to pour wine into the glass at Ferran's plateside. "Your Highness," he said quietly.

Ferran held up his hand slightly to signal he didn't want any, and Stephen bowed a little, moving away in silence.

"Good evening, Father," Ferran said at last, unfolding his napkin as the other servants began to bring the first course. *Nice and easy,* he told himself. *Be calm and collected, and tell him you want to study at the university next year. Just say the words. He might even say yes.*

The king looked shrewdly at his son. "Good evening." His eyes drifted, falling on the awkward knot of the green silk tie. Ferran looked away quickly and reached for his fork.

His uncle lifted his eyebrows and tilted his head. "I say, Ferr," Bastiano chuckled. "That's an interesting knot. Trying something new, now, are we?"

Duke Torsione glanced over. "Can't say I've seen that one before," he mused.

The king said nothing and went on spooning soup into his mouth.

Ferran tried hard not to look embarrassed. He speared several leafy greens onto his silver fork. "It was the best I could do on short notice," he said lightly. "But I'm getting better at it."

Bastiano smiled warmly. "Still haven't got the hang of that twisty one, have you?" he observed with a shake of his dark golden curls. "You'll get there. Ties are a devil of a thing 'til you've had enough practice."

"Same is true of anything worth doing," agreed Torsione, lifting his glass a little. "Language, art, music . . . war . . . women," he added thoughtfully.

The king grunted a little disapprovingly at this, but Bastiano laughed again. "In that order?" he wondered aloud.

Truffo Arlecin slouched into the room and Ferran was glad of the interruption. When the wine flowed like this, his uncle and Torsione took to philosophizing on all sorts of things that Ferran hadn't even experienced yet, and he found it tiresome and bullying of them to talk over him night after night, especially with his father glowering at the head of the table like some great Benjul tiger watching its prey.

"What have you for us this evening, Truffo?" asked Bastiano eagerly. "What on earth could possibly top your fascinating presentation last evening on the history of wallabies?"

Torsione made a judgmental sound and tipped his glass back for a deep drink. Bastiano tried not to laugh. *Like schoolboys*, thought Ferran, catching their exchanged glance out of the corner of his eye. He didn't like the way his uncle got flighty when the duke was around. Torsione was not a bad man, not as far as Ferran could tell, but there was something about him that brought out ill humor and posturing in Bastiano that made Ferran uneasy. It was as though there was some inside joke being referenced over and over again, but neither wanted to be the one to explain it.

"In honor of our most noble vessel, which wings us ever closer to our much missed, much lamented, much longed for homeland," droned Truffo with his hands behind his back and his shoulders hunched forward, "I have prepared a recitation of *The Albatross*."

"The what?" said Torsione with a wrinkle of his nose. King Alanno looked down, as if to pretend he was not listening. He seemed entirely focused on his food. Bastiano hovered one hand close to his mouth as he tried not to laugh.

"*The Albatross*," repeated Truffo with a furrowed brow. "It's a poem." Then he straightened a little and cleared his throat.

"By what poet?" demanded Torsione. Bastiano's giggle nearly broke. Truffo's mouth turned downward in an excellent horseshoe-shaped frown.

"By that poet whose name I have forgot, my good lord Torsione . . . a poet who did write this goodly, true poem about the noble bird of the sea whose name is also borne by this, our good and sturdy vessel homeward." He cleared his throat again, a little louder, and closed his eyes to prepare for the first lines of the poem.

With a resigned sigh, Ferran lowered his head and continued eating, but Truffo heard it and opened his eyes again, his brow dark and scowling.

"Come, come, Truffo," pleaded the grinning, helpless Bastiano. "You did woo us so elegantly with your history of wallabies the night past. Tell us now this poem. Say it how you will."

Although he often felt only vexation towards Truffo, whose sour moods never failed to annoy him, Ferran now felt a stab of pity for him as his uncle and the duke chuckled over their wineglasses. Truffo was nothing if not a sad sort to begin with, and teasing only made it worse.

Truffo Arlecin was neither fool nor fop, and he was neither courtier nor servant, although all four things seemed to apply to him all at once in the strangest ways. He had started as a servant in the kitchens, but they'd discovered his skills with mimicry and performance, and had hoped to encourage him toward foolery, but his ego was too delicate for full-time jestering. The courtiers often called him 'clown' or 'fool' anyway, though he'd never officially earned either title. He had been born far north of Neapolis, in a Frankish sort of country with brooding shadows, dark wines, and a more than healthy amount of egotism. His family had migrated southward and died along the way, and he had been passed into a serving family in the lower household of the king, thus working until he'd been given the post of fool some years past. He was not a juggling sort, however, and it fell upon the highest courtiers, such as Bastiano and Torsione, to needle and mock him as they saw fit.

Ferran noticed that Truffo's resolve was waning. He watched as the valet, Stephen Montanto, bent discreetly toward Truffo's ear as he passed by, and heard his quiet, gruff voice.

"Come, my boy, we're nearly home. Sing them a silly song and let it lie. Once you're through, I'll sneak you into the wine closet for a nightcap." Stephen moved away again, as smoothly as any shadow, and took up his post again in the dim corner.

Truffo drew a deep breath and looked as though he might throw a complete tantrum, but after a moment, his cheeks reddened and he let his breath out again slowly. The noblemen continued to eat, bemused. Ferran chewed his food slowly. *If Truffo would just get through his bit, I can bring up university to Father and be done with it.* His nerves were beginning to turn his stomach.

Truffo began to sing in a loud, irritable voice:

*I met a little bird,*
*Ding dong, ding dong, hey,*
*I met a little bird, oh, by the sea-shore*
*It had a broken wing,*
*Ding dong, ding dong, hey, now*
*It had a broken wing, oh, by the sea-shore!*

Ferran glanced over at Stephen thoughtfully. The older valet had a peculiar watchfulness over the moody Truffo, and had always been a solid, trustworthy sort. Stephen caught the prince's gaze, the tiniest wrinkle appearing at the corner of his mouth as he winked. Ferran smiled a little and turned back to his plate.

Truffo Arlecin's little bird song went on for eleven more stanzas, all performed with equal volume and strained tonality, despite the chuckling and eye-rolling of Torsione and Bastiano. King Alanno seemed not to hear anything that had been said for some time, but at last he lifted a hand, dropping his fork to his plate with a clatter. The fool shut his jaw quickly.

"That's enough," said the king, his expression grave. He did not seem angry, only decisive. Truffo Arlecin bowed low and backed comically out of the room, shooting Stephen Montanto a pointed look as he did.

"Your Majesty." The valet stepped closer to the king's elbow. "Do you require another cask of the wine?"

"No." The king dabbed at his mouth with a napkin. "That will be all, Montanto."

"Very good, Your Grace," murmured the valet, bowing. He and the other servants moved toward the door, clearing the room for the moment.

*It's good we're nearly home,* thought Ferran. *We're all so sick of each other. Even Torsione seems a bit bored with making Uncle Bas giggle all the time.* He sat back in his chair. *At least the food's been good.* He watched his father, trying to collect himself to say the words he'd been practicing for days.

King Alanno scraped the plate with his fork, slowly and deliberately scavenging the last bits of the triple-layered gateau from the fine china. The shrill clinking of the silver fork was the only sound, other than the hum of the ship's engines, the creaking of the wood paneling in the walls, and the settling of each of the men in their chairs as they sipped the last of their brandy.

An eternity passed as they listened to the king finish his dessert. The silence was painful, but no one wished to be the first to break it. As the time dragged on, Ferran felt muted, and he could not quite bring himself to speak up. He cleared his throat once, but no one looked up. The words danced around and around in the back of his mouth like flies, impatient but reluctant to start on their own.

At last, the king's chair scraped the floor and he got to his feet. The others scrambled to do the same as King Alanno looked at Ferran. He drew a deep breath, finally ready to make his case, but his father simply shook his head slightly and moved toward the door. The look of disappointment on the king's face snatched the words from his tongue unspoken, and Ferran's heart fell.

"Good evening, Your Grace," murmured Torsione.

Bastiano bowed his head slightly. "Good night, Your Highness."

"Good night, Father." Ferran lowered his gaze ruefully to the empty plate before him. *Of course,* he thought. *Not a chance. I should have brought it up right away. So stupid of me!*

The king was gone in a moment, and Bastiano let out his breath in a soft whistle, reaching for his nephew with one arm to hug him closer. "Don't let it bother you, Ferr. He's tired from the trip, that's all."

Ferran looked up at his uncle grimly. "I don't know what I've done to make him so cross with me," he admitted, "except that I'm just an enormous waste of his time. Now that Coralina's married and gone, I'm the only one left, and he hates me."

"He doesn't hate you," soothed Bastiano. "He really doesn't. He's always loved you, you're his son. His only son. But he's going through something, all right. Lina is his only daughter, too. And the eldest child. He just isn't ready to talk about it, whatever it is."

"Much like he still isn't ready to talk about Arthens," growled Torsione, suddenly surly. He slouched back down into his chair and put his boots up on the empty chair beside him. Reaching into his suit jacket, he pulled out a slender, bone-carved pipe—a trophy from his travels—and set about preparing for a smoke.

"You shouldn't smoke that awful stuff," Bastiano frowned. "It's terrible. I know it smells nice while you're smoking it, but it's really bad for your lungs."

Torsione looked up and met the worried gaze Bastiano had fixed on him. Without blinking, he proceeded to light the pipe and give several insistent puffs, his expression challenging. Bastiano continued frowning, but said nothing.

"What about Arthens?" prompted Ferran, looking at the duke.

"The same thing, over and over again," replied Torsione, with a shake of his head. "They're cross about your sister, still, you know. Rightfully, too." He blew a sleek stream of smoke toward the ceiling. "The Earl of Dolente can't live it down that the princess refused him."

"But she was already promised to Khalil!" Ferran liked the Tunitzan prince his sister had wed. Khalil was bright-eyed and quick to make jokes, putting everyone at ease when they'd first arrived. He'd given everyone gifts of strange and exotic birds upon their arrival, but had ordered the birds released at the end of the rehearsal dinner to signify the start of the festivities, much to Ferran's disappointment.

"Well, we know that," the duke went on, with a nod. "But they didn't. And it doesn't change the fact that the Earl's the Arthenian golden boy, and is well-in with the Greccian king. Everyone's quite upset. Easily insulted, the lot of them."

"Pity they haven't another immediate heir. Then we could patch things up," mused Bastiano, sitting down again and reaching for his brandy.

"Already thought of that." Torsione puffed a little plume of smoke away from the king's brother. "Although nobody jumps to mind, I wouldn't put it past them—any of them—to try and weasel a marriage pact out of us. Especially since Alanno's being so . . . misanthropic."

Ferran frowned. "What do you mean?"

"Misanthropic," said Torsione more clearly. "It means begrudging. Antisocial. Hermetic."

"I know what misanthropic means," interrupted Ferran. "What do you mean about another heir?"

The duke leaned his head against the high back of the chair and bit daintily on the stem of his pipe, bemusement sneaking into the wrinkled corners of his eyes. "Why, Your Highness . . . you're the next eligible royal bachelor, are you not?"

Ferran turned red as his uncle began to laugh heartily. "And that makes me what, pray tell?" demanded Bastiano, grinning from ear to ear.

Torsione cut his eyes sideways to Bastiano. "A hedonist," he purred, without letting his own smile crack too wide.

Bastiano guffawed at this, burying his head in his hands and crowing with laughter. Ferran pulled a face; he'd never been in a bawdy tavern, but sometimes the way these two talked to one another was downright unseemly.

"Good night, my lords," he muttered, sliding his chair in neatly to the table's edge and stalking toward the door.

"Nighty night, Ferr!" giggled Bastiano, still shaking his head at Torsione, who waved his brandy snifter aloft in farewell.

*We're almost home*, the prince reminded himself, gritting his teeth as he made his way back to his room. *I won't have to put up with them much longer. I can go back to my library and read for a whole week and ignore everyone. The whole library all to myself . . . it'll be like a vacation on a remote island, with no Uncle Bas, no Tor, and no Father glaring at me across the dinner table. Just me and my books. And maybe in another week or two, I can get Father alone and tell him I want to go to university.*

Ferran climbed into bed with the only book he'd been allowed to bring with him, a tattered copy of *Sinbad's Roc*, and tried to forget about the disappointment in his father's gaze. He dozed off a few chapters in, the book still propped in his hands.

He awoke to the harsh banging of the ship's warning bell.

Ferran sat up. *What time is it?* A scattered pounding of running feet sounded down the corridor. There was a knock on his cabin door.

"Yes?" Ferran said, sliding out of bed and reaching for his dressing gown.

The door opened and his father's advisor, Gonzo, waddled into the room, his brass and steel legs hissing and sighing on pistons unseen. "Your Highness," he hummed, his shining head inclined, expression as blank as ever. "They have asked us to dress and descend to the lower decks for life preservers. Also, it seems they've prepared tea for us."

Ferran stopped and stared at Gonzo. "What do you mean, life preservers?"

Gonzo bowed slightly. "It appears there is a very large storm heading for us rather quickly, and the captain would rather not take any chances with our safety. Upstanding sort of fellow. Shall we?"

Ferran moved to the wardrobe and began pulling on trousers, a shirt, and jacket. "We sailed through a storm on the way down to Tunitz, and they didn't wake us up for life preservers," he muttered.

"Yes, Your Highness, I recall that instance. However, I am led to believe that this immediate storm is a considerable threat to this aeronautical craft, and that we should prepare ourselves for an uncomfortable night." Gonzo paused and tipped his head, his round, blank eyes glowing a soft golden-green. "But they've made tea. Isn't that thoughtful?"

Ferran exhaled sharply and slid his feet into his boots. "Yes, Gonzo," he said, "very thoughtful." The mech had always had an unusually optimistic outlook, despite his neutral expression, and Ferran was glad that it was Gonzo who'd come to get him this time, and not Truffo again. This time of night meant Truffo was likely drinking as much wine as he could get his hands on.

The ship shuddered all around them, vibrations permeating the walls and floor of the cabin. There was a distant, groaning creak of metal and wood, and outside the porthole, a flash of lightning illuminated the rolling gray clouds beyond.

"Perhaps we should hurry, Prince Ferran," suggested the mechanical.

"All right," Ferran murmured, feeling the first glimmer of fear creep into his bowels. Turbulence was certainly not his favorite part of air travel. "I hope it's not as bad as they say."

"Indeed," answered Gonzo, closing the door behind them as they left the room. "It may be unpleasant, but not too much so. After all, there's tea."

# CHAPTER TWO

A great crash of thunder shattered the silence of sleep and jolted Mira awake. Gasping for air, she twisted against the canvas of her hammock and looked to the window. The world beyond the treehouse was still dark, but she saw a glimmer of lightning which illuminated the churning clouds above the canopy of trees. She put a hand to her chest, her heart racing, and frowned. Storms were nothing new to her—she always slept more soundly when it rained—but there was something distinctly strange about the thunder that had woken her up. Forcing herself to breathe more deeply, she swung out of the hammock and went to the door.

A cold front had swept through. The wind through the trees was harsh, like hands combing unruly hair, yanking forcefully on branches and boughs and making the treehouse shudder in spite of Mira's careful architecture. The little pinwheel made of leaves spun wildly on its axle, and the chimes of sea glass and shells hanging from the ceiling rang and swung helplessly in the breeze. The little house shivered and creaked around her, but Mira had spent years tying it off and supporting it with extra ropes, extra beams, extra netting. It was her home, and she had built it to last.

Another heart-stopping peal of thunder thumped against her very bones, and Mira grabbed for the tree trunk which grew up through the middle of the room. She narrowed her eyes toward the patches of sky visible beyond her windows. Although the wind blew, and the thunder was quite close, the rain had not yet come.

*This is no ordinary storm.*

Mira reached for the thatched grass cloak that hung by the hammock and the diver's goggles from the basket on the floor. Then she lifted the spear from its leaning place in the corner and stepped out of the little elevated hut, putting one foot into a rope sling and wrapping her other leg around the upper part of the rope. The pulleys squeaked and the rope began to unwind, lowering her to the ground. She untangled herself from the rope and it rose upward into the tree line again, vanishing from sight in the darkness of the pre-dawn forest.

Mira adjusted the fit of the goggles against the bridge of her nose, hefted her spear, and began to run. The diver's glasses were one of the thousand and one things she had recovered from the sea and learned to use for the better; they helped her see in the dark and underwater, depending on which knob she turned. They were her prized possession.

She ran surefooted through the trees and underbrush, heading east. The night-birds and quiet animals of the early hours were nowhere to be heard or seen—another hint that something unusual was taking place.

Lightning flashed a brilliant green through the trees ahead, and Mira slowed, crouching lower as she pressed forward through the bushes and smaller trees. Ahead, a rocky sort of cliff overlooked the lower beach of the eastern shore of the island. On the uppermost rock of that cliff stood a tall, dark shape, facing the sea.

Her father.

Mira found a sturdy young tree near the timberline and hitched herself up into the lower branches to see him better without leaving the cover of the shadows.

Mere yards away, Dante stood close to the edge of the cliff, his hands lowered at his sides, palms open toward the sea below and before him. The moon was gone, but the world seemed lit by strange glimmers of blue and green and silver that danced over the waves and through the clouds, darting like fireflies. The clouds boiled before him, churning and folding in and out of themselves. Lightning cut and splintered through the thickening thunder-heads, suddenly outlining a large, dark shape within them that turned and pitched violently.

*A ship!*

Mira's eyes went wide behind the diver's glasses. She had seen drawings. She had read descriptions in her father's books. She had seen wrecks along the ocean's bottom, scattered along the edges of the island's deep shorelines, but this was the first real ship she had ever seen in person.

It was incredible. And it was falling apart.

The storm clawed at the vessel like a cat shaking a bird and the ship spun and splintered, struggling to get away from the light-ning, from the wind and clouds and rain. It careened lower and lower, the churning waters of the wild ocean below threatening to swallow it whole.

Dante stood, appearing focused and serene as he watched the ship struggle to keep to the air. At his feet lay the long, gnarled stick he carried with him everywhere, a staff decorated with carv-ings and etchings of arcane symbols. To his right, lying open on a flat rock just behind him, was the book.

Mira watched him inhale deeply, then tip his head back, ex-haling slowly and raising his hands a little, like a flower reaching for the warmth of the sun. Lightning flashed again, and the ship's mast cracked, the sails tearing, alarm lights flashing red in the storm clouds. It began to fall.

Mira's gaze flicked from the floundering ship as it pitched downward toward the ocean to the great heavy book that lay on the rocks not far from where she crouched in the tree. She could probably get to the book before he saw her. After all this time, it was finally right there in front of her, within reach. She grasped the tree with one clammy hand and her spear with the other.

*Take it.* Her own voice in her head was quiet, calm, and collected, despite the pounding of her heart and trembling of her hands. *Take the book. It'll be easy.*

The ship hit the water with a massive splash, a fountain of smoke and flame rising into the storm from the upper decks. The propellers and enormous flight panels shuddered and screeched, and the lights flickered as they met the waves. Mira could almost hear the screams and shouts of the ship's crew and passengers.

*They're dying,* thought Mira. *My father's storm will kill them.*

If she could just reach the book, she could find out what her father had been doing all these years, hiding away in the caves and ignoring their little island life. The book never left his side, and she was certain it contained words and incantations of great power. If she could just get the book, she might finally figure out why her father kept her here, away from the rest of the world she knew must surely be out there. Her gut clenched with the weight of the decision; it was so close, the closest it had ever been, but if she didn't make herself known, the people on that ship would certainly die. Whoever they were.

*But the book . . .* she thought longingly. *The book will wait.* She tightened her grip on the spear and slid down from the tree, stumbling forward out of the bushes.

"Father!"

He did not turn to look at her; indeed, Mira would have thought that he had not heard her, except that she had encountered him in such a trance before and knew what he could and could not do while casting a spell.

"Father, stop!" she commanded, her voice raw from lack of use. She sounded squeaky and small, but she held her ground. "Those people are dying!"

He turned his head toward her slowly, as though it were an enormous strain for him to do so. For a moment, she did not recognize him, his face was so changed from the last time they'd spoken, some time ago. He certainly was not the same man she remembered from her childhood. His eyes had a gleam of lightning in them, and the strange, sleepy expression on his face was almost that of ecstatic release. Mira could not quite place it, but it seemed to her to be something like bliss.

"Mira," Dante said faintly, as though he could not bear to speak any louder. "My daughter . . . I must have woken you." His words slurred slightly, as though he were sleepwalking.

Mira squeezed the spear more tightly. "I know it's you, Father. I know you're making that storm. That ship must have passengers. There are people inside it . . . people who will die if you don't stop. I don't know why you've made this storm, but you have to unmake it!"

"Go back to sleep, my little girl," her father answered in an almost singsong tone, his eyes flashing brighter as the lightning surged again. "It's just a little rain."

"Wake up!" she screamed, as thunder shook the trees around them. "You don't know what you're doing! You have to stop!" He turned his face away, achingly slow, and resumed staring out toward the sinking ship. A light patter of rain began to fall over them. "They'll drown!" Mira shouted. "This is the closest anyone from beyond the sea has ever been to our island, and you're killing them!"

"Yes," agreed her father, raising his hands to the sky. "I am."

The ocean swelled, rising up like a snake poised to attack the ship, and Mira lunged for her father. He turned suddenly about to meet her, hands raised, his eyes masked in bright white-blue light, and the force of his mind threw her to the ground. She knocked over the book as she tumbled backwards onto the rocks, cutting her chin.

"Why are you interfering?" wondered her father, his hands claw-like. "Even if there are people aboard, why should it matter if they live or die? You are safe, Mira. That's what matters."

"Safe?" Mira spat, touching the back of her hand to her chin and wincing in pain. "Safe and isolated. You've never let anyone get this close to us before. You've kept the entire world beyond at bay to keep me safe. But you don't have to go killing people! They don't deserve to die simply because you don't want visitors! Why are you doing this?"

Something in his face changed, and the light went out of his eyes. "You're bleeding," Dante said softly, lowering his hands, muscles beginning to relax.

Behind him, beyond the shoreline, the lightning began to fade, the clouds untangling themselves and smoothing out again. The waves began to lessen, though the vessel still continued to sink.

Mira stared as her father knelt before her, the sleepiness fading from his expression, which melted into one of concern and anxiety.

"Mira, sweetheart, are you all right?" He looked at her bleeding chin, reaching for her tenderly.

She met his concerned gaze. The weathered lines of his face spoke of how tired he was, and how sad. He suddenly looked much more like the father of her memory, and for a moment, Mira considered letting him draw her into his arms and comfort her the way a father should. She couldn't remember the last time he'd come close to her. His beard was prickled with silver now, and his body was thin.

"You haven't been eating enough," she observed warily.

"My wondrous girl," Dante went on as though he hadn't heard her. "Let me look at your cut."

There was no apology, no acknowledgement that he was the one who had caused the injury, no admission of guilt or responsibility. Mira recoiled and scrambled to her feet, looking past him to where the fires of the wrecked ship were dimming.

"I hope they have life preservers," she said fiercely. She pointed her spear toward the wreck. "Or their blood is on your hands. How could you do this?"

"Their blood is on my hands?" echoed her father, unfolding himself to his full height again, his brow darkening in anger. "You have no idea what you're talking about."

"I may not know all that you know," Mira retorted angrily, "but I'm not a murderer. And I never thought you would be." She turned and fled into the woods.

\* \* \*

Dante sighed in frustration, turning to pick up the enormous, weathered book from the ground where it had fallen. He reached with an open hand and beckoned the staff, which leapt into his grasp, then turned again to look out at the ship as it slowly descended in pieces beneath the choppy waves.

Dante narrowed his gray eyes. Something had gone terribly awry, but at least the ship still sank. "Come back to me, my dainty spirit," he murmured, leaning on the staff. "Come and obey in all things, Aurael."

The light rain began to fade as the clouds moved swiftly by overhead, and the air folded and shimmered before him.

"I did perform this tempest as you bade me, my lord," yawned the spirit as he solidified into pale, translucent skin. His hair was wild from the winds, and his eyes had an iron heaviness to them. "Was there some problem that made you call it off before the Big Finale?" Although his words were courteous, his tone had a touch of steel to it, cold and sharp-edged.

Dante shook his head slowly, pulling his gaze from the wreck to stare at the spirit. He pursed his lips. "Did you hear me order you to call it off?" he asked, dangerously soft.

Aurael squinted at him, hovering and hesitating. "No," he answered slowly, "my lord, I heard you not . . . It seemed to me out there that you took control of the spell yourself and made the storm calm again." His brow wrinkled. "Was that not so?"

Dante looked darkly at him. "No, Aurael, I did not send the storm away. I had rather hoped to see the ship split into a hundred pieces in mid-air, and watch their bodies drop like stones to the sea below. Needless to say, I am disappointed."

"Wait just a second!" Aurael demanded. "I didn't do anything except exactly what you told me to do! But if you didn't stop it, and if I didn't stop it, then who did? My lord, I cannot even begin to fathom a guess, unless they had a sorcerer on board. More importantly, the deed is done. The ship is sunk, and all souls will surely perish, by shark or salt water or both." Aurael threw his hands up in childish exasperation.

"You dare make light of this?" Dante growled.

"My lord," replied his servant through gritted teeth, "I have done you great services and served you most loyally for these long fifteen years since you arrived. You promised me one thing for my loyalty back then, and you promised me this very morning that you would deliver it to me if I brought down their stupid ship with fire and brimstone." He swung a shimmering arm wide at the wreckage. "And look! I have done so."

"Yes, but there is so much more to be done."

Aurael seemed wild with anger, as though he would twist himself up into a cyclone at any moment. "I would like what is due me, my lord," he insisted, jaw tight. "I just want my freedom."

Dante burst out laughing—a dry, brittle laugh that faded away as quickly as dead leaves on the wind. "You'll have it when you've earned it. Bring me the king, his brother, the duke, and any of the other live men ashore, but scatter them about the isle so that no more than two are together at a time. Let them wonder at their friends' demises, and despair their own fates. Go now, lighter than air and faster than thought. Will you do this?" The question was a mockery, as though Aurael had any sort of say in the matter.

Dante watched Aurael seethe for a moment, steam curling up from his pale brow and vanishing into the air as he began to fade from view. "Yes," he growled.

"Yes . . . ?" prompted Dante.

"Yes, my lord," hissed Aurael, and then he was gone like breath upon glass.

With a grunt of faint satisfaction, Dante turned away from the wreckage and began his slow walk back to the caves on the south end of the island, his book under one arm, his staff in hand. If Mira wanted to meet people from beyond their island in the sea, she might meet these castaways, and then she would know the true depth of his purpose. Then she would know why he sought revenge.

# CHAPTER THREE

I n his dream, Karaburan was hunting a man. His dream—like most of his dreams—was dark and full of smells and uncertain noises, like that of a blind creature of the earth that burrows and sniffs and growls to see its surroundings with its ears rather than its eyes.

Karaburan crawled forward into the darkness on his belly, scenting the man he sought. The earth was velvety cool against his rough skin. Some parts of the ground were warm from where the sun had shone down, and some parts were cool from shade. He could hear the heartbeat of the island all around him, pulsing as quietly as though he were underwater. Far off, he heard the chime of birds singing, the faint whispering of old magic, and the gentle hum of the ocean.

He stopped, smelling the soft earth, the world around him gradually growing more and more quiet. He inhaled deeply and moved forward along the ground, still sniffing and turning his blind head this way and that, as a mole does deep within its tunnel.

His hands touched something warmer than the dirt. Skin? He hesitated, almost drawing back, but could not help himself. He moved forward, closer, feeling long and slender legs along the ground in front of him. His eyes traveled over faint shapes in the dark, his vision a limb that had been asleep and now tingled with new feeling.

Delicately, he brushed his hands along the smooth, lush skin of the legs he'd found in the dark, moving up, along the curve of what must have been hips, to a slender waist. It had not been a man he had been tracking at all, but a girl. He trembled, disbelief and anxiety blurring together as he slowly regained his sight and began to make out the vision of the girl before him, lying asleep on the ground.

She was so beautiful, her hair spread wildly out like seaweed. Her breathing was steady, her clothes utterly missing, though she was still much concealed by shadows in the darkness.

Karaburan breathed heavily and shivered, ashamed of how close he was to her and of how desperately he wanted to hold her, to crawl over her, to do something terrible that his brain could not quite understand. He wanted to press his skin against hers, but he did not know why.

The girl stirred, making a faint sound in her sleep, and he moaned in reply, terrified of his impulses. He clapped his hands over his mouth in fear, all six fingers of each hand pressing together as if to take back the sound, but she had heard him. The girl woke as suddenly as an animal, her impossibly blue eyes flying wide open in the dark and a hoarse shout issuing from her throat.

"No!" she cried out, scrambling back, but he reached his huge arms to her and yanked her close to him. "No," she repeated, louder and louder. "No! No!"

Karaburan squeezed her against himself, a strange mixture of sorrow and desire blossoming within him, as she struggled and screamed, beating at him, her eyes wider than a fish's, her mouth flapping as she begged him to stop. Just a moment more, just a little longer . . .

Then the girl's eyes went white-hot, like sunlight refracted sharply on the sea. The brightness blinded him, and he felt his

*entire body pierced by lightning. He recoiled, howling and burn-*
*ing, and the girl was gone. He was blind once again, weeping and*
*shuddering in the darkness.*

Thunder rolled loudly somewhere nearby, and Karaburan woke
from his nightmare with a start, tears pouring down his uneven,
bulging cheeks. He bolted upright, still shaking from his dream,
and found himself in the small outcrop of rocks near Dante's cave
where he had lain down the night before. He was glad to find himself in the same place—it meant he hadn't walked in his sleep. But
the dream . . . The dream was one he'd had over and over for years,
and every single time, it brought him to weeping shamefully in the
darkness for what he'd done.

A storm was raging off the coast of the island. Karaburan
watched the lightning flash through his tears for a moment before
curling up again on the rocks, barely sheltered from the light rain
that fell outside his makeshift room.

He cried until he fell asleep again, then dreamed another
dream. This time, he was playing in the springy green moss of the
forest at the heart of the island. His mother was there, picking
herbs and singing quietly in the language of her people.

As he drifted off into the gentle warmth of this new dream,
a chill wind fluttered past Karaburan's rocky shelter, whipping
grains of sand into tiny maelstroms which died down again shortly
after they began.

Aurael paused at the entrance of the crude outcrop of rock
that served as the monster's shelter for the moment. It was not
deep enough to be called a cave, but it was just enough to keep
the deformed young man dry from the rain. Aurael wrinkled his
upturned nose at the fishy smell of the monster's closeness. Even
after all this time, he was not used to Karaburan's unique stench,
and although there was no one to complain to about it, he still
pulled faces to himself.

He watched the blank sleeping face of the monster and pursed his lips in thought. It hadn't been long ago that the monster first gasped for air, pulled from his mother's womb by Aurael's own hands. And it was the fault of this ungrateful, foul-smelling wretch that Aurael had been banished to this isle himself, trapped in that godsforsaken tree by Ouberan as punishment.

Aurael's face contorted with disgust, and he tiptoed toward the sleeping Karaburan, placing an invisible finger against the monster's bulbous forehead. *I'll help you sleep*, Aurael thought with a grimace, and slipped inside the monster's mind.

\* \* \*

*"Karaburan," mused his mother, walking barefoot on the damp moss. "What do you wish for?"*

*"I wish for a playmate!" cried Karaburan, who in the dream was but a child.*

*"And what else?" Corvina smiled, her white teeth seeming even whiter against her dark skin.*

*"I wish for a father!" answered the child, whose fingers waggled in the air like so many worms peeping out of the soil after rain.*

*His mother's expression faded into one of hard apology. "You have none, child," she told him, somberly. "And none you shall have."*

*"But why?" The child put his webby hands to his mouth.*

*"For that you are a misshapen, ill-inclined, unlikely thing," replied his mother, with great seriousness, "and that you were forced upon me as a curse, and now here we are upon this quiet and lonely isle with only the trees and the birds for company."*

*The child Karaburan did not know what to make of this, but his mother looked quite distraught, so he crawled across the moss toward her skirts, which were tattered and torn and faded from the sun.*

"You are a poorly formed thing, my son," said the witch, with a sigh, crouching and setting her herbs and flowers aside to embrace him. "And yet, here we are, we two. The only two oysters in the bed."

"The only two birds in the sky?" asked the boy, putting his uneven, bubble-skinned face against her hair.

"The only two crabs on the beach."

"The only two people in the whole wide world?" laughed the boy. His mother drew back from their lopsided embrace and looked her deformed son in the face squarely then.

"Karaburan, we are not the only two people in the whole wide world," she said firmly. "You know this. I have told you many times."

"I know, but it is much more fun this way, Mother." He reached for a stick nearby that looked like a snake frozen in mid-slither, but could not quite reach it from where she held him still.

"There are others out there, my boy," fretted the witch. "And I do not know how long it will be before they find us. Or before we find them, as the case may be." She looked worried and distant. "But someday, I feel they'll come here, and stand on our shore, and know this isle as we do. I don't know when . . . or who. But I have a feeling, Karaburan, and you'll have to be ready."

"Ready for what?" asked her son, still reaching for the stick.

"Listen, Karaburan!" she rebuked with a scowl. "Look at me, and listen carefully. Someday it will come to pass that a man may come to these shores, and he will be a very bad man. Do you understand? Many men are bad, but this man will be very bad indeed. You will have to be ready."

"But you'll be there, won't you?" Karaburan looked up at his mother's scowling, worried face, his own uneven blue eyes blinking.

"I may be, but I may not be. I cannot tell, my son." She smoothed back his tuft of dark, unruly hair, which grew only on the right side of his head, thick and shiny. "But if I am not, you will have to be ready to protect yourself. This is your island, Karaburan. I will leave it to you, in your hands, and you will care for it and protect it, and it will keep you safe and alive. Do you understand? You are king over this island."

"A king, a king!" exclaimed the boy, slapping his webbed hands together excitedly.

"Yes, and a king must have a queen," Corvina went on, lifting her son's chin proudly with one finger. "When you find a woman, Karaburan, you must make her your queen."

"What do you mean?" asked her son, his head lolling heavily to one side in curiosity. "What do you mean, a queen?"

"The birds have their mates," said Corvina, "and so do the fish, but you will not have one who is your true match. You must find the one who is, and you'll know her when you do . . . Eyros' arrow will pierce your heart, and all you must do is take her for your own. All of this shall be when you are older, of course," she added.

"A queen," echoed Karaburan, pushing his hands into the dirt. "A queen for my island."

"Yes," agreed his mother, turning back to her herbs. "A queen for Karaburan."

Then the dream shifted, veering into pitch darkness from that light-filled clearing in the woods, and Karaburan cried out in the dark. His hands splayed wide to protect himself, but he could see nothing. His heart pounded and thundered inside his chest, but for several moments more, nothing happened. He dropped to all fours, no longer a child, and began to crawl forward. He crawled slowly, bit by bit, trying to get a better sense of his surroundings.

He caught a whiff of something on the air. Man! No, he thought, sniffling in the shadows, a woman. A queen.

*Karaburan moved forward, slowly as any predator bearing down on his prey, and inhaled the smell of the woman somewhere up ahead.*

\* \* \*

Aurael released his grip on the monster's head and smiled to himself. It was the one delight he took in his life these days, creating new and terrible nightmares for Karaburan. The monster didn't even know he existed, poor simple soul; all he knew was that there were some strange foul forces at work that pinched him and prodded him and beset him with visions. Aurael enjoyed it overall, as it reminded him of his early days in the world, mocking the superstitious men of ancient times.

Nowadays, men of the modern world were more likely to press through uncertainty with scientific thought and reasoning than explain things with supernatural phenomena; but here on the island, Aurael found great success in delivering torments to the simplest fish-skinned monster imaginable.

*Round and round and round we go*, he thought, and with a chill gust of wind, he vanished from the shelter, soaring out over the beach toward the wreck of the ship.

\* \* \*

### 1858

Aurael was not certain what happened to Corvina's corpse.

Her son, the deformity she called Karaburan, did not come looking for her. *Stupid thing*, Aurael seethed to himself, pressing angrily against the bark of the tree. *He probably hasn't even realized she's gone. Or if he has, he's too stupid to leave their cave, pathetic child. If only I'd finished my work before Ouberan arrived.*

His sore and angry heart beat out the words, 'Oh, if only!' a thousand times over those days that crept by like snails on the sand, and his misery never abated. He began to think he should not have tried to take advantage of her forgiving nature; now, he did not even have a soul to speak to.

After several days, she vanished, and he had no idea how. There were no footprints nor drag marks in the earth where she had been, and it frightened him to see the unbothered ground where she had lain.

After the tenth day passed, Aurael presumed the child Karaburan had died from lack of food and water. *How long does it take for a child to decompose?* wondered the airy spirit. He had no context for the matter, and indeed was robbed of his ability to observe the afterlife first hand, as Corvina's body had been politely removed from sight. It spooked Aurael right to his core, not knowing where it had gone, and the peculiar noises that sometimes came from the woods punctuated his thoughts with primal utterances and unusual song.

Aurael began a sort of hibernation, then, drifting in and out of consciousness as the tide does. It felt like years had passed as easily as hours, when a new voice interrupted the endless summer quiet of the island.

"There's a face!"

The little voice emerged from Aurael's dark and dreamless slumber, tickling his ears. He stirred restlessly, wanting to return to the darkness, but there was a replying shout from further off—a man's darker tone.

"Don't wander, Mira. Stay close to me. I have to bring up the rest of my books from the shipwreck. It will take a while, but I need you to stay close."

*Shipwreck?* Aurael thought. *I didn't hear anything crash.*

"Father, there's a face in this tree!"

Aurael cracked one eye open like a cat checking to see who was creeping up on its napping place. There was a child, a little girl, sauntering up the sandy hill toward his tree, her eyes bright and startlingly blue-green, like lightning over the ocean. Her golden-brown hair was long and handsomely done in braids and curls, and her traveling gown was a bright russet red with gold and ivory silk sleeves. She seemed a little windblown and damp from the sea, but all in all, quite well and merry. She might have been three or four, though it was hard to tell with mortals.

She saw him looking at her and gave a little gasp, stopping in her tracks as though it were part of a game. Aurael felt something strange break open inside of his sleepy, icy soul. He heard her take a few steps closer, and, after a pause, he let both of his eyes open wider by a fraction. The girl stopped again, pressing her mouth into a line to prevent her giggles from escaping.

Aurael shut his eyes again, heard her venture even closer, and then, silence. The breeze was gentle in the branches of his tree, but he heard no sign of her. After several moments, he opened his eyes fully, puzzled, and found that she had vanished. He frowned, the bark of the tree shifting to accommodate his furrowing brow.

"Are you a nymph?"

The girl was sitting on the ground at the foot of the tree, leaning against the trunk like a kitten pressing against the legs of an unsuspecting stranger.

"What?" Aurael replied before he could stop himself. "No. No, I'm not a nymph." The word tasted like evergreen sap to him, acrid and disgusting. *A nymph indeed!* He pulled a grimace in the tree bark. The little girl was tracing the patterns on the bark, deeply interested in every line.

"Are you a fairy?"

Aurael tried not to gag audibly. "No, I'm not a fairy, either."

"But you can talk. Trees don't talk." The girl looked up at him with a very serious expression. "So you must be something other than a tree."

"Are you certain this isn't in your head?" Aurael inquired, trying to see past the leaves and toward the beach, where the voice of the man had sounded. "Where did you come from, anyway?"

"A ship," replied the girl, drawing circles in the sand.

"And before that?" Aurael could hear the man walking about on the sand, and the sound of the waves, but he remained out of Aurael's eyesight. "Where before the ship?"

"Home," answered the child. "That's a silly question. Of course we came from home."

Aurael's frustration ground against the bark of the tree as he gritted his teeth, but there was something so endearing about the girl's expression as she looked up at him that he could not bring himself to snarl a reply. He sat silently for a moment, considering the new development.

"What's your name?" she asked him after a few moments. "My name's Mira."

The spirit hesitated, but the earnest expression on her face was too much. "Aurael," he murmured back, softening against the tree bark. It was against his better judgment to give up his name so easily, but she was enchanting, and he had been alone for so long.

"I like that," the child said agreeably. Aurael tried not to smile.

"Who came with you?" he asked her.

"My father," the child said brightly. "He's on the beach trying to retrieve our trunks."

As if on cue, the father called out. "Mira! Come here. I've found your doll."

Mira gasped delightedly and scrambled off down the sandy hill toward the beach. Aurael strained his branches to get a look, but could not see where she'd gone. He sighed, the branches of his tree shuddering and swaying about him, and waited for her to come back, but she did not. The airy spirit dozed in the warm sun, and slept again.

The little girl, Mira, did come back eventually to sit by his tree several times over the next few days. Often she did not speak more than a few sentences at a time, but sat quietly and drew in the sand, or played with her doll, or built stick monuments with twigs and leaves in the soil. Aurael was enchanted by her singleness of purpose, serene countenance, and unobtrusive way of simply keeping him company. It was so unlike anything he'd ever known before, and he felt as though the cares of his recent times were fading away.

"As long as it's just you and me," Aurael told the little girl, "I'm happy. Just you and me and your doll, and the island."

"And Father," added Mira cheerfully. "Father's here, too."

"Right," agreed Aurael. "But I don't want to visit with him. I only like talking to you."

Mira beamed at him, patting the trunk of the tree with one small hand. "I like talking to you too, Orryell."

"It's Aurael," he said dryly.

"That's what I said," she answered, and began to draw in the sand again.

A few days later, he startled awake just before dawn, feeling some sort of buzz along the trunk of his tree. The roots of his prison hummed with the echoes of something powerful nearby, and Aurael remembered the way he had felt the magic resonate when Corvina had been nearby. This felt similar, but amplified, as focused as light passing through a magnifying lens.

"Who's there?" he called, defensively. "Who are you?"

The birds had not yet begun to sing in the woods, but there was a rosy glow in the east that reflected across the clouds and the tops of the waves. Something moved beyond his tree, in the shadows. Aurael pressed against the tree bark, trying to see more clearly.

"I can hear you, you know," he growled.

"I know," answered a man's voice, and Mira's father came

walking out of the dark, the staff in his hand covered in faintly glowing sigils and signs. The dim gleam of bluish magic reflected in the man's eyes, his expression bemused.

Aurael shut his mouth, a chill sweeping through him.

"An elemental," mused the man, "trapped in a tree. Fascinating. I suppose you're not in there by your own choice."

Aurael said nothing. If this man was as powerful as the vibrations would have him believe, Aurael did not want to confess anything that might prove to be useful against him.

"That's all right, you don't have to speak. Yet." Mira's father came closer, studying the tree. "Hm. Someone quite strong put you in there, I see. Someone old. And . . ." His eyes fell to the ground in front of the tree, the exact spot where Corvina's body had fallen in death. The man raised his eyebrows. "Ah. Interesting." He turned to face Aurael's tree with a wrinkle at the corner of his grayish eyes. "Very interesting."

"Who are you?" said Aurael, his own eyes narrowing.

"Someone who thinks we might be able to help each other." The man leaned on the staff thoughtfully.

"Oh, really," answered Aurael flatly.

"Yes, really," replied the man. "You've been stuck there a long time. You'd like to get out. And I'd like to let you out. In fact, I'm quite certain I can free you. But in return . . . I'd need your assistance with something. A long-term sort of project."

Aurael was silent, his eyes fixed on the man's face. "You want to hire me," he said, slowly. The man smiled, and it was a kind smile, which made the coldness in his eyes all the more chilling, even to Aurael. But he was desperate.

"I'm listening," said the spirit, and the man with the staff smiled a little wider.

# CHAPTER FOUR

Stephen Montanto lay face down in the dark, the earth beneath him warm against his skin. One by one, his senses came back to him from the blackness of sleep, the first being the feeling of the hard ground and the hot sun bearing down on him.

He felt as though his entire skull had been detached, used as a bocce ball, and reattached haphazardly in something of a rush. By and by, feeling returned to the rest of his limbs and torso, along with the aches and pains of the worst hangover he had ever had in all of his fifty-some years. His body felt simultaneously hollow and full of sharp nails, prickling with discomfort as he fought to shake his mind free of the dark and remember what had happened to him.

After clearing away the trays from the king's supper, Stephen had found that the door to the wine closet was not only unlocked, but partly open. This room had strictly been forbidden to all servants except Stephen himself, and he pushed the door wider to peer suspiciously inside.

"How the—?" Stephen frowned severely down at Truffo Arlecin, who was on the flop cradling three or four bottles to his chest as though they were a litter of puppies. "Truffo, lad, you know you aren't allowed in here. How the devil did you even open the door?"

Truffo looked mournfully up at him and sighed. "I nicked your key when you told me to sing them a song."

"Why?" Stephen tried not to look impressed by the

pickpocketing. "I told you I'd fetch you a nightcap myself."

"Because!" Truffo's pink cheeks flushed darker as he rubbed one eye with the heel of his hand, trying to hold all of the wine bottles in the crook of one arm as he did so. "It went horribly. The entertainment last night went horribly. The night before went terribly. The wedding was a joke, especially compared to the damned dancing girls and fire-eaters Prince Kahlil hired for the floor show." Tears were welling in his eyes. "I'm not even a good fool. I embarrass myself. All I wanted was to stay home and be boring, Stephen. I didn't ask to be brought along."

"No, you didn't ask for it," agreed Stephen sternly, "but the king requested your presence. That's the kind of recognition that can make a career, you know. Come on, put the bottles back and let's get you to bed."

"I am not a child," sniffed Truffo, disdainfully. "I am a grown man, and I want to drink this wine." He wrestled with one of the corks.

"Good luck opening that without this," said Stephen, brandishing the corkscrew he kept on his person during mealtimes. Truffo's expression melted so quickly that Stephen almost laughed at him. "Now, lad. Put back the bottles, and away with you." He reached his free hand out to take a bottle from Truffo's arms.

"Please," whimpered the dejected fool. "Just one bottle, Stephen! Just one. Just one bottle, eh? For the end of a miserable trip?"

*Gods pity him,* thought Stephen, shaking his head as he took the other bottles and put them back into the crates where they belonged. "Truffo," he chided. "This is the king's wine."

"And he's got plenty to spare," Truffo spat. "Please?"

"You're a terrible nuisance, you know." Stephen shot him a look. Truffo folded his arms tightly and scowled. "Really. This sad clown routine is a little maudlin sometimes, Truffo."

"It's not a routine," moaned the fool, immediately unfolding his arms and raking his fingers through his hair angrily. He made a sound of frustration, like a teenager on the verge of a tantrum.

"All right, all right, quiet down." Stephen reclaimed one of the bottles from the crate and reached for his corkscrew. "I'll let you have a little as long as you promise to calm down and go to bed afterward."

"I promise," hissed Truffo, as he fixed his shining eyes on the bottle.

But he hadn't gone to bed after that, Stephen now realized. Truffo had drunk a considerable bit of the wine before insisting that Stephen drink some, too. Stephen was normally a man to drink but a few sips of the stuff before putting it aside; he was far from the lush that Truffo apparently was. He wasn't sure what had caught him off-guard that night and convinced him to keep drinking—whether it was the taste of the wine itself, or the pleading of the young fool.

That first bottle had soon become two, then three, and Stephen's normally calm, restrained nature had given way to the bumbling, brash-tongued man he'd been once in his youth—a persona released by the sweet and burning wine. Toward the end of the fourth bottle, the ship had begun to experience some turbulence, which turned into a full-on alarm of distress in the middle of the night. The ship's power was failing, and they were falling out of the sky, into the deep.

Truffo cried into his hands, hugging a bottle of his own as he sat on the ground with his knees pulled up against his chest.

"We'll die, we'll die, we'll surely die," sobbed the sad fool. "Never more to touch the sky or ask a balding eagle why, or eat my mother's homemade pie, or never fall before we fly, we'll die, we'll die, we'll die . . ."

"Hush lad," slurred Stephen, already feeling blackness at the edges of his senses. "Keep drinking. We'll go out on the wings of Dionysus together. Be brave, now." He drank from the bottle again, as though summoning the last of his own courage there.

Truffo, his boyish face tear-streaked and ruddy, looked up bleakly, mid-sob. "Dionysus hasn't got wings," he moaned. "We're going to die!"

The *Brilliant Albatross* jolted sideways, throwing both men to the floor, wine bottles clattering and rolling and breaking all around them. The lights in the wine closet stammered and went dark, and there was a scream from somewhere else on the ship as the *Albatross* plummeted toward the sea. Stephen had slipped into unconsciousness before they hit the water.

Now, on an unknown beach, Stephen Montanto opened his eyes, though the light of day was painfully bright, causing tears to slide down his sand-scratched cheeks. He tried to roll over onto his back, but an exquisite, lightning-sharp pain lanced through every single nerve in his body.

*Dead people can't be in this much pain*, he posited to himself, and breathed heavily in order to try the roll over once more. He was successful this time, but the movement made him cry out in a ragged, hoarse voice, and more tears sprang forth from his eyes.

Stephen lay on his back, panting for air, and choked with pain and sorrow as the sun beat down on him. Then he slowly started to realize that he could hear the waves and the birds and the gentle wind through the trees and grasses. *An island*, he realized, and tried to look around, shielding his raw eyes from the sun with a heavy, sunburnt hand. *I've been washed to some desert island. Perhaps I am not dead after all.*

He reflected that he had been considerably intoxicated when the ship went down, and added in the fact that, even when sober, he was not much more than a barely-competent swimmer. He let these thoughts marinate for several minutes and concluded that if he was not dead, it was by a miracle alone that he found himself on this beach. As there was no sign of anyone else nearby, he further concluded that he must be the sole survivor, and all the others had surely drowned.

Stephen gave a wordless sob. He had failed his king in the hour of true need. It was not right that he should survive—even by accident—only to know that his king was dead, and all the others aboard the *Albatross,* too. And Truffo, the poor lad. And Prince Ferran! Stephen's heart ached nearly as much as his body did.

It was too late for such thoughts. He drifted back into a kind of sleep, too pained to get up and seek out shade, and aimed to let himself be burned to a crisp by the boiling sun above.

* * *

Truffo Arlecin woke to a strangely colored bird walking on his leg. It chirruped and cawed to itself, muttering like a nosy housewife investigating a new neighbor, and taking no notice of him whatsoever as his eyes opened bleakly and his brow furrowed in concern and pain. His body throbbed dully with the soreness of one who has fallen from a great height and lived to tell the tale, and his clothing was ragged and damp.

The bird, which was yellow on top, blue on its bottom, and orange in the middle, with a sharp black marking like a mask over its face, stood about the size of a house cat. It ruffled its tail feathers as it stalked up and down Truffo's legs, poking at his clothing and cocking its head this way and that as it muttered. It did not weigh much, but its spindly feet were as prickly as a briar patch, and after several minutes of squirming, Truffo could bear it no longer.

"Hey, hoy, get off of me," he exclaimed, his voice torn and sore from salt water. He tried to shoo the bird away, but his arm was quite heavy, as though it had fallen asleep, and his shoulder screamed with pain. He abandoned the attempt, groaning in agony.

The bird clicked its long beak at him, ruffling its neck feathers and hopping from one of Truffo's legs to the other. The young man gritted his teeth.

"It hurts!" he told the bird as it tutted its way slowly up his body, prodding him gently with the sandpiper-like beak. His voice was brittle and dry. "It's unbearable."

He closed his eyes, remembering the steep pitch of the *Brilliant Albatross* as it plunged toward the waves, the clattering of glass wine bottles crashing and rolling about them, and the explosion of the airship's engine as it hit the cold sea. He knew only darkness thereafter.

Truffo opened his eyes to find the brightly colored bird settling down on his chest, staring at him with feathers shimmering. "Don't get comfortable," murmured the fool. "If I don't die in the next few hours, I'll be starving, and I'll have to eat you. Probably raw, since I don't know how to build a fire. Feathers and beak and all. Oh, gods, I hope it doesn't get cold at night," he realized, a note of panic creeping into his voice. "I'm going to need a fire. Even if I knew how, I probably couldn't . . . my arm . . ."

He craned his neck to the side, peering at his injured shoulder— a considerable amount of dark blood had seeped through his shirt, and the sleeve of his motley coat had been torn off. It felt like an arrow had buried itself in the muscle, though he could see no certain evidence of what was causing the pain. It hurt like hell.

The bird cocked its head almost disapprovingly, and Truffo frowned at it. "I told you, it hurts," he insisted through his teeth. "It hurts a lot."

The orange-yellow bird fanned out its blue tail and gave a trilling series of whistles and chirps. Then it leaned over and jabbed its beak directly into the wound in Truffo's shoulder.

He screamed, an infantile shriek that echoed off the flat beach and the rocks beyond, startling some sparrows out of a shrub. The prodding of the bird did not cease, and Truffo continued to cry out loudly, voicing his excruciating displeasure. It wasn't until he lurched upright and tried to scramble to his feet that the bird trumpeted and flapped its wings, trying to cling to him.

"Get off, get off of me," Truffo sobbed, the pain in his shoulder a flaming spike of agony that nearly caused his knees to buckle, even as he stood. "Stop, just stop it!"

The bird trilled and cawed and clucked in a myriad of different voices. Its orange and yellow wings spread and flapped and ruffled at him, its dark little claws clutching his torn shirt and jacket, and its sandpiper beak poked at his wound, causing the dark blood to flow once more.

Truffo staggered forward, still swatting at the bird, but the pain shot deeper into his body and he stumbled to his knees in the hot white sand. Black shimmering dots swam at the edges of his vision, and Truffo wondered if he had survived the shipwreck only to die at the beak of a tropical bird on a desert island.

*What a punchline,* he thought bitterly. Then he felt the bird grasp something deep in his shoulder and yank hard. Truffo sucked in air so quickly that he was utterly silenced from shock, and the bird hopped back from him, beating its wings. Much of his pain left with the bird, like a candle blown out, and Truffo sagged as blood trickled down his shirt.

The odd sandpiper dropped the offending object onto the beach beside him, and Truffo saw that it was a twisted splinter of metal, slick and shining with his blood—shrapnel from the shipwreck. His arm throbbed, as though it had been asleep and had just begun to regain feeling.

Truffo gasped for air, pushing himself up on his good arm to stare levelly at the bird, which poked at the metal on the sand once, twice, and then cocked its head at him.

"That," he panted, "was a bit clever of you."

The bird cocked its head the other direction and gave a shrill echo of Truffo's previous shriek. Truffo winced at the noise.

"Yeah, yeah, all right, that's enough of that now . . ." He hefted back onto his heels, sweat shining on his brow as he shifted his tingling, sore arm into his lap, looking down to wiggle his fingers one by one through the pain. At least this was progress.

The bird was cleaning its own feathers now, as if pleased to have been right about the shrapnel, but it looked up at him from time to time and its tail feathers flicked up and down.

"Oy," breathed Truffo, leaning forward a little. "Is there anyone else here, birdy? Scary natives maybe? A rich millionaire with a private retreat?" The bird fluffed itself as if it had no interest in him. "What about water?" His throat was painfully dry, and it was quite hot in the sun, out here on the open sand. The thought of sucking down seawater was revolting, but he was terribly thirsty. And if the bird was smart enough to have pulled a piece of metal out of his shoulder. . . .

Truffo whistled faintly to catch the bird's attention. "Yoo hoo, then," he prompted. "Polly want a cracker? Polly where's-the-water? Promise I won't eat you after," he added.

He stared at the bird as it continued to preen. After several moments, the bird clucked to itself and hopped along the sand a little ways, poking its beak in and out of the ground in search of something. Truffo groaned, pulling himself to his feet, and shambled after the bird as it picked its way down the beach.

"Go on, go on," he urged the bird, "don't mind me, but don't waste time, neither . . . You're smart enough to do surgery, you're smart enough to find water . . . or some shelter. Or help."

Truffo's dark eyes cast out toward the ocean for a moment, wondering how far away the shipwreck was from him, and how long he'd been unconscious on the sand. He tried to focus again on the bright orange bird, which had wound its way up the beach with quick little steps and turned toward the rocky upper dunes.

Truffo's feet slid about in the sand, his vision growing spotty around the edges again, but the bird's cheerful plumage was a considerable target.

*Good old bird,* Truffo thought. *Some men have dogs and others cats, but my life's been saved by a strange and hitherto undiscovered species of sandpiper.* He wondered if their new friendship would be his utter salvation, if he could teach the thing to speak—it could mimic well enough—and if it could help him survive on this spit of land.

*I damn well can't eat it now,* he thought crossly as he scrambled after it, seeing what looked like the mouth of a cave up ahead. A cave meant shade, protection from the sun, perhaps even an underground spring full of cool, clear water, and—

Something huge and dark lunged sharply out of the rocky hole and snatched up the orange bird, which trilled loudly and began to scream with Truffo's voice. Truffo fell back in fear, hitting his head on the hard ground. He gasped hard in pain and looked up just in time to see the big, man-shaped shadow snap the bird's neck.

"No!" Truffo sputtered, his vision blackening. "No, no, birdy! Oh, gods, is there no justice?"

The hulking shadow turned, the limp orange bird in its hand, and as the uneven blue eyes stared down in surprise and bewilderment, Truffo slipped into unconsciousness.

# CHAPTER FIVE

Mira broke the surface of the water, blinded momentarily by sunlight before the lenses of the diver's goggles adjusted to the gleam. She spat out the salty seawater and breathed in the clean air of the surface. Paddling her legs beneath her to stay upright, she held her trophy above the surface, turning it back and forth to examine it.

The object was partly wood and partly silver, etched with ornate curls and patterns she did not recognize. It was a little heavy, despite being quite slender, and its oblong shape sat comfortably in her palm, as if it were meant to be held there. She inspected it from every angle, noting the artful shapes and grooves in the thin sides of the thing.

There was also what appeared to be a hinge, but she was unsure how to pry it apart to see what was inside, or even how it was put together. She would need some more tools to gut it, she realized, and swam toward the shore, the clear waters rippling about her. Fish skirted by her, and a ray fluttered along the sandy bottom as the way grew shallower.

At last, Mira could stand, and she walked the rest of the way up onto the beach. She dropped the rope coil she'd been wearing across her body and stood on the warm sand, as naked as the day she was born.

She had learned knots from a book in her father's cave many years ago, and had used that skill to rescue debris from the bottom of the bay. Mira pushed the goggles back from her brow to rest on the crown of her head, her thick, tangled hair falling in a twisted, uneven braid down her back. The water beaded on her sun-browned skin like dew on a duck, and she furrowed her brow upon the little thing she'd recovered from the wreck.

Although the ship had sunk in parts and pieces, Mira had found no bodies when she dove to investigate, and hadn't seen any survivors beyond the lagoon. It puzzled her, but she soon became distracted by the fascinating array of items spread throughout the lagoon.

Over several trips to the bottom, she had spotted silverware, long-necked glass bottles—some still unbroken—and several leather and wooden trunks. This little thing of dark wood and curlicued silver had been a surprisingly easy find for its size. It had gleamed in the dark shadows of the bay as though it had wanted to be found, and now it puzzled Mira more than the missing passengers of the ill-fated vessel.

She stretched her arms above her head, working out a cramp in her shoulder, and yawned heartily. The sun was warm, inviting her to sleep, but she wanted to dive back down and retrieve some of the trunks first, to see what was inside.

Mira moved swiftly up the beach to a tree at the edge of the forest beyond the dunes. As a child, she'd hidden and found and re-hidden things all over the island, some of which she was still re-discovering. In the shade, she reached under a bundle of driftwood and pulled out another length of rope she'd placed there some time ago, leaving behind the silver-and-wood object for safekeeping.

Mira bound this rope to the first with a double fisherman's knot. She looped the large coil across her body as before, then ran splashing into the surf. She swam out to where she'd found the silver-and-wood artifact, took a deep breath, and dove down toward the wreckage.

It took some time to bring each trunk up to the surface and tow it back to shore. Had they been too heavy to swim with, she would have been faced with a difficult choice: open them underwater to try and salvage some of the contents, or leave them unopened on the ocean floor, forever a mystery. Two of these were quite light, the third being only moderately heavy, but still Mira was winded when she hefted the last of the three leather trunks onto the sand and sat down hard beside them, her arms aching.

She blew her breath out hard, and pushed her heavy braid back over her shoulder. She hoped one of the trunks contained a knife or shears of some kind—to cut her hair short and not have to drag the tangled plait around all the time would be a blessing. Who was that fairy tale princess again? The one with the long hair, trapped in the tower.

*Petrosinella,* she thought, and grimaced. *At least I have a whole island, not just a tower.*

Mira eyed the trunks beside her, wondering which would be most likely to give way and open up first. They were locked tight, but not completely unaffected by their stint underwater. She rubbed her upper arms, kneading the sore muscles, and looked out over the water, admiring the rich blue of the ocean.

It was something she never tired of. She loved the sea, even though it was equivalent to the walls of her prison. Mira felt more conflicted the older she got; some mornings she woke feeling as though the world was just right as it was, and the isle was all she would ever need. Some days she felt trapped and suspended in time, knowing that beyond the waves there was more, so much more, of everything. It frustrated and taunted her to think of the world beyond, but she loved the island, and, as there was no apparent chance of leaving, she did not struggle with the concept very often.

The soreness in her arms was beginning to subside, and, as the warm afternoon sun beat down on her, Mira thought she saw a dolphin's fin break the water a little ways out, in the direction of the wreck. She squinted, a smile creeping across her lips, but the fin didn't dip back down. Then she noticed the gulls circling overhead. She could just faintly make out their whining cries as they flapped and turned, a couple daring to swoop down at something on the surface. She pulled her glasses down over her eyes again and adjusted a knob on the side of them to focus the view for a longer distance. Something floated on the surface, though it was hard to make out what for a few moments. Then the angle of the dark shape shifted, and Mira saw what it was.

*A body!*

Without a moment of hesitation, Mira leapt to her feet, adjusting the view on the goggles as she did, and ran into the surf. *Maybe they're still alive*, she thought, and plunged into the water, kicking out with powerful strokes. She swam hard and fast, her eyes fixed on the bobbing shape. As she got nearer to the spot she'd already explored, she realized that the body was floating just a bit further than she'd swum before. She thought about turning back, but the idea that whoever it was may not be quite dead yet was too great to neglect, so she kept swimming, hoping that she wouldn't tire too much to swim back by the time she reached it.

The gulls squawked and cried at her, flapping and fluttering as she splashed noisily toward the body. Mira changed to a different stroke to keep her head more above water, slowing as she approached, and saw that it was a man—a young man, sprawled face down on a floating piece of wreck. His dark hair was short, his clothing finer than she'd expected for a sailor. His trousers were an exquisite material, his boots shined, and his shirt was very fine, other than the obvious tears and stains of blood and soot. The embroidery at his sleeves and collar was intricate and brightly colored, unlike anything Mira had seen before. She held onto the side of the raft with one hand and reached up the side of his neck with the other to look for a pulse. She realized she'd never taken a pulse other than her own before, and couldn't tell whether she actually felt one, or whether it was the bobbing of the waves, or even her own pounding heartbeat.

*Better safe than sorry*, she thought. She positioned herself behind the raft and began to swim, pushing the man toward shore with a steady, but urgent, kick.

Twice she stopped and floated on her back to rest, breathing with forced slowness as the cries of the gulls followed her, and wondered if the man was already dead, the process utterly a waste of her energy. If she wasn't careful, she could tire out completely before she got back to the beach, with or without the body in tow.

*Have to try.*

Mira gathered herself and kicked out again, taking a slower pace now, and falling into a more comfortable rhythm. The gulls mocked her progress, a few of them growing so bold as to swoop lower past her kicking legs and peck lazily at the body on the raft. She did her best to ignore them, kicking steadily, breathing in rhythm with her swimming.

*Stupid birds,* she thought, but it worried her that they hadn't given up on the body—maybe they could sense something she couldn't. If he were dead, she would have to find somewhere to bury him. Where was that wooden spade she'd built? Had she left it in her father's cave, or was it hidden somewhere else on the island?

The birds squawked closer now, and one even landed on the body as she pushed the raft toward land. It landed on the man, hopping from his back to his shoulder, pecking inquisitively at the cloth of his shirt and strands of his hair. Mira struggled to keep up her pace, prepping a splash with her right arm, but suddenly the bird's beak connected with something and the man came alive, gasping in pain and coughing wildly.

Mira stopped swimming as the gull cried out in protest and flew off, flapping its wide wings lazily. The man continued coughing, trying to catch his breath and push himself upright.

"No!" Mira cried, salt water flowing into her mouth. "No, stop! Stop it! You'll tip over!"

The young man seemed too weak to actually sit up all the way, but he craned his head around, gagging, and looked for the source of her voice, his eyes wild and glazed.

"Stop, just lie down, we're almost there," Mira cried, kicking out with her legs again, swimming harder. The young man groaned, disoriented, probably sick from the salt water and dehydration.

A few minutes later, Mira reached the shallows and leapt shakily to her feet. Her legs felt like jelly, but she couldn't rest yet—she bent and scooped him up under the shoulders, swinging the young man upward, and hefted him onto the sand. He was still conscious, but seemed completely delirious and exhausted, his breathing shallow and weak. Mira dragged him up the beach a little and laid him on his back, her long braid dripping water down her body.

"Stay awake," she commanded. "Keep your eyes open. You're going to be all right." She knelt beside him and saw that he had several shallow cuts on his chest and arms, but there was nothing to indicate he had been seriously injured, other than perhaps a mild concussion and the exhaustion of being at sea in the sun for a while. His eyes rolled up to look at her blearily.

"Your stomach is full of water," she told him as he gaped up at her. "You have to cough harder. Turn over," she said, and grasped him by the arms, rolling him to one side and hitting him firmly between the shoulders.

He coughed hard and, in another moment, had vomited a good amount of water onto the sand beside him. He groaned, holding his stomach with one arm.

The man threw up once more, though there was less this time, and it was mixed with bile. Mira held his shoulders firmly as he shuddered, exhausted from the efforts, and only when she thought he had finished did she let him lie on his back again to catch his breath. He lay with his eyes closed, his breathing labored. Her mind raced; he'd need a coconut, for hydration, and some fruit and nuts for sustenance. . . .

His eyes opened dazedly, and he lifted a weak hand to shade himself from the sunlight. Mira sat on the sand beside him, peering down into his face, her long braid hanging over her shoulder and brushing his chest. She frowned, studying his glazed expression.

"You need to rest," she told him. "We need to get you into the shade. I can—"

"Are you a mermaid?"

The young man's voice startled her into silence, and Mira stared in surprise at him for several moments, speechless. It was her first conversation with a stranger since the day she and her father came to the island and met Karaburan. Her heart fluttered strangely in her chest. His voice was like a bird call she had never heard before, and she almost didn't answer.

"I'm—no." She cleared her throat, her own breath short from the effort of his rescue. "I'm not a mermaid."

"Why . . ." he trailed off, his eyes sliding shut for a moment before reopening. "Why are you naked?"

Mira went red-hot, and her mind blanked. She stared down at him, her voice as empty as a hollow shell washed up without its crab.

"You saved me," murmured the young man, and then he slipped into unconsciousness.

Mira let out her breath slowly, grateful that she did not have to answer him. Her limbs trembled as she tried to catch her breath, shell-shocked by the realization that she had rescued this stranger from the sea. She looked about, seeing no sign of her father or the monster. She would have to hide this castaway. If Dante found him—or Karaburan—there was no telling what either of them might do. Strangers had never been here before, and if she got caught harboring one, she was certain her father would punish her severely.

Mira slid her arms under the stranger's armpits again and dragged him further up into the shade of the tree line. The first order of business was to hide him somewhere safe. Then, put clothes on and retrieve the trunks. After that. . . .

Mira swallowed as she shifted his weight in her arms. *After that,* she thought, *find out who this boy is, and make sure my father doesn't find out he survived.*

# CHAPTER SIX

B astiano Civitelli leaned back against the trunk of the tall, broad-leafed palm tree and looked down at the man lying next to him. The duke, Torsione Fiorente, was still unconscious, but his coloring was not too bad, and Bastiano had hope that he would wake soon. It had been a few hours since he awoke on the white sandy beach with the waves lapping at his feet, the unconscious Tor beside him. Bastiano had pulled him up the beach into the shade, where the sand was comfortably cooler, and the breeze off the water was reassuring and gentle.

His stomach growled softly, and he could feel the yearning for food and water growing and moving outward from his belly to his every limb and muscle. He watched the sleeping duke breathe, and fretted in silence.

*He must have rescued me,* thought Bastiano. The king's brother had come to with the duke's arm across his shoulders, which indicated as clear as day that his own life had been recovered by the duke's superior swimming abilities. *And now, he pays the price with his own health.*

He wanted to reach out and smooth back the dark, salt-curled hair from Torsione's brow. Part of him feared that Tor wouldn't make it, and that he would remain alone on this stretch of beach, with no one and nothing to show for the effort made to save his life.

Bastiano's arms prickled with goose pimples, the breeze turning cooler as the afternoon wore on. He had no idea how long he'd been unconscious, or how long the duke would remain so. He thought about getting to his feet, taking a walk up or down the beach, or up the dunes toward the forest that bloomed several hundred yards away. It appeared that they were on an island—one populated by birds and plentiful trees, but no men. It was unnervingly beautiful here, and Bastiano was grateful for the shade provided by the trees.

*If I'm this hungry,* Bastiano thought, hearing his stomach growl again, *poor Tor must be starving. Dehydrated, for sure.*

But if Torsione woke while he was gone looking for food, Bastiano would not be able to forgive himself. So he sat still and watched the waves, followed the sun as it moved across the pale blue sky, and waited.

*My brother is dead*, Bastiano thought occasionally, numbly. *And my nephew. And the others . . . all the others. There is no one here but me and Tor*. He shook his head, breathed his lungs full of clear, clean air, and closed his eyes against the bright world. *Once Tor wakes up, he'll know what to do. After all, he's the adventurer.*

Bastiano dozed, with his head bowed and his eyes shut, and waited for the duke to rouse from his waterlogged sleep.

\* \* \*

Aurael did not know what to make of the two men at first. The airy spirit had pulled them from the ocean and laid them on the sand together, since they had been arm in arm as they sank below the waves when he found them. Now, one dozed with his back against a tree, and the other slept soundlessly beside him on the sand. There was something unspoken between them, something unique about the way the upright one kept startling awake to check on the darker, prone fellow.

Aurael did not understand the complexity of most human interactions—something he'd admitted countless times in the past.

But he found himself all the more interested in watching these two men for the fact that he'd been trapped on this godsforsaken spit of land with only Dante to really talk to, Karaburan to play with, and Mira to watch from afar.

*Ah, Mira*, he thought, and wondered if she knew yet about the castaways. Aurael had already strewn several other survivors about the other beaches of the isle, spreading them out so that few would be within range of the others; but he had yet to uncover the Neapolishan king from the murky depths.

More importantly, Aurael began to wonder about Karaburan. Had the unloved, ungainly thing found the two men washed up near his hovel in the rocks? Aurael pursed his lips. *If so, there may be some sport in it.* His thoughts danced at the prospect. After all the years of carefully bending Karaburan's mind to his wills and whims, this now might prove even more entertaining than any jest he'd ever devised. The castaways would serve as pawns, and Karaburan he would capture as an opposing knight on the chess field in a gulling so foolish that it made him laugh aloud. His tinkling, shattering laugh echoed up the beach, waking the sitting man enough to make him look about in fear and bewilderment.

Aurael stood from his perch, knowing that the men would not see him, and stretched himself in the warm sun. Then, letting the breeze dissolve his semi-corporeal form into wind, he started his flight across the isle to find Karaburan and plant the seeds of insurrection, chuckling all the way.

* * *

Bastiano's heart pounded; he was certain he'd heard someone laugh. It had been a strange laugh, an eerie sound, but he was absolutely sure he'd heard it. He swallowed, his mouth dry, as he looked about and saw no one.

*Did I dream it?* he wondered. *Is the sun making my mind play tricks on me? Gods, I'm thirsty.* He put a hand to his eyes, which watered in the bright light of afternoon, and closed them again.

The duke stirred audibly, and Bastiano's eyes flew open. He turned and looked down at Torsione, whose eyelids fluttered and finally opened.

"Bas?" The duke coughed, his voice as dry as salt flats in the desert.

"Torsione," breathed Bastiano, tears springing to his eyes in relief. He exhaled the tension he'd been holding in his chest and shoulders and shook his head. "You're awake, you're all right, thank the gods," he stammered, his hands shaking as he reached down and touched the duke's arm.

Torsione tried to move and winced at the pain. "What happened? What's wrong?" he grunted as he tried to sit up. "Where are we?"

Bastiano shifted obligingly, helping Torsione to sit up with his back against the tree. "An island, I think. I've only been up for a little while," he lied. The duke gritted his teeth against some pain that bloomed and faded as he settled against the palm tree. "You weren't out long. You saved me, Torsione. You pulled me out of the water, and passed out. I'd be dead if it weren't for you. In fact, I was worried for a little while there that you would die, but you're fine, you're all right." His smile brightened, his eyes flitting over the duke's form.

Torsione sat still for a moment, with his eyes closed. "Are we . . ." he swallowed. He opened his eyes, pale blue with dazed disbelief. "Are we the only ones, Bas?"

Bastiano hesitated, but nodded a little after a moment. "I think so. I have not seen anyone else," he said, and paused again. "Nor heard any sign of them," he lied. The strange laugh from a few moments ago still jangled in his mind, but now he was sure it had just been a hallucination. He would have seen sign of any other survivors by now, he was quite sure.

Torsione blinked, his breathing shaky, and looked out at the ocean spread before them. *It may as well be the surface of the moon*, Bastiano worried. *We are lost here.*

"Have any of our belongings washed up? The cargo?" Torsione put a hand to his head. "What happened to the ship?"

"I—" Bastiano felt helpless. "I don't know."

He thought carefully. He had woken up on the beach beside Tor, but before that—before everything had gone black—he thought he remembered trying to swim, the ship splintering in the water all around them with showers of sparks and burning and smoke. The darkness of the night swallowed them all, and the ship, too.

"All I know is the ship went down," Bastiano said at last. "I was swimming, albeit very poorly, and you must have . . . found me, somehow," he managed to say, looking away from the duke's surprised gaze. "You brought me to shore, though it's nothing short of miraculous, I'd say. It was the dead of night when the ship went down, and you found an island." He cracked a smile and lifted his eyebrows, cheerfully. "Devil of a stroke of luck, that."

"I pulled you from the water," echoed the duke, as though trying to remember.

"I should say so," Bastiano chuckled: a thin, reedy sound.

"And you watched over me all this time?"

The note of wonder in the duke's voice made Bastiano look up at him again. Torsione's eyes were a radiant light blue that challenged the sky for hue, even with his battered state and his concerned brow.

Bastiano pressed his lips together and nodded again, riveted by the duke's stare.

"Bas," said Torsione, his voice broken and quiet. "That's a hell of a thing, that we've survived together."

Bastiano's heart leaped sideways in his chest, joyful and terrified. "I think so, too," he admitted, his voice small.

"Better stick together, hadn't we," said the duke, still staring at him. They were still quite close, the duke leaning on the tree now, and Bastiano just beside him, within arm's reach.

"I'd planned on doing as much," Bastiano murmured.

"So much so as to not look for food or shelter until I woke up?" Torsione closed his eyes again. "You're a very devoted nurse, Bas. Perhaps you've found your calling."

The moment had passed, and Bastiano let out his breath slowly and chuckled after a moment to mask the shuddering nervousness that threatened to overthrow him entirely. "How do you feel?" he asked, tactfully changing the subject. "Other than a headache and dehydration and such. I'm feeling those, too."

Torsione opened his eyes, considering. "Very sore. Tired. I don't remember pulling you out of the water, but that would explain the strain in my arms and legs from swimming with you in tow." He paused. "Other than that, probably all right, except the hunger and thirst."

"I'm going to look for something to eat," Bastiano decided, standing up. He shrugged out of his jacket and rolled up his shirtsleeves. "Stay here and rest. Neither of us will last very long without food."

"Don't go too far," mused Torsione, squinting in the light. "And be careful. Just because you haven't seen anyone doesn't mean there isn't anyone here."

"I'll be careful," Bastiano promised, and lingered a moment before setting off past their little grove of trees and toward the forest itself, leaving the duke to lie in the shade.

# CHAPTER SEVEN

Stephen Montanto heard crying. It was not the hysterical sobbing of an overzealous woman, nor the uncertain wail of a child. It was a quiet, hiccupping sob that did not stop, but ebbed and flowed like the waves somewhere beyond him.

He opened his eyes slowly and found himself on his back staring up at what appeared to be a rocky ceiling of sorts. He felt dry and worn out. He remembered waking on the beach alone, crying to himself about his cowardly fate. No doubt he was now brought fully into his own hell, or at least a deeper level of the afterlife, this time made of stone and lichen, and the soft, uneasy crying of a man. The echoes of his own tears, perhaps.

"Stephen?" whispered the crying voice, faltering in its sorrow for a moment. There was sniffling, and the shifting sound of fabric against stone. "Stephen, are you awake?"

Stephen Montanto shut his eyes again and stayed very still. Demons would be tricky. No doubt they would try to appear to him in his hell as faces he had known in life, faces he had no doubt betrayed. After a moment of uncertain silence, he ventured to peep one eye open again.

The woeful countenance of Truffo Arlecin had appeared over his head, and the warm salty tears of the young man fell like startled raindrops onto Stephen's own cheek and chin. He winced in spite of himself.

"Stephen! You're awake!" Truffo seemed hopeful, giving the older man an encouraging sort of jostle at the arm.

The valet grunted, his head pounding, and he batted at the younger man's hands with his own. "Don't touch me, demon," Stephen rasped, his throat dry. "Sent to torment me, are you, devil?"

"Devil? It's me, Truffo," the young man whined, recoiling from him and sniffling aloud. "You're not dead, you old fraud, you're alive! This isn't Hell—or at least, it isn't, yet." The fool gave a small choked sob and swallowed back whatever else he was going to say.

Stephen sat up slowly, using the wall of the rocky alcove for a brace. He was very sore indeed, and even as his mind caught up to his eyes in seeing his surroundings, he felt as weak as a baby bird fallen from the nest. By the saints, he was thirsty.

"What do you mean, 'yet'?" he demanded, his voice thin and rough as straws. Truffo looked toward the mouth of the little cave, where the shore and sea lay several dozen yards off.

"It'll be back soon," the fool whispered, his hands shaking. "It's hideous, Stephen—it ate a bird right in front of my very eyes! Raw! Blood and feathers everywhere!"

Stephen frowned but saw no sign of this massacre when he glanced about the sandy floor of the narrow cave. "Indeed," he grunted. "What is it?"

"Not a man nor a fish, some sea-skinned devil I've never heard the likes of before in all my life," breathed the fool. "It dragged me in and knocked me out, and when I came to, you were here, and I thought for sure you were dead!" Truffo's dark eyes brimmed over heavily with tears.

"Shush, shush now, stop that sobbing," growled Stephen, feeling an ache growing both in his stomach and the back of his skull. "We survived a shipwreck, didn't we? We'll survive this, somehow. Some luck will find us yet, you'll see, boy."

"I never thought I'd die on an island in the middle of nowhere," wailed the fool piteously. "I'm too young—too posh—too poetic for this fate!" Stephen frowned at the whining. Truffo was not very old after all; his melancholic humor and his usually lofty wit made him seem far older, but in truth the boy was not much more in age than Prince Ferran himself. Stephen's heart tugged at the thought.

*Prince Ferran!* he thought. *How young to be swallowed by the sea, and we poor servants left to carry on without the masters.*

"Come, come boy," he urged, beckoning Truffo to sit beside him against the wall. "We'll muddle through together, monster or no. But we won't get far without food or water, so we'll have to think of something. And stop crying, you'll dehydrate yourself even more."

Truffo scrambled over beside him and sat hugging his knees and sniffling quietly. Stephen sighed. *We'll have to think of something,* the valet thought, and tried not to dwell on how thirsty he was.

There was a great splash nearby, and the sound of braying laughter, followed by more splashing. Stephen's brow furrowed sharply, and Truffo stiffened beside him, his sniffles quieting to a trembling breath.

"It's back," whispered the fool.

"It?" Stephen said, as though he wasn't worried, but his mind raced. *What is it?* he wondered. *What does it want with us?*

They sat still and listened as the thing guffawed triumphantly and made its way up the beach with heavy steps and a lumbering gait, toward the mouth of the narrow cave. A smell like rotting sea-weed wafted into the cave on the breeze, and Truffo whimpered. Then the daylight that blinded them at the mouth of the cave was blocked by a huge dark shadow, and Stephen had to blink to clear his vision.

It was mannish in appearance, but Truffo had been right—its skin bore patches of peculiar bluish-green scales, fading almost to gray at the edges, as though the creature had been dipped in different jars of paint. The rest of its body was dark, and it had oversized hands and feet, with strong legs and broad shoulders. It moved a little like a gorilla, using its knuckles to balance, and its mouth was set sideways in its face, its nose feminine and small. Its eyes, though unevenly large and disproportionate to one another, were the gentlest cornflower blue Stephen had ever seen.

Stephen felt the remainder of his disbelief flee his body like steam from a kettle, and he stared unabashedly at the creature before them while Truffo curled smaller and smaller, armadillo-like, beside him. The creature stared back, its huge shoulders shifting slightly, but Stephen could not draw his gaze away from those petal-soft pale blue eyes. Finally, the creature's mouth opened in an unsettling, shark-like smile.

"You are awake!" The monstrous man's voice was more youthful than Stephen had thought it would be, and had the heaviness of a simple mind and a foreign tongue to it. "I am most glad, most glad to have you here; most glad, welcome guests."

Stephen frowned. "Guests?" he heard himself saying.

The monster bobbed its head the way a dog wags its tail. "Yes, most welcome guests, most welcome here. I am most glad, most glad to see you. You are blessed to have been spit back out by the sea."

Stephen felt his stomach shudder at the memory of drowning, and was once again quite certain that he very much ought to be a dead man.

"You are much amazed, I think, by my humble appearance," the creature went on, anxiously, "and by your own survival. I am most glad that you are both awake. I will make you well again." Their unusual host lumbered forward another step or two to hold out its large hands. In each strange palm there was cradled what appeared to be half of a coconut, filled with white fruit and a hazy liquid. "Drink these, good lords, and be well again!"

"Don't," cried Truffo. "Poison!" The creature recoiled some, surprise painting a picture of absurdity on its face.

"You are thirsty, my lords," ventured the creature. "I only want to help you. The sun is hot and you must drink."

"I've survived a bloody shipwreck only to be kidnapped by a monster," moaned Truffo, his head in his hands.

"Who are you?" demanded Stephen, although his eyes were fixed on the coconut halves, the liquid inviting even in its haziness.

"My name is Karaburan," replied the creature, sitting at the entrance to the cave like a mother bird perching at the mouth of a nest to feed her young. "I am no monster, I assure you, my lords. I am a man, truly I am, though outwardly my appearances do show me to be unlike anyone you've ever seen before, I think."

"That's an understatement," grunted Stephen, still eyeing the coconuts.

"Please, my lord," insisted Karaburan, "drink and you will feel so much better."

Stephen reached for one half, ignoring Truffo's whimpering. "If it's poison, lad, it's poison, but I can fathom nothing worse than dying of thirst right now. You'd best drink it, too. If we die, we die." He passed the other coconut bowl to Truffo, who looked pale.

Stephen brought the coconut to his mouth and drank deeply; the liquid was a little thicker than water and tasted strange, but did not seem to be bitter or vile in any way. He drank until there was no more in his coconut shell, and Truffo tasted his portion of the stuff reluctantly beside him.

After a few moments, Stephen did note that he began to feel less woozy, and his vision cleared, his headache fading away in small increments.

"What is it?" he asked the monster, brandishing the empty bowl. "Some sort of spell?"

"No magic, my lord, just the fresh water within the nut. A natural remedy to the sun's effects. Keep you from being thirsty, keep you from falling asleep in the sun and withering away." Karaburan gave him the blank, hopeful smile again. "You feel already how much better you are for drinking it?"

"Yes." Stephen frowned at the peevish boy beside him. "Truffo, just drink it. I do feel better."

Truffo did not seem to like the taste, but he obeyed, and when the bowl was empty, he looked reluctantly up at the large beast of a man.

"Is there more?" the fool ventured in a small voice.

Karaburan threw back his head and gave a strange, barking laugh, slapping his hands on the ground and on his own thighs. "More? More! Of course there's more! The island provides! Wait here, my lords, and I will fetch another." With that, the monster gathered himself up and loped away on all fours.

"What a monster!" shuddered Truffo, rubbing his face. "There are little children all over the world whose closets and under-the-beds are missing their master of mayhem! But I do feel a little better. Even if it is poisonous," he added.

"It seems a kindly monster," mused Stephen. He felt odd about the entire thing, as though he were in some elaborate dream. Now that he physically felt somewhat revived, he wasn't quite as attached to the notion that he might be dead, but it puzzled him as to why the ugly creature would try to rescue them; weren't monsters supposed to devour their unwanted guests? And where had Karaburan come from? "Perhaps it's only lonely," he said aloud, thoughtfully.

Truffo blinked red eyes at him. "A lonely monster," he drawled. "What a novelty."

"He calls us lords," added Stephen, a curious mixture of disbelief and hunger in his voice. Truffo bobbed his head from side to side as if trying to rid his ears of water.

"He doesn't know any better," said the fool.

"He doesn't at that," agreed Stephen. "And if he'll keep us healthy by bringing us water and food, why, who are we to not be lords?"

"The philosophers say a man must have a master," Truffo recited in a weary voice. "A man is wont to kneel before his betters, and allow another man to be his ruler. That is how the Great Wall of Chineh started. Or the Great Chain of Being, one of the two."

"Then perhaps we are the answer to this thing's prayers," whispered Stephen. "Perhaps our afterlife is meant to be here, on this desert place, cared for by a monster that will love us as his lords and one of us, his king." An island paradise, a willing but hideous slave—it seemed a likely enough afterlife. *The only thing missing is a woman, really,* mused Stephen.

"King?" protested Truffo. "You mean kings, plural! There are two of us after all, Stephen Montanto."

"Yes, and I am your better, Truffo. And your elder. You are a fool, and I am a valet. Was. These were our past lives. Now, *et in Arcadia ego.*"

Truffo gaped at him for a moment, slightly boggle-eyed. "You mean you get to be the king now because you used to be the valet?" He screwed up his face, one eye closing altogether. "What does it make me, then?"

"My valet," he chuckled, amused at Truffo's expression.

"And the monster?"

"Our slave," answered Stephen Montanto, and a smile began to creep across his face.

\* \* \*

Karaburan had gathered more coconuts into the canvas sack and was on his way into the forest at the center of the island in search of other nuts and fruits to offer his guests. He had crossed over to the place where the soft sandy soil became hard packed dirt, but stopped as a strange sound like clinking glasses drifted to him on a cool and slender breeze.

The sound clutched at his heart, though he could not understand why, and he found it hard to breathe, or even move. Karaburan stood still as a stone, listening with the whole of his body, and after several minutes more, the sound faded, seemingly without consequence, and he relaxed. He let out his breath slowly, shaking himself like a wet dog.

It was a funny thing, that feeling; it happened from time to time. There would be a cold shift in the air and an odd, musical sound, and then it always made him feel as though he were squeezed into a narrow space between two unyielding rocks, claustrophobia creeping into the edges of his mind and paralyzing him. No matter how hard he tried to pass through the strange pressure, it would not budge, and he found himself frozen in place until the peculiar thing passed.

Karaburan paused, sniffing the breeze that fluttered through the stray, dry dune grass nearby, his hands and toes tingling as though they'd been numb a moment ago. Then he took a step toward the forest, resuming his previous mission of foraging for his guests.

The invisible barrier took him completely by surprise. His momentum brought him face first against an unseen wall and flung him unceremoniously backward. Karaburan grabbed at his head in agony, howling in surprise and anger. As he fell to the ground, staggered by the uneven earth and the shock of the obstacle, he heard laughter like wind chimes, delicate and irksome.

"Leave me be!" cried Karaburan, scooting backward from the wall. "I've done nothing wrong!" His heart pounded, anxiety clouding his mind as he looked about for the source of the laughter. The island made strange noises sometimes, and stranger things had happened on his walks than an invisible wall springing up out of nowhere; but in general, Karaburan did not fear the island that was his home. Now, though, dread bubbled in the pit of his stomach like tar, slowing his speech and constricting his breath.

"Say 'please,' " a lazy voice trilled from a nearby tree. Karaburan swung about, searching for the owner of the voice, but saw no one. "Go on then," the voice prompted. "Say 'pretty please.' "

"Please," murmured Karaburan, frantically looking for the face that matched the voice. *I've heard this voice before,* he thought, his heart pounding like cannons in his chest. *I don't know who it is, but I've heard it before.*

"No," giggled the voice daintily. "You didn't say 'pretty.' It's 'pretty please,' these days." It erupted into peals of laughter, which echoed back at Karaburan from off the barrier before him, cutting him off from the rest of the forest.

Karaburan tried to catch his breath, but panic rose in his mind, and it became difficult to focus. "Who's there? What do you want?"

"It's me," answered the voice, "I'm here. And I want to make you suffer."

A great gust of air rushed at him, and he found himself completely bowled over backward, the sand and grasses whipping at his skin as the wind raged about him. Karaburan cried out in pain as rocks and sticks flew at his body, bouncing off of him and scattering across the ground. He crouched, covering his head with his arms, and waited for the whirlwind to pass, praying that it would not carry him away. The voice on the air roared about him, its chiming laughter echoing in his ears, until at last the rushing air faded away, dust settling on Karaburan where he lay on the ground.

His heart pounded. He had never been attacked like this before. He had heard strange things and seen peculiar visions, but he had never physically been harmed. It almost frightened him more than his nightmares the eve before: that endless, horrifying loop of hunting, finding, and ravishing the struggling girl in the dark.

Karaburan banished the memory from his mind, his skin prickling with uncertainty and revulsion as he sat up on his knees and tried not to weep at the vision. He had a light welt on his arm where a branch had struck him, and his body stung in fifty places where small stones had bit him as they passed by. Karaburan felt the terror trembling in his hands and face, and every nerve in his body screamed to run back to his hovel in the rocks, but he hesitated, recalling his guests who waited, who depended on him for coconuts and other sustenance.

Karaburan looked about, his large eyes watery, and sniffed. The bag of coconuts was on the ground a little ways off, so he got to his feet and lumbered over to them. As he reached for the canvas bag, it slid across the dirt several feet so that it was just out of his grasp. Not understanding, Karaburan moved forward to reach again, and again the sack slid a few feet out of reach. The third time, Karaburan bellowed in frustration, slamming his hands against the hard earth. That infuriating laugh danced through the leaves, mocking his anger and hurt as easily as a fish mocks the clumsy fisherman's bait.

"What do you want?" roared Karaburan. His heart thumped in distress; he only wanted to get out of here as quickly as possible. There was a rustle to his left, and he turned to look, sniffling.

Mira came walking out of the trees, her expression pitying and somber. Karaburan's heart caught in his throat, and he felt as if he might never breathe again. Dante's daughter was lean and long-legged, but her hips sloped with the early touch of Nature's growth, and she wore a man's old tunic wrapped tight at her waist with rope. Her long hair flowed and shone in the sun, dark honey-colored locks laced through with paler gold. Everything about her seemed bright and newly washed, her lips parting in a shy expression of apology as she looked down at him with her cool green eyes. She moved slowly, as though she did not want to frighten him, and he trembled in her presence.

"Karaburan, my poor friend," Mira murmured, her voice like downy feathers on a baby bird. "It's been so long since I last saw you."

"M-m-mistress," stammered the monster as he shivered, "your father bade me never look on you again, and never have I seen you 'til now." He hesitated, lingering between covering his eyes with his hands and not wanting to look away from her radiance.

"My father is an evil man. He separated us when we were meant to be together always." Mira knelt near him, peering into his face with her bright eyes and concerned brow. "You and I were such friends once, and now we are strangers. Would you rather it remain so?"

"No," croaked Karaburan, reaching out to her with one hand. "I long to serve you and be near you again. Please, please forgive me, Mistress."

"Forgive you? You are already forgiven." She took his hand in hers and squeezed it gently. Karaburan's eyelids fluttered shut for a moment, so gratifying was the feeling that swept through him.

"I did not mean to hurt you," he whispered, large tears swelling in the corners of his pale eyes.

Mira tipped her head at him. "Do I seem injured to you?"

He shook his head fervently. "No, Mistress, you are perfect and well and very beautiful."

Mira gave him a little smile. "Then you have nothing to be sorry for." She leaned in a little more. "That night when everything went wrong . . . I was young and not ready. Now I am ready. What you dreamed of will be yours—if it is what you still wish," she added with a rosy blush creeping over her cheeks.

Karaburan thought his heart would burst. "I do, I do wish it," he confessed, voice barely above a whisper.

"There is only one thing that must be done before we are together at last," Mira breathed, inching closer.

"Say what is to be done, Mistress, and your Karaburan will do it!"

"My father must die, and then his spells will break. You and I will have the island to ourselves. It will no more be a prison to us both, but a paradise for our joys combined. Kill my father, and we shall both be rewarded."

Karaburan's heart skipped a beat. He did not wish to kill anyone, for he believed, as his mother had, that all life was precious and should at least be respected, if not actively defended. But Dante was a cruel ruler of the island. Karaburan thought on how his childhood had been saved by the sudden arrival of Dante and Mira, but then how, a mere few years later, Dante had begun to treat him as a lesser creature to his own daughter. Then, when Mira was fourteen, Karaburan had made the big mistake, and Dante had banished him to servitude, forcing him to gather food and firewood for them and act as their slave. Since the night of that mistake, he had not seen Mira face to face 'til now. To kill Dante and be free—his own man—would be a blessing.

"Your servant shall do this," Karaburan growled softly. Mira smiled brightly and squeezed his hand.

"After he is dead, we will be free to do as we please," she promised him, and leaned forward. Karaburan closed his eyes hopefully, and waited for her lips to brush his own pebbled skin.

The next thing he knew, he was flying through the air, thrown by a blast of heat as though from the mouth of a volcano. He landed hard, the wind expelled from his lungs so roughly that he gasped for air, and scrabbled his hands and feet at the ground to try and right himself. His ears rang from the impact and he struggled to sit up; as his mind cleared he could hear the glass-shattering laughter from before, echoing all around him.

"Mira!" Karaburan choked, trying to get up, to protect her from the wicked thing that tortured him. "Run! Run away!"

The laughter sputtered and guffawed. "That wasn't her, you shell-scraped primordial sandwich," sneered the voice. "That was me! I am sent to torture you so long as you are a slave, Karaburan, and you are still a slave."

"I will kill him and be free!" he bellowed. He was outraged and heartsick and tired. Little stones began to rain down on him, thrown by unseen hands, as the voice cackled and giggled. Karaburan's anger flushed hot on his face, his body almost numb to the rocks, so great was his distraction. "I will kill him, and I will be free of you, of all of you!" He slammed his hands on the ground in frustration, then hobbled to the coconut bag and snatched it up before it could run away again.

*I will feed these men, and I will tell them the sadness of my story, and they will help me kill Dante.* Karaburan turned and ran toward the woods, determined to gather as much food as he could to better woo his guests to his purpose. *When he is dead, I will find Mira and tell her I love her. And I will be free.*

* * *

As the monster lumbered off into the woods, his mission fresh and furious in his mind, Aurael let his laughter dull to a smug chuckle. He smiled as he landed on the spot where Karaburan had howled with anguish, pleased at how well that had gone and how refreshed he felt.

*It's been ages since I made him hallucinate like that,* he realized fondly. *Lovely to finally stretch that muscle again.*

The monster would plot a horrible murder, Aurael suspected; not horrible in the sense of being gruesome, but horrible in that

Karaburan would probably not be very good at scheming. But he'd found some castaways, and perhaps he would be all the better for their help.

*Need to stay busy, in case his nibs calls me again,* thought Aurael with a scowl. Then the spirit stretched and yawned, sated from the encounter, and took to the air again to continue his search for survivors.

# CHAPTER EIGHT

Ferran felt sunlight on his face and opened his eyes. He wasn't sure how long he'd been asleep, but it felt like it had been years. He inhaled slowly, feeling his joints creak. Birds sang in the trees above him, strange calls that he'd never heard before. The sun was warm, but he lay beneath a particularly shady set of trees, and although the light fell dappled from above, he was mostly protected from the heat. It was somewhat muggy, and the occasional strange insect buzzed by his head as he lay there, but for the greater part, he felt quite alone and unbothered by nature.

He sat up slowly, propping his back against the nearest tree trunk, letting himself adjust to the greenery, the sunshine, the strange sounds around him. After a few moments, he thought he heard music—some sort of reedy instrument—from somewhere far off, but it faded quickly. The birdsong in the canopy and the peeping of unseen frogs in the underbrush drowned out even the sound of his own breath. It was enchanting, how warm and golden everything looked, how relaxing the sounds were. The solitude of the moment was overpowering, and Ferran let his eyes close again for a moment, relishing the sudden feeling of peace with the world around him.

In his mind's eye, he remembered the flash of lightning, an explosion; he saw rain and storm and choppy waves; he felt the cold slap of the water, the darkness that swallowed him, and the bleak loss that followed.

Ferran gasped and his eyes shot open, startled by his own memory. *I'm dead*, he realized. *How could anyone have survived that? We are all dead.* He thought about the disapproving looks his father had given him at dinner that night, before the ship went down. Ferran's stomach lurched and he dropped forward onto all fours, retching, though nothing came up.

Something shifted in the trees nearby, and his head snapped up. The pace was too decisive to be an animal wandering through the green. Ferran sat still in the leafy undergrowth, looking around for the source of the sound.

A girl came walking up the gentle hill through the trees, and she was entirely unlike any girl Ferran had ever seen. He could not see her face very well, her eyes hidden as they were by strange, boxy goggles. She had strong shoulders, and from the look of her long legs, stood some inches taller than himself. Her skin was a warm, golden olive—darker than his own skin. There was a softer, more feminine shape to her firm mouth and sharp chin than found in the lines of her arms. There was something womanly beginning in the curve of her hips, but she did not saunter or stride the way the courtiers did back home; she carried herself the way an animal does, without sense of age or gender, and no pretense.

She stopped several yards off and stood still, as if in a moment of reflection, looking down at something she held in one hand. Her other hand was clasped around a stick—no, a spear—almost as tall as her. Her wild and untethered appearance was more than a little intimidating, her hair a ratted, tangled plait of brown and gold that seemed to have never known a comb or brush. She wore a ragged, sun-bleached man's shirt and strange scraps of leather, all of it bound up with rope in the most peculiar but utilitarian sort of way. *I'll be damned,* Ferran thought to himself. *I'm not dead after all, and the island has natives!*

A bright, strange beetle flew buzzing past his nose, and Ferran recoiled sharply in surprise. The shrubs around him rustled and shifted, and the girl looked up sharply in his direction. Ferran froze, unsure what to do. The girl began to move again, taking long strides toward his hiding place. *I could run, but where to? This is her home, she'd find me out sooner or later.*

The girl was nearly upon him, spear hoisted, when Ferran leapt to his feet, hands in the air to show empty palms and nothing to hide. "Please! Don't, don't do that, I'm unarmed!"

He must have startled her, for she made a terrible noise and stumbled mid-stride, dropping the small thing in her right palm to take the spear with both hands now, her body crouched uncertainly in wary defense. The spear point was level with his sternum, steady and well-aimed.

"I'm sorry, sorry to startle you," he went on, his voice suddenly dry and ragged. "I didn't mean to. I'm rather lost. Wondering if you could help me . . ." He swallowed helplessly as she continued to aim her homemade weapon at his chest. *I'm no threat,* he thought, hoping she at least understood his body language. She didn't move. "I only speak Italesh, I'm sorry . . . I don't know your language. Whatever it is," Ferran added miserably.

"You assume much," the girl said, her voice rough and bemused. Ferran felt his eyebrows shoot upward as she relaxed her stance, planting the butt of her spear into the soil and peeling back her dark mask of steel and glass. "I speak your tongue."

"You . . . do?" Ferran felt disoriented. This indigenous girl had a face that was more the shape of one from his own country than any foreign stranger, and her eyes were an utterly strange and brilliant bluish-green.

"Yes, clearly." Her gaze narrowed in study of him. "How do you feel? You seem much improved."

"I . . . how so, improved?" His head felt fuzzy from standing up too quickly. The sun bore down on him now that he was not hidden by shady trees and close to the damp ground.

"Who do you think pulled you onto the beach?" She leaned on her spear, peering into his face. "Or do you not remember? We spoke then, though briefly, and you were much exhausted from the waves and sun."

Ferran felt his head begin to throb. "Who are you?"

"I wanted to ask you that myself," said the girl, and grinned at him. "I'm called Mira. And you?"

"Ferran," he answered, leaving out the titles and surnames for now. He did, however, offer her a slight bow, and his hand. She did not take it right away, and he looked up, already feeling foolish for having done so out of habit. She squinted at him. "It's a handshake," he told her. *I must sound pathetic,* he realized. *First contact with a stranger on a desert island and I expect her to know a courtly gesture? Stupid.*

"Handshake?" echoed Mira, staring at his upturned palm. "You aren't shaking it."

"No, you have to clasp it with your own, and then we both shake them," he explained. "Here, like this—" He reached for her hand to press it against his own.

Before he knew what had happened, Mira snatched her hand away and checked him upwards on the jaw with her elbow before backing up several paces into a ready stance, the spear held aloft with the unsharpened end pointing down at his pate. Ferran's hands flew to his jaw and face, and he blinked several times.

"Ow!" he groaned. "What was that for?" Ferran stepped back to look warily at her.

Mira stared back at him a moment, then appeared to relax bit by bit. She lowered and righted the spear. She seemed to have a hard time choosing the right words, her expression growing more frustrated as her jaw worked in silence.

"I am sorry if I startled you again," he said more gently. "I ought not to have tried to touch you. I'm sorry."

His guess had been right; Mira's expression cleared and became neutral, and then, after a moment, softened again altogether. She nodded, her mouth a thin line. "Fine," she replied. "You are thirsty and hungry, I'm sure. Come with me."

Ferran watched her turn to go, hesitating before taking a step after her. His shoe hit something hard, and he looked down. The small item she'd dropped lay in the dirt. *A pocket knife?* He picked it up carefully, and as soon as its weight hit his palm, he recognized it.

"Are you coming?" asked Mira, turning to look at him. "Or do you have somewhere else to be?"

Ferran held up the closed pocket knife. "Where did you get this?" His heart flopped in his chest like a dying fish on the sand.

Mira tilted her head, birdlike. "I found it. Give it back." She reached for it.

"Where did you find it?" He held it tightly, out of her reach. "I need to know where."

"On the bottom of the bay," she replied. "Give it to me." There was a childlike insistence to the pucker of her chin, though by her height and voice, Ferran would have placed her closer to his own age.

"Was it . . . Did you find it on a body?" Ferran felt his throat begin to close up.

"No."

"Are you sure?"

She looked at him with confusion. "I'm sure. It caught my eye. There were a lot of other things . . . silver things. Sharp things. I liked this one, so I took it."

Ferran felt his fear subside a little. "But there was no body?"

"No," she insisted, lifting her chin. "Yours is the only body I have found." She paused to study him. "What is it?"

"It's just . . . it belonged to my father. I can only imagine it came from his cabin on the ship. If there'd been a body . . ." He trailed off.

"No," Mira insisted. "What is it?"

"It's a pocket knife." He held it up, then worked the hidden mechanism to produce a three-inch steel blade from one end. The light caught it and illuminated her face for a brief moment; she recoiled a little and shut her eyes at the brightness of it. "See?" Ferran turned it this way and that.

"A pocket knife?" she repeated thoughtfully.

"Yes, you keep it in your pocket. It's handy for when you need to open something, or cut something, and you haven't got a real dagger on you."

"Hmph." Her grunt was noncommittal. "If it was your father's, then I suppose it's yours, now. I saw no bodies but yours." Her eyes gleamed like the scales of a snake. Ferran folded the blade away and slid it into his pocket, though his hand remained clamped tightly around it. "Come, I'll take you where you can rest and eat, and we'll talk more."

Ferran followed her further into the forest, his brow knit in a whirling cycle of thoughts. *Maybe they washed up elsewhere on the island. Or maybe they drowned. My mother will notice we've not been in contact. What's she going to do when she hears that we never arrived home? How could anyone find me way out here? I'm just glad that I'm not alone here.* He was grateful that Mira did not speak again until they had reached their destination.

Finally, they came upon a clear spring with a pool deep enough to submerge in and a steady little creek wandering off into the woods from there. The trees and flora grew thick and lush around it, the ground soft with springy moss and lichens. As they approached, Ferran saw some kind of furry, small mammal dart away from the pool into the safety of the underbrush, while a large, colorful bird sat preening on a rock.

Mira gave a low whistle call, and the bird stopped its preening to whistle back, cocking its head at her. Then it ruffled itself all over and took to the air, gliding to Mira's outstretched arm.

"Water! Is it . . . ?" Ferran's voice caught in his throat, suddenly overwhelmed by thirst.

"Safe to drink? Yes. I imagine you're thirsty."

He was on his knees by the pool before he could thank her, his hands cupping the cool, clear water. Much of it dribbled down his arms as he tried to drink it up, until, after a moment, Mira appeared beside him, offering him what looked like a bowl with a brown and hairy texture to the outside of it. *A coconut shell?* Ferran had never seen one up close before.

Ferran filled the shell with water several times and drank so deeply that he inhaled as he swallowed, making himself cough riotously for a minute. The bird squawked and startled but did not fly off. Mira sat down on the soft ground several feet away, the bird moving up to her shoulder to pick affectionately at her tangled hair.

"Thank you," Ferran mumbled at last, still somewhat dumbfounded to have been rescued by her. "I can't thank you enough."

Mira did not reply, her intense green eyes fixed on him with something like doubt. Ferran stared back, unsure still of what she was thinking, still wondering who she was and where she'd come from. They sat in silence a moment while the bird clucked and muttered, ruffling its tail feathers as it fussed over Mira's hair.

"Is that bird your pet?" Ferran blurted out. He felt scrutinized somehow, and did not know how to broach the subject.

"Pet," repeated his strange-eyed rescuer. She narrowed her eyes a little. "What's pet?"

Ferran swallowed. "A pet. You know. You take care of it. It belongs to you?"

Mira's eyes widened and her expression shifted to one of confusion. "No!" Her tone was somewhat bemused. "How can I own something that flies and is free?" She nudged her hand under the bird's large, dark gray talons and it climbed onto her wrist obligingly. It was so many more colors than Ferran had seen on most birds: red and blue and yellow and green, with dazzling speckles of gold hidden in some feathers' sheen. It looked around with dark, intelligent eyes and had the curved smile of a beak meant for tearing and cracking things open.

"It's beautiful. What kind of bird is it? Is it some sort of tropical eagle? It's large enough to be a raptor, but the beak isn't quite right."

Mira stared at him.

Ferran fidgeted. *Am I going to have to explain animal taxonomy to her?* "Look, never mind, I'm sorry," he babbled. "I just don't . . . Who are you? How did you find me? Have you always lived alone on this island?"

The bird ruffled its feathers as Mira shifted it back to her shoulder. "I'm Mira," she answered calmly, "and I found you floating on a piece of wreckage out near the other debris, in the bay. I pulled you to shore."

Ferran furrowed his brow at her. "You pulled me to shore? All by yourself?"

Her eyes flashed. "I'm a good swimmer."

Suddenly Ferran remembered the raft, the hot, bright sun beating mercilessly down, the squawking of birds. He remembered panicking, splashing—and a girl's voice yelling for him to stop—vomiting seawater, and the shimmering mirage of his savior's face with her bright green eyes and serious expression, and—

"You were naked," he realized aloud, and flushed as pink as his mother's rose garden.

"Ah, you do remember." Mira's tone was approving, not apologetic. "That's better. It means you probably don't have any serious damage up here," she added, tapping her own head.

Ferran's eyes dropped to his hands, his skin hot with discomfort and uncertainty. "I . . . thank you for pulling me to shore, I . . . apologize for . . ."

"For nothing," insisted Mira with apparent bravado, though there was a hint of shyness there too, Ferran thought. "There is nothing to be sorry about."

"It's not proper," muttered Ferran, even as he realized how silly it must seem to her.

Mira stood up abruptly, causing the bird to shuffle and flap its wings, taking off for another, more stable, perch in the trees. "It's my skin," she replied, with a touch of defiance. "I have nothing to hide." She moved to take the coconut shell from him and fill it with water from the spring. She drank deeply and then tossed the shell back to him; he caught it awkwardly. Then she dropped to a squat before him, quite close, and peered into his face the way a predatory animal confronts a smaller member of its pack. "Now. Ferran. You will tell me the answers to my questions."

Ferran swallowed his embarrassment and confusion. "All right?" he ventured, clutching the empty coconut.

"Where is your home?" Her eyes gleamed like fish scales catching sunlight.

"Neapolis," answered Ferran, and his stomach sank a little deeper into himself. *Though no more my home now than this strange island. I may never leave this place again.*

"And where were you traveling? In your ship? What type of ship was it? Was it a submarinal ship as well as a surface vessel, or was it just a dirigible?"

Ferran blinked. "We were heading home. My sister was just married, and now lives in Tunitz, and—"

"Tunitz? This is in Afrek?"

"Yes." Ferran looked surprised. "The northernmost country of Afrek. How did you—"

She flapped a hand impatiently. "And the ship?"

"It's an Elemental Type 43-G luxury airship. It can sail on the surface of the waves but primarily serves as aerial transportation." He furrowed his brow at the rapidly shifting expressions on her face. "Why? What does it matter what kind of ship?"

"I have never seen one so close to us before. Usually they fly or sail past our island and never notice that we're here. Occasionally, they sink out beyond the bay, far beyond, but within view. Yours is the first ship I have ever seen so close, which is why I was able to bring up some of your debris, and find you afloat."

"Debris?" Ferran stared back at her. "You mean when you found the pocket knife."

"Oh, yes, and more," she told him. "Several trunks I pulled out of the sea. I have not opened them."

"Trunks?" Ferran felt his heart beating. There could be anything in them: clothes, food, supplies, one of the Mandolinani wireless devices which could be used for contacting a rescue party . . . "Where are they?"

"The trunks? I've hidden them."

"Take me to them! I can help you open them. Please!" He instinctively reached for her hand, but stopped himself some inches from her actual skin. She did not flinch as hard as she had the first time, but she eyed him. "Please, Mira. It could be important."

"Fine. But you tell me more." She got to her feet and, after a moment, he followed. "You tell me about your world. Is Neapolis near Roma? What is it like in the mountains? Have you ever been to Troia? Landon? Gudafesct? Are these great cities as full of towering walls and elegant spires as they say?"

They walked swiftly through the woods, and Ferran huffed as he tried to keep up with Mira's long, certain strides. It was a level of activity Ferran was unused to.

"Who's they? As who says?" He felt thoroughly baffled. "Are you not native to this island?"

"No," Mira threw over her shoulder at him as they walked. "I was born somewhere else, and my father and I came here when I was very small."

"There's others on the island?"

"Just three of us," said Mira, and Ferran heard her tone grow darker. "My father and I . . . and a monster."

\* \* \*

## 1862

Mira lay on her back on the soft moss near the clear spring, listening to the birds in the trees and the sound of trickling water. A gentle breeze played at the leaves overhead, and all was calm and quiet. Several feet away, Karaburan lay dozing on his own patch of moss, curled up like a dog at the foot of his owner's bed. Her father was elsewhere, busying himself with his study of the island's native plant life, no doubt. All was well. The island was safe, and she was free to do as she pleased, even at that young age.

A voice like silvery light dancing on water whispered to her from somewhere above as the late afternoon light grew more rosy and golden with every moment. "Mira," whispered the voice. "Mira-child. Come and let's play a game! Come and let's have a chase."

Mira opened her eyes with a smile and sat up, her long, honey-brown hair spilling down her back. "Aurael?" she called softly. "Where are you hiding?"

"Come and see, come and see," chimed the unseen spirit, teasingly plucking at different tree branches to make the leaves rustle.

"Come out!" she laughed, both charmed and annoyed. "I want to see you!"

"Now, now, my girl, you know I can't do that. Be patient; someday when you're older you'll see me face to face. What games shall we have? A hunt? A chase? I'll be the fox and you'll be the huntress. Or you'll be the mermaid and I'll be the sailor."

"It's too warm for chasing," answered Mira, smiling at the sunlight on her face through the canopy of trees. "Come sit and tell me stories." She patted the moss beside her.

The cool breeze ruffled her hair and her dress, torn from wear and rearranged to accommodate her growing form. She laughed softly, and the breeze curled up on the moss beside her like a cat. She could almost see the silver-blue outline of it, its round shape, its pointed ears and bright round eyes staring up at her. Mira reached over and stroked it, causing it to purr softly.

"What stories would you have, my mistress?" asked the translucent cat in the same breathy, shimmering voice as the wind.

"How long have you been on the island?" she inquired, still stroking the cat's lighter-than-air fur. The cat stared up at her for a while before it answered.

"Probably as long as you've been alive," replied the cat, shimmering in the light.

"If that's so, why can't Karaburan see you? He's been here that long himself, he told me so. We're the same age."

The cat did not turn to look over at the sleeping Karaburan, but its eyes narrowed a little. "Karaburan is not special. He's not like you, Mira. You're the blessed one who found me in the tree, remember?" It butted its head against her hand, and she smiled.

"I'm not that special," she told Aurael, shyly. "I'm just lucky, I think."

"You're very special to me," insisted Aurael the cat, purring harder.

"Where's Karaburan's mother?" Mira asked, her voice softening. "Whenever I ask about her, Karaburan cries and won't speak. He misses her very much. And what about his father?" Aurael did not answer, and looked as if he had not heard. Mira scratched the cat under the chin, tipping its head up to look at her. "Aurael? Where are Karaburan's parents? Are they dead?"

"Yes," said the cat, and its voice sounded unhappy.

"Did you know them?"

"I knew his mother," said Aurael a little too quickly. He paused, and then went on more slowly. "She got ill and died."

"Here on the island?" Mira looked alarmed. "But I've never been ill here. Neither has Father."

"Your father . . . your father's love protects you. You are safe from much the world has to offer in the way of harm. You see? You are special."

Mira considered her next question carefully. "And where is my mother? Did she die here, too?"

"No, child. She died before you got to this island. Your father says she was very fragile. I'm sorry," the cat added, closing its eyes. Mira did not feel sad about this for some reason, and continued stroking the cat in silence, wondering why she was not mournful the way Karaburan was whenever his mother was mentioned.

"Where was I born?"

"I don't know," said the cat, looking at her again. Mira stopped petting it and swept her long hair over her shoulder with both hands, picking out the tangles that had accumulated from the wind blowing and from swimming in the sea. "Why all these curiosities, Mira? Curiosity killed the cat, you know."

"I'm not a cat," said Mira seriously, "and neither are you."

"No, indeed. That's true."

"When am I going to see you, Aurael? Really see you? I like having you as my invisible companion, and I like pretending you're different animals, but I want to see what you really look like."

"You know that's not possible," the cat said, standing up and curling its tail in frustration.

"Why not? We are sheltered here. Safe. I will love you no matter what you look like. Karaburan is ugly as a spinefish and it doesn't matter, I still care about him. That's what friendship is. Please, Aurael, show me."

The cat walked away from her, and after several steps, disappeared completely. "Your father forbids it, Mira. He has decreed that I may guard you as your friend, but not 'til you are older will you see my face. As for Karaburan, I know not. Your father is careful with his belongings and does not like to share." His voice had an edge to it like the sharp rocks that sometimes cut her feet in the shallows of the lagoon. "Alas, my dove, your present company leaves much freedom to be desired," sighed the breeze over her shoulder.

"Karaburan is asleep. He won't stir. Come sit with me and let me see you!"

Aurael did not reply at first. When he did, his voice was low and close and wary, tickling her shoulder. "He cannot see me," warned the spirit. "You know the rules."

"Rules are silly and boring," chided Mira boldly. "It doesn't matter what Karaburan sees, he's completely harmless. And who cares what Father says? This island is our home! Our safe place. No harm can come to us here."

"I cannot," groaned the invisible spirit longingly. "I am yours alone, and if he sees me, it will not end well."

Mira frowned, her expression folding neatly into a dark furrow of frustration. "But I want to see you," she insisted.

The spirit sighed noisily. "All right. For a few minutes. What other shape shall I take? A girl? A boy? A bird? A dog?"

"Just be you," she insisted. "Show me what you look like." Again, Mira was puzzled by Aurael's long silence and turned her head, listening and looking for him in the long afternoon shadows. "Please, Aurael," she added softly. "We've been friends for so long."

There was no answer. Mira sat very still, listening to the sounds of the late afternoon waning on: the cicadas hidden in the trees above the clearing and the little brook bubbling away from the pool of fresh water. She sighed and lay down on the moss again after a time. She thought about her mother, whose face and name she could not remember, and about her father, who seemed happy enough on the island, but kept to himself during the day. *I wasn't born on the island,* she mused. *So there really must be other things out there beyond the water. I want to know what they are. My father knows; he must know. He has books that tell of it, I'm sure.*

"Aurael?" Mira whispered tentatively. "Are you here?" When there was no answer, she focused on the sleeping, fish-skinned boy.

"Karaburan, wake up!" she cried, sitting up and climbing to her feet. Her playmate rolled over and groaned in displeasure at the sudden alarm. Mira pounced on him and shook his arm excitedly, her small hands even smaller in comparison to his enormous frame. Though they were the same age, Karaburan was three times bigger than she, and could carry her easily on his shoulders as he loped on all fours.

"No, no," muttered the sleeping boy-beast. "I'm not done with my supper . . ."

Mira laughed a crowing laugh. "Get up, get up, you sleepy head! We have to go to the cave!"

Karaburan startled upright, and Mira stumbled backwards, still laughing at the look of worried surprise on his face. "The cave?" he cried. "Is your father angry? Did we do something wrong?"

"No," she giggled. "I want to borrow some books!"

"Books?" Karaburan's eyes grew even larger and more fishlike with his slack-jawed expression.

"Yes, books. To read."

"But we can't read!"

"We will learn to," announced Mira. "Together. Let's go!"

# CHAPTER NINE

Truffo Arlecin sat on the warm sand, his dark eyes following the white-capped waves as they endlessly rolled in to the shore. The cawing of the dull sea birds over the water grated softly on his ears like a barber's blade against a leather strop, both soothing and irritable in turn. The bland white and gray scavengers circled urgently over a spot further out in the waves, and Truffo felt a faint pang, remembering his feathered savior.

"Birdy, I hardly knew ye," Truffo said softly to himself, putting his face in his hands. He heard a rustling in the hovel several yards behind him.

"Where's that Kabran, eh?" Stephen Montanto called as he came down the sand to stand by Truffo. "Where's that Kaliban?"

"It's Karaburan," snarled Truffo, bleary-eyed. "And it's out there, fishing for our supper." *Stephen is less witsome than I thought he'd be*, thought the fool drearily. *He is a hell of a servant, but his kingdom will be one of malaprops and malcontent.*

"Right so, right so. Kalaburn. Our goodly monster." Stephen stretched himself and breathed the air deeply.

"Why are you so pleased with yourself?" Truffo asked bitterly. Even the sound of Stephen's breathing was beginning to annoy him.

"Is it not right for a lord to be pleased over his newfound title and lands?"

"You aren't a lord—this is all make-believe, Stephen. You're a valet to a drowned king, and I'm a fool and an orphan, unloved by the world." Stephen said nothing, but continued to stretch, working out the kinks in his neck and arms, sauntering down to the water's edge to put his toes in the surf.

Truffo felt the familiar great wave of sorrow swell in his chest, threatening to overthrow him. *I should never come on this trip. Then at least I'd be able to kill myself at home in the comfort of my own room. This entire thing was a disaster. The only nice thing was that damned bird that pulled the metal out of my shoulder, and the monster ate it.* He choked back a sob, covering his face with his hands again.

"Nothing to cry about, lad," called Stephen, merrily. "We're alive, aren't we? We're alive, we've got an entire island to ourselves, and a slave to bring us food, and the sun is shining, after all. Not too shabby of a day, I'd say."

Truffo stared at the broad backside of the valet as he made a show of doing toe-touches and swinging his arms about. Stephen was not the slenderest of men; where Truffo himself seemed a bit of a scarecrow, all limbs and unkempt hair, Stephen Montanto could be called portly, and had a graying sort of dignity about the temples.

Truffo frowned deeply but could not muster his strength to bother answering the valet's jolly comment. *We're going to die here and he doesn't even care,* thought Truffo angrily, and lay down on his back, eyes closed, letting the sun beat down on him. A few minutes went by in peace, but then Stephen began to whistle an absurd melody, something that sounded like a sad drinking song set to a tempo far brighter, and a pitch higher, than normal. The scraping inside Truffo's head increased, and the black pit of his mind gaped wide to swallow the lingering bits of his sanity which clung, apelike, to the last sturdy branches of his brain. There was a great splashing in the water, and Stephen stopped whistling.

"Truffo! Truffo, look, boy!"

Truffo did not want to look. He did not want to listen to Stephen's ridiculous posturing of positivity, and he did not want to watch the wildlife while they waited for the wandering monster to come back with their would-be supper.

"Truffo, get up! Look what he's got!"

Fuming, Truffo sat up very slowly and glowered at Stephen before looking past him out to the waves. The monster had surfaced and reached the shallows. As he grew nearer, more of him reached upward out of the water, and it became clear he was dragging something with him. Something box-shaped. Truffo got to his feet awkwardly and squinted, shuffling a few feet toward the water's edge.

"What is that?"

Stephen stared out at the returning Karaburan, his expression perfectly enchanted. "A crate, boy. A crate! From the ship!"

"What are we going to do with a crate?" Truffo asked shrilly. Stephen swatted playfully at him and did a little jig on the sand, something Truffo sincerely wished he could unsee.

"Could be food! Could be supplies! Could be one of those whatdoyoucallems . . . One of those spectographical transmittance kits! We could be calling for help in an hour and be home in a day, boy!" Stephen grabbed for his arms and swung Truffo about like a rag doll.

"Could be nothing," squawked Truffo, then he shrieked in sudden pain. "Gah! Put me down. My shoulder! Ah!"

"Oh, tish. Your shoulder's mending. You really are the most terrific spoilsport, aren't you?" Stephen laughed and set him down again, clapping him on the good shoulder. "I can see why the king likes you."

Truffo locked eyes with Stephen and saw his own frowning reflection in the older man's dark eyes. Stephen's expression seemed caught between painful remembrance and embarrassed apology, and Truffo stared hard at him, letting his own anger and sorrow at remembering the drowned king boil over in his chest like a bad broth. Then Stephen looked away with a cough, and Truffo balled his hands into bony fists, wanting to hit him, and hit him hard.

*If he hadn't let me steal the key to the wine cabinet, we'd have at least drowned with the others.* Truffo ground his teeth. *It's all his fault I'm still alive.*

"What ho, Karbuncle!" Stephen waved a hand toward the monster as it sloshed through the shallows toward them. "What's that you've got there?"

"My lords! I found this strange thing on the sandy bottom while I dove for your supper-fish!" Karaburan lumbered forth onto the dark wet sand, dragging the box noisily forward as water streamed down his misshapen, scale-patched body. Truffo folded his arms tightly around himself and squinted; the wooden crate did appear to be relatively unbattered, aside from some stalks of seaweed that still caught on its corners, but it was also unlabeled.

"Let us have it then," exclaimed Stephen, pushing forward to examine the crate. "Let us pry it open, with your strong beastly arms, Karlboren!" Stephen went to clap the monster on the shoulder but recoiled as soon as his palm touched the sea-soaked, unnatural skin. "Go to, go to! Crack it open as you would an oyster, lad, gently, but with good firmness of the arm."

Truffo watched, standing a few yards off as the eager brute knelt and set about prying the crate apart with his bare hands. "What if it's explosive, huh?" he called sourly. "What if it's from the munitions locker? Or the engine room?"

Stephen made a scornful noise and waved his hands like a fishwife. "Bah, boy, you'll speak so ill, our luck will change! Close your mouth and be still awhile."

Truffo glowered back at him, shoulders hunched. *What a hypocrite! He cares for me and encourages me when we are employed and safely stowed, but now that we are alone in the wilderness with this fish-man, I am lower than a dog? Can't believe I liked him so well before.*

Karaburan eagerly peeled apart the creaking, damp wooden crate like an ape destroys fruit, then pulled the straw stuffing out in fistfuls, still miraculously dry for having been underwater. Then there was the clink of glass, and both Stephen and Truffo held their breath.

"What is it?" marveled the anxious Karaburan, pulling the bottle out of the pile of straw.

Truffo saw the widening of Stephen's eyes as they met his own.

"'Tis wine, boy," breathed Stephen huskily, and Truffo was unsure whether he spoke to him or the monster. "Wine!"

"What is wine, my lords?" Karaburan's head tilted to one side.

"Give me the bottle, and I'll show you well."

Karaburan passed the bottle to Stephen, as delicately as if it had been a living thing, and Stephen roughly took the half-submerged cork and pulled for all his might. When it burst away with a pop, Karaburan scrambled backward on the sand, terrified, and Stephen laughed. He held the bottle up as though in toast.

"By the gods, a blessing if I ever knew one," he pronounced thirstily, and put it to his lips to drink deeply.

Truffo felt his insides squirm and pucker at the sight of it. *If I'd been drunker still, I'd sure have drowned, but now I'll have it to dull the pains of survival.* In spite of himself, he stumbled forward as Stephen lowered the bottle, plucking it from his hands. "And now for me!" he cried defiantly and threw back his head to swig from the dark wine.

Stephen yanked it away again as soon as he'd swallowed, and Truffo coughed in the wake of the sudden stop. "Greedy, now, are we?" Stephen chided, but his expression was strangely merry. "Now, Karuburin, come here and kneel to your lords and swear you will be as our dearest servant." He waggled the bottle enticingly.

Truffo wiped at his mouth, happily feeling the sour burn of the dark red wine in his throat, mingling with its soreness from the hot day and rough treatment. *What on earth will it become if we make it drink?* he wondered nervously. The monster shuffled forward hesitantly to kneel and duck his head a little in deference.

"My lords, I do swear myself to you . . . as much as I may," he added humbly. Stephen's brow furrowed.

"What exactly does that mean?" he asked.

"My lords, I am your loyal, loving servant," the creature soothed, his overlarge hands spread wide in supplication. "But there is a tyrant here who keeps me for himself."

Truffo sucked in a short breath of disbelief. *I knew this was too good to be true!* His shoulder twinged, remembering the stabbing shrapnel, and he grunted in sudden pain.

"You aren't alone?" Stephen looked both anxious and hopeful. "A tyrant, you say?"

"A vengeful, twisted man who was left here by the fates to wither away, but it is he who keeps me as his slave. I gather wood for his fires, fish for his food, and protect his home from the beasts that roam this place. I do as he commands, as I am bounden to."

"Well, why?" Stephen sounded irritated. "He sounds terrible. You're much stronger than he, I'm sure."

Truffo stole up alongside Stephen as he spoke and pulled the bottle from his grasp so that he might drink again.

"He is not strong in body, but strong in mind," Karaburan went on. "He is much stronger than me, and holds much power over my simple life. I tell you, he is a tyrant. I would give myself a thousand times over in service to anyone who might rid this place of his breath and foul heart."

"You see how simple and how fond he is?" Stephen mused to Truffo, who slugged back another draught of wine from the bottle. "He wants a kindly master, not this rude and wrinkled devil. What's his name, then, monster? Who's this man?"

"I know him as my master. Once I wished to call him father, but he is no sire of mine; mine was drowned, you see, and this man made it seem that he would adopt me as his own. Until the day came that he saw my hideousness, and, disregarding my true and honest soul, he cast me out and treats me ever more as his lowest beast of burden."

"What are you even getting at?" demanded Truffo, before he could stop himself. The tediousness of the monster's toadying was beginning to wear on him, and Stephen was soaking it up like a sickly sponge. "What do you expect us to do, off him? Since you've got some kind of magic spell on you to keep you from hurting him?" He took another swig from the bottle, and Stephen and Karaburan stared at him. "What," he said, glancing between the two of them and hugging the bottle to his chest.

Karaburan lowered his pale gaze to the crate of wine bottles, as humbly as any dog hoping for a reward. "If my master dies, the spell will break, and I will be free to serve you as my trusted, my beloved, my dear lords. I would do anything to be free of him. I want a simple life, but I want to serve willingly, not because I must. And I would serve someone who does not have the darkness of spirit that he has." The beast shuddered a little, and Stephen's jaw settled sternly.

"That's what we'll do, then." His eyes gleamed, his expression serious as he turned to Truffo. "We'll set him free, and then the island will be all ours. The three of us together, eh? Karburn will help us live off the land, and we'll all be kings in our own right!"

Truffo's eyebrows flew upward, but it was not joy that seeped into his expression. He frowned a little less, but his gut twisted within him, slow and painful. "Kings . . . but only after we've murdered a man?"

"Kings are begot in blood, Truffo Arlecin," announced Stephen. "It is a good deed to help this poor and wayward thing claim his freedom. And besides that, we're the only two left alive from the wreck of our former life. We may never go home again—and if we don't, let's make the most of it, eh?" He squeezed Truffo's good shoulder gently, a glimmer of paternal coaxing passing through his dark eyes, and Truffo realized that he could no longer tell if this plan was driven by justice or greed.

# CHAPTER TEN

The sun was still hot and high in the sky, and Ferran stood under the thin shadow of a spindly tree, breathing in the sea air. He watched as Mira reappeared through the tall grass, dragging another leather-bound trunk with her. "Here's the big one," she said. "It's lighter than the others."

He nodded eagerly. "Are any of them particularly heavy?" Ferran was hopeful that they might have more than just clothing in them, although the clothing would be nice, if it were dry and in wearable condition. His thoughts ran through the other possibilities: food, tools, a spectrograph, maybe?

"Depends on what you mean by 'particularly heavy,' " she replied, and her bright, serious eyes fell on his skinny arms. He blushed and crossed them over his chest.

"I mean, do they feel like there might be a machine in any of them?"

"Are they yours?" Mira tipped the trunk over onto its side and brushed the dried seaweed from its brass corners.

"They're from the ship, so yes, technically."

"Was it your ship that sank?" Mira sounded almost impressed, and Ferran straightened his back a little.

"Technically," he affirmed.

"What's technical about it? The ship is either yours or it isn't." Mira's eyes were traveling, possibly retracing her steps to the trunks.

"It's—was—my father's ship."

"Then it's your father's ship. Not yours." She began to move off, counting her steps under her breath.

"It is, too, mine," Ferran insisted. "Everything that's his is mine, as is rightfully so for the son of a king."

Mira was halfway down the ridge of sand dunes in search of another trunk and stopped, turning to look up at him with something like surprise. "You're a prince?"

Ferran set his jaw firmly and stared back at her. Her green eyes traveled the height and shape of him, and he felt again like a butterfly under glass. He hadn't intended to reveal this information in the form of a brag, or a declaration of . . . what? Importance? He exhaled through his teeth and looked down at the trunk.

"You were a prince," said Mira at last, making him look up. Her expression was even and judicious. "Now, you're whatever you want to make of yourself."

"What do you mean?"

"Your ship went down, yes, but it set you free. This is your chance to be what you will, not what others tell you that you are."

"I was supposed to be king someday, but I never thought—I never thought I'd be very good at it."

Mira took a few steps back up the embankment and looked at him without judgment. "What did you think you were good at?"

"The natural sciences," said Ferran, without hesitating. "Studying plants and animals. I wanted to travel the world and find new species, to understand the delicate balance between mankind and its natural environments. My father thought it was no place for a prince to become a scientist, and although my mother didn't mind, she tried to get me to study something else, something more likely for my father to approve."

"Was your mother also on the ship?" Mira asked. Something about the lowering of her head made Ferran think of a deer tentatively passing through an open clearing.

"No." Ferran shook his head. "She stayed in Tunitz with my sister for an extra week, hoping the climate would affect her conditions. She took ill after I was born and has been battling with the illness ever since. She was quite well for a while, but the last several years have been difficult for her. Her doctors recommended she stay longer."

Mira fell silent, apparently unsure of what to say after that. Ferran swallowed. "So, the trunks?" he offered.

"Yes," said Mira, and moved off quickly down the dunes for the others.

Ferran let out his breath in a frustrated sigh. He wished that there was someone else with him. Someone who wasn't a strange-minded, island-raised girl with a penchant for long stares and heavy silences. He thought about his Uncle Bas and his throat tightened. *No*, he thought, bending down to examine the locks on the large trunk. *Don't dwell on it. Move forward. Always forward.*

The trunk was a leather-bound steamer trunk, large enough for him to fit inside. It appeared to have been battered about quite a bit in the shipwreck, but even with the new scrapes and dents, Ferran did not recognize it. *So, it isn't mine*, he thought. *Duke Tor's? Or . . . Father's?* He pulled out the pocketknife and set about trying to pick the first lock.

Mira reappeared, dragging two smaller trunks with her. Ferran glanced up as she approached. *Even if those aren't heavy, she's still stronger than I am*, he realized, glancing at her arms and the ease with which she moved. *No marvel, then, she was able to drag me to shore.*

"What about these?" Mira slid the trunks onto the sand near him, and Ferran's eyes widened.

"Yes! I mean, I think so. That one looks like mine." He abandoned the large trunk and scooted over to work on the smallest trunk.

Mira perched on top of the abandoned trunk like a lizard on a warm rock, watching him in silence. After a few minutes, she said softly, "I am sorry you've lost so much. I hope you find some of it again."

Ferran paused his lock-picking and looked over his shoulder at her, but her eyes were closed and her face was turned up toward the sun as though she hadn't spoken at all. "Thank you," he said, then added just as quietly, "I'm very grateful that you found me. I owe you my life." He turned back to the trunk, and after a moment more, the lock sprang open and he unhitched it. "Let's see," he said, warily opening the lid. "Ah! It is mine!"

The air which belched forth from the trunk was musty, like the closet in his cabin on the *Brilliant Albatross*, with a faint hint of campfire smoke from the wedding feast. The trunk was full of clothing he'd worn on the way down to Tunitz and during the festive week before the wedding.

"Your clothes?" Mira was peering over his shoulder at them with intense interest.

"Yes. I never thought I'd be so happy to see my dirty laundry," he laughed. She looked at him quizzically.

"Laundry," she echoed.

"Yes, laundry; it's . . . clothes that I have worn recently and haven't washed yet."

"Washed."

"Yes, with soap and scrubbing and such. They aren't clean."

Mira stared at a shirt he was holding, and then looked down at her own strange tunic and short trousers, most of their color and movement lost over time and weather. He suspected she didn't have much else to wear.

"Here," he said, "look at this." He unfolded the shirt and held it up. "That might fit you. We aren't too different in size. And let's see about trousers." He dug through the clothes. "I'll want to change, too, but we can share, there's no reason not to."

"You want me to wear your clothes?" asked Mira, looking deeply confused.

"Why not? I know they aren't entirely clean, but I thought they might be more clean than . . . well, I mean . . . if you want to, that is, you don't have to," he added hurriedly.

"I have never seen new clothes before," Mira explained slowly.

"Well, this isn't really new. It's not what the ladies are wearing nowadays, but it'll do. And you won't want skirts anyway right now, I'm sure they'd only be a burden on the island. I don't even want to think about a bustle or a corset," he added.

"What are those?" Mira wondered, pulling the shirt on over her own tunic experimentally. It was a pale, canary-yellow linen thing, with festive dark blue and green embroidery at the collar and cuffs. She ran her fingers over the stitching incredulously.

"That? That's blackwork. Well, it's called blackwork, but it's obviously not black. It's a kind of embroidery."

"No, bussel. Corzit."

"Bustle? Corset? Underthings. Ladies underthings," he added apologetically. "They're complicated."

"Complicated how?" Mira reached past him for a handsome gold and green sleeve, one of his fancier doublets. As she passed him, Ferran caught the scent of her hair, which smelled of sea salt, moss, and some flower whose name he did not know. It was unusually pleasant, and caught him off-guard.

"They're . . ." he faltered. "Corsets are like a very stiff shirt that laces up the back very tightly to make your waist small. The bustle is like a cage you wear on your backside to . . . to . . . floof up the skirts, I guess." He picked out some brown trousers for himself and a plain white shirt.

Mira's face was a wrinkled raisin of disbelief. "I don't know what half that means, but it sounds ridiculous. Why don't ladies wear pants?"

"I don't know, they just don't, really. Some do, I suppose, if their occupation calls for it, but they generally don't."

"What else do they wear?"

"Big hats," Ferran told her, then added, "or tiny hats. Depends. Lots of feathers and ribbons. Ah . . . I don't really know what else."

"But you know about bussels and corzits and underthings." Ferran flushed, but her expression was oddly bright, and he realized after a moment she was teasing him. He laughed awkwardly, but the brightness in her gaze only increased, her mouth curving until a smile broke like a whale breaching the surface of the sea. *So she does have a sense of humor!*

"How old are you?" he blurted out.

"I don't know. How do you know?"

"You count. You, or someone, keeps track of how many years you've been alive."

Mira looked down at the handsome sleeves of the doublet, which were still unbuttoned and hung down like wings from her shoulders. "I don't know. It seems like a long time, but I am not so old as my father is, of course, so maybe it hasn't been so long."

"Your father," Ferran pressed curiously. "What's he like? Why haven't we seen him?"

Mira did not answer right away. She tipped her head back toward the forest, as though listening intently for something. After a moment, she seemed satisfied, and looked him in the eye. "He can't know you're here."

Ferran was confused by her sudden dark tone. "Why?"

"He'll . . . he just can't. That's all." She pointed. "Trousers?"

Ferran turned back to the trunk and offered her his dark green breeches. "I expect you don't want long pants."

"You are observant," she told him approvingly, and accepted them, pulling them on over her home-made short pants. "How do I look? Like a man? Like you?"

Ferran sat back and looked at her. She certainly did not look like a man. She did look a little silly because of the way things fit her, but with some adjusting and coaxing, it would be quite a handsome look for her. Strangest of all, perhaps, was that before, when she had been in her own sand-stained, sun-bleached rags, she had seemed much less . . . real. Like some wood nymph from the fairy tales. Or like Hartemys, goddess of the hunt. But now, wearing a motley assembly of his own clothing, she seemed like an illustration in a book come to life, ungainly, but suddenly solid and real.

"No, you rather look like a storybook character," he admitted, blushing a little. "Like a heroine who's had to dress in men's clothes to disguise herself while she's on some journey."

Mira's expression of amusement faded into curiosity and she moved toward him, the long sleeves flopping. "Why would she disguise herself? What story is that?"

Ferran paused, trying to decide how to explain. "In some stories, when bad things happen, the hero, the girl-hero, has to go on a long journey to make things right. Sometimes she dresses up like a man so that no one will bother her when she travels."

"Why can't a woman travel alone? Why must she dress like a man?" There was something insistent about her voice, something intense in her gaze that made Ferran nervous.

"Because—well, in many places it isn't safe for a young woman to be alone. There are bad people in the world, who do bad things, or, people make mistakes, or—"

Mira's brow grew dark, her green eyes clouding over into a bluer tint. "What bad things? What mistakes?" she asked, her voice very quiet and deeply serious. "What do they do?"

Ferran's words stuck in his throat, and he realized what it was that was giving him trouble about the explanation. *How do I explain this? I don't want to upset her.* "They . . . hurt . . . or they might take away a woman's innocence. Her freedom, her . . . I'm sorry, I don't know how to . . ." He swallowed, his mouth dry, the sunlight suddenly too hot on the back of his neck and the top of his head, which he was positive were already sunburnt. Mira peered into his eyes, her mouth a thin line, and after several moments, she lifted her chin a little.

"Ah. I know what they do," she said quietly. "Those kinds of monsters."

Ferran flushed hotly, but couldn't look away from her hard green eyes. "You—you do?"

"There is a monster here. I told you this before."

Ferran's eyes widened. "You mean . . . you didn't mean a monster-monster, you meant . . . you mean . . ."

"I try not to think of it much. My father cursed the monster to never lay eyes on me again, nor come within my sight for the rest of his days. That is why you have not seen his face. And my father keeps to himself. He cannot know you're here."

*What isn't she telling me?* Ferran searched her expression for further clues. "Mira . . . did the monster hurt you?"

Mira fixed her eyes on his like a bird of prey targeting its supper, but her mouth was still a thin, weary line. She nodded.

"Oh, my gods," Ferran muttered. "I'm . . . so sorry. I'm so sorry, I-I shouldn't have said anything. That's terrible. It's just awful." He looked sharply away then, his eyes burning from having stared into hers for so long. *No wonder she didn't like it when I tried to take her hand before. I shouldn't have assumed I could just . . . touch her.* He felt suddenly cold all over, as though the sun had gone out, and strangely helpless. He didn't know what else to say.

"You didn't know," she said simply, at last. "And it wasn't you." Her tone had grown brusque. "Do these hang down like this, or are they worn differently?" She flapped one of the green sleeves at him.

"There are buttons," he said, his eyes still averted. "You button them over your shirt sleeve, so the shirt pokes out."

Mira held out her arm. "Show me," she said, and he looked up. She seemed as calm and unperturbed as though they'd never discussed the presence of monsters in the world.

"All right," he agreed, and reached for the first button.

\* \* \*

Aurael left a while after the foolish castaways had convinced Karaburan to drink from the bottle of wine. He soared away, leaving them carousing on the beach, whooping and cheering themselves on in an increasingly drunken blur. Each man thought he would be a king, and all three were committed in wine to murdering the unnamed tyrant of the island.

*Ah, and I will be free as the sun when Dante's blood flows down the rocks to the sand.* He flew toward the forest in search of Mira. He had been hard at work both for and against Dante's will all day. Did he not then deserve a glimpse of his beloved, his guiding star?

He startled some birds from a fruit tree as he soared by, rattling the round yellow fruits to the ground. Soon, all would be ready, and soon, all would unravel. His burden and his enslavement would be reversed, and he would be free to do as he wished. Although Ouberan had trapped him indefinitely in the tree, loopholes in the laws of faerie magic had allowed his escape: if any should come that were strong enough to free him, he should be enslaved to them until such time as he was freed by their will, not Ouberan's.

Dante's conditions for freedom, of course, had involved a period of service, though that period grew longer and longer with each passing year. Aurael was convinced that Dante never meant to free him at all, and so the only reliable path was for Dante to die.

*It would be so much simpler if I could do it myself,* he thought on more than one occasion. *But if I kill him, my lord will surely know, and I may as well be dead myself.*

It had been a long time building up to this. Aurael had hoped to mold Karaburan into a murderer years ago, but as a child, the misshapen creature had been so overly gentle, so unjaded by the balance of his life on the island, that no nightmares or sweet dreams could coax him to mutiny. Karaburan had doted on Mira and worshipped Dante, no matter how many times Aurael slipped into his mind in the form of his dam, the Psychorrax. He had plagued Karaburan's darker dreams with a fervent constancy, dangling the things the monster longed for before his eyes and then tossing them away again into darkness, sending Karaburan chasing them uselessly night after night.

He had come so close to finally breaking him, that night in the thicket where the blackberries grew. Had Aurael been a younger, more sympathetic imp, he might have done things differently. He might not have used his beloved Mira as the bait for Karaburan's fall from grace. He hadn't meant for Mira to be truly harmed in any way. But things had gotten away from him so quickly—

"AURAEL."

A sudden, bone-shattering gong sounded in his head, and Aurael dropped like a rock from the sky, landing in an unseen heap on the ferns. The birds and beasts of the island carried on about their daily business, as though the noise had never happened. Aurael rolled over onto his back, groaning and clutching his head with both long hands.

The spirit sat up, the voice in his head booming. *Yes, my lord Dante?* He gritted his teeth hard as a horse refusing the cold bit but anticipating the sting of the whip.

"ARE MY BETRAYERS SCATTERED SAFELY ON THE ISLAND?"

Aurael nodded, as though Dante could see him. *Yes, my lord. They are as broken shells upon the beach; the pieces which fit together are separate and confused and not to be reunited by natural cause.*

"ON WHAT BUSINESS DO YOU ATTEND?"

Aurael did not hesitate to lie. *Laying the traps for the drunk ones—they found some of their wine casks in the wreckage and are praising their good fortune even now, my lord.* He did not want Dante to know that he was on his way to look in on Mira. Dante was convinced—or at least, he was pretty certain that Dante was convinced—that Aurael was blissfully uninterested in Mira or Karaburan, and his only wish was to serve Dante's will to earn his freedom.

"THE TIME APPROACHES, AURAEL. WE MUST BEGIN. WHERE IS THE KING?"

*He is trapped on a rock off the coast, master. The tide changed, and he cannot swim to shore. The sun brings him delirious visions, hunger, and thirst, and he lies there as if he were Promythia, and the eagle is coming to pick out his liver.*

"GOOD. BRING THE KING TO ME—ALIVE, BUT AS HE IS, WHETHER BLOODY OR NO."

The airy spirit unfolded himself from the ground, his body shifting and growing and expanding like a hot air balloon. He stretched as high as his ties to the island and Dante's power would allow him, and when his invisible leash grew taut, he sighed and soared downward again, seeking the unfortunate king.

* * *

"Mira," said Ferran, after a while. "Just how long do you expect to hide me from your father?"

Mira heard him, but made no indication of it, and did not answer right away. She was fiddling with the gnarled braid of hair that hung over her shoulder. Some of it shone dimly in lighter gold tones than the rest, which was a softer honey color. *All my life, I've grown this hair*, she thought. *This braid, this tangled knot.* She pulled on it a little, and it resisted firmly as any sailor's rope.

"Mira?"

*It weighs on me. Like the monster, like my father.* She looked up, meeting Ferran's quizzical gaze, his funny slender eyebrows reaching upward in wary curiosity of her stare. *Why should I keep it? Why should I carry it? I have new clothes, why not new hair as well?*

"Are you all right?" Ferran looked concerned.

"I'm fine," she answered him, and looked down at the larger chest. "Shall we pry this one, too?"

"It seems pretty secure," admitted the boy, running his hand lightly along the back of his neck, red from the sun. He gleamed pinkishly all over, in fact, which made him seem the more wide-eyed, innocent, and childlike to her. His skin was unused to so much raw, open sunlight, and the glare off the water was powerful.

"There must be a weak point. It did sit on the bottom of the lagoon for much of a day." Mira crouched to examine the large lock on the side. She was still testing the limits of the clothing Ferran had given her, and so far was pleased with the functionality of the trousers and the sleeves of the doublet, which could be removed at will. Crouching was manageable and comfortable. She would have to test it with tree-climbing, soon.

"Maybe," agreed Ferran, kneeling on the sand beside her and feeling the edges of the trunk for weak spots. "It'd be a nuisance not to open it."

"Let me try the lock." Mira held out her open palm to him.

"With the knife?"

"Unless you have another set of tools I don't know about."

Ferran blushed—or was it simply more sunburn? It was a strange thing, this boy and this situation. She had often wondered what it would be like for a foreigner to wash up on shore of their island, for her to have a conversation with that stranger, and learn things of the outside world. She had not thought that one would actually come, let alone that it would be a young man about her own age, whose features reminded her too much of a handsome, but still ungainly, young animal, like the baby foxes she saw from time to time in the forest, or a dolphin's child in the lagoon.

He handed her the pocketknife and she turned it over a few times in her hand before opening it to reveal the blade. She carefully set about prodding the lock's opening with the blade's point, and after several moments, there was a click.

Ferran looked thunderstruck. "What! Don't tell me it's already undone!"

Mira pulled a long face to resist smirking a bit. "Hm," she grunted, and tried to lift the lock. It was still attached, but definitely seemed looser. "Don't twist yourself up," she told him archly, secretly pleased that she had gotten lucky with it. His expression of disbelief amused her. A few more minutes passed and there was nothing, so Ferran got up and wandered off a little, stretching his arms and legs as he moved.

"What have you been doing all this time?" he wondered aloud, and Mira glanced at him over the dunes.

"What do you mean?"

"I mean," he called back, "what do you do all day? Swim, eat fresh fruit, drink fresh water, swim some more, have a nap? It sounds so boring. Restful, maybe, and relaxing, but boring."

Mira stopped poking the lock with the knife and gave him a hard stare. "Is that what you think I do?" she demanded.

His expression shifted immediately to contrition. "No, I mean, I just . . . I have no idea," he shrugged helplessly. "But I'm curious."

"When we came here, my father brought books," Mira began. "A great many books, in fact. I have read them all, some of them twice, some of them ten times. I know the names of the stars and constellations, I know the names of the plants and animals on this island, and some that aren't here, too. I know the history of Alejandra the Great, and Djengos Con, and the story of Homer's Oddity. I know how to cure minor ailments with herbs, and treat a snake's bite or a jelly sting. I build things and take them apart and build them again, but differently."

She glanced at him. "I understand that the Earth is built on hot magma and stone, and that the oceans are bigger than any one piece of land, and that we revolve around the sun, thanks to Capricornus' model. I have read that airships are the height of technological and military advancement, but yours was the first I have ever seen so close. There are terrors beyond this island that I cannot fathom from so far away, and there are wonders, too. So I read, I consider, I observe, I annotate. I build, I seek, I understand. I swim and climb and run and hunt and study. I wait. Someday, I will leave this island and walk the entirety of the world." She looked down, lightheaded as a young bird fallen from its nest. There was a pause.

"Walk the whole world?" Ferran teased.

"And fly, and run, and swim, and sail," she added. "Did you know that when some fish are kept in a small place, they only grow as big as the space will let them grow? That is why some fish are enormous. Because they have the entire ocean to grow into."

"Whales are quite large," admitted Ferran.

"Whales aren't fish," said Mira quietly, looking at him with her head tipped back a little. His expression shifted as though he wasn't clear if she were teasing him or not. Mira lowered her chin to meet his gaze more squarely. "They breed live young. So do dolphins."

"How do you know that?" Ferran sounded intrigued.

"I've seen them. They sometimes come to the edge of the lagoon to birth in shallower water. It helps the babies, who are prone to not understand which way is up when they've first come out. The others gather and push them up to the surface to breathe." She indicated this process with her hands, one palm down, the other sliding in underneath it to push it upward in the air.

Ferran gave a stunned sort of laugh. "Extraordinary," he muttered.

"I'm surprised you didn't know that," confessed Mira, taking up the knife again to pick at the lock.

"I told you, I don't study much of the natural sciences these days," Ferran said defensively. "My father put me on a political track. Theology, philosophy, and the strategies of war."

"You sound as though you don't like that much." Mira cut her eyes sideways at him. He was staring out at the water, probably thinking of his father again. She studied his expression, noting the mixture of regret, shame, and grief that formed on his face every time his father was mentioned.

"No," agreed Ferran, moving to stand in the shade again, leaning on the roughened bark of a tree. " 'All knowledge is worth having, but some things are more worthy than others.' That's what he would always say when I told him I wanted to travel abroad, study more languages, explore." He kicked at the sand halfheartedly. His boots, undoubtedly made of very fine leather, were already beginning to look decades older from the salt, sand, and sun.

"We share that," observed Mira, focusing her eyes on the lock. "That longing, wanting to learn."

"I feel like a caged animal."

Mira looked up at this. She recalled several sketches in a naturalist's journal her father had, drawings that depicted a tiger, a peacock, and an elephant in some Anglish king's menagerie. In each illustration, the animal in question was housed in an elaborate cage embellished with curlicues and jewels, and each animal had its mouth open in a cry of protestation.

"I have never known a cage," she replied, at length, "except for this island."

Ferran furrowed his brow in sympathy. "And now it's my cage, too."

A strange silence passed between them, the words having lost their momentum, and Mira continued to fiddle with the lock and the knife.

"Mira," said Ferran again. "How long can this go on before your father finds out I'm here?"

"A while," she insisted, not looking up.

"Mira. There is so much you haven't told me."

She almost met his gaze then, so sudden was the concern and anxiety in his voice. She pressed the tip of the knife a little harder against the inner workings of the lock.

"Mira, I'm stuck here. Please. I need to know. You don't have to tell me everything, but why are you so worried about your father?"

The lock clicked and sprang open, startling both of them. Mira almost dropped the knife in surprise. She glanced at Ferran as he moved closer.

"You're sure this one isn't yours?" she asked him. He shook his head.

"Might be my father's," he murmured, repeating his earlier impression. "I don't know. It's bigger than most of our regular trunks. Here goes nothing, I guess," he added, reaching for the lid and pushing it up and back. The hinges creaked in protest, and the heavy lid thumped backwards onto the sand.

Mira stared, her jaw slackening. Inside the trunk was a man.

# CHAPTER ELEVEN

## 1846

"My ass is sore," groaned Dante as he slid from the saddle and swung to the ground. His mount sidestepped, making him stumble on already rubbery legs as he reached for the reins.

"You're the one who insisted on riding," laughed King Alanno as he stepped out of the little cart, handing the reins to the boy who sat on the bench beside him. "Hold these still, Stephen. Can you do that?"

"Yes, milord," answered the young valet. Stephen was a stout lad of twenty who wore the livery of a groom, but was really more of an all-purpose servant. "I'll keep them still."

"Good lad." Alanno smiled and adjusted his wool driving cap. "Shall we inside to see what our maestro has made?" He rubbed his palms together eagerly.

Dante regarded the king with a wry expression. Although Alanno had just turned thirty a week ago, he still had the spritely blue eyes of a child, and his handsome bearing and fit form from his love of sport gave him a lean and youthful appearance. Despite being five years younger than the king, Dante always felt that he looked like the older of the pair of them, and more than once on casual outings such as this he'd been mistaken for the more important man in the room. Alanno thought it was funny, but it embarrassed Dante every time.

Dante tied his dark brown mare to the hitching post nearby, and she immediately dropped her head to graze at the sparse but bright green grass that grew within reach.

"Ah!" sighed the king loudly, stretching his arms wide. "I love the country!"

"No, you don't," Dante reminded him.

"Be quiet, Duke Fiorente! I am your king, and if I say I love the country, then so I do! Also, it is my birthday, and so you must agree with me." Alanno's voice boomed in the open air.

"It was your birthday," Dante groaned, "a week ago! You've already got the whole kingdom over me, Alanno, give it a rest!" But he smiled as they walked up the lawn to the house. It was good to see Alanno in high spirits again. He'd been rather down the last few years, ever since the queen, Isabella, had hurt her legs. Alanno doted on her, but he feared that unless she was able to regain much of her strength and constitution back, their chances of producing an heir would be less likely.

"Doesn't look much like the richest place in town, does it?" said the king, pursing his lips. "Have you ever seen him in person?"

"No." Dante glanced over the property. "It's cozy enough. I hope he's not some kind of hermit."

"Hermit? He's a genius. You'll see."

If one had a task for the inventors of the kingdom of Italya, a task that one did not want shared or broadcast among the masses, one inevitably sent word to the village of Orologio. There, one could employ the nation's finest clockmaker, architect, intellect, engineer, and scientific mind that could possibly be found, and all of these were but one man. His name was Alfareo Garriley, and he was the chiefest among thinkers and polymaths of the day.

It was widely understood that Garriley had been born in Pirano, but that, as he got on in years, he had abandoned his city life for the gentle countryside, and only rarely left his beloved Orologio. He had not quite achieved hermit status, but he was comfortably on his way to such a title as the number of social appearances he made lessened year after year.

Alanno had written a letter—in his own royal hand—to Garriley, asking for his keen mind to come up with something that could help Queen Isabella to regain her physical strength and mobility, insisting that money was no object in helping his wife grow strong and healthy again. The longer they went without an heir, the easier it would be for rival nations to try and take the crown. Garriley had not written back immediately, but had considered it at length, and at last sent the king a polite but brief missive inviting him to the villa in Orologio for a meeting.

Alanno, always eager for an adventure, had roped Dante into coming along. Dante, beholden to his king and his best friend, had reluctantly agreed, although he would have rather stayed behind to continue courting his own lady love, Sophia. They had made a great outing of it, the queen and their attendants lingering at some lord's villa several hours' ride away while the king and the duke trotted out to Orologio, in the middle of nowhere.

"We don't even know if he's agreed to do it," muttered Dante with a shake of his head, as they stepped up the short stair to the villa's door. It really wasn't even a villa—it was much more of a small mansion.

"If he planned on refusing us, why would he have asked us to come all the way out here?" Alanno sounded confident, jauntily ringing the bell.

"I don't know." Dante suddenly felt uncomfortable about the whole thing. "We should have brought the guard. We shouldn't have come all this way on our own, Al."

Alanno put his hands in his pockets casually. "Relax. You are such a worrier, Dante. Everything's fine, I'm sure. Besides, he's the foremost in nearly every field you've ever studied as far as invention goes. Don't you want to meet him face to face?" His blue eyes gleamed.

"Well, yes," blustered Dante, "but there are so many rumors that he's a crackpot."

"I certainly hope so," agreed the king, as the door latch unbolted and the knob turned.

"Your Highness," said the man at the door, "My lord. Please come in."

The king's smile faded, and Dante's eyes widened. The man at the door wore the plain suit of a country servant, neat and tidy, in rustic browns and grays, but his skin gleamed a most magnificent rosy brass color, like polished metal. At first glimpse, his hair was black, and so neatly combed that it did not appear to move in the slightest. After a moment, Dante realized the coif was molded to the man's head. He did not appear to breathe or blink or shift in the way that normal people do, but stood perfectly still, holding the door open with one gloved hand and the other out to welcome them into the foyer.

"Sweet Jove," breathed Dante, before he could stop himself.

"Please come in, Your Highness. Maestro Garriley is very pleased you're here." His voice had a faint echo to it, and his lips and jaw did not move, but the words came from somewhere within him.

Dante's mind raced. He stared at the man before him, analyzing the materials, theories, raw observations, trying to make sense of what his instinct was telling him.

"Come now, let's not keep the maestro waiting," beamed Alanno. Dante shot him a look as they stepped over the threshold, and the gleaming servant bowed slightly at the waist.

"You little imp!" Dante exclaimed, thunderstruck. "You knew! You knew exactly who—what—who was going to answer the door, and you brought me all this way for this."

Alanno chuckled, removing his hat and looking like the cat that got the cream. "Don't know what you mean, old boy."

*Well, this wasn't how I thought today would go,* Dante fumed as the servant moved past them at a smooth but slow pace. *Automatons aren't just possible, now they're apparently already in production! That's the last time I place a bet against Alanno.*

They followed the man-machine down the carpeted corridor into a sitting room, which was simply decorated, but for the shelves and shelves of books on all four walls. Alanno flopped into a cushioned chair with a grin, but Dante's eyes were fixed on the servant.

"I will fetch him at once," the servant intoned in a clear voice. It bowed slightly again and went out of the room.

"Dante, what on earth's the matter with you?" Alanno beamed innocently at him.

"You know perfectly well what. That," growled Dante, pointing to the now-closed door, "is an automaton."

"No!" cried Alanno, as though insulted. "You're overreacting, Dante, surely! Simply because he doesn't blink doesn't make him any less of a man!" But his eyes danced merrily as he tossed his hat back and forth from hand to hand. "I knew you'd be surprised."

"Surprised enough. I'm not paying you for that bet, by the by. Alanno, what precisely did we come here for?"

"I already told you! My commission, silly."

"You said it hadn't been approved yet by the Mae—by Garriley."

"Well," said Alanno, hedging. "That particular commission isn't the one we're here to pick up. There's another one."

"Another? But what about Isabella?" Dante frowned.

The door opened and the metal man stepped back inside with a curt half-bow. "Maestro Garriley, your guests: King Alanno Civitelli, first of the Italyans to bear his name, and the honorable Duke Dante Fiorente of Neapolis."

The maestro himself, Alfareo Garriley, stepped into the room, smiling a peculiar, knowing little smile. He was a small, slight man, but had roundish features that indicated a well-stocked cupboard and many long, lush meals over his lifetime. His hair and beard were white, but where his beard was neatly trimmed and well-kept, his wild hair was like a baboon's crested mane. He wore simple country clothes: a shirt, waistcoat, and trousers in ordinary cotton and wool, and a longer, lightweight jacket like a driving duster that appeared to be faintly stained with old marks of oil, soot, and possibly blood. His eyes gleamed the same coppery hazel as the servant's skin.

"Welcome to my home, Your Highness," said the inventor, bowing at the waist. "And my lord duke."

"Ah, Garriley!" Alanno beamed, lounging in the armchair while Dante stood surprised at his elbow. "Thank you for having us. It's good of you to allow us to meet in private this way."

"Certainly, Your Majesty. It is my pleasure entirely." Garriley looked at Dante, his hands lightly clasped at his back. "Duke Fiorente has a lot of questions for me, I think."

"Bosh," said Alanno, waving his hand dismissively. Dante pressed his mouth into a thin line. "That can wait. First, is it done?"

The inventor inclined his head to the king. "Yes, Your Highness. It's done. The first round of Royal Guard are complete and ready to ship."

Alanno smiled widely. "Oh, most excellent. That is very good to hear."

Dante felt his insides coil tightly with uncertainty. *The cat has got the cream after all,* he realized, looking from Garriley to the king. "There is already a Royal Guard," he said. "What do you mean, they're ready to ship?"

Alanno stood up and straightened his own jacket, giving Dante a lofty, almost scathing look. "Yes, but our current guard are soft, permeable, and basic. They can be bettered, built upon. They can be improved." His eyes gleamed, but the mischief and mirth was now gone, replaced with determination and pride.

"Alanno," Dante ventured. "Why didn't you tell me about this before? Why bring me here under different pretenses? Is there even a machine to help the queen?"

"There is," interrupted the inventor. The king looked surprised.

"Is there?" Alanno seemed agitated.

"Of course, Your Majesty. I've built her a pair of leg braces that will renew her muscle strength and make her legs stronger. In addition to your ten Royal Guardsmen."

"You'll be paid extra, as agreed, if my wife recovers her movement." Alanno's mouth quivered a little, though his voice held steady.

"I wasn't aware," Dante interrupted lightly, "that our country's technological capabilities were so . . . advanced as to include the completion of fully functional, speaking, and obedient automatons."

Garriley inclined his head a little with a slight smile. "Your technology isn't, my lord. But mine is."

"I told you, he's a genius," breathed the king, pleased and reveling in his satisfaction.

"You are indeed widely regarded as truly excellent in your fields," Dante admitted. "But you must allow a measure of skeptical concern at the significant promise you have made to His Highness."

"Your lordship is truly a scholar. Would you care to view the guardsmen in my workshop before we adjourn for lunch?"

"An excellent idea," agreed the king, nodding.

Dante held the inventor's gaze firmly, but Garriley did not shift, he merely smiled. "Very well," Dante agreed. "Let's see them."

The metal man by the door led the way out of the sitting room and down the corridor. At the end of the hall, they turned, and turned again, then came to a door which was barred with iron and marked with strange carvings in the stone arch and wood. Dante thought he recognized some of the shapes and patterns.

*Prayers,* he thought. *No—spells?*

His own research had taken him through the basics of alleged magical practices some time ago. He had read about the druids and the more primitive historical groups who used magic to heal ailments and shape reality, but it was all academically considered incomplete data, unlikely to have been fact. It was more likely that the 'magic' had simply been drug-induced perception, but of course that didn't keep him from wondering if the real thing was out there, waiting to be discovered.

They passed through the doorway and descended a well-kept stone staircase into the lower layers of the mansion, emerging into a large, cavernous room with rounded ceilings and impressive industrial lights—the new electrical kind, Dante noted. The inventor led them past tables and workbenches, easels and blackboards, past a carriage prototype and several small scale models of cities and airships spread over one particular table. At last, they came to an open area of the work room, and Garriley stopped, the metal servant coming up alongside him.

"Well?" asked Dante. "Where are they?"

Garriley inclined his head and produced from his pocket a small handheld device with a series of small buttons, one of which he pressed with his thumb. A small door set into the wall opened, and the Royal Guard marched neatly into the room to stand in formation before them. They were unarmed, but their garments were uniform, their movements precise, and they cut an impressive picture, tall and imposing.

"They're perfect," breathed Alanno.

*They're terrifying,* thought Dante, but he immediately understood the reasoning behind their creation. *These are the real guard. The guardsmen made of flesh and bone can be stopped, or silenced. These men are more . . . formidable.*

"I'm glad Your Highness is so pleased by them." Garriley smiled. "They're perfectly obedient. They don't speak, but we can add voiceboxes if you'd like."

"They're impenetrable by bullets, aren't they," guessed Dante.

"Of course."

"And waterproof?"

"Yes. They're perfectly capable of standing watch out in the rain. They're self-winding, too; their inner workings will run for a very long time before they wear down."

Dante looked at him. "How long?"

"Oh, years." The inventor waved a hand. "This one's lasted a decade so far, and his wiring is a little more primitive than theirs." He gestured, and another mechanical man came shuffling out of the corner, its features rounder and distinctly simpler than the smooth cheekbones and hard jaws of the Royal Guard. It was shorter, too, the same height as Garriley himself, and thus a comical companion to the tall and stately guards. Its eyes gleamed greenish-gold, bright and pupilless, its vague expression almost sheepish.

"A decade!" crowed the king, clapping his hands and bouncing toward the tall guards to study them up close. "Ah, Garriley, you're a wizard!"

Alanno wasn't looking, but Dante saw the peculiar expression flash over Garriley's face, before vanishing. "Thank you, Your Highness," the inventor said, tight-lipped. "But you know I truck only with science and mathematics. Hard facts. The impossible is achievable when the mind works hard enough," he added, moving closer to the line of guards and the joyful king. "Let me show you the schematics for your new warship, Your Highness."

"Ooh!" exclaimed the king, and they moved off toward an easel with some drawings on display.

Dante stayed behind, lingering and staring at the lineup of tall, perfect, gleaming brass guards. *Creepy.* Dante didn't like their cold stares, their eyes lifted just over his own head. Then he let his eyes drop to the short, almost stubby, mechanical man just off to one side, whose green-gold gaze held steady as any lantern. The littler mech was benign, almost apologetic in its physicality, as though it was concerned it was taking up too much space. Dante moved closer, warily.

"Do you speak?" he wondered aloud.

"Yes, my lord," it answered, its voice similar to the mech-butler upstairs.

"Do you have a name?"

The short mech tipped his head to one side a little. "The master calls me Gonzo."

Dante held back a laugh of surprise. "After the children's story?" Gonzo was the name of a fool in a fairy tale, whose hunger was so insatiable that he was able to eat his own body as easily as though it were a plate of pasta.

"I do not know if that is the reason why," Gonzo went on, "but it is a reasonable hypothesis, my lord."

"You know me?"

"Duke Dante Fiorente, Lord of Neapolis and trusted friend of the king, His Royal Highness Alanno Civitelli, First of His Name."

Dante raised his brows. The little mech's ease and humble tone of voice were somehow endearing. The round face reminded Dante of the masks in commedia dell'arte. *He's no Arlecchino,* thought Dante, impressed by the mech's ease of speech. *He's hardly a hungry fool. He's much more the Pedrolino—something of a thoughtful, sad clown about his features.* Oddly, Dante felt a strain of interest in the peculiar contraption.

"Aren't you a little short for a guardsman?"

Gonzo drew up to its full height—five foot three, if Dante had to guess—and its odd brass eyebrows slanted upwards even further. "I wasn't made for their jobs, my lord," said the mech, almost indignantly.

"Well, then? What exactly do you do?"

"Nothing much, my lord. The master doesn't have much use of me now that he has upgraded the model." Gonzo shrank back down again to its hunched, rotund posture, and peered up at him. "But I do excel in chess and all manner of puzzles. And I can recite *Paradise Lost.*"

"You've read *Paradise Lost?*"

Gonzo folded its flat, hinged hands primly. "I liked it."

"Maestro," Dante called, turning and moving toward the inventor and the king at the easel. "I am much impressed with your craftsmanship. What would the little round one cost?"

Garriley removed his spectacles and squinted at Dante shrewdly. "Well, my lord, I am very pleased you like it so well, but I hadn't planned on selling him."

"What purpose does he serve?" Dante used his most easy tone, and his most calm, assuring smile.

"He is . . ." Garriley hesitated, and then shifted his tone to one of curiosity. "What would you have him for, my lord?"

Alanno crossed his arms. "Yes, Dante, what do you want with him? If these were hounds, he'd certainly be the runt of the litter." He chuckled.

Dante shrugged. "He says he can recite *Paradise Lost* and play chess. He'd be such a charm about the court, don't you think? I want to see what else he can learn."

"Chess, you say?" Alanno rubbed at his chin. "I'd bet he's a dash hand at memorizing strategies, then."

Dante could practically hear the wheels turning in Alanno's mind. "I should think so. I'd expect he's a fine example of a balanced, objective opinion."

Alanno twisted his mouth up in thought. Garriley stared at Dante, a thin smile on his lips. At last, the king nodded. "All right!" he cried. "We'll take him, too."

Garriley did not lift his eyes from Dante, but gave a slight bow. "As you wish, Your Highness. Shall we pause for lunch?"

The king and the inventor moved past him, and Dante turned to find the short mech was shuffling toward him. "You'll be an excellent counterweight," he said, pleased at himself. *If Alanno is clamoring for conflict, he'll need more than just flatterers at the council table.*

Gonzo lifted his round chin a little and recited:
*"I will place within them as a guide*
*My umpire Conscience, whom if they will hear,*
*Light after light well us'd they shall attain,*
*And to the end persisting, safe arrive."*
Dante smiled. "Perfect."

# CHAPTER TWELVE

N o more stalling," Torsione admonished. "Truth or taxes?"

"All right," Bastiano chuckled. "Truth, then."

Torsione considered his options, leaning on the hearty branch Bastiano had found to serve as a crutch. His left leg pained him and was difficult to put his full weight on. He worried that it might be broken. "Hmm," he mused. "What about Hortensia?"

Bastiano choked on his laughter. "The Duke of Skicilia's niece?"

"The very same."

"Gods, no!" Bastiano shook his head so fervently that little droplets of perspiration flew from his temples. "What an awful match! How could you be so cruel, Tor?"

It hadn't taken long for the two men to get on their feet, combing slowly through the forest on the island, looking for food and hopefully fresh water, or civilization of some kind. To pass the time, they had been trading truth and taxes, telling tales and making bets on things they would or wouldn't do when they got home. It wasn't much, but it kept them talking, and Torsione always liked to make Bastiano blush.

"Hortensia is a very becoming woman," insisted Torsione, keeping his smirk at bay. "Except for the mole, she's really very lovely."

"I wasn't talking about the mole. I think it's a terrible match, that's all," Bas recovered quickly, holding a low branch aside for Torsione.

"Why? Are not her features comely? Is not her dowry worthy? Is her nature not sweet, her accomplishments not impressive?" Torsione went on. "I find her a well-rounded woman in many areas."

"Hortensia is a very lovely person." Bas seemed embarrassed, a color blooming in his cheeks which Torsione thought rather handsome.

"She would be a fine wife to either of us. What could possibly be your objection?"

"She isn't . . . inclined to like us," Bas fumbled.

Torsione paused, leaning on the crutch, and looked back at him with innocently raised brows. "Speak for yourself," he snorted. "I'm utterly capable of that level of seduction, and you know it."

Bas fidgeted with a leaf between his fingers, his sunburn blending with his blush. "No, no, I mean she's . . . she likes women."

Torsione knew that, of course. He feigned surprise, though, for Bastiano's sake, and looked away from him, as though in disbelief. "Really?" he murmured. "I mean, are you sure?"

"Yes," said Bas gingerly. "We danced at Coralina's birthday last year, since everyone had been trying to get us in the same room for months, and she told me. Well, she told me after we'd danced and had several glasses of wine. She had her eyes on Lady Leontes."

"Well, that's certainly something. Was your pride quite hurt by her rejection?"

"Oh, no, not at all," gushed Bas. "It was a bit of a relief."

"Relief?"

"Yes!" Bas' mouth caught up to him, and he hesitated. Torsione imagined Bastiano's little rabbit heart pounding, his blue eyes round and anxious. "I, ah . . . wasn't terribly keen on her. No chemistry, you know. Can't be taught."

Torsione stopped abruptly and turned about quickly enough to be nose to nose with Bastiano. "Of course it can be taught," he purred. "I was top of my class in chemistry, you know."

Bas gulped. "Were you?"

"Can't you tell?" Torsione kept his expression as serious as he could, though he wanted to laugh as Bas squirmed silently for a moment.

"I . . . this is no time for your teasing," said Bastiano. "Shipwrecked on an island, and you're being just as much of a creep as you were at home." He smiled cheerfully and gave his friend a jaunty jab to the shoulder, stepping around him to keep walking. "It's my turn, isn't it?"

Torsione felt oddly disappointed that Bas had evaded him. He hadn't meant anything by it but to make him blush again, but there had been a little fizzle of something there, something peculiar between them that Torsione had always thought to be—what, fictional? They had argued and quipped and sparred verbally all their lives, and Bastiano had always been the more sensitive of the two, but it never occurred to Torsione that the blushes and flustered laughter were worth anything.

"Truth," said Torsione challengingly.

"Hum," Bas mused. "The most scandalous conquest you've ever had?"

He bit back his immediate reply—*the Empress of Chineh's sister*—and quietly answered, "Hasn't happened yet."

Bastiano made a sound of disbelief, but did not look back. "Come on, the truth. That's the rule!"

"Rules! Rules? Here?" Torsione scoffed. "Desert island, Bastiano. Hardly the place for rules."

"Don't you silver-tongue your way out of this game! I know you better than that. Just because you don't want to answer doesn't mean you're allowed to stray from the task at hand."

Torsione paused to look behind them. "Did you hear something?"

"Very coy of you. No, I didn't. Nothing but the sound of your cowardice!" Bas laughed.

*He thinks he's bested me this round,* thought Torsione, but he was still listening to the forest around them. The hum of insects, the song of birds, the breeze in the leaves of the canopy above them. . . . *Nothing unusual here.* But Torsione felt with certainty that they were being watched.

"Tor!" Bastiano was several yards ahead of him now. "My gods, come and see!"

He hurried to meet him, his uneven strides aided awkwardly by the makeshift crutch. Just ahead of them was a clearing, shady and cool, and at the center of it was the most unbelievable banquet table Torsione had ever seen. Even in all his days of diplomatic ventures and social enterprises, those feasts were put to shame, dissolving to dust in the corner of his memory as he took in the table before them.

Mountainous platters of fresh fruit rose up between dishes of roast pork, turkey, beef, and venison. Enormous soup tureens balanced out broad salad bowls, and trays of bread, fine cheeses, and vegetables were arranged in circles around the larger dishes. A goodly number of wine casks seemed to sprout up like sapling trees from the tabletop, and there was a glimmering freshness to the whole view, as though it had just now been arranged, the finishing touches clean and still new.

*It can't be,* thought Torsione. *Where could it possibly have come from?*

"It smells amazing," whispered Bastiano.

"It does," muttered Torsione, and his stomach groaned. "I'm so thirsty that I had all but forgotten how hungry I am." Bastiano was moving through the line of trees toward the table with a light step, as though his burdens had been lifted. He smiled giddily in relief.

"Bas, wait, don't!" Torsione reached for him, his fingers just missing the sleeve of Bas' shirt. "The stories," he added, stumbling on the words.

"Stories?" Bastiano hesitated in confusion. He was already halfway to the table.

"Yes. Stories. The old stories, the fairy tales? A magical banquet appears, although the hero has been warned to touch nothing."

"But we haven't been warned to touch nothing," Bastiano protested. "And this isn't a fairytale, Tor. We're stranded and starving. This means there's someone here! Someone else lives on this island, and they either prepared this for us or they did it for themselves. In either case, we should eat what we can and thank them later." He moved toward the end of the table for the nearest cask of wine.

"Wait," called Torsione thinly, but as soon as Bas uncorked the bottle and began to drink, his hesitation evaporated entirely. He moved as quickly as his pathetic crutch could carry him and fell forward, catching himself on the table's edge and grabbing a handful of carved, glazed beef. He took the first bite and his mind exploded into color and ecstasy; it was delicious. Tears began to gather in his eyes as he shoveled food into his mouth, chewing and swallowing faster than ever before in his life. Cheese and fresh bread and soft pears and warm quiche—it was utterly divine.

As quickly as he could bring the food to his mouth, Torsione was scooping up more again with his other hand: handfuls of dates, sugar peas, wild strawberries, a ladleful of stew, a chunk of soft buttery bread. Glancing down the table to his right revealed towering plates of desserts, and Bastiano standing with one hand on the table to steady himself. He chugged down wine, which spilled from the corners of his mouth and ran rivers down his throat.

*Something's wrong.* The thought flashed through Torsione's mind but he couldn't hang onto it. He tore into a perfectly golden-skinned turkey leg, and instead of savory ecstasy, he felt a sudden stab of realization in his gut. *The wine is clear. It's not red or white, it's not even rosé, it's . . . invisible.* Bastiano's shirtfront wasn't even damp, save for his own sweat.

Torsione stopped chewing, the bits of turkey tumbling from his lips. His thoughts were beginning to catch up with his body, his stomach still groaning at the incredible smells that wafted up from the banquet table. He looked down. Bits of the food he'd been shoveling into his mouth piled at his feet, broken and mashed. His hunger swelled with the sudden discovery. *I haven't eaten a thing.*

"Bas," he rasped. "Bas, stop!"

Bastiano did not hear him, but choked on the wine, gasping for air and reaching for another bottle, uncorking it quickly.

"Bas, stop it, listen to me!" Torsione dropped the turkey leg and lurched forward, groping his way down the table on weak knees and wobbly hands. Pain seared through his left leg, worse than before, and he threw himself forward, knocking the wine from Bastiano's hands. Bas roared in frustration, startling some birds out of the trees nearby.

"I am so bloody thirsty!" he bellowed, tears welling in his eyes.

"It's not real, it's not real," slurred Torsione, desperation pitching his voice higher as he grappled with Bastiano, trying to force him away from the table.

"Let me go!"

"No, Bas—"

"Let me go, I say!"

"Stop it!"

A loud growl caught them both by surprise, resonating in their bones. Torsione craned his head around at the noise and felt the hairs on the back of his neck stand up as a prickling fear spread throughout his body. He squeezed Bas' arms. The growling faded, but left utter silence in its wake. No cicadas buzzed, no birds chattered. Just silence.

"What was that?" Bastiano's voice was fragile as a glass ornament.

*Sounded like a tiger if I ever heard one,* Torsione thought. He looked nervously at Bas. "We should go," he muttered, his pulse racing.

"Go? Go where?" Bas breathed.

"Back. To the beach? I don't know. Just . . . quietly."

They managed a few steps toward the way they'd come, but then there was a buzzing, hissing sound somewhere just ahead of them, and they stopped short.

"Rattlesnakes?"" Bas sobbed softly.

"I don't see anything!" Torsione turned this way and that. "I hear something, too, but I don't see it."

"What do we do?"

"That way," Tor pointed to the far edge of the clearing. "Go that way!"

They both turned and began to run, legs jelly-like in disoriented fear, and they had almost reached the forest when the sky went black and the beating of mighty wings stirred a cold whirlwind all around them. Bas cried out and recoiled as tree branches whipped at him in the gusty air, and Tor felt the wind pushing him back into the clearing, away from the tree line. He lost his footing, falling onto his back, and saw it above him. He profoundly wished he hadn't.

The sky above the clearing had filled with black fog, as dense and dark as the deepest ocean trench, with sizzling crackles of electric white and green that illuminated the churning clouds. Enormous talons uncurled from the blackness. Lightning flashed to reveal impossibly hideous teeth spread wide in a predatory smile, and Torsione felt his insides go completely slack. It was enormous, larger even than the elephants at the wedding in Tunitz.

Its face and head were human in shape, but its body was more like that of a massive bird of prey, whose wingspan was too large to see all at once, and whose plumage looked more like bronze and silver knives made dark with time and dried blood. Its eyes were as dark as its claws, terrifying and shiny when the lightning shone, but otherwise so black they appeared missing entirely. It was as though the deepest, most hideous and impossible nightmare had been plucked from the farthest reaches of his imagination and brought to life before him.

Torsione couldn't breathe. Then Bastiano screamed, and the horror descended from the fog to land on the table in the middle of the feast. A stench like that of a spoiled corpse in the desert rolled over them, and Torsione felt his stomach heave sharply as he scrambled to get up.

"Angels and ministers of grace, defend us," he choked, covering his mouth and nose with a sleeve. It didn't help much. The thing perched on the feast table smiled wider, and Torsione watched as the food began to rot before his very eyes, blackening and crumbling, fouled by the very presence of the monster.

*YOUR PRAYERS ARE AS WEAK AS YOUR BODIES,* said the hideous creature, without moving its mouth. Both Torsione and Bastiano clapped their hands over their ears and cried out. The words scraped the inside of their minds, invasive, scratching their eardrums and grinding noisily in the hollow places of their bones. *YOU DARED TO TASTE OF THE FEAST LAID OUT FOR ME? POOR HUNGRY MEN. WERE I A WILLING SORT, I WOULD LET YOU FEED BEFORE I KILL YOU, BUT IT IS NOT MY WAY. I MUCH PREFER TO PLAY WITH MY FOOD BEFORE I DINE.*

Piles of mush and refuse slopped off the sides of the table as the harpy strutted, rooster-like, back and forth. Torsione retched again, and he could hear Bastiano sobbing softly. *We've gone mad,* Torsione thought helplessly. *Completely and utterly mad.*

*YOU ONLY WISH YOU WERE MAD,* sneered the harpy, fixing its black eyes on Torsione. *YOU AREN'T MAD YET. BUT YOU WILL BE, FOR A BRIEF AND SHINING MOMENT, YOU WILL BE PERFECTLY MAD, AND THEN I WILL EAT YOU.*

Torsione caught his breath, and the metal bird wings unfolded again, vast and gleaming. The harpy chuckled, a sound that made his skin go cold and his gut clench. Then the monstrous creature swooped at them, and he screamed.

# CHAPTER THIRTEEN

I don't know," said Ferran for the fortieth time, as he set down his end of the trunk. "I don't know what to do with him."

He and Mira sat down on the spongy moss in a small thicket to examine the metal man in the trunk. Mira had wanted to hide him, take him deep into the forest, away from anywhere her father might accidentally find him. They had dragged the box out of the sun, but now found themselves at a loss for how to proceed.

"What did you call this thing?" Mira prompted him as she lifted the lid.

The metal man lay inside the trunk, for all appearances completely shut down and somewhat battered from his journey. His legs were detached, oddly enough, and he bore several dents in his chest plate, possibly from his own legs jostling about during the wreck of the *Brilliant Albatross*.

"Gonzo," said Ferran tenderly.

"Gonzo?" Mira shifted the name in her mouth like a sour berry. "It has a strange name."

"He. He has a strange name," corrected Ferran a little sharply. "And it's not that strange, it suits him." It was good to see the serene, round features of the king's most primitive mech, even if Gonzo's round eyelights never regained their startling green glow.

"It is not an animal or a man. Why do you call it by name and assign it a gender?"

"Because he has a mind and a personality of his own," Ferran said coolly. "Gonzo is the most valuable courtly advisor my father has ever had. He was my tutor when I was a child. I could never win when we played chess, though. He always thought faster than I did." He smiled a little.

Mira was silent a moment. Then she said, "Are you sure it—he—cannot be repaired?"

"I'm no engineer. I don't know how I could reattach these, especially without the right tools." He examined one of the dislocated legs.

Mira bent forward suddenly, placing her cheek against the smooth brass chest plate. Ferran looked at her in bewilderment and opened his mouth to ask what in the world she was doing, but she shushed him before he could speak. After a moment of silence, she gestured at him to lean closer. He stared closely at the weathered metal, but Mira reached across and turned his cheek with one hand, pressing his ear firmly to the brass.

"Hey! Ow!" he exclaimed, more startled than anything.

"Shh!" Mira commanded.

Ferran frowned, but then he heard it. His eyes widened. A faint whirring came from within the metal casing. Occasionally, there was a solid click that made Gonzo's chest vibrate a little, buzzing against Ferran's skin.

"He's alive!" Ferran exclaimed, sitting upright again, relief flooding through him. "This could change everything!"

Mira made a face. "Alive? It's made of metal. It can't be alive. But it is possibly still functional," she admitted.

"He's as alive as we are," argued Ferran. "Trust me on that. We have to find a way to restore him." He picked up one of the metal legs. It did not seem to have been torn off by the crash of the

*Brilliant Albatross*, but rather intentionally separated in order to fit Gonzo into the case.

"If that's so, why is he in a trunk?" Mira examined the other leg.

Ferran thought about it for a moment. "We heard the ship's alarms going off, and Gonzo came to my room to fetch me. We went down into the hold and the servants made tea, and we were instructed to wait until the captain gave the order to abandon ship." He paused, and Mira looked up. "Then someone said that something had gone wrong, that the lifepods had been ejected without us."

He swallowed, remembering. "The ship dropped out of the sky, and I blacked out. I've never been good with heights. Or speed. When I came to, it was starting to get light out. The water was cold, and I was alone. I kept smashing into bits of the ship. The water was trying to pull me back down. I found that piece of hull and held on, hoping it would stay afloat. After that, I must have passed out again, and the next I knew, you had pulled me to shore."

Mira stared at him, an odd mixture of emotions on her face. "But the trunk?" she said finally.

Ferran shrugged. "I don't remember him being there in the hold with us. He came down with me, but he must have left. I don't know who put him in the trunk." He looked down again at the metal man, laying a hand on the smooth brass arm. "Poor Gonzo."

Mira stood up suddenly. "This is foolish. You're mourning a machine."

"He's not—he's not just a machine." Ferran furrowed his brow, frustrated at her inability to adjust to the concept. "I know that's hard for you to understand. But he was like a family member."

"It is just a machine." Mira narrowed her eyes. "We should open it up and use its parts. We could build countless other things from it, depending on what's in working order." She looked down at the prone metal body. "If those eyes still work, we could use them for lights at night—head lamps! I can finally study the night-walking animals. And the night-blooming flowers. And diving! Diving at night!" Mira's eyes widened excitedly, and she leaned over to examine the dull green optical orbs.

"We can't scrap him!" Ferran was mortified and swatted her hand away from Gonzo's face. "No! I won't let you!"

"You're being foolish and sentimental," exclaimed Mira, incredulous. "It has many parts that would be very useful, perhaps the difference between living and dying here. You haven't even spent an entire day here. You don't know what the elements can do. Or the animals. Just because you haven't seen the tiger yet doesn't mean it isn't out there. There is so much good that could come of these parts, if put to other uses. This place, this island is wild. There is no one here to shelter you. There is no palace. Do you understand that, prince?"

Her eyes were fixed on him, and for a second, Ferran felt swept away by their unusual blue-green color; but the way she emphasized his title made Ferran's skin crawl uncomfortably. "He's mine. You can't use him for scrap," he growled defensively, grasping one of the legs tightly.

"What are you going to do, drag it around all day? What about when night falls and you're asleep? Why shouldn't I just pick it apart then?" She laughed then, and it was a strange, airy sound, as though she did not do so often.

Ferran stood up, too. He felt his cheeks hot with sun and anger. "You will do no such thing. I am your prince and that is an order."

There was a pause, a hesitation in the argument. Mira's expression was as stunned as if he'd raised a hand to her. Then her brow darkened.

"I," she said fiercely, "am not your subject."

Her gaze flashed with an unnatural brightness that hurt Ferran's own eyes, and before he could stop her, she hauled off and slammed the leg she was holding into the metal man's chest with a resounding clang. A bright flash of blue-white light exploded on the impact, sending Ferran staggering backward, shielding his eyes. The clang shuddered and buzzed in his ears, fading slowly, and he lowered his arm.

Mira looked surprised, but not as shocked as Ferran felt. Their eyes met, her blue-green stare devoid of the white light now. Then there was a noisy clicking sound, and they both looked down.

"System reloading," announced the nonchalant voice of the mechanized man. His eyes, round and faintly green, began to glow from within, slowly becoming the familiar bold beacons they always had been to Ferran.

"Oh, my gods," breathed Ferran, his heart leaping into his throat. "What did you do?"

Mira did not speak, but took a calm moment to drop the metal leg and examine her hands, back and front alike.

"Gonzo," Ferran muttered, dropping the leg he held. He leaned closer, crouching down. "Gonzo, are you in there? Gonzo!"

The brass face tilted to the side to look at him as though he were a poorly sighted person without glasses on. "One moment please. Your patience is indispensable." The whirring picked up speed from within the metal torso, and Gonzo's eye-lights flickered and brightened.

"What was that?" demanded Ferran. He stared up at Mira, his feelings rapidly shifting from awe to joy to anger, and back again. "What was that light? How did you do that?"

Mira's expression grew colder, but she did not reply. She turned and walked off into the trees determinedly. Ferran didn't bother to call out to her. *She'll be back.* He frowned and retrieved the leg she had dropped.

"Your understanding and patience are most gratifying," announced the metal man in the trunk. The round, coppery-colored head shifted again. "My name is Gonzo, how may I assist you?"

Ferran looked down and smiled. The sound of Gonzo's voice filled him with a strange mix of relief and new pain. His eyes burned. "Gonzo, it's me," he said gently.

The mech looked up slowly, as though his neck was stiff from traveling so uncomfortably. "Prince Ferran! What . . . I beg your pardon, my lord. What happened? Are we home?"

"No, Gonzo . . . the ship went down," Ferran answered quietly. He tried not to choke on his words. "We washed up here."

"No!" exclaimed the mech in his tinny voice. He paused, and Ferran could hear the gears clicking and turning even though Gonzo's expression did not change. "Where are the others?"

"I can't find any of them. It was only by a miracle I survived, and we found you by accident."

"Your Highness, you say there are no other survivors and yet you also use the plural 'we.' Who else is with us now?" Gonzo was keen for answers. He was always quick with observations.

"My savior," said Ferran with a sigh, sitting down. It was strange to have to explain all of this to Gonzo. "A girl. She pulled me from the sea, and you, too."

Gonzo made a quiet noise of contemplation that was halfway between a hum and the ding of a bell. Then, "Prince Ferran, why are you holding my legs?"

Ferran set them down carefully on the ground. "They were detached in transit, I believe. It's how I found you. I'm sorry, Gonzo, I don't know how to reattach them, or even if they'd work after I did."

Gonzo made the thoughtful noise again. Then he tried to sit up, awkwardly grasping the sides of the trunk with his brass-articulated fingers. Ferran helped him until he found a balancing point, and tried to keep a calm expression as Gonzo looked down at his legless pelvis, his green eyes glowing dimmer for a moment, then back to their normal contrast.

"I am sorry, Prince Ferran. Are you quite sure—the king . . . ?"

Ferran shook his head. "You know him, Gonzo." His voice shook a little. "He's been so frail. So tired. And he was never a swimmer. Something went wrong with the lifepods on the ship. I don't think anyone made it." He felt a dampness on his cheek as Gonzo stared at him.

"So, the old king put me in this trunk to keep me safe," announced Gonzo softly, "and the new king delivers me from it once more. Long live the king."

"No," Ferran blurted, "no, I'm not the king. He—he put you in the trunk?" He frowned.

"Yes, when the lifepods failed." Gonzo looked out to sea for a moment, then turned back to Ferran. "You are the king of Italya now."

Ferran sat back a little, the words filling him with cold dread. "No, no. I'm not. My uncle would be, before me. But I guess he's gone, too. Gonzo, there's no way off the island. We're alone, and we can't go home. I'm not the king if we can't go home."

Gonzo tilted his head a little. "No, my prince. You are the king now. And you must go home. Somehow, we must find a way for you to return."

Ferran floundered a little at the idea of going home now, with nothing, and telling his mother and the court that the king—that his father—was dead. It seemed impossible and terrifying. *I feel like such a coward, surviving when the others did not.*

"But Mother is still the queen," he protested.

"Your mother may not be queen for long if she does not have a reason to keep fighting." Gonzo sounded serious. "She is tired, Prince Ferran, and she loves you very much. What do you think will happen if she receives word that the ship was destroyed and all souls lost? What do you think will happen to her, or to the nation?" He shook his head by slowly rotating it back and forth. "We must get you home, Prince Ferran."

"But your legs," said Ferran weakly. He was losing the argument. He realized then he would rather stay on the island than go back and be king. He could live simply, the way Mira did, even if she was currently cross with him. "How are we going to attach your legs?"

"I suppose we could examine the detachments more closely," Gonzo answered. "And if your friend was clever enough to save us both from the depths of the ocean, perhaps she has some insight into how we can survive this together."

"I don't know about that," Ferran sighed, exasperated. "She's stubborn, and she's lived here almost her whole life. She doesn't remember a time before the island."

"A native?"

"No, she was born somewhere else. But she lives here with her father—sort of. She said he's kind of dangerous, not to be trusted. She said he can't know I'm here."

"That's peculiar, indeed." Gonzo shifted his weight, tipping his head quizzically.

"She's the most peculiar girl I've ever met," Ferran confessed. "I don't understand her, sometimes. She's still and quiet and focused like an animal. She sees through everything. She's incredibly strong, too. Stronger than me. But there's something about her father that scares her, I think, or makes her angry. She looks upset every time he's mentioned."

"How unfortunate," said Gonzo. "Where did she go off to?"

"Mira went off that way," Ferran gestured vaguely. "I bet she'll be back."

Gonzo stopped turning about in the trunk like a child in a bath basin and looked at him slowly. "Mira?"

"Yes. Her name is Mira."

Gonzo made an unusual clicking noise, and Ferran saw the green eye-lights flicker. "What is the name of her father?"

"I don't know," admitted Ferran, feeling suddenly uneasy. "Why? What is it?"

"My prince," began the mech, but stopped before he could complete the thought. Mira came stalking out of the woods, carved spear in hand, looking somewhat calmer. She stared at Gonzo as she approached, her gait seemingly careless and confident.

"It works all right?" she asked, sounding a little impressed as she came to a stop near them.

"His mental functions seem to be operational," Ferran nodded. "His speech, too. The only thing is his legs, we were just discussing—"

"Miracolo!" Gonzo sounded almost awed.

Ferran and Mira both looked at him in surprise. "What?" said Ferran, confused.

Mira fixed her eyes on the mech. "What did you say?"

"Miracolo," repeated Gonzo, quietly. "Miracolo Vittoria Sophia Fiorente. You have your mother's nose and chin, but your father's cheekbones."

Ferran's eyebrows shot up. "What?" he exclaimed again.

"How . . . do you know that?" asked Mira levelly, and though her expression fought to remain still, she looked deeply unsettled. Ferran watched her squeeze the decorated spear tighter.

"You poor child," Gonzo said. "Of course you would not remember. Has your father never told you where you came from?"

"Gonzo, speak plainly. What is the meaning of all this?" Ferran demanded.

"My prince, this is Miracolo Vittoria Sophia Fiorente, daughter of Sophia Volans and the former Duke of Neapolis, the exiled traitor, Dante Fiorente."

Ferran felt his jaw slacken entirely and he looked at Mira, who stood motionless, her expression stunned. "Is this true?" he demanded.

Mira stared at the metal man, then looked at Ferran helplessly. "I don't know," she confessed in a small voice. "My father has never spoken to me about it. I don't know where we lived before the island, I was too young."

"How old are you, child?" asked Gonzo gently.

Mira shook her head. "I don't know."

"Don't you know when your birthday is?" Ferran marveled. She shook her head at him again.

"The former duke's daughter was born approximately eighteen years ago, and the former duke himself was banished approximately twelve years ago." Gonzo turned his head from side to side slowly. "It was a complete scandal."

"Scandal? Why?" Ferran asked. "What happened? I've never heard a word about this from anyone. Not my father, not Uncle Bas, not even Duke Torsione, and he's the current Duke of Neapolis."

"Your Highness, Duke Torsione is the younger brother of former duke Dante. That would make him your uncle," Gonzo added, looking from Ferran to Mira again.

"But this is outrageous!" Ferran couldn't process the idea. "Why on earth would my father banish a duke and a young child to a barren island in the middle of nowhere? What could he have possibly done that would warrant that?"

Mira looked at him almost apologetically, then, as though she had a feeling what might be coming. Gonzo tipped his round head to the side.

"Black magic, my prince," said the mech. "And ambition."

# CHAPTER FOURTEEN

Karaburan crouched at the foot of a tree, three dead fish at his feet. He had eaten the bird on the beach this morning, much to Truffo's insult, along with a few fish, but he was hungry again. It was the usual way of his day-to-day activities. He picked each one apart slowly, the eyes and fins first, then the flesh, then the bones and other crunchy bits for last. From time to time, he looked up at Stephen and Truffo, sitting across the little clearing from him.

They stared at him, eating their own food much less vigorously than he ate his, as though distracted by his display of savoring the meal. Both Stephen and Truffo bore expressions of pale disgust, eyes round and glazed, mouths slightly agape as he slurped and gulped his food down. He sucked one of the fish's eyeballs out of its skull carefully, and saw both men blanch at the sight of it. *These strange, soft men do not like it simply because it is not flame-burned. It is a foolish thing to be choosy about, when building a fire is work and there is enough food to be had without a fire.*

"Are the berries to your liking, my lords?" asked Karaburan in as sweet a voice as he could muster. "Or can I offer you some of my meal as well?"

Truffo made a terrified guttural sound, his hand halfway to his open mouth with another round yellow fruit.

160

"No, no, monster." Stephen shook his head. He had taken to calling Karaburan 'monster' as his inebriation grew stronger. "That is not necessary. We are quite content."

"It does not do for kings—no, gods! It does not do for gods to go without meat." Karaburan said a little mischievously. He had seen Dante prepare meals over an open fire, and had seen evidence on scorched bits of earth and ashen pits that Mira, in her ranging about the isle, had done the same. Karaburan was not sure why he didn't mind the raw fish, but it was amusing to him. "Please, my lords." He held out two of the half-torn fish carcasses. "Let your servant feed you!"

Truffo gagged audibly. Stephen stood upright too quickly and staggered back into another tree trunk, catching his balance there and shutting his eyes firmly, as though dizzy.

"No, truly, that's enough of that, monster, we want none of it!" Stephen cried, holding his hand over his eyes. "Indeed, please finish your meal quickly. Tasty though it may be, the sight of it is most insulting to our senses." Truffo groaned in agreement and put his face into his arms, as though he might be sick.

"I would not wish to offend your lordships," Karaburan laughed, and eagerly tore into the remaining fish. Truffo rolled over and began crawling hurriedly away into the bushes, possibly to escape the sight of raw fish being pulled apart, but Stephen remained stalwart, gazing in horrified amazement as Karaburan ravaged his food.

When the last bones crunched between Karaburan's teeth, he spotted Truffo peeping out from between some broad ferns, looking somewhat relieved, but still wary.

"Are you still hungry, my lords?" asked Karaburan, crouching. "I can go and fish for you! Perhaps a bird or two?"

"Not necessary," Stephen managed to say, closing his eyes for a moment. "We are quite without hunger, now."

"What, then, would please you most, my lord?"

"More wine," said Stephen, his expression darkening as he crossed the little clearing to the crate they had dragged up from the beach. Karaburan lumbered closer to watch as Stephen stumbled toward the crate, then caught his balance again and reached for a bottle.

"More wine, and then to our purpose?" Karaburan tried not to sound too eager. He liked the taste of the wine well enough now that they had drunk so much of it, but it did not affect him the same strange way it seemed to affect Stephen and Truffo. It had fascinated him at first, the way their words slurred, their eyes clouded over, and their ability to stand, sit, and move normally became more and more difficult.

But as the afternoon wore on, Karaburan felt increasingly anxious that their window of opportunity to kill the tyrant slipped away. If they could surprise him sooner rather than later, they might stand a better chance. If they waited, Karaburan feared that something would change, that Dante might sense their ill intentions and punish him for even thinking about rebellion.

"Purpose is relative," grunted Stephen gruffly as he wrestled the bottle open with a pop. His cheeks were red and his eyes were distinctly shiny. He moved past Karaburan, toward Truffo, who had just come crawling back out of the underbrush to sit with his back against the trunk of a tree. "Thirsty, lad?"

"Yes, but not for wine," complained Truffo, batting at Stephen with his hands as he came closer. "My gullet is dry for water, Stephen, without which we wandering woeful wretches won't win wars when wars would want winning."

Karaburan tipped his head to one side at the impressive string of syllables. *They talk so strangely!* he thought, wishing he had someone familiar to discuss it with, but knowing he was quite as alone as ever, even in the company of these men.

"But the tyrant," protested Karaburan.

Stephen made a sharp gesture with his free hand. "I will hear no talk of him!" he snapped. "It is time to drink, not to commit murder."

"But you promised." Karaburan began to grind his teeth. Truffo looked startled at the sound, but Stephen seemed only to be scornful.

"I am your new king, and I will not have you make demands of me, monster."

"You will do as you swore to do," snarled Karaburan, drawing himself up to his full height. "If you knew how long I've been tormented—"

"And that torment is nearly at its end. So, why don't you sit down and celebrate like a real man?" Stephen drank from the bottle.

"Don't talk to it so!" Truffo hissed. "It's so much bigger than we are!"

"This monster will not harm us, lad," Stephen went on calmly. "It is a goodly and gentle monster, and will do us no harm. Isn't that right?" He waggled the bottle at Karaburan, who did not take it, but simply glowered and went back to sit on his patch of earth across the clearing.

*Some lords they are,* he thought to himself. *They are not strong or wise, they are not kind, and they certainly do not seem powerful. All they want to do is drink that wine. If they will not kill Dante, I ought to turn them in, and kill him myself while he's distracted by them.* Karaburan cocked his head to one side. *Now there's a thought. Yes, I can always give them up . . . and his back will turn as he studies them like specimens, and I will be there, ready . . . ready to twist his neck so sideways it will stop his heart. Finally.*

Somewhere in the trees a strange piercing screech went up from a flock of birds, startling the men.

"What was that?" gulped Truffo. He grabbed at Stephen's sleeve, nearly spilling the wine.

Karaburan gave a little gurgling laugh at how silly they both looked. "It's only the birds, my lords." *They fear their own shadows!* "Very large birds with large claws and hooked beaks for tearing fish in half," he added experimentally.

Truffo looked nervous, but Stephen was unchanged. He took a swallow of wine. "An eagle or a hawk. Such birds of prey we have back home," he declared unsteadily, but with great conviction.

*Oh, I can't kill them now,* Karaburan thought, entirely amused. "Their wings stretch wider than my own arms," Karaburan said, standing up to his full height and spreading his arms apart. "And their eyes are like the moon, shining and blind-white."

"Blind birds? That's silly. Birds can't go blind." Stephen frowned. "How could they fly?"

"They aren't blind. They see the sounds they make, and hear the smells, and fly on wings like flints."

Truffo looked horrified. "That doesn't even sound possible," he stammered.

"I've seen them," assured Karaburan cheerfully. "It's true."

The afternoon was waning on, the daylight becoming warmer in color as the sun traveled farther toward its inevitable sunset. Karaburan tried not to smile too widely at the fear that began to glimmer in both men's wide eyes. *Fear makes men desperate,* he had heard Dante say once, a long time ago. *Desperate men do almost anything if they think it is their only option.*

"Bah, birds. What else?" Stephen wanted to know, lifting his chin a little in defiance. Karaburan shrugged his lopsided shoulders and crouched comfortably again.

"Many things, my lord," he answered, and glanced around them into the forest for a few moments, listening and watching. Then he turned back to them and lumbered closer. "The most delicate and beautiful insects, but deadly to be bitten by."

Truffo paled and clung closer to Stephen's trouser leg like a spooked child. Stephen swayed, trying to keep the bottle aloft. He squinted at Karaburan. "Monster, I do insist you tell us the truth of it," he said, carefully and slowly. "There is nothing to be gained by frightening us unecessh . . . unnessy . . . unarcsissa . . . without reason."

Karaburan lowered his head soberly. "Yes, my lord. I promise to tell the truth," he vowed, amused that his words had held such power over them for a short moment.

"Now speak truth," Truffo blurted out, "Is there aught on this damnable land that can devour us whole?"

Karaburan shook his head. "No," he said.

Something moved in the trees, and Karaburan heard a low growl. He turned to look over his shoulder, seeking the source of the noise. There was nothing there. It had certainly sounded like something, but there was nothing there, so it must be nothing.

"What," Truffo demanded, pushing himself up to his feet awkwardly, "was that?"

Stephen squeezed the bottle of wine tightly. "Monster," he said cautiously, "what was that noise?"

Karaburan was very still, listening to the leaves rustle in the breeze. He looked at Stephen, his own eyes a little wider. "I don't know," he murmured.

"Monster, you promised," whispered Truffo. "You said! He said there was nothing out there!" Truffo turned his attention to Stephen, scrambling to his feet.

There was another growl, closer this time.

Stephen's lips worked silently. Truffo trembled like a dry leaf, and Karaburan turned around again in search of the source of the noise.

"Monster," Stephen said in a tiny voice. "Should we run?"

Karaburan saw the leaves moving, the lower branches of trees and bushes swaying as though forced apart by the body of an animal passing through the greenery. For a moment, he was at a loss. He had only seen the tiger once, and hoped never to see it again. The isle had proven big enough—or at least tricky enough—to keep him from encountering the biggest of the beasts since that day. He wasn't sure he could best the tiger. He had wrestled with fish and water-dwelling things over the years, had climbed trees and wrangled birds, and chased the littler mammals over the paths and through the forest. But the tiger frightened him.

The growl increased in closeness and pitch, then rose to a series of sharp barks. Karaburan had never heard that sound before, and it frightened him.

"Dogs?" Truffo exclaimed. "Wild dogs?" Other barking voices joined the first, and the sound of running feet approached the edge of their small clearing.

"What is a dog?" asked Karaburan.

The leaves shook and the barking was nearly upon them.

"Run!" bellowed Stephen.

The three of them turned and ran the other direction, into the forest, away from the wine crate, the clearing, and the barking, but the animals followed. Karaburan, more accustomed to the uneven terrain of the island, quickly passed Truffo, and then Stephen, and was now in the lead of their desperate flight. The barking escalated to snarling and howling; the sound of snapping jaws, louder than any beast Karaburan had ever heard, echoed at their heels, even as they ran on.

"What are they?" cried Stephen in terror.

"I don't know," yelped Truffo, "I can't bear to look!"

Karaburan had a thought then, an idea that almost surprised him more than simply the fact that he had an idea in his head at all.

He veered to the left and heard the men yelp. "This way!" he cried, and heard them crashing through the trees after him.

Truffo was a relatively good runner, from what Karaburan saw each time he glanced back, but Stephen was crimson-faced and puffing as noisily as any whale breaching the water for air. The dogs snapped their jaws and howled, and Truffo began to sob in between leaps over uneven ground and fallen branches. Stephen was falling behind.

"Take heart," called Karaburan, "we are nearly there!" There came a yelping, and it sounded as though one of the dogs had tripped, interrupting the momentum of the pack. The dogs snarled at one another, lagging in their speed. The barking and yowling began to fade.

"We're losing them!" Stephen sounded giddy and short of breath.

Karaburan found what he was looking for and began to slow, pulling tree branches aside with his large hands so they could follow him.

"Hurry," he urged, revealing the dark alcove of rock.

"Gods bless us, a hiding-hole," cried Stephen in relief, staggering toward the stony entrance.

Truffo followed, wordless and gasping, and Karaburan heard the last barking cease as he followed them inside the cool, dark cave.

Stephen had fallen to his hands and knees, sucking in air like a drowning man. Truffo was pressed against the wall of the little cave, his body trembling with effort. Karaburan stood with his back to the entrance they'd used, catching his own breath. *They are so fragile,* he marveled. *So foreign to the island, they cannot even survive a short sprint. Lucky we were so close to the caves.*

As they stood panting in the cool shadow of the cave, Karaburan felt something in his gut begin to sink. His plan was not the best one he'd ever had. Now they were all three in the caves together. He had hoped to stir them to action and leave them to their murder. He had hoped to stay out of it, and now he was inevitably a part of it.

*I hope we find him before he finds us,* Karaburan thought anxiously. *If we surprise him, we may stand a chance.*

"What," gasped Stephen, "was that?" He turned to look up at Karaburan, exhausted.

"I don't know," repeated Karaburan apologetically, and made a show of checking the entrance for sign of their pursuers.

"You didn't tell us about the feral dogs," whined Truffo. "I want to go home!"

"Any suggestions as to how?" Stephen looked sourly at him.

Truffo pulled a pained, tired face. "You know plain well I haven't."

"We're safe for now," murmured Karaburan, watching their expressions in the dim light of the cave.

"Do you hear something?" Truffo hissed, and they all held their breath for a moment. From somewhere further down the dark, narrow passageway was a sound like running water, or perhaps a wind chime.

Stephen sniffed. "Do you smell something?" There was a distinct smell like roast chicken, and Karaburan saw their eyes grow wide and hungry.

"I'm so hungry," Truffo said meekly.

"Let's have a look, then," Stephen whispered, and began to move forward.

"Wait, lords!" Karaburan growled. "Be wary—we have found the lair of the tyrant. Perhaps he will be distracted and we can catch him unawares."

Karaburan saw the doubt flicker over Stephen's face, and resolved to do what must be done. *If they do not do it, Dante will kill them, and I'm not strong enough to stop him.* He remembered the time he'd stood up against Dante's orders, the look in his master's eye, the whiplash of magic that scored his back and his arms with burning pain.

"So be it," agreed Stephen, and unlooped his belt.

"What's that for?" demanded Truffo.

"Garrote," said Stephen, as though that were a stupid question.

"That's not a garrote, it's a belt."

"Well, we'll have to make do! We don't have a real garrote." Stephen swatted at him. "When we find him, you distract him, and I'll throttle him with this. And you get him by the feet."

"How?" Truffo looked stunned. "What'll I get him with?"

"I don't know, tie his shoes together if you have to, boy!"

Karaburan nodded eagerly. *Dante doesn't wear shoes,* he thought, excited at the thought of Truffo's misfortune on that front. It was strange, but as soon as they'd stepped into the cave, Karaburan felt his mind shifting, his allegiance to these strange castaways melting. It was as though that vision of Mira had never held sway over him. He felt giddy and anxious, but somehow pleased, as pleased as a shark that has cornered its prey in the lagoon.

Stephen began to creep forward, heading deeper into the cool shadows of the cave with Truffo clinging to his shirt and Karaburan bringing up the rear. They moved carefully down the narrow passageway until it opened up into a wider sort of chamber with several passages branching off.

"Which way?" whispered Stephen.

"Straight ahead," Karaburan answered, and hoped it had not sounded too eager. "His chambers lie at the heart of the caves. Go on and I will follow you."

"Shouldn't you go first, since you know which way is which?" Truffo demanded.

"Shush!" Stephen admonished with a wave of his hand, the belt flopping in his grasp. "We go forward." He headed toward the middle path, Truffo whimpering behind him. Karaburan hesitated, listening carefully.

*He's here somewhere,* thought Karaburan. His insides churned in both fear and elation. Stephen and Truffo soon vanished into the dark shadows ahead, leaving him standing behind in the larger room. He moved to follow them, but a voice stopped him.

"Karaburan," Dante whispered, stepping out of another passage.

*Oh, no.* Karaburan crouched, cowering in his usual show of obeisance. Fear pulsed through him, overriding the joy he'd felt mere moments ago. "I brought them to you," he mumbled quickly, betraying his new lords before he could stop himself. Being so near his master was agony, like a pressure inside his mind that he could not drown out with sound or thought. He lowered his eyes. "I found them, brought them here to you, as you did order long ago: any men washed ashore, living or dead, must be brought before you, Master."

Dante moved into the room, as silent as a shark in the shallows. His slender form was shrouded in his rags and tatters, and his ragged cloak swept the rocky floor of the cave, a haunted whisper of fabric that bounced off the ceiling of the chamber. Karaburan saw that Dante's brow and hands were covered in black soot. He had seen this soot on him once or twice before, and knew that it meant he had been hard at work with some black art or another.

Karaburan kept his head down, stealing small glances at his master as he glided toward him. At last, Dante stopped and placed a hand on Karaburan's patchy shoulder with a surprisingly gentle touch.

"Well done," Dante said in his quiet, distant voice, and Karaburan felt his insides sink in equal measure with his thumping heart, pleased to have done well by his master. It made his head hurt, the way he could feel both pride and shame at the same time over this.

*Oh, I am a terrible thing . . . those men will die at his hands,* he thought trembling. *Oh, Mira! I could not do it . . . I am sorry.* Karaburan watched as Dante strode past him and down the passage after Truffo and Stephen, into the cool shadows of the cave.

# CHAPTER FIFTEEN

## 1854

Corvina woke in darkness, with only a fleeting memory of the look in the duke's eyes before he struck her with her own staff. Her bones ached and rang like a gong that had been hit too hard, and her stomach churned like an ocean within her.

The dark was disorienting—she could not tell where she was or what time of day it was, or even how long she'd been unconscious. She felt at herself in the dark, her hands weakly seeking out her clothes and hair. Other than her pounding headache and unhappy stomach, she appeared to be unharmed. She groaned as she shifted her weight and tried to sit up.

The room was very small, and she could not quite get her balance, even while seated. She sat still a while, breathing slowly to center herself. She wasn't sure how much time had passed when light spilled suddenly into the little room. She recoiled, covering her eyes quickly with her hands.

"Oh, dear, is that too bright?"

She peeped through her fingers, her eyes watering at the brightness. The man in the door was broad-shouldered and tall. His voice was cracked and roughened, and the smell of salt and brine came in through the door with him.

*Oh,* Corvina thought, as she recognized the creaking of the walls and the smell of the sea. *I'm on a ship.*

"Ever so sorry about the cramped quarters," said the man, with a sneer that made it quite clear that he was not sorry at all. "The duke said to give you the finest chambers we could manage, you know, but this ship's got a lot of folks down below what need the space themselves, see. A lot of folks. And besides that, we wouldn't want the likes of you mingling with the likes of them . . . no telling what a witch like you might do, Lady Psychorrax."

Corvina shut her eyes, the light piercing her closed eyelids and burning at the borders of her mind. She remembered the duke, and the storm which had ceased to rage the moment the little baby was born. *Psychorrax!* he had said. *Heartbreak!* Witches, like Corvina. *Psychorrax!* Even though she had tried so hard to keep the duchess alive. She had tried everything she knew, and it hadn't been enough. That storm had been too strong, and the baby had to be born. Corvina pressed the heels of her hands against her eyes, as if to wake herself from a nightmare.

"Oh, don't you fret, milady," simpered the sailor in the doorway. "I'm here to see you gets special attentions, see. The others downstairs ain't got nothing. But you're special, at least 'til we get to the colony, you are. You'll all end up on the same block, you know. But for now, I'm here to make sure you've got everything what you need for a comfortable, pleasurable journey. Courtesy of the duke himself."

Corvina's stomach lurched again, and she forced herself to look up, even in the bright light. *No,* she thought, but she couldn't find her voice. The sailor chuckled, slipping inside the tiny room and closing the door behind him. *No. No, no. Not this.* The sound of his belt coming undone brought bile to her throat as she scrambled to a corner, the straw on the floor shifting and whispering beneath her.

*Stop,* Corvina thought as he knelt. *Please stop.*

She could not speak, her throat was so dry, but even if she had screamed aloud, she did not believe he would have stopped. Her chest constricted and she struck out in the dark, but he only chuckled calmly, like a farmer bridling an unruly horse.

Afterward, Corvina lay in the small room, feeling the ocean push and pull at the ship that held her, and, for days, drifted in and out of a restless, painfully sore sleep. Time had no meaning any longer, though she knew it must be passing still, for occasionally she would wake with a bucket of mushed food or grog in the cell with her. She tried to tell herself that the conditions of the slave ship were definitely worse below decks, outside of her small chamber. She tried to tell herself the voices sneering "Psychorrax!" and "Witch!" were only the sailors passing by her cell, and not voices trapped within her own mind. She wept from time to time, but she was so dehydrated and exhausted that she could do little but lie still in the straw.

She huddled there in the dark, each moment passing as an hour, each hour as a day, and, like grains of sand through an hourglass, she wasted away, her dreams, thoughts, and very self, crumbling and slipping away through the cracks. The darkness bore down on her and confused her mind until, by and by, she did not care anymore how dark it was or how long it had been since she'd had fresh air, fresh clothes, or clean skin.

Sometimes, Corvina slept like a corpse, unmoving and dreamless. Sometimes she could not sleep, because the sailor was there with her, touching her, moving in the darkness. It was all a nightmare.

* * *

Rain pummeled the upper decks of the ship. The hull creaked and groaned in protest of the harsh treatment, but they sailed on nonetheless. Corvina was sick to her stomach in the tiny room, trying to ride out the rough weather. She focused her mind inward, steadied her breathing, and tried to summon any last bit of energy she had to calm her nausea, to soothe her pains and aches, and try not to think about how she would either die at sea or die as a slave.

Great waves sucked at the ship's hull, like an enormous lizard scavenging an egg, but the ship strained onward, buffeted by wind and lightning. Corvina shut her eyes and begged whatever little power she had left within her to wake.

*Do something,* she pleaded feverishly to the nameless magic. The ship lurched again. *Do something! I can't, I can't . . . I want one more chance. One more, please, just one.*

Corvina braced herself in the corner of the small, stinking room. She mumbled invocations of power, the words tumbling tonelessly from her lips like the beginning of a flood breaking through a dam, and shut her eyes hard to block out the lurching walls. Her palms pressed against the rough wooden floor as the sea threatened to toss the entire ship over.

There was a great crack of thunder and, for a moment, Corvina's stomach leapt up into her throat before crashing back down again. The ship had been airborne, thrown high by a wave, and then dropped down again like a child's toy in the bath.

Corvina opened her eyes, gasping at the pounding of her own heart. *I won't survive this,* she thought, faintly. She thought of the poor duchess and the tiny little girl that had been born, who stopped the rain in Neapolis. *Bless her, even if her father betrayed me, used me . . . Bless her, and bless me. I'm done for.*

She shut her eyes. The sounds of the raging weather went silent. She opened her eyes again.

The ship no longer rocked violently around her, and the roaring sounds of the storm were muffled now. Her stomach calmed, her nerves soothed, and the soft silence descended around her, as though she were not quite attached to her body.

*Am I dead?*

"No," said a voice cheerfully. "You're on pause."

Corvina's voice caught in her throat.

"You seem to be in trouble," observed the voice primly. "I might be able to help you."

*Who are you?* she thought, staring into the dark room. *Where are you?*

"I'm right here," said the voice, suddenly soft and lush and kind. A cool, smooth hand rested on her cheek, and she flinched as he unfolded from the darkness like a mirage in the desert.

He was very beautiful.

He held a cup to her lips and helped her drink—the water was clean and cool. Corvina gulped it down, grasping his wrist with both hands to steady the cup. When the water was gone, she sank back against the wall and gasped for breath. Her visitor smiled at her, crouching as lightly as an animal, his pale gray eyes impossibly bright in the darkness.

He was slight of figure and not quite as tall as she, but his brightness filled the room, making her feel small. His hair was windswept, voluminous but short, and silvery-blue, darkening at the roots. His skin shimmered like light over water, translucent and pale as porcelain. His mouth and nose were smallish and round, and his eyes were dark and alluring. His build was lean but strong, and he was, for all she could tell, quite naked, although his appearance blurred if she moved her eyes away from his face.

He gave her a serene, gentle smile, and she felt calm radiate from his hands, which smoothed back her hair and cupped her face.

"A spirit," she said, softly.

"Yes," he replied, lifting his brows and beaming at her, his teeth perfectly neat and gleaming. If he had been taller, he might have been one of the statues Corvina remembered seeing in the temples in Greccia during her time there—handsome, smooth, well-muscled. There was a delicateness about his hands that was almost feminine. She wondered for a moment if it was a female. As if hearing her thoughts, he chuckled and batted his long lashes at her.

Corvina let her head rest back against the wall of the cell and shut her eyes, confused and exhausted.

"Poor thing," cooed the spirit, still touching her face with his breezy fingertips. "What a long path that has led you here. What troubles you've seen, and still see."

Corvina let her eyes open by a slit, and studied his face. He was all innocence and proper sympathy. She didn't like it. "Who are you?" she asked again.

He smiled brightly, like the moon coming out from the clouds. "A spirit, as you say, sweet lady. You are unwell, and you are likely to die here if you don't find a way out soon. Dangerous weather out there," he added, eyeing the ceiling.

"And you can help me?" Corvina was unconvinced. The storm was bad, yes, but trafficking with spirits was an unruly business, and she had never liked them to begin with. They were tricky.

The spirit tilted his head like a bird and took her hand in both of his own softly. "I would like to," he admitted. "I would very much like to help you, if you can find it in your heart to let me."

"Let you?" echoed Corvina. The spirit smiled coyly at her, brushing his thumbs along her hand and wrist lightly as feathers.

"I'm sure a lady of your kind has something to offer me," he mused softly, looking into her eyes. "In fact, I know you do." One of his pale hands left hers and landed softly on her stomach.

Corvina's eyes went wide, then narrowed sharply at him. She pulled her hand away and tried to push him back. "No, I don't," she said, gruffly, feeling suddenly groggy from his close proximity and the lack of sound outside of the little room.

The spirit laughed softly, like wind chimes. "How can you be sure? How many times has that sailor lain with you? How long have you been trapped in here? How many times have you been ill?" He rose, and walked—glided—about the little room thoughtfully, watching her as calmly as any predator.

"No," Corvina said through gritted teeth, but there was dampness on her cheeks, her eyelashes, and she put her hands over her belly in fading denial. "No, no . . ."

"You've always wanted a child," he remarked thoughtfully, his expression growing somber. "And now you'll have one . . . if you can get out of this mess, that is." His head tilted to the side again. "Oh, how sad. How sad, sorceress. A child of rape is still a child, and it's still yours. Don't you want a second chance? Wouldn't you like to see that child live? Or better yet, perhaps . . . give it the chance it deserves to live a better life than even you might give it?"

Corvina stared back at him. "Speak plainly, spirit. Tell me exactly what you want."

"I want your child. I will give him to someone who really, truly wants a baby, someone who can't have what they want. It would be a blessing, truly, it would. You'd be a hero."

"And in exchange?" Corvina's head swam.

"I'll save your life, sorceress. I'll deliver you from this place and bring you somewhere you can live in peace, unhindered by men and politics. You'll be free."

"That's all?" Corvina sat up. How could that possibly be all? "I agree to give you this child, and you will bring me to a safe place, where I can live in peace?" She narrowed her eyes at him.

The spirit's eyes were round and shining, his little mouth somber with promise. He nodded several times, childlike. "Yes, exactly. That's all."

"Tell me what will become of the child." Corvina wasn't sure why she wanted to know—perhaps because the spirit was right, that the child was hers, no matter what else was true now.

"My lady does desire a child to care for. Her lord would give her one to make her happy, but he has been unsuccessful. I would bring your child to my lady, and she would be eternally grateful to your kindness of heart, from one woman to another." The spirit laid a hand on his chest, where his heart ought to be.

Corvina did not like the simplicity of this. Spirits were usually the opposite of simple. There was more he wasn't telling, but her mind was reeling; consequences were distant and difficult to grasp now. "And I'll be safe, and unharmed, and alive?"

The spirit nodded somberly again. "Yes, of course. I know an island not far from here. We can go there long enough to let you bear your child, and then I will take you wherever you like in the world, and you'll be safe for the rest of your days. So help me," he added, making a foreign-looking sign over his chest with his fingers.

Corvina closed her eyes for a moment. She had been raped, that was true. And if she was to bear a child, she may as well pay for the spirit's rescue with it. She could do little to care for a baby now. Perhaps if things had gone differently with the duke and duchess . . . but they hadn't. And in the end, if she refused the spirit, she would die a slave, whether aboard this ship or in some colony.

A bargain with a spirit was never ideal. But it was an option, and it was theoretically better than staying in this godsforsaken place, waiting to give birth as a slave.

"All right," said Corvina quietly. "All right. Take me to the island, and after I've given birth, you can have the child."

"Thank you," the spirit answered softly, moving closer to her again. "Thank you for letting me help you."

Corvina didn't like the way he said that, but the next thing she knew, he had wrapped her up in his arms in an embrace, his whole brightness covering her and making her shut her eyes. A crash of thunder rang out. She kept her eyes shut tight, felt a warm, gentle wind passing them by, and the sounds of the storm faded away into the dark.

* * *

Corvina startled awake.

"Shhh," soothed the voice of the spirit beside her. "You're safe. Relax now."

Corvina exhaled slowly, feeling the warmth of the sand seeping up through the blanket she lay on, and closed her eyes for a moment. The air was fresh, the breeze was warm, and dawn was coming, the sky already beginning to lighten and change its midnight shadows for rose and gold. She relaxed, stretching the faint aches in her feet and arms and neck.

The spirit hummed something faint and soothing, and Corvina opened her eyes again with a yawn.

"Thank you," she murmured. "Thank you for saving me."

"Oh, you're very welcome," replied the spirit lightly. "Do hold still."

"Hold . . . still?" Corvina tried to sit up and found she could not. "Spirit . . . what are you doing?"

A bright light shone just out of her line of sight, the glimmers of it dancing below her chin. The spirit crouched beside her, and appeared to weaving the very air itself while he hummed quietly.

"Spirit," asked the witch again, her voice cracking. "What . . . are you doing?"

"Helping you give birth," replied the spirit, turning to smile at her widely. "Isn't it funny? You were a midwife, and now I'm your midwife."

He laughed, and the light shimmered brighter. Corvina tried to lift her hands, but they were heavy as dead weights in the sand.

"I don't understand," she said hoarsely. "I'm not full term."

"You weren't full term," corrected the spirit. "You will be in a few more minutes."

"But . . . no, you can't . . ."

"I can," whispered the spirit, still smiling in the dark. "And I am. Just lie still. He'll be out in no time."

"Please . . ." Corvina felt the pressure growing in her abdomen. Spirit magic was unruly at best, but powerful in most cases, and if this spirit was speeding up her pregnancy. . . . "Please be careful, I—" she cried out as the pressure in her abdomen peaked.

"Be still," scolded the spirit, still moving his hands over her body.

Corvina gasped. "Have you ever done this before?" she demanded, straining to keep her eyes on him.

"Quiet!" His tone was harsh, but he did not turn to look at her. "It's coming."

Her lower half was mostly numb, but she could feel the pressure within it coiled like a spring wound far too tightly, ready to burst. The pain took her breath away, but it was over as suddenly as though she had fallen from a great height and slammed into the ground at full force. The light snuffed out, and the voice of an infant screeched and gasped for air.

Her skin gleamed with sweat. Her vision was blurry, and there was a pounding in her head that might have been her own heartbeat.

"What . . . what did you do . . . ?" she panted, trying to sit up. Her limbs felt too heavy to move, but she could roll her head to the side a bit, and saw through her haze the shape of the silvery spirit, crouched in the sand near her, holding the infant in his hands. He muttered in a foreign language she could barely hear. "What are you doing?" Corvina coughed.

The infant writhed and flailed its little arms, crying aloud, and then Corvina saw the impossible—its legs stretched, its hands widened, its head bobbed, and the baby grew before her very eyes. As the sun rose over the strange and foreign island, the infant sprouted up like a morning glory, unfurling and speedily blooming into a toddler by way of a magic she could not even begin to understand.

The baby, still half-infant, blinked and breathed and wiggled in the spirit's grip, staring up at the silvery, grinning creature whose magic conducted this affair. It burbled and laughed and hiccupped in a tempo faster than that of normal life, and Corvina tried to catch her breath on the sand. The magic did not appear to be hurting the infant-thing, so she did not speak. Darkness crept in at the corners of her vision.

The spirit grinned like a cat who'd caught the fattest fish in the pond, the glowing magic poured from his hands into the baby, and Corvina began to slip into unconsciousness.

"Grow on, grow on," hummed the spirit to the child. "Grow on, grow up, you ugly thing, and away to my lady I'll take you to be a Frankish boy . . ."

Corvina's eyes slid heavily shut, overcome by her exhaustion.

Lightning struck the sand at the spirit's back.

"*Aurael,*" intoned a voice like heavenly thunder. "*What have you done?*"

The spirit nearly jumped from his skin, hastily steadying the child in his hands and halting the process to turn and look.

A tall, bald-headed man stood behind him on the sand, looking down his nose at Aurael. When he moved, lightning-bright patterns and sigils danced over his dark skin, gleaming from his round skull and reflecting in the dark depths of his eyes. He was impossibly handsome, and more imperious than any lord of men. He wore a garment with tailored shoulders and straight-legged trousers, pale, pin-thin stripes running vertically throughout the fabric.

The silver-blue spirit held the toddler in his hands like a half-eaten sandwich and stared up at the King of the Faeries.

"My lord," he breathed emphatically through a wide, plastered grin. "How nice to see you . . . So unexpected!"

"*Aurael,*" boomed the king, barely moving his lips. "*You are much discovered, spirit. Speak truth now and your punishment—though inevitable—will be less harsh. What have you done?*"

"Done, my lord? I have not done—"

"*DO NOT PLAY THIS GAME,*" bellowed Ouberan, grabbing the spirit hard by the throat. The half-toddler, still in Aurael's arms, began to cry again.

"My lord! I did this for you, my lord, all for you! Let me explain!"

The mutated infant bawled, and the Faerie King stared at it a moment. He released Aurael, who slumped, coughing, on the white sand, and took the child from him, studying it carefully.

"*What is this,*" asked Ouberan flatly.

"A mortal child, born of this woman here and a mortal man on a ship at the bottom of the sea," gagged Aurael, touching his throat tenderly.

Ouberan turned the sniffling infant over the way one might turn a broadside or a news pamphlet over, to glance at it from all sides. "*It is hideous. Not all mortals are this hideous,*" said the king. Aurael sat up, clearing his throat violently.

"Yes, indeed, my lord, for I have not done fixing it yet," he piped up. "I was speeding it up a bit that it may resemble better the Frankish boy my lady has adopted and would raise in her train. Thus, we can change that boy for this boy here, and you will have the lovely Frankish boy, and she will have this changeling."

The King of Faeries made a low sound of contemplation, which distracted the oddly-shaped infant from its sniffling and made it look up at him in curiosity, its hand in its mouth.

*"Aurael,"* began Ouberan, *"How am I to be sure that once you have worked your magic you will not give me this changeling and leave the real boy to my wife?"*

He widened his eyes. "My lord! I had not even thought of that!" he protested in soft, earnest tones. He paused. "I do not suppose you would be so easily fooled," he observed, tapping his finger to his mouth. "My lord is much too clever to be wooed by such illusions as I, a lowly air sprite, might muster . . ."

*"But my wife . . . ?"* prompted Ouberan, with interest.

Aurael shook his head heartily, his flyaway hair bouncing. "Oh, my lord Ouberan, your wife would be as easily fooled as a sheep to give suck to a lamb that is actually a goat's kid. Or vice versa. Or a cuckoo to nest the wrong eggs. Or a dachshund to mother a Great Dane!"

Ouberan smiled like moonrise—silver-white and perfectly aligned. He chuckled a little, looked down at the deformed child in his hands, and laughed a little more. Then he looked at Aurael, held up the baby, and guffawed to his heart's content, and Aurael laughed his own broken-glass wind-chime laugh.

Then lightning struck the airy spirit's feet, and Aurael shrieked and shot backward across the sand, grabbing for his singed toes.

Ouberan was not laughing anymore. He glared down at Aurael, his eyes full of anger and insult.

*"Aurael,"* growled the King, *"You are hereby exiled from our realms to this island indefinitely for the plotting of treason against myself and the queen, for insulting my wife's intelligence, and for sticking your turned-up nose where it doesn't belong."*

"What!" Aurael squealed, pig-like, and scuttled back further in the sand. "But you can't! I was trying to help! I wanted to help you, my lord!"

*"I think you wanted a promotion. In fact, I really don't doubt that part of it,"* said Ouberan with a sigh, lowering the toddler-sized

baby down to its mother's sleeping arms. *"But really, Aurael, you should know better than this. You shouldn't have tried to get involved before anyone asked you to."*

"But no one was going to ask me to!" protested the air sprite. "No one ever asks me!"

*"Exactly,"* growled Ouberan, advancing on him. *"You're selfish and cannot be trusted. You always pick the wrong battles, and look where it's got you now. A lovely desert island with a mortal woman and a misshapen, magic-molded baby."*

Aurael's brain raced. He could beg and sob and play the tragic card while the king was still here, and then as soon as he'd left the island, Aurael would simply run. Run away, far away, and never return. Easy. Banishment was a blessing, he thought darkly, as he allowed tears to begin to shine in his large pale eyes.

*"Now hold still,"* said Ouberan, reaching for him with an arm that seemed to stretch infinitely.

"No, my lord, please, please don't—"

*"I said, HOLD STILL."*

Aurael squirmed, but could not slip through the Faerie Lord's fingers. "I beg you, Lord, don't—" He made a squishing, squawking sound when the king's hand closed around his throat. "HfngAK! . . . pleeeease," he croaked as Ouberan walked, carrying him by the throat. "What . . . gughhfk . . . my king, please!"

Ouberan stopped walking at last, holding Aurael up by the neck, the air sprite's pale hands clutching and clawing at the king's, to no avail. His gleaming eyes leveled with Aurael's, and Aurael felt the rough bark of a tree dig into his back.

*"Welcome to your own private island, Aurael,"* said the king. *"If you're very, very good, and I'm in a better mood, perhaps I'll change my mind later and let you out."*

"Good?" gasped Aurael, "You mean, quiet?"

"*That's precisely what I mean,*" purred Ouberan, his smile cold. "*Very, very quiet.*"

"But King Ouberan," sputtered the air sprite. "If I'm very, very quiet, how will you know if I'm very, very good? If I'm quiet, won't you just . . . forget about me?"

Ouberan's smile widened, and Aurael felt his last little burst of craftiness slip out of him like water from a drainpipe.

"*Perhaps I will,*" agreed the King of the Faeries. "*Perhaps I will forget all about you. Goodbye, Aurael.*"

"No, no, my lord! My—"

Ouberan pushed Aurael against the tree trunk hard, and there was a tearing sound like a sail slashed apart by a sharp and jagged blade. Aurael squeezed his eyes shut and screamed. It was an exquisite, splintering pain, and he felt as though he'd been shoved into a coffin too small for even his slender form.

As the throbs of pain subsided gradually, he opened his eyes. The king had vanished. A little ways down the beach, he could see the prone form of the woman and the smaller form of the child, both sleeping soundly. The sun was rising to the east, painting the island in strange, rosy colors. It was a peaceful scene.

Aurael moved toward the mother and child. He'd wake her and force her to undo whatever his lord had done. Surely she had some power left, even if it killed her to do it—he stopped, finding that he hadn't moved at all. He was still exactly where he was. He could see everything around him, but there was a hard boundary between himself and the world that he could not understand.

The tearing sound jangled in the echoes of his mind.

*The tree.*

Aurael threw himself against the hard, invisible wall, clawed at it, screaming in a frenzied fury. It was no use. He was trapped.

# CHAPTER SIXTEEN

Bastiano jerked awake, the sudden motion paralyzing him with pain for a searing moment. He relaxed, trying not to groan aloud. *Where am I?* Pain ran all the way through his limbs, sharp and throbbing, and he felt the sting of open cuts on his face and hands. He was covered in dirt, leaves, and broken branches.

*Where is Tor?* Bastiano tasted the dirt in his mouth, coughing. He tried again to sit up, and some of the leaves slid away from his face. He looked up at the base of a massive hill, a steep incline reaching up to the sky, covered heavily in greenery. *Gods! What a fall,* Bastiano thought to himself, feeling lightheaded and sinking back. His shoulder throbbed with pain.

"Bas," coughed a voice from nearby. "Are you all right?"

"Tor!" Bastiano turned over onto his side, looking for Torsione. "I'm here!"

"What happened?" Tor was a few arm's lengths away, swiping at the debris that covered him. "Did we lose it?"

"Lose it?" Bastiano paused, breathing hard. *The harpy.* He shuddered. It had flown at them, picked them up, and tossed them like empty purses. They had run from it as it taunted them until they fell down the cliff, where it had apparently left them for dead. "Yes, I think we lost it," Bastiano winced, crawling through his agony toward Tor.

"Are you hurt?" Torsione's cheek was stained with blood from where the harpy, or the fall, had cut him. His eyes were cloudy.

"Yes, but not badly," Bastiano lied. "Your face—!"

"It doesn't hurt," Tor said, and let his head drop back onto the ground.

"Maybe it thinks we're dead." Bastiano pulled himself closer across the rustling leaves.

"It's a harpy, Bas. Harpies live on carrion. It's out there somewhere, waiting. It wants us to think we're safe."

"Aren't they basically extinct? I thought they hadn't been seen in decades."

"They haven't. I heard of one once in the Chineh mountains, but it was old and feeble, according to the locals. Not like this one." Tor paused. "I don't think we're going to survive this."

"Don't say that. We're alive, now." Bastiano moved some more of the leaves away from Torsione's face and neck, furrowing his brow at the cuts.

"And for how much longer, Bas? We have no food, no fresh water, no weapons, no help, and a gigantic harpy that's going to eat us. And we're injured." Torsione shook his head stiffly. "This certainly isn't as lucky a day as we thought it was."

Bastiano pulled himself to an upright position, despite the screaming of protest in his arms, and continued clearing the debris from Torsione's prone form.

"I won't let us go down without a fight," Bastiano said through gritted teeth. "It's not so bad. It'd be much worse if we were apart."

"I don't know about that," Tor replied. "I think you'd have a much easier time hiding from that thing without me slowing you up."

"Your ankle will be fine. It just needs time."

"I'm not talking about my ankle, I'm talking about the fact that we just fell down this cliff here," Tor said sharply, then exhaled. "Bas, I'm not sure . . . I don't know if I can walk anymore."

Bastiano moved a larger branch from across Torsione's legs and saw from the angle that one of them was almost certainly broken. His chest tightened even further, and his throat threatened to close up with terror.

"I can make a splint. Out of sticks and my shirt." Bastiano couldn't look away from the broken leg. The cloth of Tor's trousers was stained even darker with blood.

"Bas, you're not a field nurse, stop acting like one. You're going to have to leave me. You have to find some kind of shelter. There must be food on the island somewhere, fruit trees or something. We keep hearing birds. They must survive on something. You can survive on them, if you catch one."

"Stop talking like that." Bastiano heard his own voice harden. "I am going to keep you alive. I'll take you with me. We can do this together."

"Bas, you've got to be realistic," Tor snapped, looking up at him in frustration. "I'm not going to make it, but you've got a good shot at it, if only you'd—"

"No. I am not listening to this—"

"Bas, please, don't be ridiculous, I'm—"

"No, no, I'm not listening, you great idiot, shut up—"

"But Bas, if we both slow down to my speed, the harpy will find us. If you go, you have a better shot at surviving, that's a raw fact; just go, for heaven's sake—"

"No!" Bastiano roared, "I am not going to leave you here, Torsione, I can't live without you."

For a moment, Tor stared up at him with wide, suspicious blue eyes under a deeply furrowed brow. Bastiano's heart pounded so hard he thought his chest would burst. *Well, now I've done it,* he thought weakly, and drew a shaky breath.

"I-I can't do this without you," he stammered. His words tumbled out of him like ripe apples from a tree. "You have to stay alive, we have to find a way to survive together, Tor. I love you. I have loved you since you first rolled your eyes at me at court when we were boys. This life has no meaning for me if you are not there. I have lost everything, everything except you, Tor. I will do anything to survive this, as long as I survive it with you. Now stop being a child and let me make your splint." He finished with a huff, unthinkably embarrassed. He had never intended this confession to happen, let alone happen like that.

Torsione was silent. Bastiano felt the flush of heat across his own cheeks and found that he had no more words left. He made several frustrated attempts to tear one of his shirt sleeves into strips for bandages.

"Bas."

Bastiano kept pulling on the fabric, using his teeth now to try and leverage the rip.

"Bas," Torsione repeated quietly.

He avoided Tor's gaze and finally coaxed the sleeve into tearing twice more, unevenly, but well enough to use as ties. He began looking around for a branch flat enough to serve as a splint.

"Bastiano!" said Tor, sounding pained.

"What?" He turned sharply, feeling defensiveness boiling up into his throat.

"Why didn't you tell me?" Torsione sounded apologetic— ashamed, even. His expression was deadly serious.

"How could I?" Bas whispered, the blazing heat of his defense melting into shyness. "How could I even consider telling you that? Every time you went away and came back home, there were new stories, new conquests, new marriage deals broken by your untamable personality. How could I even think that it would mean anything at all to you, if I said that out loud?"

Torsione closed his eyes. *He's revolted by me,* thought Bas weakly. *It doesn't matter. I have to help him.* "I need to find good sticks for your splint."

"Bas, wait," Torsione opened his eyes. "I'm in pain, but it may not be that bad."

"You just said you don't think you can walk," Bas countered.

"Just . . . pull up my trouser leg and see if the bone's sticking out," commanded Tor, wincing as he tried to adjust his position on the ground. "If it isn't, we can keep going in search of shelter. The good news is that my ankle doesn't hurt anymore." He looked at Bas, the faintest twinkle passing through his gaze.

Bastiano carefully rolled back the fabric from Tor's leg. The blood and dirt were like stains on a napkin after a particularly messy feast, and it turned Bas' stomach a little. *What do I do?* he thought. *I'm not a medic.* There was no bone sticking out, but the angle did not look quite right.

Tor lifted his head. "How bad is it?" he asked quietly.

Bastiano swallowed. "Not bad. That is . . . it doesn't look broken."

"Are you sure?"

Bastiano nodded, then shook his head and looked back at Tor. "I can't tell," he confessed, "I don't know. It may not be so bad. We have to be very careful with it, but we can't just stay here. How does the rest of you feel?" he hurried on, looking him over.

Tor exhaled slowly and tried to move again. "Tired, in a lot of pain, but not dead," he admitted, reaching for Bas' arm for support.

Bastiano moved to help him sit up, but gasped sharply as his left shoulder flared with pain, and let go. Tor caught his own fall and helped himself the rest of the way upright, his expression filled with concern.

"What is it?" Tor asked, his hands already carefully exploring his friend's arm.

Bastiano winced and recoiled a little. "My shoulder, it's . . ."

"Dislocated," said Tor with a frown. He took a firm but careful grasp. "I can fix it. Done this before."

"No, it's fine, I . . . " Bastiano trailed off, gazing back at him. "It'll hurt, won't it?"

"Oh, yes. A great deal," said Torsione levelly. "But it will hurt worse if I don't fix it."

"Your leg, my shoulder. What are we coming to?" he mumbled weakly, his heart stammering against his chest.

"Close your eyes."

He obeyed.

"Try not to cry out," Tor added at the last second. "The harpy thinks we're dead."

Bastiano opened his eyes in alarm, but Tor smiled at him, and he felt a piece of himself relax instantly.

"I'm joking," Torsione said, his voice low. He smoothed his hand up the side of Bastiano's bare arm. Bastiano felt flares of warmth as Tor gently moved his other hand over his shoulder, his mouth dry as he looked back at him in disbelief. Tor's eyes were steady, his expression calm and knowing as he leaned toward him. Bastiano's breath came short as his heart pounded harder, and his eyelids fluttered shut in anticipation.

There was a sudden pressure, something clicked loudly back into place, and the pain vanished. "Oh," said Bastiano, and looked at his shoulder in surprise. "Was that it?"

"Yes," Tor chuckled, and sighed. "The look on your face!"

"That's not funny!" exclaimed Bastiano, completely astonished that it had been so easy, so painless. "What on earth is wrong with you?" He recoiled instinctively, feeling the strength return to his arm.

"You big buffoon," murmured Torsione, shaking his head as his pale eyes traveled over Bastiano's face. "You should have told me sooner."

Bastiano flushed. "I thought I was rather obvious on more than one occasion," he admitted breathlessly.

"I baited you so many times, and you never bit."

"How could I?" Bastiano echoed his earlier sentiment. "You are this . . . legend of romantic triumph. I'm just me. I thought you'd laugh at me, tell me it was a phase. Or worse."

"Worse? Tell you it was unholy?" Tor's blue eyes flickered, his mouth becoming a firmer line. "Never, Bas. And I'd never laugh at you, either. At least, not unless you let me. And you are not 'just you,' you are exactly you. You know you're my oldest friend and greatest companion. And if I'd have known this—"

"You don't have to say anything else," Bas interrupted, looking down, his cheeks burning. "It's all right. We're friends."

Torsione took his chin and lifted it firmly again. "We are friends," he agreed. "But you have saved my life in more ways than you know. You have no idea what I think. What I feel." He paused. "Do you think it's a phase?" he asked quietly.

"No," choked Bastiano, his hand grasping Tor's reflexively. "No, heavens, no. It's—it's just you, Tor."

Torsione nodded. "Good. Because I haven't been breaking off engagements with princesses and duchesses for nothing, you know."

Bastiano's heart leapt. *Everything could really turn out all right,* he thought, ecstatic. He opened his mouth to speak, then closed it again.

"So. How about that splint, then?" Tor chuckled, lifting one eyebrow.

*HOW ABOUT NOT?*

The explosion of wind and noise threw them apart, sending them spinning away from one another like pieces of a house picked up and redistributed violently by a tornado. Bastiano landed hard on his stomach and gasped for air. Leaves whirled and rocks flew past him. He lifted his head, squinting against the onslaught of debris, and saw the harpy standing where he'd just been, walking with black clawed feet toward Torsione's crumpled body.

"No!" Bastiano bellowed, scrambling to his feet.

The harpy smiled at him and lifted Torsione in its talons. *DON'T WORRY. YOU'LL BE NEXT.* It beat its wings twice and soared upward, into the sky over the trees, vanishing with a smell of burnt metal and lightning.

# Chapter Seventeen

Mira had never dreamed her father's history would be so astonishing. Gonzo told them the tale of the midwife, a woman who came from Algyrs, near Tunitz, but had traveled all across the sea and the great nations to make her living helping women with their births.

"She was dark-skinned," Gonzo said, "and covered in intricate tattoos, and her eyes were pale blue. Dante had employed her to help the duchess give birth, but had other plans for her as well.

"At first the courtiers whispered that Duke Dante must certainly be having an affair with her, an average dalliance while his wife was abed with her swollen belly. But there were other things, too. Several times, I witnessed the duke levitating objects or burning papers with a flame that appeared from his bare hand. The duke often cheerfully wrote it off as a malfunction of my optical cortex, but it was nothing of the sort. I was certain."

When Mira was born, and Sophia passed away, Dante got rid of the midwife. No one quite knew how, but Gonzo—whose business was to know many things that he did not divulge freely within the court—had seen her taken from the palace by guards, and it was a safe bet she had been disposed of or sent to a colony as slave labor. Whatever happened to the midwife, Dante began his downward spiral into the beginnings of madness. He remained unseen for days on end, barely eating any meals brought to his chambers, and would not attend council meetings or courtly events.

"At the behest of the king, I attempted to find out what Dante was doing in the workshop, but it was challenging. Dante was adept at making sure his comings and goings went unnoticed. It wasn't until Torsione, the duke's brother, broke into the workshop that the truth of the matter was discovered: Dante was exploring black magicks, with a heavy influence on possessing power over life and death." Mira's heart pounded, and Ferran frowned deeply.

"But that's absurd!" he exclaimed. "Insane, even."

"Yes, indeed. The king was sure that the loss of his wife had driven Dante mad, and banished him to a colony for an indeterminate time. He sent Dante away with servants to keep an eye on him and his young child, along with a great many books unrelated to his dark arts, and some supplies. A week after the ship departed, word reached the king that it had gone down in a storm, a terrible tempest, and all souls had been lost, according to the ship trackers the Royal Aeronauts used."

"There was a great storm," Mira recalled, "and the ship did go down, but we were brought safely to shore. I remember my father standing on the beach with his book and his staff, speaking to the winds and the water for hours. I remember waiting what felt like an eternity for him to finish, and the next thing I knew, we had a very comfortable cave filled with books and my father's little inventions. We had food, supplies, and a hearth. It was quite comfortable. I never asked how it all happened, because I knew he would not tell me." She looked from Ferran to Gonzo again. "He is protective of his magic."

"So he is, indeed. We were all quite sure that you had both perished," finished Gonzo. "If we had been given any indication that you might have survived, there would have been a great search party dispatched. The king loved your father as a brother, long ago."

Ferran looked utterly exhausted. "It's so extraordinary," He shook his head. "This is an impossible coincidence."

"Now you know," Gonzo said simply, still looking at Mira. "You must do what you can to keep Prince Ferran safe. Do you understand? If his father has drowned, as it is believed, then he is the heir to the Civitelli line, and must return to Neapolis to ascend the throne. The threats of war from Arthens and abroad will not stop simply because the king is dead. There are innocent lives to protect."

From the corner of her eye, she saw Ferran turn to look at her, but Mira did not meet his gaze for several moments. She sat turning it all over in her mind, studying Gonzo's round brass face and glowing eyes.

"Are you all right?" Ferran's voice was gentle.

"What happened after he was exiled?" Mira said abruptly. "After he left?"

Gonzo nodded once. "His younger brother, Torsione, was given the dukedom, in addition to his already significant contributions as a courtier, council advisor, and diplomat. Even when they were younger men, Dante was studious, where Torsione was charming. In fact, Torsione was the one who initially thought that Dante's mourning was beginning to seem unusual, noting that his brother kept peculiar hours and did not take care of his duties as duke. When Dante heard that Torsione was informing the king of his movements and strange studies, Dante challenged him, but the king would not allow it. That was the beginning of the decision to exile him."

Ferran shook his head. "It's all so terrible," he said. "I can't believe it."

Mira exhaled slowly. "I think I can."

"Is he really like that?"

"Yes." Mira's jaw tightened. "He's cold. He cares only for himself. I keep well out of his way, now that I'm older."

"But what about when you were younger? He must have taken care of you then?"

Mira paused, thinking back. "No . . . It's so strange. I don't exactly remember, except that it feels as though he had help of some kind."

"Like a nanny? A governess? Perhaps one of the servants survived."

"There are no signs that anyone else was with us." Mira's gaze grew cloudy. "But the point is, he doesn't love anything. Least of all, me. He must have loved my mother very much, to have her death twist his mind so completely, but now, there's nothing left of that."

"Child, you must understand," Gonzo said gently. "You were never intended to be raised unassisted on a desert island. Your ship was headed for a colony, one with a great deal of people and some comforts of home. No, this shipwreck was not meant to take place. Had your father been sentenced to death, they would not have sent you, too. You would have had a home, at court."

"I am not a child," said Mira, her words hard. Then she stood up. "We shouldn't just sit around here." She gestured at Gonzo. "We can hide you, but if we're to try and fix your legs, we'll need more tools. I will go back for the other trunks, and in the morning, I will dive again and see what's left on the bottom." She looked at Ferran for the first time, noting the strange mixture of pity, apology, and confusion on his face. "What?"

"This must be so difficult . . . shouldn't you probably take some time to think this over?" Ferran looked away politely. "We can go get the rest of the tools and trunks tomorrow, if you'd like. I'm so sorry."

Mira studied him, squeezing the carved spear in her hand, then lifted her chin. "I don't know what you think of me," she replied levelly, "but I don't need time to think this over. I'm very capable of taking care of myself. And now I have to take care of both of you, too." She felt her chest tighten in a way she wasn't used to. "Stay here," she added curtly, and started walking back toward the beach and the copse of trees where they'd left the other luggage. She was out of sight before either Gonzo or Ferran could say anything in reply.

*My father grew cruel and cold because my mother died . . . that night with Karaburan—he acted as though he'd barely even noticed what was really going on.*

Mira didn't realize she was holding her breath until she was several strides beyond the clearing. She exhaled too quickly, feeling dizziness rush to her head, and her vision blurred. On the one hand, it didn't seem so bad—at least her father had a reason for his passion.

*None of this would have happened if my mother had lived.*

Tears stung her eyes as she tried to catch her breath, but she did not slow down, the carved spear tight in one hand as she moved rapidly through the trees. Her determined strides slowed by and by, and she felt a sob bubble up in her chest. She paused, feeling very small, blinking her way through the tears. She drew a deeper breath, smelling the cool air coming up from the beach ahead of her. The shadows lengthened as the evening wore on. Once it got dark, she would have to return to the treehouse and keep an eye on Ferran and Gonzo. *I have to keep them safe.*

*Why? Why should I care?* she pondered. *Because they need me to survive. Well, perhaps not Gonzo. He's metal. But Ferran can't live without my help, not here . . . and if my father finds him, it will all be over. I'm risking my neck for them now. We'll all be in danger if he finds out about them. They need me to survive, and if I don't help them, I'll never see another human being as long as I live.*

The trees and shrubs grew thinner along the path as she emerged onto the higher dunes overlooking the shore, the sky beginning to turn brilliant shades of coral against the darkening blue. Mira made her way toward the clearing where they'd left the trunks, but as they came into view, she stopped short and dropped into a defensive crouch.

A huge tiger stood on the sand, her large head lowered to sniff warily at the leather trunks, long tail flicking from side to side occasionally.

*The tiger!* she thought, her pulse racing. *Karaburan was right all along!*

The beast was massive, her pelt a rich orange with thick, inky black stripes all over and perfect white spots behind each dark ear. Mira rose cautiously to one knee.

She watched, her heart pounding in her chest, as the tiger pawed gently at the trunks, sniffing at them halfheartedly, each movement as smooth and heavy as the ocean's tide. Then the tiger turned and looked right at her, as though she had known Mira was there all along.

The tiger's eyes were a shocking, but somehow familiar, pale blue.

Mira felt her breath catch as she stared back at the huge cat, frozen to the spot. She could almost certainly not outrun the tiger, and she was not strong enough to take her on if she were to pounce at her. She was, for the first time in perhaps a very long time, utterly at a loss for what to do next.

The tiger looked at her, her whiskers twitching as she caught Mira's scent on the air. Beyond the dunes, the waves crashed against the shoreline, and farther off, the birds gave their dying cries of evening over the sea. The weight of the tiger's stare bore down on her. Mira felt a tremor build in her left arm, as she forced herself to stillness.

Suddenly, the tiger broke her gaze and looked away, as though she had heard someone calling her name. Then she looked back at Mira and took several heavy, graceful steps toward her over the warm sand, stopping just out of reach.

Mira had encountered larger fish and dolphins briefly before on her swims, as well as the occasional shark. But this was by far the largest predator she'd been within range of in her entire life.

*She doesn't seem interested in attacking,* Mira thought in surprise. *If we'd met when I was still a child, though . . . there's no telling.*

The tiger flicked her tail idly and turned in a lazy circle, as though she would lie down. As she turned, Mira saw something strange in the thick striped fur. For a moment, the black stripes changed shapes, shifting and morphing as she watched. A definite pattern of shapes almost like glyphs or runes materialized, but when the tiger stopped turning, the stripes were nothing but stripes once more.

*What was that?* she thought, unsure of whether she could trust her sight. *I shouldn't leave Ferran alone too long,* she realized, wondering how long this stalemate had gone on, and how long it might continue. *If my father catches him . . .*

As if on cue, the tiger gave a huge, lazy yawn, showing off massive teeth and a wide pink tongue. Then she licked her whiskers and padded away as disinterestedly as though Mira had not been standing there all along.

Her heart thumped in her chest, but as soon as the tiger was out of range, Mira rushed forward and gathered the first two trunks. She made her way back up into the forest, her hands trembling from her giddy thoughts.

*The look on Ferran's face when I tell him there's a tiger! I bet he's never seen one, either. She was so beautiful . . .*

Mira's head snapped up as a cry of alarm rang out ahead of her in the trees. She dropped the luggage and bolted forward, spear at the ready. As she neared the treehouse, she slowed, ducking off to the side of the thin trail and peering through large ferns.

Ferran lay on the ground, groaning.

Her father loomed over him.

"Please," Ferran said, his voice clear despite his obvious discomfort. "I've done nothing wrong."

"Sins of the father, sins of the flesh," said Dante, holding the magic staff in his right hand as regally as any king. "Don't worry yourself too much about what you have or haven't done, my boy. It won't matter much longer."

"Please, stop, I mean no harm to you, sir!" Ferran pleaded. "I washed up ashore and have been looking for food and water all day . . . I didn't know anyone lived here until I found this," he lied, gesturing to the treehouse.

"A handsome little liar," Dante mused coldly. He advanced on Ferran, even as the boy scrambled backward in the dirt.

"Please, I have nothing! I have lost everyone. My father and uncle drowned in the shipwreck!"

Dante smiled then, and Mira shuddered. "Don't be so pessimistic, boy," Dante advised with a dry, reedy chuckle. "You haven't lost everything yet. Your father's still alive. For now."

Ferran's face went white. Mira took it as a cue and leaped into the clearing, spear pointed at her father.

"Stop this!" Mira commanded. Dante turned lazily over his shoulder.

"Daughter, you will stay out of this," he said calmly.

"No, I will not," she retorted, grinding her teeth at his tone. Rage began to fill the pit of her stomach. *After all this time, after all that's happened, he's to blame.* "Let him go."

"Why on earth do you care, you ungrateful child?" Dante asked, suddenly interested, turning away from Ferran completely to face her, his ragged cloak swirling like clouds in his wake. He laughed coldly at her. "You've only just met him, haven't you?"

"The first human I've ever met that wasn't insane or a rapist?" Mira's voice echoed back at her from the trees as she raised her volume. "Trust me. I care." Her eyes narrowed. "Let him go."

"You knew this moment would come since you first took him in," Dante said, pursing his lips. "You knew that I would find him, and still you did it. You probably even knew I would do something terrible to him when I found him." His smile returned for a moment. "You were right, daughter. I'm going to kill him. They will die for what they've done. It is destined."

Ferran threw Mira a terrified look, but she did not back down from her father's gaze, just as she had not backed down from the tiger's strange blue eyes. She pointed the spear at him like an accusatory finger.

"Your books speak of laws and justices and judges and rules. You are no law, no justice. You are a man, as is he. He deserves no punishment, least of all death at your hands. This is madness."

"The threat of insanity bears little meaning when you have already passed the point of no return," shrugged Dante, and turned back toward Ferran, who had uneasily gotten to his feet.

Before Mira could move, Dante swiped the air with one hand, his fingers trailing symbols in fire, and Ferran went flying across the clearing, slamming into the base of the tree that held up Mira's shelter. Dante drew closer, raising both arms like a fisherman raising a net, and Ferran was dragged upward into the air, groaning in pain.

Mira lunged, sliding her hands down toward the base of her spear and swinging it like a bat, the broad shaft connecting with Dante's side. There was a crack like thunder, and he staggered sideways, bellowing in anger. Mira spun the spear again and struck his hand, making him drop his staff. She advanced on him, but he turned and flung a hand at her, throwing her backward several feet. Her own spear went flying. The stone spearhead broke clean off the shaft and vanished into the bushes.

"Mira, don't!" yelled Ferran, from above.

Dante flung his other hand up at Ferran and gestured. The prince fell and hit the ground hard with a shout.

"Stop this now!" Mira cried, regaining her balance and straining against the magical grip her father trapped her in. Her hands balled into fists, and she pressed hard against the invisible force.

"You will not interfere!" Dante cried, looking simultaneously furious and incredulous that she fought back. A great wind kicked up all around them, and the smell of lightning burned in Mira's nostrils. "You cannot stop what is already in motion."

"No," agreed Mira, pressing harder, "but I can slow you down!"

Something snapped, and Mira soared forward like a stone from a slingshot. Dante snatched at his staff and made a sharp gesture at Ferran, and with a bellowed word that Mira did not recognize, both her father and Ferran were gone. She hit the ground, tumbling forward on the rough earth, and lay on her back, gasping for air.

"Gonzo," she gasped, sitting up. "Gonzo?" She got to her feet, her bones thrumming and her palms tingling from the fall. "Gonzo!" She searched the bushes at the edge of the clearing for the metal man and, after a few moments, found him.

Gonzo had been torn into two large pieces. Some of his wiring and innards had spilled out, shining on the dark ground. His eye-lights had only a residual dim glow to them, and his jaw appeared to be unhinged. It was as though he had fallen from a great height, or been hit with something very heavy. His legs lay under a fern several feet away.

"Gonzo?" Mira knelt, her body still trembling from the skirmish. *Ferran will be devastated.* "Gonzo, please . . ." She tried to turn him over, but his broken insides clanked and tinkled like a chandelier in pieces, so she stopped. "I'm sorry," she said help-lessly. *He's only made of metal,* she reminded herself. *Maybe he can be repaired.*

She gathered him up into a pile and took him up to the tree-house bit by bit, carefully laying him out in the shape he once had been. She went down again to check for any last cogs or coils, and saw her spear lying on the ground where it had fallen, now missing its stone point. Glad it was not otherwise damaged or missing, she moved to recover it.

As she grasped the wood, lightning seared through her body. The etchings on the staff illuminated in brilliant blue-white, and she felt her own vision go bright-hot and blind. Hot pain seared her palms, and at the same time, a sensation of beautiful strength and ease swept over her. Power coursed through her as powerfully as an eagle in flight, soaring effortlessly through the air. At last, the blindness passed and the burning evaporated, and Mira gasped for air again and staggered backward a step. She stared at the stick in her hands.

*This isn't my spear,* she thought, her mind full of thunder and rolling clouds as she turned the stick back and forth. It was like her spear, tall and hefty, with careful and deliberate carvings all over it. But unlike her spear, this staff made her palm warm as she held it, and buzzed with something unseen when she let go and shifted it to the other hand and back again.

"His staff," she whispered aloud, realizing. She had never been allowed near it, even when she was a child, and her father had never explained why it was forbidden. Was it because of this? Did he know this terrible feeling would come to her if she held it? Mira shivered.

"Now what do I do?" she breathed.

There was a cold breeze that made her skin prickle, and a voice answered her: "Command me how you will, my master, I am—oh!"

Mira turned, brandishing the staff as she would her own spear. A youthful man stood in the clearing, his features handsome and blue-tinted, with windswept hair, and a translucent and half-complete body, like a painting unfinished. He stared at her as though he could not believe his eyes.

"No," he breathed, a powerful, desperate sound of hope. "It can't be!"

"What are you?" Mira demanded. "Where did you come from?"

The bluish man fell to his knees, his palms up in supplication. "I am your humble, loving servant," he cried rapturously, "Aurael!"

# CHAPTER EIGHTEEN

## 1869

Aurael curled up on a smooth patch of stone still warm from the heat of the day, tucking his long tail around him and pricking his triangular ears toward Mira, who lay on the grass a little ways away, reading some book or other. He found himself taking on all sorts of different animal shapes lately: hound, bear cub, goose, pig, and now, a cat. In any shape, Aurael would follow Mira about and keep an eye on her from day to day. Occasionally, she would play along with him, riding on the bear cub's back or chasing the pig around until he squealed.

There were other days—like today—where he felt somewhat invisible to her, as though he were not chief of all things on her mind. He doted on her, even on the days where she seemed not to notice him. Those days were far too frequent of late, and he found his best option was to be an animal when near her, or she wouldn't even notice him. If he spoke as a formless voice on the wind, she did not hear, and if he shaped himself as a man, she did not see him. She only saw the animals, and that worried him. He didn't understand what caused it, though, and so he carried on, trying constantly to win her affection and attention as different beasts and birds.

"Mira," called her father from just inside the cave. "Bring that book in. I don't want that one in the dirt."

"I'm almost done with this part," Mira replied, with a smile. "I'll bring it in again in just a moment."

"Mira!" Dante moved to the mouth of the cave, his eyes like dark clouds. "I will not repeat myself."

"Father, I am so close to the end of this chapter," his daughter pleaded, sitting up on the grass with her long legs splayed. The dress from her childhood she had long outgrown, and now she wore its torn and repurposed remains as a bodice of sorts, with her skirt comprised of sailcloth and burlap and linen. "Please, please let me finish reading, Father!"

Dante hesitated, and the cat Aurael watched the tension in his master's jaw shift in thought. Then Dante set his mouth in a firm line. "Do not tarry too long," he commanded brusquely. "Finish your reading and replace it on the shelf as soon as you can. If you linger, I will be displeased," he added, moving off into the cave again with a begrudging frown.

Aurael lay his head back down, watching lazy dragonflies circle in the air above Mira, who began reading again. *He does love his child,* Aurael thought to himself. *I'll give him that much. It's not so bad, being his slave. If he loves Mira that much, he's sure to set me free eventually.* He yawned with his tiny cat jowls and closed his eyes. *Especially if I convince her to beg him for it.*

"Mira, Mira, Mira, Mira!"

Aurael's eyes snapped open. Mira sat up as the misshapen beast Karaburan came crashing through the ferns, startling a few birds and banishing the dragonflies. Cats cannot frown, but Aurael tried to anyway.

"Kabu? What is it?" Mira closed the book.

"I had the most terrible dream!" Karaburan cowered like a frightened dog, his head lowered, shoulders trembling. Aurael hated the sight of him, but it was unavoidable that Mira was fond of the fish-skinned creature.

"Come here, it's all right," Mira coaxed, and Karaburan crept forward and sat in a huddled heap nearby, his face in his six-fingered hands.

"It was horrible," he groaned, shuddering.

"It's over, now," Mira said, gently patting Karaburan's bulky shoulder. "You're safe, all is well. There's nothing to be frightened of."

*Funny*, thought Aurael. *The maiden comforting the monster. I didn't send him that nightmare; he must have had one all on his own.*

Aurael enjoyed crafting detailed and sumptuous dreams for Karaburan, usually involving the long-dead witch Corvina as well as elements of torture and deception. He didn't do it very often, but when he did, the dreams were expertly executed and utterly horrifying, unlike the beautiful dreams he gave Mira.

Her nights' visions were filled with soaring through the clouds on wings of her own, or swimming to the depths of the sea with whales, or climbing highest mountains with nimble-footed goats. Mira's imagination was well-equipped to take on its own adventures in the dreams, once he gave her the gentle nudge to do so; Karaburan's mind was so weak that Aurael felt like a play actor, performing and strutting through those visions with gusto and fury.

"I feel so awful," fretted Karaburan, his teeth chattering. "I never want to sleep again!"

Mira shook her head. "Don't overreact, Kabu. You'll sleep again, and you'll sleep soundly. One bad dream does not cause all dreams to become bad dreams. There are always good dreams and bad dreams. It's really going to be all right. Besides, if you realize that it's a dream while you're dreaming it, you can do anything!"

"Anything?" echoed Karaburan, dubiously.

"Yes. I fly sometimes in my dreams. You only have to realize you're dreaming, and then you can take control. I fly over mountains and deserts and cities and oceans."

"But there are no cities except in those books you showed me," Karaburan said, furrowing his brow. "There is nothing out there but our island." He hugged his legs to his chest.

"Kabu, you know that's not so. We've talked about this. I showed you the maps!" Mira's eyes sparkled with fondness and excitement. "There's so much more out there beyond our shores. And someday, I'm going to see it all!"

"You want to leave the island?" Karaburan looked stricken.

"Not now," Mira assured him. "Not anytime soon. But someday. That's what I dream about, you know. All of the things that could be out there." She paused then added a little more gently, "I'm sorry you had a bad dream."

"I don't want to dream that ever again," Karaburan whined, quivering in fear. He seemed to be calming down, but his pale blue eyes were wide and still clung to his fear.

"You don't have to sleep right away," Mira told him, standing up. "I have to put this book back, but then we can play a game. Would you like that? We can play a game, and then later you can sleep on the moss near me instead of going back to your shelter."

Karaburan looked speechless. Aurael's hackles went up instantly. "Oh, may I?" whispered Karaburan. "You won't make me go sleep alone on the rocks?"

"Not if you don't want to. Just this once. I don't see why not. You'll see what I mean—nightmares come and go. They're just dreams."

"But won't your father be angry if he sees me here? He told me to stay by the rocks at night."

"He only said that because you smell like fish, sometimes," she explained simply. Karaburan looked thoughtful, but nodded. "It doesn't bother me so much. Besides, we're friends, and I don't want you to feel like you're alone. Let's put this book away, and then we can go look for crabs 'til it gets dark!"

Karaburan followed Mira into the cave, past Aurael, heading for the library where Dante's books were carefully kept away from the elements. Aurael stood still in disbelief, his tail upright, staring wide-eyed after them. *Unbelievable. This hideous beast is more welcome to her company than I? It's as though she's forgotten me. She can't have . . . Can she?*

\* \* \*

Karaburan slept on the grass beside Mira that night in peace, with nary a hint of bad dreams. Since no nightmares startled him awake, and since Dante did not notice Karaburan's presence, Mira declared that he would stay with her whenever he liked.

It became routine: before night fell, he and Mira would play a game, or talk, or Mira would read from a book, and they would fall asleep together on the grass. It was too cold to sleep in the stone cave, so Mira liked to sleep in the open air. At first, Karaburan couched himself several feet away from Mira, but as the days passed and turned into weeks, he drifted closer to her, until at last they slept side by side, like young animals in a nest together. Night after night, Aurael watched and seethed with jealousy at their growing attachment.

*I ought to break open his mind and let the nightmares take over,* he thought maliciously. *I ought to crack him like an egg, and then Mira will see how dangerous and loathsome he is, and Dante will banish him for good, and then we'll see who Mira turns to for friendship!*

When at last a month had gone by, Aurael made his move. He waited until Mira and Karaburan were asleep, side by side on the soft grass and moss outside the cave. The fireflies danced in the darkness, reflecting the gleaming stars in the sky, casting strange flurries of light on the prone form of Mira and the curled-up lump that was Karaburan, snoring softly beside her. There was no sound but the insects chirping faintly in the dark, the occasional night-bird in the trees, and the gentle breezes passing through the ferns.

Aurael stepped into the dark place of Karaburan's mind and pulled him into a dream about his mother.

In the dream, Karaburan sat on the grass like a dog, eagerly attending his mother's words. Aurael used Corvina's semblance as a puppet, dictating a speech to her son about growing up, becoming a man, and being lord over the entire island all to himself.

"But, Mother," Karaburan interrupted eagerly, "I am not alone! My friends are here."

Aurael, as Corvina, stopped and looked closely at Karaburan. "What friends?" said the witch.

"The kind man, Dante, who let me live, and his daughter, Mira, who is my best friend in all the world."

"But, my son," Corvina said, puzzled. "You cannot be friends with those who belong to you! You are a king, you are an emperor of all this isle. Do they not know who you are?"

"They know my name," said Karaburan, happily. "We are great friends! I am very glad they're here."

"My son, my noble son," Corvina purred. "What is Mira?"

"My friend!"

"No, Karaburan. She is a girl. She will be a woman. And you will be a man."

Karaburan made a strange face, thinking very hard on what that could possibly mean. Aurael could practically hear the gears turning, even in the dreamscape. Suddenly, before Aurael could stop it from happening, the dream shifted and spun into darkness, and there was a roar as from a great jungle cat.

Aurael was flung unceremoniously from the witch's puppet-body and into dark space, spinning uncontrollably like a top. He dug in and tried to grab onto something in Karaburan's mind. *A tiger? What the devil is that doing here! I must be losing my grip on the dream.*

Aurael's momentum slowed at last, and he could hear Karaburan whimpering in the dream-shadows. He slunk closer, listening with one ear for his unexpected attacker.

"Karaburan," he whispered in a voice that was not his own.

"Who's there?" cried the man-beast.

"I'm you," lied Aurael. "From the future."

"What!" Karaburan's tears dried instantly, and he crawled forward in the dark, sniffing and pawing at the shadows. "Where are you?"

"I'm here, within you." Aurael made himself very small. "You—I—we are king of the island!"

"We are?" Karaburan exclaimed, stopping and making a joyful noise.

"Yes, yes, we are! But do you know what we had to do to become king?"

"Oh, what? Tell me! I want to be king. Will I be king soon?"

"You will if you do this," promised Aurael.

"What is it?"

"Mira."

"What about Mira?" Karaburan was puzzled.

"She is our queen! She loves you and does not know how to tell you. To become king of the island, you must show her you love her."

"I do love her! How do I tell her that?" Karaburan scrambled about blindly in the dream space, and Aurael felt the air growing warmer with his excitement and confusion.

"You don't need to speak it," assured Aurael. "You need to show her. You know what you want to do, way deep down. Follow your instincts."

"I don't understand," protested Karaburan, but Aurael wearied of waiting for the beast's simple mind to grasp his meaning. He reached way deep into the monster's psyche, grasping several strands of emotion and base instinct and twisting them together sharply. Karaburan gasped, and Aurael kicked off from the surface of the dreamscape, veering upward, out of the dream altogether, until he crouched on the moss in the clearing again, with the fireflies overhead. He soared backward, perching high in a tree, and watched as Karaburan writhed on the ground and woke with a start, his breathing labored and shallow.

Aurael felt breathless and dazed, but triumphant. Then he saw Karaburan roll over on top of Mira, and his triumph vanished like a cold dousing of water.

Mira woke, startled, but groggy. She said something in a blurry voice and began to push at Karaburan, then to kick and flail her arms and legs. She thrashed in protest, but Karaburan was large and heavy, and his body covered hers like an octopus envelops its unsuspecting prey.

*What have I done?* Aurael saw the gleam of moonlight in Mira's eyes, suddenly wide with terror, and knew he'd made a mistake.

Aurael whipped the air at the grass around them as though he could blow Karaburan away. He changed shapes in quick succession, wanting to drop down and tear the misshapen boy away from her with iron claws and snapping teeth, but he could not do it— Dante had commanded that he never reveal himself to Karaburan. Dreaming had been Aurael's only access to Karaburan's mind over the years. Without Dante's direct orders, Aurael was as powerless as though he were not even there.

Panicking, he dropped from the tree and threw a bolt of cold air into the cave. It struck and toppled a stack of books and a metal bowl, causing a clatter loud enough to wake the sleeping man.

Mira made a strangled noise of terror, and Karaburan moaned, then Dante appeared with a crack of thunder, his staff gleaming blue in every scratched rune. His eyes were like wildfire, and with a single sweep of the staff, he knocked Karaburan across the clearing and dropped him at the foot of a tree, crumpled and terrified.

Mira lay on her side on the ground in shock, her hands shaking, trying to catch her breath. Dante stood over her protectively, fixing his furious gaze on Karaburan.

"Please, sir, what have I done?" cried Karaburan. He looked completely stunned, as though he had been startled awake by Dante's blow.

Dante knelt beside his daughter. "Mira," he said in a very grave, quiet tone. "Are you hurt?"

Mira hesitated, but after a moment she shook her head. Aurael thought his own heart would burst. She did not look hurt, but surely Karaburan had been too heavy, too strong. Her frightened face and trembling hands made Aurael wild with worry. *I thought he would have some kind of fit, cause a scene, not try to take her by force!*

Dante stood again and pointed the staff at Karaburan. "What exactly did you think you were doing?" he demanded.

"Doing? Nothing! I was asleep! If I hurt her it was a mistake, an accident! I did not mean to hurt her," pleaded Karaburan. "I did not mean to do anything! I love her, she is my true and only friend. I would never hurt her!"

"Be still," said Dante coldly. "You have broken my trust," he declared at last. "And you have broken hers. You have destroyed what peace you had, and you have done it on your own terms. You will never lay eyes on her again." The runes on the staff grew blindingly bright. Karaburan's sobbing and hiccuping slowed, and his eyes grew glassy.

"You will go to your rocky hovel on the beach, and remain there, asleep, until dawn. You will not return unless I call for you, and you will never see Mira again. You will remain permanently divided from her, as your punishment; she will move freely about the island, but you will only be able to move wherever she is not. If she passes you by, you will be rooted to the spot where you stand until she has gone elsewhere, out of your range. You will be enslaved to my service until your days have ended."

"Yes, Master," answered the hypnotized Karaburan.

"Now go, and speak no more of this night."

"Yes, Master," repeated Karaburan, and lumbered off as casually as though he had only been a wild animal passing through.

Aurael could scarcely believe it. *That's it? His big punishment is an avoidance spell? Why won't Dante just kill him?* he seethed, but his insides were as loose and watery as the tide as he looked down at the terrified girl below. *What have I done, what have I done!*

"Come, daughter," said Dante, turning to head back to the cave.

"Father," Mira stammered, eyes wide. "Why did he . . . What just happened?" Tears glimmered at the corners of her eyes, wavering on the brink.

Dante's expression was stoic. "It doesn't matter," he answered coolly. He raised one hand as though to calm her down. "It's done. You have nothing to fear. You will act as if it never happened."

"But it did!" Mira's voice squeaked in the night air. She shook violently as she reached for her father, seeking comfort. "It happened! That was real. It was. He . . . He was going to—"

"Hush. No more!" Dante's eyes flashed. He tightened his raised hand into a fist for a moment, before relaxing and lowering it to help her stand. "Come inside and sleep upon the bed I've made for you. It is no place for you to sleep with insects and fish and creatures of all sorts." She did not take his offered hand, so Dante took her by the arm and pulled her upright. She shook free as she got to her feet, recoiling from his touch.

"That's all you have to say?" Mira whispered, her voice tiny and terrified.

"Daughter, you are not hurt, and he will never come near you again. You are quite safe. There is no need for you to be hysterical."

Mira stared at him in tear-stained amazement, and Aurael could almost hear the twang of a string breaking somewhere in her heart. After several long moments, she went inside, shocked into silence.

Aurael put his face in his hands. *I have ruined her,* he thought desperately. He felt a strange heat on the backs of his hands and peered down. Dante was staring up at him where he perched in the tree. His expression had grown darker, the lines of his face deeper and harder. Aurael felt suddenly extremely exposed and vulnerable. *Oh, dear,* he thought.

"I had a vision this day would come," Dante murmured. "I foresaw the betrayal of the beast-child, and I foresaw the change in my daughter's innocence. There are forces at work here other than you, Aurael, and I will not have it. I will not brook any further mischief. And as for you, you will leave her alone, do you hear me? She will forget you as easily as a dream."

"Master!" Aurael exclaimed aloud, swooping down and landing on his knees at Dante's feet. "Please! I can help, I can protect her, I can—"

"No," declared Dante. "She has outgrown her imaginary friend."

Aurael's soul cried out in agony. His voice, reed-thin, pleaded once more, "Please!"

"From now on, no more games. You are my servant, Aurael. I am your master. If you want your freedom, you must work for it."

He went away into the cave, his strange and weathered cloak flowing like the night sky behind him, leaving Aurael to cry to the fireflies and night-birds in the darkness.

# CHAPTER NINETEEN

Ferran drifted into consciousness and heard a faint but steady dripping of water nearby. He felt hard, uneven stone against his back, his muscles sore from the not-quite-flat position he lay in, with rocks poking into his back and neck. He opened his eyes to darkness and tried to sit up, but found that his ankles were bound, as were his wrists before him. A pain spiked in his ribs as he tried to turn over onto his side, and he caught his breath hard. Soreness bloomed throughout his body, various bruises throbbing in reminder of their presence. The sound of his sore grunt echoed back at him from the walls and low ceiling.

*A cave? What happened?* Ferran tried to think back, reaching into the dark fog of his mind for answers, but nothing materialized.

There was a scraping sound somewhere in the dark. Ferran lay very still, listening. Someone was coming. He shut his eyes, hearing the heavy footfall of someone coming nearer. Whoever it was sounded as though they were dragging something big. The unseen stranger stopped somewhere in the room and dropped the load, then sighed heavily and lumbered away again, the steps sounding fainter and fainter down the corridor.

Ferran waited a few more moments then opened his eyes again. His eyes began to adjust to the darkness, and as his world came into focus, he found himself in a small cavern, with several large stalagmites protruding from the ground. Although his feet and hands felt completely bound, he could see no rope or ties of any kind.

*What prison is this?* Ferran craned his head carefully to look at what the stranger had left behind and saw that it was a man, lying in a crumpled heap with his back facing Ferran.

"Hello?" he whispered. "Who's there?"

The man on the floor lay motionless and did not reply. Ferran felt his heart pounding. *Captive in a cave with a possible dead body,* he thought worriedly. *This does not look good.*

The footsteps approached again, and Ferran quickly shut his eyes and shifted back to his original position, hoping he would continue to go unnoticed. The stranger came along again, dragging more cargo.

*Another body?* thought Ferran. *Who are these men? Castaways from the* Albatross . . . *or something else?*

He risked peeking one eye open as the stranger dumped the second body near the first, and Ferran caught his breath audibly. The stranger heard his small gasp and turned to peer into the dark warily. Just before he could shut his eyes again, Ferran saw its face, and froze.

It was a monster.

It was a man, more or less, though unlike any man Ferran had ever seen. Tall and wide, it was covered in dark skin mixed with pebbly rough patches, like a fish's scales, that gleamed in the dim light. It wore a rough hempen cloth wound about its waist and legs like makeshift short trousers, and there were six long fingers on each hand and six toes on each huge foot. Its eyes were unevenly placed and Ferran was surprised to note they were sky blue, startlingly pale against the creature's unusual, patchy body.

The creature looked hesitantly about the cave, not noticing Ferran's stare then, seemingly dismissing the sound, turned back to the bodies on the floor, moving them closer together as a sailor arranges barrels of cargo in the hold. Finally, it gave a sad sort of shake of its lopsided head and slouched out of the cavern again, its huge feet stomping down the passageway, out of sight.

Ferran tried to keep his breath quiet, his heart pounding wildly in his chest. *The monster that hurt Mira,* he thought. *That means I'm in her father's caves. I could be hundreds of feet underground.*

In a flash, Ferran recalled Dante's arrival in the clearing by the treehouse and the subsequent attack when Mira tried to stop her father from taking him away. He shivered.

*He's going to kill me,* thought Ferran. *Unless Mira finds me, or I escape.*

One of the bodies on the ground groaned softly, startling Ferran.

"Hello! Psst! Are you all right?" Ferran whispered frantically. There was no telling how long they'd be lying here in the cold and the dark, how long before Dante came to fetch them. *If they're not too injured, perhaps we can help each other out of this mess.*

There was another groan, worried and pained, and one of the bodies rolled over a little.

Ferran's heart leapt. *It can't be!* he thought as the man's face came into view. "Truffo?" he whispered, voice cracking.

The bruised, rumple-haired young man opened his eyes. It most certainly was Truffo Arlecin, but he looked so different now: tired, hunted, and almost empty. Ferran was reminded of his childhood hound, and the look it had given him the day before it had given up on living and died of old age.

"Truffo," Ferran whispered again. "You're alive! I am so glad to see you!"

"Prince?" muttered the fool, his eyes fluttering closed again.

"Yes, it's me, Prince Ferran. Wake up! We have to get out of here!"

"Can't escape . . . there are monsters . . ." Truffo's head lolled with exhaustion.

"Truffo!" Ferran was desperate. "Please! Stay awake!"

It was no use. Whatever had happened to him had worn him completely out. Thinking on Dante's soulless stare and the creature that had brought the bodies in, Ferran could hardly disbelieve Truffo when he claimed there were monsters about. Exhaustion overwhelmed him, and he drifted into a kind of dreamless sleep, waking some time later to the faint smell of something burning and the tinkling of a distant, unseen wind chime.

Somewhere deep in the caves, a man screamed in pain, and Ferran felt the last of his courage vanish completely. With great effort, he rolled over onto his side and saw that Truffo and the other body had disappeared. He was alone.

*I have to get out of here.* Ferran looked toward the passageway where he'd seen the monster enter. There was another scream, and, without another moment of hesitation, Ferran began to wriggle desperately toward the uneven passage in the rock ahead of him, praying that it was not far to the cave's exit, and that he could make it outside before he was caught.

\* \* \*

"I said, stay back, ghost!"

Mira adjusted her grip on the staff, feeling it buzz in her palms. Although there was no sharp head on this staff's point, something about having the staff in hand was comforting in the face of this unexpected development.

"Please, do not be alarmed," the sheer-skinned man pleaded, still kneeling. His eyes were full of starlight and endless night skies, and his voice shook with something possibly like joy. "I'm no ghost. I mean no harm to you, Mira. I owe you my life."

"You . . . what?"

"I beg of you, please remember me." He looked pained. "Think hard, think back to your early days. Remember when you came to the isle, when you were but small. Do you remember your very first friend?"

Mira hesitated, furrowing her brow in deep concentration. "I remember my father and the monster, and . . ." The glimmering creature before her looked hopeful. "And there was someone else . . ." Mira felt her heart leap in confusion.

"I am an airy spirit, born of the sky and wind and clouds," the spectre said, spreading his arms wide. "My name is Aurael. I was bound here, imprisoned in a tree, until you and your father arrived and freed me. You found me first, and you were such a little thing, so bright and trusting!" He smiled, and Mira felt something brush up against her memories, familiarity dropping like a pebble to disrupt the surface of a pond.

"I . . . don't remember everything, but I think I remember you," she said slowly. She could not quite place the exact memories, but it felt true. "What happened when we freed you?"

Aurael sat back on his heels with a happy sigh. "We were insepa-rable! We spent all of our time together, and as you grew and explored the island, I kept you safe from harm. Do you remember the games we used to play? I sometimes was a bear to walk with you, sometimes a dolphin to swim with you. I was always at your side, Mira."

Mira lowered the staff so that it rested upright on the ground, and she leaned on it a little. "I don't remember," she said again, al-though there were echoes of truth to his words that made the lights on the staff's runes glimmer and spark as the shadows around them grew darker. *It will be night soon, and Ferran is in trouble.*

"Try. Think back." Aurael's sheer, pale blue form did not fade or darken, but he seemed to glow from within himself, pale against the twilight of the forest. "I was with you all along." His expression was full of—what? Adoration? Mira felt her skin prickle.

"You were?"

"Yes," breathed Aurael, smiling. "I was your constant companion."

"Where did you go?"

"Why, anywhere you wished me to!"

"No." Mira's jaw tightened. "Where did you go when you left me alone." She watched his silvery blue smile fade slowly into a kind of neutral puzzlement. "You say I set you free from that tree. You say you watched over me, cared for me, kept me safe from harm. So, where did you go? Why did you let Karaburan do that to me?"

Aurael's expression was childlike with guilt at first, and then the same pleading look took over again. "Mira, you don't understand," he began in a careful, soothing voice. He raised a hand, palm toward her in supplication. The gesture made her chest constrict sharply. Her father had done the same thing that night when Karaburan assaulted her. Her grip tightened and she narrowed her eyes on Aurael.

"Then explain it to me! Why did you let that happen?"

Aurael's brightness flared and his soft handsome features went sharp and angular as a thornbush for a brief moment before smoothing again. "My will is not always my own, sweet girl," he growled defensively. "Your father's price for freeing me from that tree was to take me as his long-indentured slave, until I had earned my freedom. What was meant originally to be a few small tasks became a mountain of work, and has stretched across the years like weaving upon a loom, ever in progress, never complete."

Mira gripped the staff tighter and stared him down. "That doesn't answer my question. Unless you mean to tell me my father ordered you to stand by and watch Karaburan violate me—"

"Your father did no such thing," Aurael's voice was rigid. "But that monster's foolishness caused me to be banished from your side. Your father decreed that you would not remember me again, and he made a spell to keep your mind from thoughts of me, your once-beloved playmate and humble servant. He banished the monster, too, in another way; he bade the creature forget his ambitions and cursed him so that wherever you would roam on the isle, he could not follow, nor even coexist in the same region."

Mira looked closely at him. *Another curse? So many curses. But that would explain much of my avoidance of the creature.* "This you swear?" she prompted him fiercely.

Aurael nodded. "Yes, I swear it."

The staff flared warmth, then sudden cold, against Mira's hand, and she glanced at it quizzically. *A lie?* she wondered. "My father forbade you to interfere with Karaburan's attempt on me?" she asked, her voice even.

"Yes, and his punishment was to banish me from your company. There were lessons he wanted to teach, both to you and that slack-jawed demon."

The staff cooled drastically in her palm, and Mira squeezed it, steeling herself for the next question. "And why would you aid me now, when his will was made so clear?"

Aurael shook his head. "You command the staff, and so you command me. And because I still owe you my life, even if it was your father who freed me from that tree and made me his own slave."

Mira narrowed her eyes at the spirit. The staff was lukewarm. *A partial truth,* she decided. "Tell me the truth," she said, keeping her voice level. "I am tired of questions. My father wants some kind of revenge, and Ferran's life may be at stake. Tell me the truth about what's going on." The runes on the staff shimmered, and Mira saw Aurael's expression grow humble and almost glossy.

"I love you," Aurael answered immediately. "You are the brightest star I have ever seen in any sky in the hundreds of years I've been alive. I want to make you happy, to give you whatever your heart desires . . . but I can do so little when I am still bound to your father's will. As long as he lives, I am his. Unless he releases me."

The staff blazed warm. Mira took another step back, her jaw tightening. *That was all true.* She didn't know what she was supposed to feel about this confession, given so plainly from such a strange and unexpected person. She took a moment to breathe. "Then you'll help me now, and I'll see that you're set free."

Aurael's face shifted like the sudden clearing of clouds after the rain. "You would free me?" The hunger and awe in his voice were palpable.

Mira nodded. "I need your help. I have to stop whatever it is my father has set in place, before any more damage is done."

Aurael fidgeted. "Command me, and I will obey," he promised.

"Tell me what my father intends."

"He wrecked that ship to murder his enemies, but something made the storm abate, and his mind was changed. Dante had intended for all aboard the ship to die, but when he changed his mind, a few were saved: some servants, the elder prince, the younger prince, the duke, and the king."

Mira's mind flew back to Gonzo's description of their history. *The king is Ferran's father, the duke is my uncle . . . This was all my father's plan.* "Go on."

"He bade me torture them, separate them, dangle their survival just out of reach as bait on a hook. Then, when they were right upon the verge of madness, I was to bring them home to him, to the caves, for some ritual or other, I know not what exactly." Aurael shrugged. "Presumably, he's going to kill them all."

"You will stop him." Mira set her jaw firmly.

Aurael looked surprised at her blunt order, and he bowed, his form melting as suddenly as though a strong wind had blown him away. Mira remained, holding the staff tightly in her right hand.

"And if you don't, I'll have to stop him myself," she told herself softly, unsure whether Aurael had actually gone to obey her or to rat her out to her father.

A faint crack and rustle of leaves sounded behind her, and Mira turned, again brandishing the staff like a spear.

The tiger stood on the edge of the clearing, gazing at her with those stunning pale blue eyes.

Mira held her breath then let it out slowly. *Not once in all this time, and now twice in a day,* she thought. *What could have prompted this?*

The tiger moved slowly toward her, crossing the clearing with long, liquid strides, and stopped several feet away, just out of reach of the staff. The enormous cat then sat down as neatly as a housecat and curled her tail around her feet. Mira blinked, confused, but the tiger looked at the staff with interest.

"Some magic this is," Mira observed, warily, and the tiger looked up at the sound of her voice, and nodded at her.

Mira's eyes widened. "Speaking the language of beasts is not one of my skills," she murmured. "What, then? The staff? The staff's power now lets me speak to you?"

The tiger purred softly, a low rumble that resonated in Mira's bones.

"Have you been on the island all this long while? I never knew you were even here." Mira shook her head slightly. The power flowed through the staff and into her palm like a steady river, but it made her feel as though she were dreaming.

The tiger nodded.

"Do you have a . . . a family? Are there more tigers?"

The tiger got up and moved toward her. Mira stiffened. Every instinct told her this was a wild beast with claws and teeth, and the simple conversation she was having with it a mere trick of her imagination. The tiger's stripes shone in the reflection of bluish light from the staff's runes, and as the tiger circled her, Mira found herself watching the ink-black stripes change and morph again as they had before. Then her eye caught a symbol she recognized, and her breath went out of her as quickly as a doused candle.

*The runes on the staff.*

"Who are you?" Mira demanded. "What are you?"

The tiger stopped circling and leaned close, pressing her gigantic head softly against Mira's leg. Mira gasped as her mind filled with pictures: a spider's web, a baby being born, a storm cloud filled with lightning, a metal bird flying through the sky, the glowing staff, dark arms covered in darker ink tattoos, a terrible shadow with grabbing hands, the island, a dry and crooked tree with a face peering out of the bark, and at last, Karaburan as he had looked as a child.

Mira stepped back on watery legs, away from the touch of the tiger's head, gasping for air as her vision blurred with tears. *What is this? What is happening to me?* She fought to catch her breath, leaning hard on the staff for balance. "I don't understand," she coughed.

The tiger pressed in close again, still purring, and when the thick fur made contact with Mira's skin, she saw again the baby being born, held by dark arms as the storm abated outside the window. She felt her chest tighten, her breathing shallow as she looked at the bed and saw the lifeless body of the woman—the duchess. Mira felt the swelling fear and sorrow that welled up within the midwife as she held the newborn and turned away toward the window, where a wild storm raged outside. The midwife whispered softly in a strange language that Mira did not recognize, and she watched the newborn stop crying, yawning into sleep, its skin as bright as the lightning that flashed beyond the windowpane.

The glow faded as the door opened and Dante came into the room, stunned with grief. He took the baby from the midwife and sent it away with a servant. Mira felt the midwife's fear spike even higher, pulse racing, as Dante took the staff, the same staff as in her own hand now. The midwife's hands buzzed with magic, an attempt to defend herself, but Dante moved without hesitation, and viciously struck her down.

"No!" Mira bellowed, her throat raw. Her stomach surged sickeningly, her skin crawling with gooseflesh, and she dropped to her knees hard, gasping and sobbing. The clarity of the visions paralyzed her, and she crouched, trembling. "No more, please, no more!"

Mira looked down at her hands, and for a moment her skin was as dark as the woman's in the vision, covered in tattoos. She cried out and dropped the staff, pawing at her arms as though she could wipe the stranger's skin away, but the tiger moved to support her, twining about her like a housecat would.

The contact sent another shockwave through Mira's mind and body. She saw darkness and felt the world plunge and sway beneath her, and then there was a man in a small dark room with her. The smell of sweat and damp straw was overpowering, and her stomach dropped sharply as the man moved toward her, crushing her in the dark. She tried to push him away but he held her down, her mind spinning as the ship lurched around them.

Mira screamed in terror and pain, and the vision shifted sharply to the island, where there was a baby in her arms—a misshapen, blue-eyed child. She felt her own self slipping away.

# CHAPTER TWENTY

## 1858

Thunder broke loudly nearby, and the cave trembled all around Corvina. She startled awake with a gasp, immediately reaching out to her son in the dark. Karaburan lay sleeping beside her on their thin bed of leaves and grasses, utterly unperturbed by the storm outside.

She put a hand to her heart to slow its wild pounding, and exhaled slowly. The rain never ended, it seemed. Perhaps it was simply the location of the island, its proximity to different air currents, which created the storms, or perhaps there were other forces at work. All Corvina knew was that the island was frequently plagued with rain, and she was grateful to have found the caves.

In fact, she had found that, despite the drastic change of living conditions from Neapolis to the island, somehow she and the boy were getting by. She often thought about what they didn't have, only to find some of those very things on the island or washed up on shore, leftovers from previous marooned sailors or rumrunners or shipwrecks. It almost felt that the island was providing for them, that it wanted them to survive. She thanked whatever magic lay in the isle's roots, and did not question it.

Corvina began to drift off to sleep again when the voice came to her.

*Psychorrax. Psychorrax. Psychorrax.*

She opened her eyes and reached for the spear she'd fashioned from a hearty branch and a tooth-like sharpened stone. She did not bother looking around the cave for an intruder; she knew exactly where the voice came from.

She gathered one of the lengths of canvas sail she'd discovered in the caves about her like a cloak and went out into the rain, her hand squeezing the hefty stick where she had begun to carve little sigils and signs in the wood. The spear warmed a little to her touch, but the buzz of power was no stronger than a single candle flickering in a dark house.

Corvina longed for her old staff. She'd spent decades honing it and carving it, feeding her energy into each line, each glyph. This spear she had roughly cobbled over the last three years was crude, and she had lost almost all of her own magic simply by trying to survive. The island cared for them in its own ways, and there were few natural predators to fear, but life was not easy, and often it was far from comfortable.

The truth of it was that when she had struck the deal with Aurael, she had lost much of her remaining inner power. It was a flickering ember now, clinging to life as the fire of her magical self died slowly.

*At least I'm free*, she thought, *and no man's slave. And Karaburan is a good boy.* She hadn't wanted it to turn out this way, but she was grateful for the small things she did have, and loved her boy, even with all his peculiarities.

The rain fell lightly but steadily as Corvina passed out of the forest and toward the copse of thin, unwieldy trees on the rocky edge overlooking the beach. Below was the water's edge, where she had given birth to Karaburan the night that Aurael had rescued her from the slave ship. And it was here, at the edge of the overlook, where Aurael's tree remained.

*Psychorrax.*

Corvina stopped near the tree, her face a mask of a defensive frown. The rain fell lightly around her, the night made darker by the storm clouds covering the moon.

"What do you want?" Corvina asked, already knowing the answer.

The thin and twisted branches of the tree swayed in the dark, and the weather-worn bark of the trunk blurred in the shadows, forming a face.

"Corvina," sighed the face in the tree with Aurael's voice. "How kind of you to come. "

"You woke me up," replied Corvina flatly. "Now what is it?"

The tree face shifted and took on a demure and apologetic expression. "I am sorry to have troubled you . . . maybe it was your subconscious? Your guilt for leaving me alone out here keeping you awake?"

Corvina squeezed the spear in her hand. The glyphs did not glow as the ones on her old staff had done, but she did feel a tiny nudge of warmth in reply to the squeeze. The magic flickered almost nervously at being so close to Aurael's prison.

"Aurael, you know full well how long it has been, and how I have tried so hard to free you. I have nothing left to give. I keep my child healthy and safe as any mother does, and that's all I have. I am tired. Aren't you?"

The rain fell between them in the pause that followed. Aurael's tree expression squeezed into a pinched, haughty look of suspicion.

"Well, yes, I'm extremely tired of being trapped in this tree," Aurael sniffed. "And your insistent ingratitude is quite tiresome. I saved you, Corvina. You and your baubled brat. And you've done nothing but flout your freedom in my face ever since!"

Corvina knew he wanted a rise out of her. She squeezed the spear again to dull her anger, although there was tension in her jaw and shoulders. He was being perfectly childish. His sudden shifting moods made Corvina feel as though she were speaking to an entire collection of commedia dell'arte masks. Aurael shifted as easily from one vice to another, as slippery as an eel, and villainously cunning.

"Aurael, I tell you again: I have nothing left. I have used all I have to try to free you, and what's left I've used to stay alive and protect my son. I have nothing left in me now. You have to let it go. I'm sorry."

Aurael's brow bent inward sharply, his scowl deepening in the tree bark. "I have been in this tree for three years! Don't you care? Do you have any idea what this is like? Of course not! You have your freedom and your precious son."

"Freedom?" cried Corvina, stamping her foot on the wet earth. "I am trapped for the rest of my life on this island! And my son will likely never know the outside world! You think this is freedom simply because it isn't a slave ship? This is purgatory. Of course you don't understand. But you will," she realized, tipping her head back a little to look at him from a new angle, his frown seeming fretful and worried now. "You'll understand someday, Aurael. You did save my life. And you did help my child into this world, although it was your magic that shaped his deformities. But I am not strong enough to free you from this tree. There is nothing left that I can do."

There was another pause as Aurael stared at her. Thunder growled overhead, like a hungry belly, and Corvina's thoughts shifted to her son asleep in the cave. She should return and see to him.

"I'm sorry," Corvina said again. "The work of your faerie lord is too powerful for me to undo. We're stuck here together."

Aurael's tree-face twisted and wrinkled like a raisin, sour from his defeat. The tree swayed in the rain, and he said nothing.

Corvina sighed. "Good night, Aurael," she said, and turned to head back to the cave.

"Corvina," called the spirit, and his voice was so thin and pleading that she stopped. There was a note of desperation, of fear, that she hadn't heard from him before. "Corvina, please . . ."

She turned to look back at him, and his expression was like that of a child not wanting to be alone in the dark. "What is it?" she asked, warily.

"There are things on the island," he blurted, as though he'd been afraid to tell her. "Things you can't always see. You can hear them sometimes, or feel them, but . . ." His eyes darted past her, then off to the right. "Please, I'm—I'm sorry I've been horrible. And I'm sorry for Karaburan, too." He sounded pained, like a violin string stretched and about to break.

"I can't help you," repeated Corvina, though he had begun to worry her. "I'm sorry, Aurael, there's just nothing I can do now." What did he mean by things on the island? She had felt something when they'd first arrived, and yes, the birds and insects of this place made stranger noises sometimes than ever she'd heard in her travels.

"I know," choked Aurael, his voice dropping to a whisper. "I know you can't, I know. Please, I've been trapped here for three years, and we've fought and squabbled, and I'm so alone. I apologize. I am sorry for everything I've said."

Corvina furrowed her brow. He sounded genuine, and that made her even more worried. *Something is wrong.* She was sure that he was indeed lonely—she recalled how vibrant and bold he'd been when he swooped into the ship's cell to rescue her. Now, he was just a knot in a tree trunk, warped and weathered.

"What do you want me to do?" she asked quietly. "You already know there's nothing I can do to free you. And you don't eat or drink, so I can't exactly feed you. What do you need?"

Aurael seemed to be holding back tears. Corvina waited while he gathered himself.

"It is foolish," Aurael whispered. "But I have not felt anything but the bare elements in so long. Occasionally, a bird will come and sit on these branches, but not often. Will you put your hand on the bark? Just . . . touch the tree?"

Corvina lingered, uncertain, but considerably less wary now that the request had been put into words. She had feared something less mundane. "But you're an air spirit. Can you even feel?"

"I have never been one to crave physical contact," confessed Aurael, closing his eyes. "But I'm also used to not being frozen in one place like this. There are sensations when flying, or soaring under the water, or passing through solid walls. Air has its own way of touching things. I have felt nothing but the bark of this tree for three years."

Corvina could hardly believe it, but his words moved her. She took a few steps closer to the tree, but Aurael's rough face remained somber and humbled. *Perhaps we've both been cursed after all,* she thought, and sighed. She had expected him to cheat her somehow, back on the ship, but she had never expected him to be cheated as well. Corvina reached out a hand and gently placed it on the bark of the tree, just to the left of the puckered, sad face of the spirit.

Aurael sighed, too, and the branches swayed feebly in the rain. "Thank you," he whispered, very demurely. "I never intended us to be trapped here. If he hadn't caught me—well, you'd be free, too. Everyone would have won."

"I know," Corvina murmured. "We can't change it now." She moved her hand along the tree trunk a little. "Can you feel that?"

"Sort of," Aurael replied, and shifted his face toward her hand as a plant turns toward the sun. "There . . . that's a little better."

"I should go back. Karaburan will be hungry when he wakes."

"Thank you," the spirit mumbled, in the most piteous voice Corvina had ever heard. "I'm sorry I woke you. Good night."

Corvina hesitated for a moment, then leaned over to plant a kiss on the rough bark of Aurael's cheek.

Aurael turned his face as she did and their lips—hers soft and cool from the rain and his hard and roughly hewn from bark—connected in a sudden kiss. Corvina's eyes flew wide open and she jerked away, only to find that she couldn't move. She was paralyzed, and felt something being wrenched from deep within her, like weeds from a garden. Her heart leapt into her throat and panic spread through her veins, but she was held fast by whatever trick he had used. Thunder rolled again overhead, and sudden lightning nearby blinded her. The rain began to fall harder, and Corvina strained against the spell to break free, but Aurael held her fast, their lips touching, something deep inside her being sucked away.

*Stop, stop it!* she begged him in her mind, and remembered saying the same thing to another three years ago in the cell on that ship.

*Relax,* said Aurael's voice in her head, and the bark twisted into a smirk even as he held her still with the kiss. *It's just a little loan. I'm just borrowing a little until I'm free. Then you'll get it back.*

*No,* Corvina thought, *no, don't! I told you there's nothing left— I'm . . . I can't . . .*

*I'm almost done,* scolded the spirit, but Corvina felt her knees begin to buckle. He reached not just for the last strains of her magic, but the very force of life itself.

*You'll kill me,* she realized, darkness creeping into the corners of her vision.

Aurael stared back at her unfeelingly. *So be it.*

Thunder cracked hard, directly above them, and lightning lashed out at a tree several yards away. The light faded, and Corvina crumpled to the ground in a heap, her spear rolling away into the underbrush.

*Karaburan will die without me,* thought Corvina, dimly, as her heartbeat slowed.

"Damn you!" cried Aurael, the branches of his tree thrashing in anger. "You couldn't hold on for just one more minute! I almost had it! I was almost free!"

*Karaburan,* Corvina called with her mind, knowing he probably couldn't hear her. *Be good, my son. I'm sorry.*

"Damn you, Corvina!" raged Aurael in his tree. "Psychorrax! Psychorrax! Witch!"

But she was already gone.

\* \* \*

"No!" Mira's own voice startled her out of the vision. She recoiled sharply, tearing her mind away from the tiger's memory, and a roaring sound like the sea filled her ears. Her sight began to adjust to her actual surroundings again, and her whole body shook from the release of emotion.

The tiger pressed close to her, purring softly. Mira crumpled against the warm fur, her body racked with sobs. Tears streamed down her cheeks as the images dissolved, and she put her arms around the cat's neck. She wept, and, as her tears fell, her limbs became her own once more, her confusion and panic beginning to subside.

When at last she could speak, she drew a shaking breath. "You were my midwife," she whispered, "and Karaburan's mother." A swell of sorrow grew in her chest. "And my father . . . betrayed you, as Aurael did."

The tiger nodded again, and Mira felt a wave of satisfaction and relief emanating from the beast.

"I'm so sorry," Mira cried. "None of that should have happened to you. If you hadn't been my mother's midwife, or if my father hadn't found out about your power. . . if my mother hadn't died."

The tiger turned her big head around to look at Mira. Then she pressed her broad face against Mira's still-trembling body.

"I don't know what I'm supposed to do," Mira murmured, wiping at her face with her hands. "My father's got them in the caves somewhere. My father's magic is more powerful than I thought, and I don't know how to stop him."

The tiger purred louder as Mira's hand stroked the thick orange fur. Mira saw in her mind's eye the glowing staff that she held, the staff which had once been the midwife's own. Then she saw her father's book, the huge tome worn by time and weather.

Mira furrowed her brow. "My father's staff—your staff—and his book? I've got one of those already. He mistook my spear for his staff by accident. But the book never leaves his side, he protects it with his life. I can't get to it without help. And Aurael! He betrayed you, and he said he'd betray my father—how do I know he won't betray me, too?"

The tiger's eyes shone paler, and Mira could see Karaburan in her mind.

"No," said Mira, shortly. "He . . . I can't."

The tiger stopped purring, and Mira felt as though she were being cradled in a woman's arms, a powerful sense of comfort and reassurance passing from the cat into her own body. She saw dark shadows that looked like herself and Karaburan, playing as friends and lying down to sleep, and Aurael above, high in a tree, boiling with jealousy.

He transformed into a mist, soaring down and slipping into Karaburan's head. After a few moments the mist seeped out of one of Karaburan's ears, and the patch-skinned monster rolled over on top of her younger self. Mira jerked her hands away from the tiger's fur and pressed them against her eyes to block it out.

"It was Aurael? Aurael made him do that?" Her insides churned at the memory, knowing now that Aurael hadn't just been a bystander, but the architect of the assault. *He'll pay for that.* "What do I do?" she asked the tiger, her voice hard. "I can't trust him now."

The tiger's pale eyes met hers, and she licked her whiskers thoughtfully. Then she stood up and stretched regally.

"I can't trust him, but perhaps I can use him. . ." Mira stared back at the tiger for a moment, her brow still furrowed. She picked up the staff again and got to her feet. "I need Karaburan to get to my father's book. And I shouldn't trust Aurael. Can you help me?"

The tiger gazed back at her in silence. Mira opened her mouth to ask another question when a gust of cold wind blew at her back, and Aurael's voice announced, "Sweet mistress, your father has the shipwrecked men in hand, and soon his spell will reach its highest peak. The moon is rising now, and when it reaches the skylight of his cave, Dante will drain them and use their blood."

The tiger had growled low and vanished like smoke at the sound of Aurael's voice, and Mira swung the staff around to face him, her expression hardening. The runes began to glow brightly.

"Be not concerned, Mira," Aurael went on eagerly, "Together we can stop him. I will show you where within the caves—"

Mira swung the staff at him, violently, and Aurael split himself in two to avoid the blow. He looked shocked, and stumbled backward.

"My love!" Aurael protested. "What's this? I have begun what you bade me!"

"You are a twisted, shameful, deceitful spirit," Mira spat, her frustration coming to a head. The staff hummed in her hands. She felt the memory of the tiger's anger and hurt mingling with her own, and her breath came short and fast.

Aurael recoiled in fear. "Mira!" He squeaked. "Please!"

"You have betrayed my father, you have betrayed Karaburan, and you have betrayed me. You lie and cheat and shift the world around you as though there are no consequences for your actions. But there are." She narrowed her eyes at him. "You will do exactly as I say, or by this staff, I will destroy you for what you've done to me, and what you did to Karaburan and his mother."

Several different reactions flitted hurriedly across Aurael's face. "I have done nothing that was not deserved," he hissed through his teeth.

"Did I, a child still, deserve to bear such an assault from a creature too simple to know what he'd done?" Mira glared. The veneer of anger cracked, and Aurael flinched. "You made that happen, Aurael. You. You are no fairy, no dainty spirit of the old folk tales. You are a devil in your own right, and by all the gods, I pity your empty, shriveled heart."

Aurael's eyes shone with what might have been tears. "It was a mistake," he confessed in a whisper. "When you have lived in bleak, unfettered disappointment for as long as I have, it is much harder to remember how human psyches work. It was an accident, I swear. I only wanted to get him out of the way so that you and I would have each other!"

Mira lifted her hand. "Enough," she growled, and felt the staff warm in her hands as though readying itself. "I will break these curses and set things right again. Bring Karaburan to me unharmed. You will both help me retrieve my father's book."

Somewhere distant from the island, thunder rolled softly. A storm was coming.

# CHAPTER TWENTY-ONE

M ira crouched, the soft but steady rain drumming down on her thatched cloak. She kept her eyes on the dark opening in the rock several yards away. When they had arrived on the island, the cave had only been one chamber, with one wide-mouthed entrance facing south. As time went on, her father had found ways to reshape the rock and carve out new chambers and rooms in the darkness. He had still been in the process of doing so when she left to build her treehouse several years ago.

*A whole labyrinth, probably. There's no telling what the inside looks like,* she thought. *Without Karaburan and Aurael to guide me, I might wander in the dark forever. Aurael said something about a skylight . . .* She peered up through the trees, trying to follow what must be the roof of the cave. The moss and misty rain were illusory, though, and she found herself blinking rapidly to clear her blurry vision of its distractions.

She heard the soft purring of the tiger somewhere in the bushes nearby and glanced over her shoulder, but did not see the beast.

"How will I know what to do?" she muttered nervously. "I'm not a wizard."

The tiger only purred louder, and Mira shook her head. There was a glimmer of blue ahead, and Aurael half-materialized in the rain. He beckoned Mira closer to the narrow opening in the rock, and, after a moment, she sprinted to him and pressed her back to the rock face beside the passageway.

"The book is just lying on the floor," said Aurael, "he isn't using it at all. If we can get in there, one of us can surely get to it."

"Where's Karaburan?" Mira looked back the way she'd come. "You said he was here."

Aurael's face flickered, and he made his mouth a thin line. "He was. Maybe that curse isn't broken."

"So break the curse," she commanded, but Aurael laughed snidely at her and crossed his arms.

"You're the one with the staff, dear girl," he replied loftily. "Maybe you ought to try harder."

Frustrated, Mira closed her eyes and shifted her grip on the staff, feeling it buzz in response. She reached out into the rainy forest with her mind, hearing the patter of drops on leaves and listening for the breathy, uneven presence of the monster.

*Karaburan isn't a monster,* Mira reminded herself as she searched blindly for something, anything that felt like him. *He was manipulated. He was forced. He deserves a chance at peace without curses and without magic.*

She paused, hearing a quivering sob. *That feels like him . . . Why is he crying?* She wondered, and with her mind, she reached toward him and gave a gentle tug on Karaburan's mind, beckoning him to where they were. Just a simple little pull, and she felt as though a single thread had snapped. Mira felt him startle, his blubbering growing quiet. She pulled at him again, carefully, and he began to move toward her.

Mira opened her eyes, and the patch-skinned Karaburan came loping miserably out of the trees, a quizzical look on his face. He stopped when he saw Mira by the cave's entrance, and his jaw went slack with disbelief.

"No," he murmured. "No, no, not again, not again!" He started to retreat back into the forest.

"No, wait!" Mira threw out a hand to stop him, and he froze. She drew a shaky breath, the staff's energy pulsing through her. Her heart beat erratically; it had been years since she'd seen him, and now that she knew the truth about what had happened that night, she wasn't sure how to feel or act. She dropped her hand, and saw his posture release and relax. "Please don't go. I need your help."

"I did what you asked, I did, I tried! I tried to do what you asked!" Karaburan covered his face with his long fingers. "Leave me in peace!"

Mira frowned. "What is he talking about?" She looked over atAurael quizzically, and saw that the spirit had become mostly invisible, his shape fading chameleon-like into almost nothing against the stone wall. "Aurael," she growled warningly, and his face became visible again, the picture of innocence.

"Yes, my mistress?"

"What is he talking about?"

"I'm sure I have no idea," said Aurael, looking as though he wanted nothing more than to flee.

Mira made her hand into a fist at him, yanking on his silvery aura. He made a sharp, uncomfortable noise and cleared his throat.

"I may, or may not, have pretended to be you, but it was for a very, very good reason, I promise you," Aurael choked. Mira squeezed her fist a little, feeling the anger and disgust rising in her chest. "A very good reason!" Aurael squeaked.

Karaburan gaped openly at Mira, as though entranced. "Voices," he stammered to himself. "Voices on the air, and false visions!"

"Explain!" Mira snapped.

"I convinced him that if he killed your father, you two could reunite, and you would forgive him." Aurael rubbed at his non-corporeal throat and scowled. "I was only half wrong, wasn't I? This is all for the greater good, you know," he added nastily.

Mira felt her insides churn. *The more I find out, the worse this knot tangles,* she thought, trying not to let the anger rise again in her chest. Her eyes flew to Karaburan, who cowered, trembling in the rain. She exhaled slowly and moved cautiously forward. Karaburan did not look up as she drew closer, and she stopped just within arm's reach, feeling her pulse quicken. Her instinct screamed at her to get back, reminding her of his weight, his scaly skin, his strange smell, but she tightened her jaw and stayed still.

"Karaburan," she said, quietly. "I am not an illusion. I'm real. I'm me." He did not raise his head, but shuddered. "This is important. It's more important than you and me. Listen to me, Kabu."

The long-unused childhood nickname made him lift his eyes toward hers in disbelief, and they were the same pale blue of the tiger. Mira resisted the urge to recoil, her free hand balled into a little fist to keep it from shaking. *Fight it,* she thought. *Fight whatever lies have been woven over us. We were best friends before Aurael used you.*

"Mira?" Karaburan's voice was hushed, his eyes suddenly focused and clear of whatever madness he had borne. "Mira? I'm sorry . . . I think I was very bad."

It was as though the last few years had never happened, and Karaburan looked up at her with the decided love and loyalty of his childhood. It was deeply strange, after these long years, to face him in this way. Mira had often wondered what would happen if they ever met again by accident. At different times, she had felt wrathful, then sorrowful, then demanding, then neutral, and never knew for certain what she would do or say if face to face with Karaburan once more. As time passed, she had stopped wondering, and had known with certainty that she would never forgive him.

*But he was manipulated by magic. He was forced.*

"I know," Mira said aloud, and swallowed. "You . . . You have a chance to do something good now. Something important."

Karaburan put his hands down and tipped his head to one side, the rain sliding down his uneven face. "What is to be done?" he asked, his voice timid. "I will do it."

"My father's book. The big, old book he carries when he's . . . working."

Karaburan's eyes widened as he nodded. "I know the one," he murmured.

"I have to get it. I have to take it away from him before he does something very bad. I need your help to get the book so I can destroy it." Mira held his gaze. "If we destroy the book, no one else will get hurt, and we'll all of us be free. You won't be a slave, and neither will Aurael."

"Who?" Karaburan made a face of confusion.

"He doesn't even know you're here?" demanded Mira loudly, her patience waning as she glared at the spirit.

Aurael shrugged and became more opaque, his expression one of frustrated impatience. "So it's my fault his mother never introduced us?" he muttered. "Dante told me I wasn't to manifest before him, so I didn't."

Mira turned back to Karaburan, who looked thunderstruck at the sudden appearance of the spirit. "Kabu," she said, pulling his attention again. "My father has kept you and Aurael as slaves these last several years. He has kept me an unwitting prisoner, in ignorance of the past, and of the world beyond our island. He has done all of us a great injustice, and now he aims to murder several men. I need your help for this. Will you help me?"

Karaburan looked frightened still, and ashamed, but he nodded after a moment. "I will try. If it means we all go free, I'll try."

Aurael crossed his arms, his disgust written in his frown. "We could have done without him," he muttered to Mira.

She turned and met his gaze, watching him melt and cower a little before her. "No," she said decidedly. "We couldn't. We need him to enter unnoticed."

"Unnoticed?" Aurael's dark eyes narrowed.

"You will disguise yourself, take the shape of a mostly drowned sailor. Karaburan will bring you into the cave, telling my father that he has found one more body on the shore, while you remain unconscious. You will grant me your invisibility, and I will follow you both in. While Karaburan goes for the book, we will rescue the men, unseen. Then we destroy the book."

"What if he catches us?" shuddered Karaburan. "I'll be beaten . . . we all will."

"He will destroy us if we fail," agreed Aurael.

"We have no choice! He has wronged us, and he's going to kill Ferran and his family. Do you understand?" Mira drew a deep breath. "If we go, then we all go down together. If we do not try, we will never be free."

There was a silence, except for the gentle rain. Thunder rolled overhead. At last, Karaburan nodded slowly.

"We go," he agreed.

Aurael sighed through his nose, and, with a shimmering like light through water, he vanished, re-appearing on the ground in a crumpled heap. His new shape wore torn trousers and a blood-stained shirt, his face obscured with long damp hair and wounds where perhaps sharks had nibbled away at his flesh. Karaburan recoiled at the sudden change, but Mira only raised her eyebrows.

"How authentic," she said dryly.

Aurael made the castaway's face contort in disdain, then re-laxed again into neutrality, feigning death.

Karaburan made a startled sound and stepped back, looking all about him in nervous disbelief. "Mira?" he cried, his eyes wide. He shifted his weight anxiously like a dog on a leash, turning his head this way and that.

*Aurael must have made me invisible already,* she thought. "I'm right here," she answered, putting out her hand to touch Karaburan's shoulder. He stopped fidgeting and stared at the rain in front of him blankly. "Can you see me?"

"No!" breathed Karaburan in amazement. "It's good magic."

"Of course it is," sneered Aurael from the castaway's puffy mouth.

"Quiet!" Mira patted Karaburan's shoulder and then stepped back, out of his way. "All right. Drag him in, I'll follow behind. But don't let my father know our plan, Kabu. Just get us in there, and get me the book."

"I'll try." Karaburan wiped a scaly hand across his eyes to clear away some of the rain, and shook himself a little. Then he bent down and hefted the sailor's body over his shoulder, cautiously making his way into the cave.

Mira paused at the thin passage into the stone and shed her woven cloak onto the ground. She slipped into the cool, damp cave after Karaburan and Aurael, and squeezed the staff tightly in her free hand, willing it to give them the strength and speed they needed to do what must be done.

*Hold on,* she thought, picturing Ferran in her mind. *Hold on, we're coming.*

\* \* \*

Despite his every nerve and sinew begging to remain unconscious, Ferran drifted awake, the pounding in his head too steady and too loud to be natural. He forced his heavy eyelids open and saw, through a black fog, a massive clock face set into the rock across from him. The heavy tick and tock of the exposed, rusted gears was the source of the rhythmic pounding echoing in his skull.

*What happened to me?* His palms stung and throbbed painfully. He vaguely remembered crawling and struggling down the narrow passageway of the cave in an escape attempt, scraping his hands and knees on the rocks. There was an echoing pain at the back of his head. *An ambush,* he remembered, and as he blinked, the black fog in his vision cleared a bit.

Ferran was held upright with his arms and legs splayed, pinned by unseen chains to the rock wall behind him. His shirt was missing, and blood coursed weakly down his cheek, throat, and chest. A painful spot swelled on his head. The cavern he was in now was much larger than the previous one. This room was round and vast, and on the wall, evenly spaced along the points of a diagram which occupied nearly the entire vast floor space, were several other men, limbs splayed as Ferran's were, heads bowed in unconsciousness. All bore recent injuries, bruises and drying blood painting their bare chests and arms as though they'd been through war. Between each man, a torch burned, illuminating the eerie scene and darkening the shadows in the room.

The diagram was composed mostly of foreign shapes and letters. It had many points, and spiraled inward toward the center of the room, with strange runes drawn out around the perimeter. Directly adjacent to Ferran was a series of makeshift shelves and crates, some unusual-looking handcrafted tools, and various clay jars and bowls filled with powders, herbs and who knew what else.

Several weather-worn books were stacked on the ground, the topmost of which lay open to a page showing the same diagram which was painted on the floor. At the center of the chamber was a faint patch of light from a hole in the ceiling that acted as a sort of skylight. The moon was not bright enough yet to show, but the dim gleam of night danced on the raindrops that fell down through the hole and pooled on the floor of the cave.

*This does not look good,* thought Ferran weakly. Stories of human sacrifice and black magic rituals fluttered through his mind like nightmare moths, making his palms sweat and his stomach churn.

Ferran suddenly recognized one of the men along the wall: Truffo. The prince inhaled sharply, causing hard pain to flare throughout his body. He winced hard, gasping for air, and, as the moment passed, he realized that he knew all of the prisoners: Truffo Arlecin, Stephen Montanto, Duke Torsione, Uncle Bastiano—and Ferran's own father, King Alanno.

*Father!* Ferran could not even cry out. His voice was as empty as a dying wind, gagged by his exhaustion. He tried to call again, but no sound accompanied his breath. *He's not dead yet; he can't be! Oh, gods, Father! Please don't die, don't die yet, hang on . . . Please . . .*

A scraping sound echoed from the passageway, and Ferran let his head loll forward again, feigning unconsciousness. From under the cover of his hair, he watched with one eye open as Dante emerged from the dark, dragging a large, sharpened tool of some kind. It looked to be carved out of ivory, with a well at one end, almost like a soup ladle. Ferran had never seen a bone that big before, and wondered nervously what kind of animal it had come from, and how Dante had come by it in the first place.

Dante was muttering to himself, but did not seem agitated as he moved across the chamber to the set of small clay pots. He drew a pinch of some dark powder from one and sprinkled it lovingly over the instrument, then rubbed it in with his hands as gently as any healer performing rites for the wounded. This process he repeated several times with different powders, calm and methodical. Ferran studied the man, finally having a chance to really look at him.

Ferran could not imagine this weathered, sun-soaked man as a decadent duke, but he must have looked very different, long ago. Dante's hair was mostly dark gray, only partly tamed by what may have originally been a gentlemanly queue, but over time had tugged looser and looser by the wind, giving him a wild, unkempt look. The cloak he wore was salt-stained and ragged, composed of many different fabrics sewn and tied together. The colors ranged from black to blood red to midnight blue, with hints of what must have been gold and silver embroidery once upon a time. Dante's hands shook visibly when he moved, and even more so when he stood still; Ferran hadn't noticed it before, and wondered if those hands had shook when Dante first attacked him in the woods.

*If I did not know better now,* Ferran thought, *I would think him a gentle and kind-faced old man. Perhaps he was even handsome once, like his brother.* But there was something about Dante's calm that terrified him.

"Your thoughts are as loud as your breathing, Prince," said Dante quietly, turning to look at him. "There is no need for panic, yet."

Ferran's blood ran cold. He swallowed, his mouth kept firmly shut, but he lifted his head to meet Dante's eyes.

"You have grown much since last we met," Dante observed, turning back to continue his business with the bone. "In height, in weight, in mind . . . And yet, not grown enough in spirit to please your father, I understand. At least, that's what I hear from your father's dying dreams." He nodded toward the king's limp body. "His impressions of loss and disappointment are powerful. It must be difficult for you to shoulder your father's dismay as you do."

The sting of the remark prickled Ferran's skin like hedgehog spines, but it was nothing compared to the pain he still felt pounding through his head and pulling at his wrists and ankles. He said nothing.

"So. A prudent prisoner." Dante smiled. "That's fine with me." He went back to the clay pots.

After a time, Dante moved across the room, dragging the ivory instrument with him, and approached the unconscious Torsione where he was slumped upon the wall. Ferran strained to see what he was doing, and Dante gave him a tired, wry look.

"Curious, too? Even in the face of death? I need a little more blood from each of you. All part of the recipe, you understand," the old man explained calmly, pressing one end of the bone instrument to Torsione's chest. The sharp end of the instrument sliced delicately into the skin. Torsione did not stir or wake, but his blood slid brightly down the grooves in the pale bone. "From my brother, for his treacherous ambition." He repeated the process with Bastiano. "From the king's brother, to balance my own brother."

Ferran strained against his invisible bonds as Dante turned toward him next, still carefully tilting the bone so that the samples of blood remained in the well at the bottom of the shaft. The old man's gray eyes were bemused and strangely glossy as he peered into Ferran's face.

"And some from you, too, boy," Dante murmured. "Son of a king, to balance the sons I never had. My wife died, you know. You were too small to remember it. That was the start of it all."

Ferran felt a tickle in the back of his throat. He swallowed several times as Dante studied his face.

"There's no way you wouldn't have been brought into this," Dante was saying. "It was your destiny, so there's really no use in thinking on alternate situations now, worrying about how things could have been. Your fate always would have brought you here. It couldn't have been your sister; it had to be the son."

Ferran furrowed his brow, still surreptitiously twisting at his restraints. *What is he talking about? What is it all for?*

"You're confused, and rightly so." Dante tipped his head to one side thoughtfully. "You'll forgive me if I spare you the unfortunate, lengthy details, Prince Ferran. You would not understand them. I have been hard at my studies for such a long time to keep them all in order." He tapped his temple and chuckled airily. "So to be brief: I will conquer death itself, so that never again can it take from me anything that is precious."

Ferran felt the tickle rise in his throat again and he made a soft sound, much to his own surprise. Dante raised one brow.

"What's that? Finding your voice, are you? I have a moment to spare for your words, if you make them brief." He beckoned with a trembling finger, and Ferran's throat cleared of the tickle so suddenly as to make him cough.

"What . . . what's left that is precious to you?" he croaked at last, his voice unsteady. "You have destroyed yourself, ruined Mira's life, broken all bonds. Now you will kill your remaining family and once friends? You cannot hope for your wife to return, sir," Ferran coughed. "She is gone, and you remain. Mira remains."

"You do not know what I am capable of." Dante's sneer was abrupt. "You are just a boy."

"And you are an old man. If you kill us, you'll have nothing left." Ferran saw Dante's eyes narrow a fraction in uncertainty.

There was a fretful sound, like a groan, from somewhere further down the corridor, and Dante flinched slightly. He turned away from Ferran without completing the task, clutching the bone in his shaking hands. Ferran exhaled softly in relief.

The large, scaly-skinned man appeared once again, slumping out of the passageway with an anxious expression on his face. He carried another body on his shoulders, and he gave another little groan again as he met his master's eyes.

"Karaburan," Dante said through gritted teeth as the castaway was delivered carefully onto the floor. "Did I not ask that you leave me to my work in peace? Without interruptions?"

"Yes, Master," mumbled the creature, his pale blue eyes watery and worried. "I did think you might be unhappy that I returned, but you told me to bring all of the bodies to you, and I obey in all things! I found one more," he explained, gesturing to the sailor's body.

"He's no one," Dante frowned, stalking over to the corpse and eyeing the dingy clothing. "It's just a sailor, you mongrel; I don't need him."

"But I obeyed!" protested Karaburan, worriedly. "I did not want you to think I disobeyed solely for the fact that you already had what you needed!"

Dante sighed through his nose. "Very well. Turn him over," he commanded. "But I am sure I do not need him. Everyone is accounted for."

Karaburan knelt and turned the body over, the unkempt wheat-gold hair tangled with seaweeds. He reached up and pulled the weeds away from the sailor's face and made a strangled noise of terror. Across the room, Ferran craned his neck, trying to see the face. Dante gasped and almost dropped the bone instrument, and, as he fell to his knees, Ferran finally saw the sailor's face.

*Mira!*

# CHAPTER TWENTY-TWO

**W**ell, thought Mira, *that was rather dramatic.* She stood near Ferran, holding the staff in one hand, watching Karaburan fall to the floor in tears upon recognizing the body.

It was an unusual sensation, looking at her own dead body. Mira felt oddly amused at the sight and paused a moment, despite her urgent purpose to free the men and stop the ritual. There was a great swath of rope and seaweed tangled about the corpse's throat and torso, and her eyes stared blankly at the ceiling, a dull cold green. Her face still shone purple in the dim light; it appeared very much that she had strangled and drowned.

Beside her, Ferran made a soft, choked noise. Mira looked at him and saw tears begin to pour down his cheeks. Karaburan was sob-hiccupping in terror, his large, six-fingered hands patting uselessly at the body. Dante set down the ivory instrument with one hand, trembling as he reached out to close the corpse's eyes. He looked as pale as the bone beside him.

"How could you," whispered Dante, rocking a little over the body. "My daughter, my only child." He looked at Karaburan. "How could you?"

"Me?" sobbed the creature, "I didn't do this! I could never have killed her!" His fat tears pooled and slid over rough cheeks. "I did not even know it was her," he squealed in agony.

*Ah, poor thing,* she thought. *He didn't know that bit was coming, either. Quite the performance, though. And my father!* She couldn't help but be intrigued by his emotional outburst. It was more real feeling than she'd seen from him in years.

Dante cursed loudly, pressing his hands to his eyes in pain. Karaburan lowered his head to kiss the corpse's lifeless hand, but Dante looked up again sharply and swiped at him.

"Get away, beast!" The force of his gesture flung Karaburan across the room, toppling the shelves and crates, dumping books and pages and artifacts onto the weeping creature. Dante bent forward over his daughter's corpse, mumbling something insistent and forceful, but whatever incantation it was, there was no flicker of life in the body.

Mira focused her mind on Karaburan in the pile of books and crates, reaching out with the power of the staff. *Kabu,* she called with her mind, and heard his sob turn to a yelp as he struggled to get out of the debris. *It's Aurael's trick. I'm still here. Bring me the book!*

Beside her, Ferran shut his eyes, seeming unable to keep his head up any longer. He had stopped straining against his invisible bonds.

*Right,* thought Mira. *Ferran.*

She covered his mouth with her hand, and Ferran's eyes snapped open in panic, shifting from side to side frantically, but did not see her.

"Shh," she breathed in his ear. "Don't speak. I'm not dead. Just follow my lead, and stay quiet."

Ferran gave a tiny nod and looked straight ahead, watching Dante attempt to revive the corpse. Mira reached for his wrist, feeling the binding spell and attempting to unravel it with her mind. It took several moments for her to figure out how to unlock it, but once she did, the bindings at his other wrist and his ankles were easy to remove. *The others won't take long, now.*

"Don't move until I give the signal," she whispered, and touched his chest briefly to plant him in place with her own spell, intending to cut him loose as soon as it was safe. Ferran looked startled at the touch, but then exhaled softly and nodded again. Mira moved quickly to undo the holding spells on each of the other prisoners, glancing over her shoulder at her father and Karaburan as she did so.

Dante looked up at the ceiling of the cavern, his cheeks pale in the torchlight. His eyes were cold and dark, his mouth a grim line, but otherwise, he seemed as though nothing had happened. The hole in the roof showed the first glimmer of moonlight beginning to peep through, brightening the spot on the floor, and he stood carefully.

He retrieved the bone ladle, moving away from the corpse on the ground as though it were not even there. Karaburan half-crawled away from the corner where he'd been thrown, limping awkwardly, as if hurt. A second glance revealed that Karaburan clutched something under one arm, trying to hide it by hugging himself tightly as he made his way back toward the tunnel exit.

Ferran shifted his weight, and Dante looked over at him before getting to his feet. "Be still, poor prince. We are all destined for the same dark end, all of us—except for myself, of course."

"You can't cheat or conquer death," Ferran croaked. "Postponing it isn't the same thing. A wise man would know that."

"Then I suppose I am not a wise man," Dante replied bitterly, gathering up the bone instrument from the floor and checking to be sure it had not cracked or leaked.

Moonlight shone more brightly through the ceiling now, and Karaburan was almost to the passageway when Dante turned toward Ferran with the bone's sharp edge.

*Almost done*, Mira thought at Ferran as she unbound the last of the men. *Keep talking!*

"What will you do with our blood?" Ferran demanded, wincing as the instrument moved closer to his skin.

"It's very technical."

"Humor me," insisted Ferran, balling his hands into fists.

Mira dashed toward Karaburan, her bare feet light and silent over the stone floor, her heart pounding in her ears. *The book, the book, the book, the book!*

Dante sighed through his nose. His gray eyes were dull as he looked at the prince. "The blood of my betrayers to counterweight me. I am to call upon Death, and when He comes, I will barter for my wife . . . and now my daughter, too. I will try to retrieve them both, but if I must choose, I will choose my wife." He glanced over his shoulder sadly to where Mira's body lay on the stone floor.

It was gone.

"A trick!" Dante whirled, his eyes flashing. "What's this?" he hissed, and looked toward Karaburan. "What have you done?"

Breathless, Mira reached Karaburan just in time. *Right here,* she told him silently. Karaburan's blue-gray scales gleamed in the moonlight as he turned, lifting the book up to hand it to her.

"Stop!" commanded Dante, lunging at him, but it was too late.

Mira took the book with her free hand and the invisible glamour melted away, revealing her in plain sight to the others' eyes. She stared defiantly at her father, feeling the staff pulsing with energy in her hand, the glow from the runes pouring into her arm and spreading throughout her body. The sensation filled her with sudden strength and power and her knees nearly buckled in surprise, but after a moment, she caught her breath and the magic began to settle within her like a bird upon a perch, ready to take flight when ordered.

Her father seemed frozen to the spot, his jaw slackened in disbelief. She lifted the staff and slammed it down; an earsplitting clap of thunder shook the walls of the cavern, snuffing out several torches. Dante staggered, thrown off balance by the force of it. Ferran and the other prisoners dropped down to the ground, released from the temporary binding spell.

"Mira," breathed Dante, his gray eyes wide. "You're alive!"

"I am," she answered.

"Daughter," he swallowed cautiously, eyeing the book, the staff, and the cowering Karaburan at her side. "Whatever you think you're doing . . . Give me my things back. Now."

"Or what?" Her voice was amplified by newfound power, rippling throughout the cavern and echoing back again. She held the book close to her chest and tipped her head to one side. "You'll punish me, Father? You already have."

"Obey me," stammered Dante, his entire body trembling like a leaf in autumn as anger seeped into his voice. "Give me my book. And my staff. You will obey me!"

"I will not," Mira replied curtly, and felt a surge of new power wash through her. She drew a deeper breath, exploring the feeling of control. "I wondered why you never let these old things out of your sight for all these years. They're filled with your anger, your hunger for success, your sorrow. Was that how you were planning on courting Death's favors? By bullying her?" Mira shook her head, her heavy plait swinging. "Hardly politic of him, don't you think, Aurael?"

"Quite rude, indeed," agreed the spirit, stepping out of thin air behind Dante and grasping him about the throat and by the hair. His eyes were dark as pitch, and when he smiled, it was both happy and terrible. Dante gasped for air, clutching at his throat where he was held tight. "Don't struggle, you'll only make it better for me," crooned the young man.

"Aurael. Not yet," Mira warned him.

The spirit rolled his dark eyes and sneered down at Dante. "I will wait only a little longer," he promised, through gritted, gleaming teeth.

Mira walked toward the pattern painted on the ground and shook her head. "Even if you brought my mother back," she said coolly, "what good would it do? What would you say? How would you excuse yourself to her for sending in so many other lives so that she might live again?" She gestured at the prisoners on the floor about the cavern. "Perhaps you should have used me to start with. Surely my blood is strongest in this case, being both yours and hers. If you had trapped me instead, you wouldn't have lost your precious book." The harshness in her own voice surprised her for a moment, but the thrumming flow of light and warmth from the staff made Mira hold her ground. "Either you stop this spell now, or I will."

"Please," begged Dante from the headlock. "I did it for you, my daughter, I did it for us. They took everything from us because they were frightened of my power. They are nothing more than cowardly, backstabbing animals. You deserve a mother and we deserve to be a family, Mira, please . . ."

"Please," echoed Mira coldly. "Stop. Your lies are useless now. I heard you tell Ferran you'd choose my mother over me." A light went out in Dante's eyes, his breathless expression turning to a sneer for a split second before being overwhelmed by tears. "You went mad long ago, Father, and there's no changing that now. I have to end this. You will gain nothing from this path, and yet you would lose everything."

"But I protected you!"

"From what?" She frowned. "From the world? Yes, you did well to keep me hidden away on this island, using your magic to sow seeds of vengeance instead of new beginnings. You could have brought us a ship years ago, but you would rather have stayed here and played a god over me, over Karaburan, over Aurael." Anger slithered through her limbs, making her tremble, and she swallowed back the curse that crept up the back of her throat. "You felt nothing when I needed you. You would not even so much as comfort me after Karaburan attacked me."

Dante's voice was gentle and sickly sweet. "You were unharmed, and I needed time, Mira, sweet girl. And look at you now! So grown, so strong and intelligent. You would be a fine duchess. Your mother would be proud of you . . . she will be proud, when she arrives." His gray eyes were pleading. "Please, let me do this, daughter. It is my fate to see her once more, to bring her back. Don't you want to see her, too?"

Mira hesitated, fighting for control of her nerves. "And murder all these people for one small chance?" she asked. "No. Destroy the spell, Father. Now." She shifted her grip on the staff.

"If she lives," Dante vowed, "I will set things right." He held her gaze, and Mira felt a twinge in the back of her mind. She almost wanted to believe him.

"Mira," Ferran coughed, but she did not look at him, her eyes fixed on her father. "He'll kill us all! Your mother isn't coming back!"

"It will work," said Dante, his voice calm and powerful. Aurael squeezed him tightly in his arms, but Dante did not struggle, staring at his daughter. "It will work, Mira, I promise you. I learned my magic from the very best. I will not fail to bring your mother home to us."

"Learned your magic? Or stole it?" Mira inhaled deeply and felt storm clouds brewing inside her. The staff and the book shook in her white-knuckled grip. "You learned your magic from a woman who you later banished to slavery."

Dante's expression changed, his eyes darkening. "That's not true."

"I hold the book. I have the staff you took from her," Mira went on, fueled by her disgust, "and I have since had visions of my own. You betrayed her. You took what you wanted from her and left her to die . . . but she didn't die, not right away. She was raped on that slave ship, Father. Raped, and shipwrecked on an island. This island."

Dante was shaking his head, slowly at first, but more and more emphatically, his eyes glassy with denial. "No," he muttered, "No, no, no . . ."

"She had a child as a result of that rape. Have you guessed what became of it?" Mira tilted her head sadly. "He's here now."

Karaburan crouched near Mira, staring at Dante, his expression contorted with pain and anguished memory. Mira felt the echoes of the tiger's feelings in her heart, emotions swelling and coiling tightly again.

"You have woven your web too tightly, Father, and now it chokes you. Give this up, let them go, and use what power you have left to restore their health."

"If your mother had done her duty and kept my wife alive," Dante snarled suddenly at Karaburan, "we would never have been in this mess! You would never have even been born!" He strained as though to lunge for the creature, but Aurael had wrapped him up tight as a python.

Karaburan recoiled, making a sound of anguish.

"Damn you!" Dante snarled furiously.

"If you will not fix it, I will destroy the spell myself," Mira warned her father again, taking a step closer.

Dante laughed—a bitter, raw-throated sound. "You may have the book and the staff, but you're hardly capable of wielding them properly, child. I studied for years to master their powers and strengthen my own. You've held them for mere minutes and have no inherent magical ability."

"Doesn't that frighten you? Anything could happen if I try to stop the ritual." She narrowed her eyes, pointing the staff at him levelly, frustration blossoming in her chest. "And how exactly can you be so certain I have no power? Am I not your daughter?"

"I'm certain," spat Dante, but his voice wavered as he eyed her suspiciously. "I would have known when you were young if you'd inherited anything at all."

"Did you test me or study me? Did you even try? Or was it worth nothing for you to even find out, since my mother was dead? From what I hear, you could focus on little else."

Dante narrowed his gaze. "You would not hurt me," he whispered. "I am your father, and I am all you have left in this world."

"You're right. I won't hurt you," Mira replied and swung the staff toward the ground, where the pattern smeared against the stone and dust. "But I warned you, and I will end this now!"

The runes shone brightly, and Mira's heart leapt. *Break this ritual,* she thought, focusing her mind. *Blast it clean away.* Lightning shot out from the staff, clawing at the floor of the cavern. When the crackling light faded, there were thick black scorch marks and cracks spread across the floor, shattering the pattern and the spells it contained.

"No!" Dante bellowed with rage, struggling, but Aurael laughed in a shrill voice and held him tighter.

"Everything you have done has been to hurt and destroy. It ends now," declared Mira, leaning on the staff. Euphoria from destroying the spell rushed through and around her like a floodgate opened wide, but after a few moments, it ebbed, tempered with a shuddering exhaustion that built in her legs. *I don't know how much longer I can do this,* she thought, her hands shaking.

There was a rumble from deep within the rock. Mira looked around, the staff trailing streams of blue light in the air as she moved. Karaburan gave a little moan of worry, whirling about in search of the sound's source.

"What was that?" Mira demanded, turning to her father.

"There are wards in place in case my conjuration is broken by another's hand," raged Dante, his gray eyes wild and angry. "For your insolence, the cave will swallow us all!"

"I warned you to give this up!"

Another rumble from deep within the cave shook the floor beneath them. Karaburan howled with fear, but Mira tapped the staff against the ground, already thinking fast. "Be still!" she commanded him. "I will make the men light so that you can carry them all at once. We must go before the walls come down. Now!"

Mira threw her energy at the men's bodies on the ground—*only as heavy as a bundle of firewood*—and little flares of light danced out from the staff to envelop each man. Karaburan lurched forward like a startled racehorse and gathered the fallen bodies in his large arms as easily as if they had been rags. Aurael scooped the struggling Dante up off the ground and soared toward the exit. Ferran clambered to his own feet, limping toward the exit after the others.

"Go now!" Mira commanded. Aurael and Dante vanished down the passageway. Karaburan followed after them, carrying the men draped over his shoulders and in his arms. Ferran staggered forward like an ungainly colt, his legs like rubber as he ran, and Mira came after him.

# CHAPTER TWENTY-THREE

The rumbling and shuddering of the ground grew more violent with every step they took, and the darkness of the long passageway seemed to stretch on forever. Rocks broke apart and tumbled over one another, crashing like waves in their wake. Ferran cried out in pain, struggling to keep pace.

"Faster!" Mira grabbed hold of his arm and pulled him along with her. Her grip was strong, and her strides made faster by the magic within her, so Ferran let himself be swept forward by her momentum. Dirt and rocks tumbled down from the ceiling ahead of them as they ran. Cracks ran through the walls like shattered glass, threatening to cave in as they raced onward.

"Go!" bellowed Aurael from somewhere up ahead. "Run, mortals, run!" The ceiling shuddered wildly and began to crumble, even as the exit loomed ahead.

"We won't make it!" Ferran gasped, stumbling. Aurael and Dante vanished through the cave's mouth, and Karaburan, with the men, followed. "Mira, we're trapped!" Rocks began to fall, filling up the darkness ahead of them.

"No, we're not! Shut your eyes," Mira said sharply, and Ferran obeyed. *Through the wall as softly as though it were water.* Mira leapt forward, yanking Ferran with her, and felt her stomach drop as they met the barrier. There was a brief pressure, like squeezing through a partly-closed door, and then they were out the other side, running down the open beach, away from the cave and the forest.

"You can open them," Mira panted, ecstatic that it had actually worked.

Ferran did, and they both glanced back. Dante's magic illuminated the cave as it dissolved inward on itself like quicksand. The destruction spell sucked the stones, the trees, and the landscape down into the sinkhole with a hungry rumbling sound. Bluish-white magic snapped and flared like hot coals, barely lighting the way down the beach, away from the disaster.

"It's disappearing!" Ferran gasped. "The whole thing is vanishing!"

Mira did not answer, dragging him onward, still sprinting after Karaburan, who, in turn, huffed and puffed alongside Aurael, flying low in his harpy form, carrying Dante like prey in his claws. One of the men—Stephen—slipped from Karaburan's shoulders and Aurael doubled back, snatching the body up in his talons.

Mira pulled Ferran onward until they reached a spit of beach where the sounds of the cave-in were faint and far-off, and there they finally stopped. Karaburan crouched on the damp sand, depositing his cargo and gasping for air. Aurael lowered Stephen and Dante to the ground and sat over them, his claws trapping them on the sand as firmly as bars on a prison cell.

They all looked back to watch the last of the rubble churn downward into the hole, which at last seemed to have filled itself in, leaving only a few trees and a small hillock where the outer entrance of the cave had been. It was all gone. They panted in silence for a few moments, shaken and breathless.

Mira let go of Ferran, carefully lowering him to the sand, where he winced and pressed his hands to his sore sides.

"My work," moaned Dante, trying to get up. "My work! You'll never know how long I labored," he snarled miserably.

"How long you labored?" demanded Aurael, tightening his claws around Dante's ribs. The old man cried out and writhed, pushing at the talons with his trembling hands. "I did all the work! I did your every little errand and bent to each of your stupid, delusional whims. You were a slave driver! A madman!" His harpy's wings flared and ruffled, the iron-sharp feathers shining in the pre-dawn glow. He ground his sharp teeth together in rage. "You made my life a living hell, all because you couldn't have a couple of things that you wanted. Did it never occur to you that you were exiled for being a complete—"

"Aurael! Stop this." Mira slammed the staff down on the sand. "It's over."

The bushes along the tree line shifted and rustled. A tiger stood at the edge of the trees, watching them. "Mira," Ferran hissed, spotting it. "Mira, look!"

Mira looked up as the tiger moved smoothly down the beach from the treeline, her fur gleaming in the dim light, blue eyes luminous and pale.

"It's huge!" Ferran breathed, trembling as he crouched on the sand.

"It's all right," Mira said in a quiet voice. She felt a wash of relief upon seeing the tiger again. "She won't hurt us."

Aurael frowned. He tossed the unconscious Stephen off to one side but did not release Dante, crouching over him. Karaburan made a tiny sound of wonder and fear as he stared at the tiger. The huge cat was as silent as an eel, moving toward the unconscious bodies on the sand. She paused by each of the men, lowering her head and touching her velvet nose to their bodies, as though inspecting them. Long silver whiskers shimmered as the tiger sniffed at them.

"Look," Ferran whispered, his voice creaking. "Oh, look . . ."

Each man's blood faded quickly, flowing backward and vanishing beneath hair and muscle and sinew once more. The bruises bloomed in reverse, growing pinker and then returning to each man's own healthy shade of skin. They breathed normally, and slept soundly.

The tiger looked briefly at Mira, then turned her head at last toward Dante on the ground, and growled softly.

"What is going on?" Ferran wheezed, pressing a hand to his sore side again.

"A final ghost-to-face," Mira announced a little wryly, looking down at her father. "Do you know her? She knows you." The tiger bared her teeth at Dante, who flinched and quivered, then moved past Mira to where Ferran sat.

"Oh. Oh, dear. Oh, no," Ferran stammered as the cat came close. She purred as she sniffed at him, though, and he flinched visibly when she nudged him with her broad head. After a moment, he raised an unsteady hand to stroke the thick neck, and met Mira's eyes in astonishment.

At last, the tiger moved to stand in front of Karaburan, her pale blue eyes wide. Strange expressions played across Karaburan's face as he stared back at her in silence.

"Have I been bad?" Karaburan whispered. "I'm sorry if I was bad." The tiger padded forward and he put his arms around her neck like a child.

Mira looked down at her father. Dante lay exhausted and shivering on the sand beneath Aurael's gleaming claws, as the sky began to lighten with the first glow of dawn.

"You see?" she said gently. "Now there is healing."

"It was my destiny, child!" Dante wheezed. "And yours, too. We cannot fight what is already woven for us."

Mira paused and looked at the huge, ragged volume in her hands. She glanced back at Dante. "No, Father. There is no such thing as destiny. There are different little paths for all of us to choose from, but we create what is, and we determine the endings. You chose your paths, and those paths brought you here. Aurael," Mira went on, turning to look at the harpy-shaped spirit, "I free you of your slavery to my father, and bid you do no ill will toward any present here."

Aurael looked ecstatic, then confused. "Wait. You won't let me avenge myself?"

"No. Enough trouble has been made here. Go, and be a free fae once more." Mira gestured once with her hand, and the spirit shuddered, his harpy's wings and claws melting away until he was a slender, silver-blue boy once more. He looked simultaneously relieved and frustrated, and sat awe-struck on the sand in silence. Aurael turned to look at the tiger, squinting as though he recognized her from somewhere.

"Karaburan, I free you, too." Mira gestured with her hand at Karaburan as well. "No more curses, no more slavery, no more deception. You are the king of this island now."

Karaburan nodded his head somberly, his pale eyes watery and full of awe.

"Father." Mira turned just as Dante struggled to sit up. He fell back on the sand, breathing shallowly. She moved closer and knelt beside him. He looked frail and winded. "Father, what is it?"

"You fool," Dante growled. "Your breaking of the spell has weakened me. Give me back the book and the staff, so I can heal myself." There was a look of fever about him, and his eyes were shut as he lay quivering. "I was so close to the end . . . Let me finish my work."

"No! I won't give them to you," Mira cried, furious. "Don't you see this is killing you? Look what you've become!" Ferran moved to put out a hand to steady her as she shivered, her own body weary from escaping the caves.

Dante groaned, and his tone grew softer. "All I wanted was Sophia, to see her smile again. I would have traded you for her in a heartbeat . . . and for that, I am sorry. Perhaps if I had taught you my art, you would not betray me now." His face twisted with pain, and he opened his eyes to gaze up at her.

"You treated me like a pet until it became inconvenient to take care of me," Mira protested through gritted teeth, tears swimming in her eyes. Ferran could feel her shaking. "When I was endangered, you did not comfort me."

"I wanted you to grow strong, and so you did." Dante coughed again, shutting his eyes from the brightness of hers. "I was strong, too . . . before I poured my soul into my instruments."

"Mira, the book," Ferran murmured. "And the staff. He must have put so much of his own will and force into the book and the staff that they were keeping him alive."

Dante opened his eyes again, fearfully looking up at his daughter.

Mira's jaw worked silently for a moment. "What happens if they are destroyed?"

Her father did not answer for a long moment. "You would murder me, child."

Mira looked at the glowing runes on the staff in her hand, searching for some answers in the design. She glanced back at the tiger, who watched in silence.

"If I break the staff, she goes, too," Mira said grimly. "The staff was hers, once, before it was yours. Before it was mine." She squeezed it 'til her knuckles turned white, and then she relaxed her grip once more.

"Don't send me away, daughter!" Dante murmured, his watery eyes frantic. "We can still make things right. We can still bring your mother back if we work together, child. Save me!"

"He will rise again if you let him live!" cried Aurael shrilly, his silvery face sharp with anger. "We'll be trapped here forever!"

"He'll beat us," whimpered Karaburan, from beside the tiger.

Ferran's mouth was a thin line. "It's the only way to end all this," he said firmly.

"I am dying," Dante croaked. "But if you use the book, you could bring me back. You could heal me, fix me, daughter. Please . . . the book!" His eyelids fluttered.

At this, the tiger gave an insistent growl, moving out of Karaburan's arms and padding on huge paws toward them. Ferran recoiled just behind Mira's shoulder, but Mira did not flinch back.

"Father," Mira said again, her voice breaking. "I won't—"

Dante opened his eyes again to look at her, and her words stuck in her throat for a moment. She sat in silence, trying to summon the words to tell him how she hated him. For all those years he had manipulated and controlled her, and most of all, ignored her very existence. And yet, as he stared at her, new words formed on her tongue, and although it was the last thing she had intended to do, now Mira couldn't stop herself from begging.

"Please," she blurted out, reaching for the tiger. "Do something. Help me fix him! You healed those men, and you healed Ferran and Kabu." She felt dampness on her cheeks, unable to tear her eyes from her father's. "I know he was wrong, I know he betrayed you, betrayed all of us, but we can fix him, can't we? Please . . . Help me heal my father, please, I'm begging you. I don't know how to do this on my own!"

"Mira, are you sure?" Ferran was shocked. "You just said—"

The great jungle cat interrupted with a growl and turned back to Dante, whose breathing came ragged and shallow, his face etched with agony. The tiger bent forward, long whiskers brushing at Dante's body. She paused, hesitating over his chest, and looked at Mira. Mira nodded without looking down at her father.

"I trust you." She had no idea what would happen next. Nor could she remember why she had hesitated to save his life. "Please."

The tiger bent her head down, placed one paw on his stomach, and sank her teeth into Dante's chest.

Mira recoiled in alarm and Ferran made a sound of horrified disgust. The tiger did not ravage Dante, she simply bit into him as delicately as a dog might reach into a hole to retrieve a bone. Dante struggled under the weight of the tiger's paw on his body. No blood spurted forth, no skin or viscera tore off, but the tiger dug down to something buried deep in his chest, her head passing like a ghost through his solid form.

"What on earth!" Ferran breathed in amazement.

The tiger lifted her head slowly again, and something oily, black, and snarling writhed in her jaws. It squirmed and coiled like an octopus, hissing in anger at being removed from its housing, and writhed in protest even as the tiger pulled it out of Dante's chest. It flailed its wispy tendrils, lashing at the tiger's maw. Dante lay wheezing softly on the sand as the tiger shook her head violently, trying to rid herself of the black thing.

"What is that thing?" Ferran cried.

"I don't know!" Mira had never seen anything like it.

"Curses and hatefulness," moaned Karaburan. Mira lunged forward to reach for the black thing, but the tiger yanked it out of the way.

"Don't touch it, or you'll catch it, too!" Ferran yelped. "She's stuck! She touched it and now she's stuck!"

Karaburan shifted his weight back and forth, seeming torn between backing away in fear and wanting to save his tiger mother.

"We have to get it off of her!" Mira commanded, grabbing the staff and reaching out to scrape the writhing dark shadow off of the tiger's face.

"Gods help us, it's growing!" Ferran cried in horror. The thing made a squelching noise, its tendrils stretching even longer and whipping out to begin to envelop the tiger's face. It hissed and squirmed away from the staff when it came near, and the tiger danced backward, shaking her head frantically.

Mira swung at it again and again, but it dodged, slipping out of reach. Finally, she feinted to the left and struck to the right, connecting with the squelchy thing. With a shock of blue-white light, it squeaked and released the tiger's face, flopping down onto the sand, curling and uncurling its tentacle-like arms. As it began to scuttle away, Mira swung again, missing several times. Frustration seared through her, and she hauled back, slamming the staff squarely into the creature's center. The black thing made a cracking sound, dissolving into a fine powder.

The tiger growled irritably, and lay down on the sand, looking worn out and dizzy. Karaburan hurried over to stroke her fur, fretting over her.

"What was that?" muttered Ferran, completely confused.

Mira shook her head. "I don't know. A curse?" She looked at the tiger anxiously. "Or maybe just the corruption of his spirit?"

"Did it work?" Ferran peered over at Dante.

Mira touched her father's shoulder cautiously. "Father?" she asked. His eyes were closed and his mouth was slack. "Father, can you hear me?"

After another moment, Mira pressed her palm to his chest to make sure his heart still beat, and then Dante drew a deep breath and opened his eyes slowly. He looked younger now, healthier, and he gazed up at Mira with an expression of relief and gratitude.

"Mira," he whispered, as though surprised to see her. "My daughter!"

"Did it work?" Ferran asked again, anxiously.

"Oh, gods," Dante breathed. "What have I done?"

Mira frowned, her chest tight with uncertainty. "How do you feel?" She moved her hand to where the tiger had bit him, but there was no mark, no trace that the teeth had pulled a strange black shadow from his chest.

Dante simply gazed at her in breathless joy, smiling as his gray eyes filled with tears. "I feel tired . . . but I am so proud of you," he whispered. "And I am ashamed. I am so, so sorry for what I've done." He looked dizzy from the realization.

Mira's throat constricted. "Father," she stammered, not knowing quite what to say. "Are you all right?"

"I feel as though a great weight has been lifted," he told her, his voice soft and full of wonder. "And it's all because of you." He reached his hand up to touch her cheek.

Mira took his hand and held it for a moment, her eyes stinging with tears, then reached for his shoulder to help him. "Sit up. Here, let me help you."

Ferran moved to the other side and helped steady the older man as he sat up, looking nearly like a completely different person. The hard lines of Dante's face had softened, and his eyes were full of light where they had previously only held ice and hard shadows. Mira hardly recognized him. *Was this what he was before the island? Before my mother died?*

"I am so sorry," Dante told Ferran, breathless from his revival, "for all of this terrible ruin. I should not have done this, Prince Ferran." He leaned forward, trying to get to his feet, but Mira stopped him.

"Father, you have to take it slowly," Mira insisted. "We've just been through a lot, and you'll need time to heal and rest."

"I never let you fret over me before," Dante muttered, shyly. "You've grown up so much. Mira, child, I can never earn your forgiveness for this. Nor can I earn theirs," he added, nodding to the unconscious men on the sand a few yards away.

Mira shushed him. "We must take things one step at a time," she admonished, shaking her head. "There was something black deep inside your heart, and she pulled it out." She gestured to the tiger. "Do you understand? Even though you betrayed her in her past life, she still saved you."

The tiger parted its eyelids to glare at Dante, who reached to take Mira's hand in his own. "I am sorry for you, too," Dante told the great beast. His voice was meek. "I have wronged you, too. But perhaps I still have a chance to redeem myself with my daughter." He looked at Mira. "Please give me a chance to be the father I never was."

Mira sat back on her heels, studying his face. She struggled to find the words, her feelings ranging from relief to confusion. "Yes," she answered finally. "You have much to atone for . . . but you are still my father."

A groan arose from behind them. Ferran and Mira both turned to look; several of the men were stirring. Mira saw Ferran's expression shift to utter hope as one of the older men raised his head groggily.

Ferran held his breath, peering at the man in the dim early morning light. Then his father's voice cut through the quiet air and he felt his fear vanish, relief pouring into him.

"Oh, gods, what happened?" King Alanno struggled to sit up, appearing stiff and disoriented, but no longer brutally injured.

"Father!" Ferran scrambled to his feet, hurrying across the sand. He stumbled, but did not stop running until he reached him. "Father, are you all right?"

"Ferran, my boy!" croaked the king, reaching for him, tears springing to his eyes. "My boy, oh, you're safe, you're well?"

"I'm fine, are you?" Ferran steadied him as he sat upright, kneeling at his father's side. "I thought you were dead. I thought you'd drowned!"

"I'm not dead, not yet anyway. Oh, my boy," murmured the king, pulling Ferran toward him.

Ferran put his arms around his father and shut his eyes, his heart pounding. *Thank the gods,* he thought. *We're all here. We're all together and safe again.*

Torsione opened his eyes and sat up, too, wincing as though stiff from sleep. "What time is it?" he murmured, hazily, and then saw Bastiano beside him. The sight seemed to snap him out of his fog a bit more. "Bas! Wake up, man. We're alive!"

Bastiano stirred and mumbled, but Tor shook his shoulders gently and Bas opened his eyes. "What? Alive?" Bas blinked and looked around. "My gods, look! Alanno!"

Alanno opened his eyes, still hugging his son, and looked at Bastiano. "Brother!" he breathed. "Thank the gods."

Bastiano's eyes welled up with tears. "And Ferran! He's alive! You're alive," he added, excitedly, turning back and touching Torsione's cheek. "We're okay."

"I'm more than okay—my leg is healed. And we're all here," marveled Torsione, in hushed tones, his expression full of amazement. He ran a hand along his leg, feeling the healed limb. "All of us, together. It's unbelievable . . ."

"Oh, I don't know about unbelievable. Amazing, yes. Wonderful? Absolutely." Bastiano shook his head, beaming, and pulled Torsione close, hugging him tightly.

Ferran raised his eyebrows at the sudden display of affection.

"Well, that was rather a long time coming," muttered Alanno, and Ferran laughed.

Bastiano was blushing bright scarlet, but his eyes were full of light, and he smiled widely. Torsione closed his eyes, pressing his forehead to Bastiano's. He let out his breath with a laugh.

Alanno exhaled slowly. "Ferran, my son, forgive me. Please forgive me, my strangeness, my words . . . You are my only son and

I love you. I thought I'd lost you. I thought we were all done for."
He searched Ferran's eyes.

Ferran half-laughed, half-sobbed in reply. "It's all right. It's all right now," he said, and opened his eyes to look over his father's shoulder toward the sea. "I'll explain everything in a while. All that matters is we're all right."

Beyond the dark waves, the pink and gold rays of dawn glowed through the clouds as the sun came up again at last.

# CHAPTER TWENTY-FOUR

Mira watched as the men woke from their bespelled slumbers and reunited with one another. From a distance, she watched over the sleeping servants, the weeping king and his son, and the embracing lords. She heard their exclamations of joy and gratitude and disbelief, and felt as though she were a million miles away.

*What now?*

The words thumped quietly in her mind like a heartbeat. She had done the impossible—saved Ferran and his family and friends, and found a way to restore her father's sanity. But now it was as though she stood on the edge of a precipice in the dark, and although she knew she had to take the leap, she was unsure what would meet her at the bottom.

*What now? What now? What now?*

"Mira." Dante's voice was hushed, humbled.

She looked at her father beside her, and found his expression somewhat frightened as he watched the joyful reunions taking place mere yards away. "What is it?" she asked.

"I'm so ashamed," he confessed, "of what I was . . . of what I intended to do."

"It's over now," Mira said dismissively as she met his gaze. There was a strange weight in her chest as she said it. "Everyone's all right. It'll be like it never happened."

"But my brother, and the king!" Dante protested, and began to cough. "My head is swimming."

"Here," Mira said brusquely, helping him to lie down again on the sand. "Just rest. You're exhausted. I'll go fetch them." Glad of something to do, she scrambled to her feet and moved quickly down the beach, past Karaburan with his arms around the tiger's neck.

"Sweet merciful—who is that?" Bastiano exclaimed as Mira approached, the staff in hand.

Ferran stood up to meet her, brushing sand from his hands onto his trousers. "Mira," he said, a little breathlessly. "Is your father—?"

"He's recovering," she replied, glancing from face to face as the castaways stared up at her in confusion and awe. Their eyes were uncertain, a little afraid, even. Mira felt oddly powerful in that moment. "As are we all," she added.

"Mira?" The king looked perplexed, peering up at her from under his wrinkled brow. "Did you say Mira?"

"Yes, Father!" Ferran looked excitedly at the king. "This is Mira. She saved me, she saved all of us. We owe her our lives."

"But where did she come from?" demanded Bastiano, astonished. "We walked all over the island and saw no signs of civilization, no one at all . . ."

"Except for the harpy," breathed Torsione. His expression shifted to one of horror, as though it could appear at any moment. Bastiano squeezed his hand gently.

"The island does strange things to the mind," Mira admitted, and felt her voice falter a little. "When I was young, I tried to map the whole thing, and every time I went back over my steps, I found my notes were wrong. I tried to sketch it with charcoal on canvas and the backs of pages in books, but no matter how I tried, the maps always turned out wrong or rearranged. The island doesn't care much for logic, I think."

Bastiano and Torsione exchanged puzzled looks, and Mira met the king's gaze at last. Alanno sucked in his breath.

"My gods," he murmured. "Those eyes! Forgive me, my dear, you . . . remind me of someone. A dear friend we lost long ago."

"Sophia?" Mira's heart pounded. *Do I really look like my mother?* The idea reassured her.

Alanno paled. "Yes." The others looked amazed, studying Mira even closer now.

"Sophia was my mother," Mira answered, finding the phrase strange but gratifying to say aloud. "My father . . . was the Duke of Neapolis."

"No! Dante?" Torsione staggered to his feet, thunderstruck. "Is he here?" There was desperation in his tone, but also something like anger.

"But we received word that the ship was wrecked and all aboard were drowned!" Bastiano protested.

"We didn't. My father . . . his powers brought us here safely." Mira took a step back as Torsione rounded on her.

"Where is he? Where is my brother?" His voice was hoarse and shrill.

"He's over there," Mira pointed with the staff, "resting a little ways up the beach. He's very weak."

"Weak?" Torsione frowned again.

"Exhausted. From escaping the cave-in." Mira looked from face to face, seeing the confusion etched upon them like carved stone. "We stopped the ritual."

"What on earth are you talking about?" Alanno asked. "The last thing I remember was the ship sinking."

"That was my father's storm," Mira confessed.

"I was taken by the harpy." Bastiano shuddered. "Just after Tor was. I don't remember what happened after that."

Mira was dumbstruck for a moment, but Ferran leapt to her aid. "He had us all in a cave, bound and shackled, and we'd all surely be dead if Mira hadn't saved us," he said, fiercely. "Dante had a spell, a ritual of some kind. He meant to bring back his wife."

Alanno frowned softly. "He intended to give us to Death in exchange for her. I had thought sending him away for a time might help him recuperate some of his senses . . . but I see that only made things worse."

Mira was at a loss for words, studying the sad face of the king. "He was already on a dark path when you sent him away," she replied finally. "He may not have been saved by staying where he was. He may have continued to choose the darker path."

"Perhaps," said Torsione, his voice wavering, "but we could have chosen to try harder. He's my brother."

"You tried," protested Bastiano.

"I should have tried harder."

"He pushed you away!" Bastiano looked indignant. "You tried as much as you possibly could, Tor. All you can do now is try to reconcile, if he will hear reason."

They all turned their eyes to Mira again, and she swallowed to push the uncertainty back down to the pit of her stomach. "He is much changed. We broke more than his ritual, I think. Come and see him; he asked for you," she added, and turned to lead them back up the beach.

Karaburan cried out in alarm, and, from a distance, Mira saw the huge form of the tiger leap toward her father's prone body.

Mira's heart stopped. She sprinted toward them, the sand shifting and slipping beneath her feet. The tiger pounced at her father, snarling, but even as Mira skidded closer, the tiger was flung backward onto the beach, tumbling tail over snout. Karaburan staggered to help the tiger up again, and Mira saw what had prompted the attack.

Aurael had Dante by the hair and throat, his shimmering lower body entwined about Dante's torso like a gigantic serpent. Dante gasped for air, his arms pinned down by the spirit.

"Aurael, stop!" Mira cried, stabbing the staff into the sand. The runes flickered brightly for a second, but Aurael did not recoil. He tilted his head to look at Mira, his eyes filled to the brim with a starless, deep black void. His smile was humorless and hungry.

"Oh, no, my love," he hissed through his gleaming rows of teeth. "There's not a thing that could stop me now."

"I command you to stop!" she called out hoarsely, but the runes on the staff only glowed dimly. *Why isn't this working?* She brandished the staff as though it were her old spear again.

Aurael's laugh was like broken glass. "You've only got half the toolkit, precious girl," he told her, "and besides—you freed me, remember?" The serpent tail of his lower body curled around Dante one more time. Mira saw that, wrapped in the very end of the tail, was her father's book, shuddering with energy as the snake-body squeezed it ever tighter.

"Don't," she begged. "Please don't, Aurael. He's my father. He's been a terrible, awful man, but he's my father!"

"All children must bury their parents," the spirit snarled. "Isn't that right, Karaburan?"

The tiger lay in a jumbled heap on the sand, Karaburan at her side, distraught. Aurael smiled again.

"Please, Aurael," Mira insisted. "Please. I have one more chance to have him as my father, a real father. One last chance. Don't do this."

Aurael's face contorted as he squeezed both Dante and the book tighter in his coils. Dante made a hollow, painful sound, his eyes rolling back into his head.

"Say 'please' again," hissed the spirit.

"Please!" Mira couldn't help it. Her father's face grew redder and redder. "You're killing him, please, Aurael!"

"I vowed when I was put into that tree that once I got out, I would never be trapped again. And what happens? Your selfish, pathetic father snares me by a trick of words and makes me his slave. For fourteen years I served and suffered, and now I am free at last. This is my final duty from a servant to a master."

"Please!" Mira's voice hardened. "I know we have all been trapped, but you don't need to—"

"Trapped? You, who have never known the ecstasy of a pure wind and the open sky? You, who have never seen the stars from above, the seas from below, the earth from its core? You are mortals. I was trapped. You were simply inconvenienced." Aurael sneered. "You are nothing compared to me! I am a god. You are as ants to a titan!"

"Show him mercy," Mira pleaded. Aurael's shimmering brightness, the gleaming of his teeth and dark stare made her own eyes water and burn. "Please, Aurael! For whatever love you bore me as a child, please!"

Aurael glared back at her, but his churning rage began to flag, his coils loosening around Dante's body, and the old man gasped weakly for air as the spirit let him go, bit by bit.

"Gods be merciful," breathed Bastiano from somewhere behind Mira.

Dante sagged onto the sand, choking on the air that rushed too quickly to his lungs now that he was loose. The spirit slid back a little from the old man, eyes locked with Mira's, his tail still coiled about the heavy book.

"Be free, Aurael," Mira commanded, her breath shallow. "Go away and never come back."

"Free," echoed the spirit, sounding dazed. He looked down and saw the book still in his grasp. His eyes narrowed. "Yes. Now, I am free."

Aurael squeezed hard, snapping the book's spine and weather-worn cover as easily as driftwood. A flash of light burst from the book as it split. A spark caught fire on the pages, blazing with sudden brightness and consuming the book as it fell into pieces on the sand. Blue and white sparks flew, the heat keeping Mira at bay even as she dove to save it.

"No!" Mira cried out in anguish. Ferran yanked her back from the flames, stumbling on the sand with her. *Not the book!* Burning pages of the old volume fluttered to the ground as Aurael opened his snake-jaws to strike.

An echoing roar erupted from off to the side. The tiger leapt onto Aurael's back, sinking her claws and teeth into him. He howled and, with a blast of wind, shook her violently off. She scrambled to her feet again, but the spirit slapped at her with the length of his thick tail. Something cracked, like a huge branch snapping in two. The tiger collapsed onto the sand in an orange heap, motionless. Karaburan screamed, and Mira felt her entire body go cold. She looked up to see Aurael crush Dante in the folding coils of his silver-blue scales. She stared, paralyzed with disbelief, as her father's body vanished into the serpent's grip.

*No,* she thought, *I was so close. I almost fixed it.* Darkness crept in at the edges of her vision, overwhelming her. For a second, she thought she smelled something burning, then a powerful wind knocked her down. A bright light ahead of her chased the blackness away from her sight.

Mira shook her head to clear her vision and found herself on her back, blinking up at the most gorgeous woman she could possibly have imagined.

"By the gods!" breathed Torsione.

"She's beautiful," whispered the king.

She wore a plain ivory gown like the Greccians did in ancient times, her black hair in tangled, sweeping locks adorned with flowers and vines. Unnaturally tall and willowy, the woman's skin was warm brown with mossy green undertones. Her eyes were bright, polished gold, lined with dark kohl, and her expression was that of the housecat who has captured the last mouse. Dread clenched Mira's stomach, but then the woman smiled, and she felt a warmth spread throughout her body.

"*Well done, storm-child.*" The woman's voice was like water in a marble fountain, resonant and clear. "*The sins of the father are paid for, the monster is absolved his crime, and the imp will face a punishment greater than his own revenge.*" She shifted slightly to look back over her shoulder at where the tiger, Karaburan, and Dante were scattered on the sand. Mira sat up quickly, and found that Aurael was no longer a massive silvery snake, but a twitching, goblin-faced imp suspended in the air. He looked nothing like the handsome, smooth-cheeked boy he'd been to Mira, his features uglier, more twisted. He whined and panted, hanging above Dante's fallen form.

"Who are you?" Mira winced, her body tender from the fall. She looked around to find the other men sprawled all over the ground around her, with Ferran off to her left, trying to get his bearings again after the fall.

"*A gambler,*" said the woman, and laughed as if she had made a joke. "*My lord husband often places bets on the losing pony, and when he does, I am the one to collect. It's especially true when the loser is one of my husband's little lackeys. Isn't that right, Aurael?*" She reached for him, and the spirit soared to her hand, jabbering and snarling. The woman held him aloft and peered at him as a fisherman examines his catch. "*Oh, would you have words with me, imp? Very well, speak.*"

There was a faint popping sound and Aurael groaned, snapping his jaws in frustration. "Please, my queen, I can explain . . ."

"*You can always explain,*" she tutted at him. "*But that does not mean anyone will believe you. That is your real tragedy, Aurael. Your tongue is so silver that even your truths are falsehoods.*"

"Please," Aurael begged. "Don't be hasty, Your Highness!"

Mira held up a hand to her brow, her head still echoing with the strange burst of power. "You're a queen?" she prompted. "I don't understand. You're a spirit, too?"

The tall woman looked at her and smiled a little. It was a beautiful smile, but a dangerous one. *"Among other things, storm-child. I have many names, as do we all, in our lifetimes. If you will excuse me, I shall remove this imp from this awful little island and leave you all to your utterly confusing mortal moralities, or whatever else it is you do in your short little lives."*

"Wait!" squawked Aurael.

"Wait!" cried Mira, putting up one hand. The queen looked at her in mild surprise. Mira hesitated, unsure how to properly address the faerie queen. "Please, Your Majesty. I ask you for your assistance."

*"Do you? Very well, I will hear your request."* She seemed utterly amused at the concept of demands from a mortal child.

"I have several." Mira held the queen's gaze a moment, hoping that the faerie queen would know how badly she needed what she was going to ask for. She drew a deep breath before kneeling to the crumpled body of her father. Dante's face was pale as the sand, his cheeks sallow. Mira's insides went watery, and she took his limp hand in hers. *He's gone. Aurael destroyed the book, and it's too late to save him.* "Can you reverse death?"

The queen's amusement left her like a bird from a windowsill. *"Only Death can reverse death, and she is not likely to do it anytime soon. I am sorry you have lost your father, child, but there is nothing more to be done for him."*

Mira drew a deep breath and let it out again, feeling tears prickle her eyes. The lords nearby exchanged wary, amazed looks. "I understand," she replied, shakily. "And the tiger?"

The queen glanced at the tiger, eyebrows raising in surprise. *"Why blessed be,"* she murmured in astonishment. *"Corvina!"*

Karaburan was sobbing piteously over the tiger's blood-soaked face. He cowered as the queen's eyes passed over him.

*"Do not cry, witch-son,"* the queen said gently, waving a hand as though she were wafting perfume toward herself. The tiger's fur shimmered and faded, and, for a moment, there was no tiger at all, but a dark-skinned woman covered in tattoos lying on the sand. Karaburan's tears slowed in astonishment, and he gaped at the sight. *"Your mother served me well in her younger days,"* the queen told Karaburan. *"For that, I will shift her. Her spirit stayed here to guide you all in the body of this tiger . . . but now that body, too, has failed her. Her spirit is now part of the very island itself, so that she can be troubled no more, and can continue to watch over you."*

The queen beckoned, and the gleaming, rune-carved staff soared through the air to her hand. She broke it in half as neatly as a twig of driftwood, and Corvina's body faded into a hazy sky-blue shape, which sank into the sand. The two halves of the staff gleamed blue, shimmering into dust, and the queen scattered it to the wind.

She looked at Mira with an arched brow. *"Well, storm-spawn? What else is on your shopping list of boons?"* she asked tersely.

"Can you repair a shipwreck?" Mira got to her feet with Ferran's help, keeping her voice steady as she did so.

Someone made a noise of agreement behind her, and Mira saw the men nodding hopefully out of the corner of her eye.

"Our trunks," murmured Bastiano. "All of our clothes, our food, our supplies."

"The crew," Ferran added, looking sad. "The servants. Oh! Gonzo!" He turned to Mira, eyes wide.

"I picked up all of the pieces," she told him with a shake of her head. "I have no idea if he's fixable."

"Gonzo?" The king looked confused.

"Dante . . . he smashed him," Ferran explained, and the king's face fell. "I'm sorry."

"But how is that possible? If the ship went down, he ought to have gone down, too."

"I found the trunk he was in and brought it ashore," Mira interjected. "He was already in pieces, but now he's in shards, I'm afraid."

"His inventor is long dead," Alanno sighed. "And Dante was the only other one who knew much about his anatomy, unfortunately."

Mira looked at the queen, and the others turned to follow her gaze.

The queen eyed the men haughtily. "*Hm,*" she mused, as though bored by the very suggestion. "*That's an awful lot of gears to piece back together, but I suppose I could make it work. As for the shipwreck . . . perhaps I could bring you something a little smaller? A smoke signaler?*"

"You're joking, right? These men need passage home, not a slightly larger chance that a passing ship might pause to pick them up at an undetermined point in the future!" Mira leaned on Ferran and exhaled sharply in frustration. "Please. Anything you can do to help. Surely it is a small matter to someone as great as you, Highness?" she added.

"*You've got an awful lot of fire in you, storm-child,*" the queen said icily, and Mira held her breath, wincing inwardly. There was a considerable pause. "*All right, fine. There shall be a ship on your horizon much sooner than you think.*" She flapped one hand carelessly.

"A working ship?" she ventured. The queen hesitated a half second, then smiled.

"*Of course. I'm not heartless, after all. It would not do to rescue you all from one shipwreck only to place you into another one.*"

"Thank you, Your Majesty." Mira bowed her head, exhaustion beginning to creep into her limbs.

The queen laughed a little snidely. "*Ah, mortals. So surprising. Sometimes they ask too much, sometimes too little. Well, I will give you one thing more for all your troubles, storm-child.*" She glided toward Mira and looked into her eyes. Mira felt the massive, ancient presence of the faerie queen, and tried not to let her uncertainty show. "*I will let you keep what's yours,*" said the queen, and smiled again. She turned away, still holding the squirming, desperate Aurael aloft with one hand.

"What does that mean?" Mira frowned.

"My queen, please," choked Aurael. "Queen Titanya, I beg you!"

"Your Highness," Mira interrupted. "I don't understand. There is nothing here that is mine to keep."

"*That isn't quite true,*" replied Titanya, still smiling. "*There are many things that are yours alone: your body, your mind, your soul, and more within you will find, in time. You have already used your power several times today, or have you forgotten already? Your father, too, had power within him, but it was his choice to use it for great ill. So this is my blessing on you, storm-child—that your power remain with you to grow as you see fit, and to bend to your will so long as your intent is pure.*"

Mira felt a ripple of bliss start somewhere in her chest and flutter outward to her fingertips and toes. She blinked rapidly, startled by the sudden flush of euphoria. "Thank you," she said, curiously. It seemed a good blessing to have received, even though it had been accompanied by such a peculiar sensation.

"*I am sure you will use it wisely. Goodbye, mortal children.*" Titanya winked at the men. "*And as for you,*" she continued, looking now at Aurael. "*Now that you have served your sentence here, it is my duty to inform you that your punishment will continue at home. Poq cannot wait to get her hands on you. You've really got her goat this time, Aurael.*"

The airy spirit's eyes went wide. "Poq? But that was two hundred years ago! That's ancient history!"

"*Not for her, it wasn't*," Titanya chuckled, and bopped Aurael on the nose.

"No," he pleaded, thrashing in her grasp like a worm on a hook. "No, please, please my queen, not Poq, don't send me to Poq, anything but that, anything but that, please! *Aaaauuuuugggghhh!*"

Titanya threw her head back, laughing as brightly as birdsong over Aurael's scream, and, with another sudden great whirlwind, they were gone. Gulls began to cry in jarring tones somewhere out over the water, and there was a faint rumbling noise. Mira turned to look, and as she did, she saw the men follow suit.

An airship broke through the clouds, soaring toward the island, flying the king's colors from the mainmast.

"My gods!" cried Bastiano, leaping up joyfully. "We're saved, we're all saved!" He and Torsione whooped and hollered with giddy laughter, exhausted relief flooding their features.

"Thank all of the gods for getting us out of this mess," sighed Alanno, squeezing Ferran's shoulders and smiling. "We'll see your mother again, lad. She may not have even left Tunitz yet . . . we may beat her home still."

"It'll be good to go home," agreed Ferran, his voice cracking. Tears shone in his eyes, Mira noticed, but still the prince smiled.

Mira turned back to look at her father's body, and found that it had vanished. Panic gripped her and her knees buckled. She sat down clumsily, as though the floor had shifted to meet her, and saw that where he had lain now stood a great funeral pyre, burning a steady golden flame whose smoke rose high into the sky as a beacon for the ship that approached the island. Her panic dissolved into a deep, bone-jarring sob.

*He's gone.* Her breath came short and painful in her chest, and although tears blurred her vision, they did not fall. *No,* she told herself, *he was gone long ago, and now it's over. Oh, gods, it isn't fair* . . . Anguish surged within her and she slammed her fists down onto the sand, bright bluish-white light erupting from her and sparkling out across the beach before fading.

Karaburan lumbered toward her with a sober expression.

"We are both orphans now," he said, his voice timid.

She nodded. "So we are. I suppose all children grow up to be orphans at some point in their lives," Mira mused, watching the flames, dazed with exhaustion and grief. "Aurael was right. It is the way of life that children must bury their parents."

"That doesn't make it less sad," replied Karaburan, and sat down in the sand at her side, just out of arm's reach. They watched the pyre burn for some time in silence.

"Mira?" Ferran wandered closer to them, keeping his distance, as though he feared to interrupt the moment. His expression was hopeful as Mira turned to face him. "I know this is a huge . . . well, I understand that there's a lot . . . Will you come back to Neapolis with us?"

The question shook her from her reflective reverie. Mira raised her eyebrows, her heart surging in her chest at the idea of leaving the island. Suddenly, the day's tumultuous events seemed distant, and her mind raced as she considered the offer.

"Neapolis is your home, too. I mean, it should be. You were born there, you're still a citizen. And . . . you shouldn't stay here forever, not alone like this, now that your father's gone. And besides, it's what you wanted, isn't it? To travel?" he added, his cheeks growing a little pink as he said it. His hands balled into fists at his sides, as if they weren't sure what else they should be doing.

Mira got to her feet, swallowing her mixed feelings of excitement and confusion. She looked over at Karaburan, who eyed her sideways with an innocent expression.

"I'm the king of the island," he said, as if that explained everything. He spread his six-fingered hands wide in an awkward shrug.

Mira tried not to laugh. "Yes, you are. What do you think?"

"I'm the king of the whole island," he repeated, carefully. "I cannot abandon my kingdom. My mother's spirit rests here, and so must I."

Mira furrowed her brow. "Won't you be lonely?"

Karaburan shook his head imperiously. "No. You would, but I won't."

"And what should I do instead?" she asked quietly.

Karaburan turned his whole hulking frame about and eyed Ferran a little shyly. Then he ran a hand over his head and scratched his shoulder, fidgeting. "If you want to see what's beyond the water, you should go beyond the water and see it. Whatever it is," he added, as though he could not fathom it himself.

Mira drew a deep breath and let it out again slowly. "That about settles it. Thank you, Your Highness," she added.

Karaburan's pale blue eyes lit up like candles, and he smiled an uneven, timid smile.

"All right," Mira said. She turned to Ferran, who looked as though he were trying not to smile too widely. She raised her brows at him. "What?"

"I'm glad you're coming," he confessed, and looked around sheepishly. "I'm glad we made it out of this, y'know, alive."

Mira said nothing, sensing what he was getting at. She looked back at the island thoughtfully, the trees painted with the colors of dawn. "So am I," she agreed. Sorrow, relief, and resolve battled equally within her, but riding at the forefront of those emotions was the thrill of anticipation.

"Are you all right?" Ferran asked in a quieter voice. "I mean, a lot has happened."

"I know. I'll be fine." Mira took a deep breath and smiled, looking over at him. "There is much to do."

"Is there?"

"Oh, yes. First things first: when that ship lands, I need you to show me how everything works. And I mean, everything. After that, I am going to need some piloting lessons."

Ferran laughed. "And after that?"

"After that," Mira replied, "I'm going to see every inch of this brave new world."

# ACKNOWLEDGEMENTS

I didn't intend for this to be my first novel. I've written (or attempted to write) several before this, but this one happened at just the right time, and it had the right challenges for me. These challenges could not have been met without a lot of help, a lot of encouragement, and a lot of love. If you're reading this: thank you.

Specifically, I have to thank the incredible friends I have who have supported my every creative move, especially those which led me to this moment. Thank you beyond words to Nika, Jessi, Meg, Lev, Kim, Bobby, Dora, Chels, Kyle, Matt, Kathy, Chris, Elyse, Meghan, Sarah, Laurence, Atra, Becka, Ilana, Warwick, Deborah, Ken, Mary Jo, Josh, Benjamin, Andy, Dave, Nicole, Kurt, Stephanie, Deborah, Nathan and Mel for their friendship and support, for offering to feed me when I was eye-deep in revisions, for offering to booze me when I was tearing out my hair with frustration, and for offering to read the final product when I was ready to let it all go out into the world. Thanks also to Brian, Beth, Gary and Cathy for keeping the Fan Club alive. Love you guys!

Thank you to The Book Cellar in Lincoln Square, Red Eyes Cafe in North Center, DemiCon in Des Moines, and the indomitable, magnificent TeslaCon in Madison—TeslaCon brought me into the world of Steampunk in person, when I had only ever experienced it in books before, and made my imagination explode with possibilities. Cheers to you all: Will and Karen, Alexis, Kait, Kat, Shane, Joseph, Eli, Elizabeth, Evan, Tab, Ansel, Adam, the Prussians, Neal, Rachel, Aelf, Heath, Katherine, and Eric of course. Love and thanks!

To the Plan 9 Asstronauts (sic) and fan family for weird shimmies and your unfathomable love for my mortal grossness.

To the Piccolo Theatre family for taking a chance on me as an actor and for making me one of your own, and for bringing me into a whole new family for a whole new chapter of my life.

To the great weird excellent massive unstoppable force that is the Bristol Renaissance Faire: Kristen said leap, so we must leap. The net will appear! (Thank you Kristen!) Naomi, Lara, Greg, Kate, Chris, Steven, Juli, Drew, Gwen, Jiggins, beloved commedia, all of the directors, all of the cast, all of the photographers . . . everyone who has been a part of the Bristol bubble of creative joy. Thanks.

To Danielle, for letting your peanut gallery help my peanut gallery find their voices, and for being such a wonderful cheerleader.
To T. Stacy Hicks for (sometimes unknowingly) providing historical context and finesse.

To Dr. Robert O. Bucholz, for being an unparalleled pillar of inspiration for me and countless other students you've had throughout the years. Your storytelling is infectious, and your friendship and encouragement has been utterly amazing.

To Jon Balcerak, to whom I would have dedicated "Lavenza" if I'd have been given a space to do so. This is all your fault for teaching me to speak up and write better and enjoy this kind of thing.

To Grandma Sally, who gave me my first journals and taught me to love writing every day, and to savor each story worth telling.

To Grandpa John, Who took me seriously as a writer when I was seven, and who will never get the chance to read this, but whom I hope would be proud.

Thank you to my impossibly wonderful editor Jessica, whose ability to decipher my theatre-brain and my GIF-laden emails with ease is amazing. I am so grateful that your humor is like my humor, or this would have been a hell of a lot more difficult. Thanks also to Rie, Kristina, McKenna, Heidi, Penny, and the Xchyler Publishing family—I feel like the Velveteen Rabbit as a writer sometimes, and you guys made me a Real Writer.

To Tee Morris and Philippa Ballantine, for giving me an open door and their open hands to help me take the first steps, for being my Steampunk fairy godparents, and for the laughter and love even across the miles. Kia kaha and thank you.

To Tom Charney and Ann-Elizabeth Shapera, two of the most giving and inspiring and encouraging human beings I have ever known, for tunes, for noms, for hugs, for unyielding support and care even when we were mostly strangers still. I am unfathomably grateful for your presence in my life and I will always reach higher because you believed in me.

To Emily, for being the best cosmic hetero-lifemate the universe could possibly offer me. You are my constant, my touchstone.

To Claire, for being an anchor as well as a buoy, for taking very, very good care of me and for helping me be better in so many ways.

To Alexis, for allowing me to drink wine and shout things while she helped me fill out the project management workbook and try to organize this novel like a grown-up. Spreadsheets make me dizzy, and without you, I wouldn't have been able to fill them out. Also, thank you for everything. Just everything. La la la la la la la.

Thank you to Mom, Dad, and Ben, without whom I would not be telling nearly so many stories or be nearly so dedicated to my dreams. If you hadn't told me I could do it, I wouldn't have tried. It's that simple. I love you all.

# ABOUT ALYSON GRAUER

**A**lyson Grauer is a storyteller in multiple mediums, her two primary canvases being the stage and the page. On stage she is often seen in the Chicago area, primarily at Piccolo Theatre, Plan 9 Burlesque, and the Bristol Renaissance Faire. Her non-fiction work has been published in the Journal for Perinatal Education for Lamaze International. Her short fiction can be found in *Tales from the Archives (Volume 2) for the Ministry of Peculiar Occurrences* and in two anthologies from Xchyler Publishing, *Mechanized Masterpieces: A Steampunk Anthology* and *Legends and Lore: an Anthology of Mythic Proportions*. Alyson is a proud graduate of Loyola University of Chicago and hails originally from Milwaukee, WI. This is her first novel.

Twitter: @dreamstobecome
Facebook.com/AuthorGrauer

# ABOUT XCHYLER PUBLISHING

At The X, we pride ourselves in discovery and promotion of talented authors. Our anthology project produces three books a year in our specific areas of focus: fantasy, Steampunk, and paranormal. Held winter, spring/summer, and autumn, our short-story competitions result in published anthologies from which the authors receive royalties.

Additional themes include: *Losers Weepers* (spring/summer 2015) and *Worldwide Folklore and the Post-modern Man* (winter 2016).

Visit **www.xchylerpublishing.com/AnthologySubmissions** for more information.

**Look for these releases from Xchyler Publishing in 2015:**

*Winter Storm,* the third installment of the *Grenshall Manor Chronicles* by R. A. Smith. February 2015.

*Vanguard Legacy: Fated,* the conclusion of the three-book series by Joanne Kershaw. April 2015.

*Blondes, Books and Bourbon,* an anthology of short stories set in the *White Dragon Black* world of Jonathan Alvey, by R. M. Ridley. April 2015.

*Everstar* by Candace J. Thomas, Book 3 of the *Vivatera* series.

To learn more, visit **www.xchylerpublishing.com**.

A Xchyler Publishing Sneak Peek

# Lavenza, or the Modern Galatea

## ALYSON GRAUER

**From Mechanized Masterpieces:**
**A Steampunk Anthology**

My name is Elizabeth Lavenza, and I am dreaming the same dream that has haunted me since I was a child.

I am lying on my back in my bed, and my skin is hot with fever. There is a sound like metal clicking, and a gentle voice is humming some unidentifiable, soothing tune. I open my eyes slowly, the room around me blurry and swimming with too-vibrant colors. My body is heavy as lead, my limbs limp against the mattress as someone peels back the sheets from my prone form. Gentle, firm hands cradle my head and prop me up against a pillow, and I can see before me.

My mother, beautiful and serene, is there beside me, her touch loving and careful. She is the source of the humming, the melody some foreign lullaby that calms me despite my inability to move my body. She pulls a pair of goggles down over her eyes, and there are gloves on her slender hands. She pushes aside more cloth, and my vision blurs again, the room spinning.

She has a set of small, strange tools on a tray beside her, and she is using them on me, somehow, in a way that I cannot quite make out from this angle. My heartbeat is loud as a metal drum, and there is a whirring of gears and clacking of cogs.

I am suddenly afraid, for I do not understand what I see with my own eyes, but then the fever takes me into blackness once more.

Then I awake, and I am whole and well, with no trace of fever, no sign of any surgery upon my form, and my mind is full of questions.

I have had this recurring dream since I was a child, but it is not the first thing I remember. If I am to tell this tale, I ought to start from the beginning of my life.

I was once an orphan, brought to be the ward of a well-off couple when my poor Italian foster family could no longer afford to keep me. This fine couple, whose name was Frankenstein, told me that I was the daughter of a German lady and a Milanese nobleman, an illegitimate child and the cause of my mother's death.

For as long as I could remember, my new parents determined that I would one day wed my foster brother, whom I have called 'cousin' all my life. He and I were playmates as children, the best of friends, and it did not seem unusual that we should one day be man and wife.

Despite my rise from destitution to comfort, from abandoned to loved, I had always understood my own existence to be average in every way. I was comfortable and happy, and there was nothing strange or out of the ordinary about me or my adopted family.

Oh, the lies we tell to protect the ones we love!

After my adoption by the Frankensteins, my childhood was very much a warm and happy one. My dear cousin Victor was a deeply inquisitive, quiet, intelligent soul. We were constant companions, and I often found my own curiosity piqued by his. He revealed unto me endless wonders of the world and its habits, and we explored the way children do: fearlessly and often, without stopping to rest. We spoke of stars and mountains, rivers and caverns, of flame and electricity, of steam and iron.

Victor was fascinated by the progress of invention, and I found myself often peering over his shoulder at things he studied, curious in ways of my own. More than anything, however, I loved his passion, the gleam in his eyes that spoke of rushing, fathomless thoughts too quick for even his own tongue to keep up.

I suppose I always knew he would be a scientist of some sort; a scholar, definitely. His father wished for a doctor, or lawyer, and indeed, my Victor could have achieved all this and more. But, Victor wanted the thrill of discovery, the sleepless nights of research and experimentation. He wanted a more difficult path.

Victor always got what he wanted.

When we were still quite young, I contracted an illness, that which went by the name of scarlet fever. I was quarantined in my chambers upon diagnosis, to suffer it through or be taken to the arms of God, and my adoptive mother was barred from caring for me as she so wished, on the chance she might contract the fever too.

I remember little of this time spent in dim firelight, rolling in the sheets in a haze of heat and weakness and worry. And then I woke to find my mother there, feeding me soup and giving me water to drink, and dampening my brow with a cool cloth.

"But Mother," said I, fearful, "the doctor said you could catch my fever!"

"Better to catch your fever, my angel, than let you suffer alone," said she, then continued to care for me as bravely as any soldier on the front lines of a war.

Again, I dipped into dreamless, fuzzy sleep, and was lost for a time in darkness and warmth. Once, I thought I opened my eyes and saw my mother there, bent over my abdomen with gloves and spectacles on, using a tiny set of metal tools to fix something, like a surgeon. I slept again in confusion.

When I woke again, my mother was there, looking weak and tired herself. I felt somewhat better. The little tools and gloves and spectacles of magnification were nowhere to be seen. I wished to ask her why I had seen these things, but had not the courage to do so, lest I be seen as mad.

"You will get well now, my Elizabeth," said my mother, smiling distantly. "Your fever has broken and you will mend."

"Are you well? Have you had the fever, Mother?" My voice was filled with dread, but she only smiled.

"I am still here, am I not? We have so much to do together," she added. Then, she drifted off to sleep in her chair.

But my mother did catch the fever from me, and though my strength and appetites quickly returned to me, a healthy pink to my cheeks, she grew pale and weak and warm to the touch. When she was confined to bed, I could not bear to leave the room, for fear of losing her, as she had nearly lost me.

When she was at her weakest, she held my hands in hers and lay on her side in bed, smiling at me. I felt full of emotion and fear and worry, but she calmed me as she always had with her steady eyes and gentle hands.

"I have lost one mother," I said. "I do not want to lose another. Please get well again." She squeezed my hands. "Illness is unfair, but you should rejoice, Elizabeth, for you will never be ill again and all will be well."

"How can you know this?" I wondered, perplexed by her words.

My mother's reply was one I did not expect or quite understand, at first. She told me that she had given of herself to make me whole, and ensured that I would never fall prey to sickness again, and that it had, by some turn of events, made her ill, too.

"But I need you," I protested. "I cannot let you die this way for saving me."

"But death for a loved one is not a death wasted," my mother said, gently. "And Victor needs you. Without you, he will be lost. Always remember that, Elizabeth."

When Victor was summoned to join us, that our mother might say her goodbyes, he was anxious and pale as any son who fears for his mother. She held our hands in hers and smiled bravely.

"It is my wish and that of your father, that when you two come of age you should be wed. You are meant for each other. Keep each other safe and happy, that's all I ask, and your father will be comforted."

When she died, our father mourned deeply, as did we all, for she was beloved in our household and our town. Victor and I sat in the garden in our mourning clothes, watching the wind in the grass and the clouds passing quickly overhead; a storm was doubtless on its way.

"She went peacefully," I said gently. "She wasn't angry or upset. That's good isn't it?"

Victor said nothing for a while, but I could see the familiar gleam in his eyes, full of thought and pressing need.

"We shall miss her," he said. His chin quivered a moment, then was still.

"Yes, but we have each other. We shall always have each other, Victor. I shall always be here for you."

"I know you will. But you will stay here, and I shall be going away to school." When he spoke, his voice had lost its childlike bounce and fervor, and now withheld a tremble of determination, unusual in a child our age.

"Will you study medicine or law?"

"Both, I should think. And science. There are so many questions, Elizabeth, and I must answer them all."

"You will be brilliant at whatever you do. And you will come back to me, and all will be well."

From our mother's death, I had no wishes but to serve and help the family. I acted as mother and sister and daughter. I was a well-mannered young woman as I grew older, selfless and as kind as I could be to anyone and everyone I crossed paths with. I took over much of the house management, and was well used to the care and keeping of our rooms.

When Victor went off to school, we said a hopeful, but teary, goodbye. When his coach disappeared down the road, I felt a peculiar pang in my chest. For the first time, I wished I was going with him, and learning all the things he would learn. But it was not my place, and so I continued to exist in the small world of our home, waiting for his return, and writing him letters from time to time.

I never thought about the fever dream of my mother with the tools again—not until I found the letters. I was airing out the cupboards in her private rooms which had been locked by the house staff since her death.

My mother's room felt like just another room in the house, for years had passed, and I was older. I missed her daily, but taking on her responsibilities had helped me to see my place as I grew into adulthood.

This day was different from my usual cleaning routine. Something caught the toe of my shoe while I crossed the room, and I stumbled. On investigation, I discovered that the offending object was the corner of a loose board in the floor. Without hesitation, I knelt and began to pry it out, curious to see what had caused it to come loose.

In the hole beneath the board was a cloth packet, tied with string.

I reached down and pulled it free, and after a moment, decided to unwrap it. The old, stiff cloth peeled away heavily to reveal a leather journal and a stack of letters in envelopes. Most were sealed, many unaddressed. Two were addressed to me, but the second of these had the heading "On Your Wedding Day."

I opened the first.

*My dear angel Elizabeth,*

*If you are reading this, then I am gone, and I must yield unto you a part of my deepest self, and reveal several things which may come as rather a shock to you. You must not reveal any of this information to your Victor or to my husband, your father. If you cannot promise me these things, you must hereby burn these letters and bury the journal in the soil. There is no shame in this, my dear one, but if you choose to read on, you must be strong, for all our sakes. Flesh of my flesh and bone of my bone you are, Elizabeth, and from your state and mine shall never be parted, bliss or woe, no matter what happens.*

I paused in my reading. This was most unprecedented. But even as I pondered the meaning of this, the vision of my fever dream, my mother in spectacles and accoutered like a surgeon over my prone form, sprang before my eyes.

There was no way about it but to read on, know the unknown, and keep my mother's secrets.

When my mother was a young girl, she wrote in her careful, sweeping hand, she and her family, called Beaufort, encountered a small company of gypsies on the road to Paris. The gypsies had broken a wagon wheel, and it was such that my mother's mother longed to hurry by without stopping.

But my mother's father was a kind gentleman, and he ordered the coachman to slow warily and ask if the little ragged family was well or if they required assistance. Mrs. Beaufort insisted that this was a certain invitation for trouble and robbery, but Mr. Beaufort refused to hear her.

It was such that the gypsies were not of ungrateful stock. The patriarch of their patchwork family doffed his cap and thanked the gentleman kindly for his offer.

"Our wheel has broken, monsieur," announced the gypsy man, "and we can go no further. We are too far from town and my wife is with child. We cannot walk."

He gestured to the woman, seated on the slanted wagon, her belly round and full. She had a sad, knowing look about her, and when Mrs. Beaufort peered out the coach window to see with her own eyes, the gypsy woman sat up straighter.

"Your own daughter, madame," pleaded the gypsy woman suddenly, reaching out to her. "She is your life's light, your only joy. You would do anything to see her comfortable and happy."

Mrs. Beaufort was doubtful, for she feared that there would be dishonesty behind the sentiment, but the pregnant woman seemed gentle and true, despite her destitution.

"If your servant assists us," said the gypsy man, "I will offer a few coins to spare, although it isn't much to the likes of you. But my wife, she tells fortunes."

There was then an obligatory squabble between my mother's parents regarding the legitimacy of the offer. Mr. Beaufort, in his infinite kindness, agreed to let one of their servants step down from the coach and assist the attachment of a new wheel to the gypsies' wagon. When the deed was done, Mrs. Beaufort held out her hand from the window, saying, "Very well, read my palm."

The gypsy woman slowly came alongside the coach, and squinted at the palm proffered to her. "You will have your heart's desires," she said, "but it is not your fortune I am meant to tell, madame. It is hers."

"Whose?" demanded Mrs. Beaufort.

"Your daughter's."

At this point, my mother, a polite girl of eight, stood up inside the coach and peered out the window at the gypsy with curiosity. The gypsy woman smiled at the little girl.

"Your mind exceeds your heritage, child," said the woman kindly, "and your accomplishments will be grand and extraordinary, though few will credit them to you. Do not be disheartened by this, for your own son someday will be an extraordinary mind, too. His dreams will see fruition, but it will be at a terrible price which cannot be avoided."

"This is foolishness," said Mrs. Beaufort, upset. "Caroline is but a child!" Mr. Beaufort shushed her. The gypsy had more to say.

"There is one thing that may redeem your son: your daughter. When you have a daughter, she will be an angel from heaven, if you have the means to save her. Do not let your own brilliant mind be wasted in preparing for your children's future." The gypsy turned away, leaning on her husband for support, and the husband thanked the couple for their generosity again.

"What does that mean?" demanded Mrs. Beaufort, but the fortune was told and done.

For years, my mother toiled over what the prophetic words could mean. As she grew older, she read a great many books and was considered 'unhealthily educated' by her mother. Thinking perhaps the gypsy meant there would be something wrong with her daughter when the girl was born that would require fixing or even prevention, she read all she could about surgery and medicine.

She studied anatomy and engineering and sciences to further her understanding of life, the mechanics of the human body, and the untapped potential therein. The words regarding her son were full of praise and success, linked inexorably to the fate of her daughter. If she could save her future daughter, her son would also be saved.

When her father died, my teenaged mother was taken into the care of her father's friend, a man called Frankenstein. A romance bloomed there, and ultimately, they were married. She bore him a son, Victor, so-called for his predestined victory in whatever field or profession he should chose. The next child to be born was also a son, whom they named Ernest. My father would have been quite settled with these two healthy boys, but my mother was determined that a daughter should be born.

"Then, my dearest Elizabeth, the unthinkable happened," wrote my mother. "I was, at last, with child again, but tragedy struck me, and the infant was lost. The doctor revealed to me after the incident that it had been a female child, and I lost much of my health and ability to carry on, thinking very much that I had failed my prophecy. The doctor advised your father to take me to Italy for warmer, more temperate climes, and so we went. It was there, my dearest girl, my true angel, that we found you."

I realized that I had been holding my breath for a little too long. I sat back and breathed, closing my eyes for a moment to clear my head. The rest of this letter was professions of faith and love, and reassurances that I would be well all the days of my life if I entrusted myself to Victor faithfully, and cared for him in deepest love and honesty.

I studied the second fat envelope, marked "On Your Wedding Day." This first letter was the hitherto untold story of my mother's journey up to her most generous adoption of myself. What else could possibly lie unsaid? Curiosity spread through my veins like poison, and I ran my fingers over the paper. I wanted very badly to open it and read it, though it was not my wedding day. With Victor away at his studies, I had no idea when that day would come, I realized with a sad twist in my gut.

I shook my head to clear it of confusion. My mother hid these things knowing—or at least hoping—that I would find them someday, and I must trust her to know when the truths would be most rightly revealed.

I hid the journal and letters back in the floorboards, replacing it and carefully dusting everything with a rag, so as not to betray any one place that had more or less dust than the hiding spot. I would wait. I had to wait. I would continue to do her proud by caring for the family, and loving Victor, even in his absence, and waiting for the day of our marriage.

**Continued in**
*Mechanized Masterpieces: A Steampunk Anthology*
**2013 Xchyler Publishing**